The PROMISED ONE

Acknowledgments

The author wishes to thank his wife, children and grandchildren for their help, patience and encouragement during the writing of this book; Pauline, Richard, Helen, Michelle Balmer and Christine Naegele for their help with the manuscript; Catherine for her editorial skills; Sue Boland for her help with the original illustrations; his three young test-readers Clio Adam, Alanna Cockburn and Jonathan Jackson for their forthright and invaluable advice; John Harrison for his encouragement and practical assistance; and Suzy Jenvey for having both faith in the book and the courage to act on it.

The PROMISED ONE

DAVID ALRIC

Illustrated by
David Dean

faber and faber

First published in 2004
by Bladon Publishing
12 New Street, Chipping Norton, Oxfordshire OX7 5LJ

This edition published by
Faber and Faber Limited
3 Queen Square, London WC1N 3AU

Design by Mandy Norman
Printed in England by Mackays of Chatham plc, Chatham, Kent

A CIP record for this book
is available from the British Library

ISBN 978-0-571-23484-4
ISBN 0-571-23484-4

DISCLAIMER: With the exception of the historical characters, any resemblance
between the people and animals in this book and any real person, living
or dead, is entirely accidental

2 4 6 8 10 9 7 5 3 1

To my wonderful grandchildren:
Clare, Lucy, Sarah, Benedict, Henry and Christopher

Contents

Preface   ix

Prologue   I

1   A Promise Fulfilled   3

2   A Villa of Villainy   32

3   Discussions with Dolphins   44

4   Some Mysteries Solved   59

5   Some Lessons in History and Geography   76

6   A Crash in the Jungle   94

7   Kidnap!   108

8   An Unplanned Trip for Lucy   122

9   An Eventful Flight to Cayman Creek   138

10   An Uncomfortable Day at the Creek   156

11   Jungle Telegraph   169

12   Richard Drops in to Stay   179

13	Cruising with Crocodiles	205
14	Waiting to be Eaten	215
15	Jungle Quest	225
16	Into the Valley of the Mighty Ones	240
17	Christmas in the Jungle	262
18	An Even More Uncomfortable Day at the Creek	268
19	Operation Jungle Sting	293
20	Sad Farewells	306
21	A Flutter on the Stock Exchange	319
22	Home – to More Revelations	339
	Lucy's Lexicon	357
	Notes on the names in the book	361
	Glossary	367
	Unit conversion table	404

Preface

The first edition of this book was produced without the assistance of a children's publisher and consisted of a limited run of hardback copies. To my great pleasure the story proved popular with both children and adults, and with teachers interested in its literary and educational content. I am now delighted to collaborate with Faber and Faber in producing a new paperback edition of the book which will be available to a much wider readership than the original version.

My aim in writing this story was to provide young people with an enjoyable and exciting read that would also present them with something of a challenge in its use of English. To this end the language has not been 'dumbed down' in terms of either grammar or vocabulary, and to assist younger readers I have included a glossary of those words and phrases in the book with which they may be unfamiliar. As dictionaries are themselves sometimes difficult to understand, I have tried in this glossary to provide explanations that are easily accessible to such readers, and hope that in doing so I have yet managed to retain sufficient accuracy to satisfy the language purists.

In addition to those regular words in the English

language that may be unfamiliar to the younger reader of this story, there is a set of words that will be new to *every* reader. These are descriptive words such as 'furriclaws' and 'fledgiquill', which I have created in an attempt to convey the wonder and novelty of Lucy's communications with her beloved animals. These neologisms are, I believe, clearly part of the fantasy element of the book; I hope that they will not confuse or mislead a generation of children that has been brought up in a world full of the bizarre names, amazing fantasies and special effects that modern technology has brought to our television and cinema screens. To assist in the interpretation of these names that Lucy learns from, or assigns to, the animals, a lexicon of such appellations is included at the end of the book; I hope, however, that most readers will have some fun in trying to guess what they mean before trying to look them up. The same applies to the list of characters' names which follows the lexicon.

It is perhaps worth saying at this point that, in those areas of the book that are obviously *not* fantasy, I have endeavoured to be as scientifically accurate as possible and that the statistical, ecological and biological details given in the story reflect, to the best of my ability, our current state of knowledge in these fields. This academic note brings me on to the slightly vexed issue of units of measurement. Children, particularly those in the younger age groups, are now properly taught to think in metric rather than imperial units. My grandchildren refer to lengths in centimetres, not inches, and metres rather than feet or yards. Older readers still probably use some 'old' units, however, particularly for distances and heights, and I rather suspect the adults in this story such as Richard, Helen and Julian would do so as well. For this reason I have attempted a compromise in the book whereby specific anatomical lengths (e.g. 'a wingspan of three metres') are given in metric units, while the older units are used for what would be said naturally in conversation by the adults when referring to things such as the height of a cliff or the width of a crater. To help the younger readers through the complexities of this compromise (which, after all, only reflects the reality of everyday life in many countries, including Britain), a short conversion table is included at the end of the glossary.

Nothing more remains but for me to hope you enjoy reading about Lucy's adventures and to promise that she will soon be setting off once again to wield her unique power for the good of all living creatures and the planet.

David Alric, London, 2007

Prologue

The time was 8.25 a.m. in a London suburb. The girl was eleven years old; the boy was fifteen. She was walking to start her first day at secondary school; he was driving a stolen BMW at fifty-six miles an hour along the suburban streets. She was excited and a little apprehensive; he was drunk, drugged and high. In a few seconds both their lives would change for ever and the world would never be quite the same again.

A Promise Fulfilled

At last, almost three weeks after her terrible road accident, the wonderful day arrived when Lucy could leave hospital. Her grandfather came to pick her up while her mother and grandmother got everything ready at home, and he had to make two trips from the car to the ward to collect all the cards and presents she had received.

Lucy wept tears of relief when she walked back into her own room. During her stay in hospital following her brain operation she had wondered at times if she would ever see it again and, kind though everyone had been, it was wonderful to be back home again. Her mother had clearly been very busy during her absence. The room was spotless, and properly tidy for the first time since Lucy had been responsible for tidying it herself. Some spaces had appeared on shelves now that her books and CDs had been arranged neatly, and the tea stain on the carpet had been shampooed away – she wouldn't have to leave her shoes and clothes lying on the floor any more to hide it, she thought to herself. There were new curtains, a vase of fresh flowers on her desk, and her childhood soft toys, dusted and freshly fluffed up, sat in a row on a shelf looking at her as if glad to welcome her home.

As she got into bed that evening she glanced at the card on her bedside cupboard which her father had sent just before her accident. She was sad that he was abroad but was sure he would be back soon. The card had obviously been chosen with Lucy's love of animals in mind, showing all manner of exotic and brilliantly coloured South American fauna, with a magnificent jaguar as its centrepiece. She'd had a particular fascination with these animals since being given one as a fluffy toy when she was little and her father had clearly remembered this. For the rest of her life Lucy would treasure this card and wonder whether her father had chosen it through some uncanny presentiment of what lay in store for them both in the weeks to come.

She suddenly felt exhausted. The excitement of coming home and the journey had made her tired and now in her own bed in her own room she felt utterly secure. She cuddled close to Jackie the jaguar, and within a minute or two was fast asleep.

In the sitting room Joanna Bonaventure put her feet up with a cup of tea, relieved beyond words to have her daughter back at home, safe and sound at last.

'It's a miracle she's made such a good recovery,' she said to her parents, 'but I'm going to make sure she's completely better before I think of letting her back to school.'

'Well, when you think she's fit enough to travel you know we'd love to have her come down and have a little holiday with us at the seaside,' said her mother, and her father nodded in agreement. They were going to return to their cottage at the coast the following day.

At that moment Clare, Lucy's elder sister, came in from the kitchen where she had been clearing up the supper things.

'Has anyone seen Tibbles?' she asked, a puzzled look on her face. Their cat normally spent the evening in the sitting room cuddled up next to one of the girls. Since Lucy's return, however, she had been behaving oddly and was now nowhere to be seen. Sarah, the youngest of the three sisters, ran upstairs to look for her and returned to report.

'Well, I never! She's sitting next to Lucy's bed just watching her.'

'Maybe she's missed her,' said her mother, 'and is now worried she might go away again.'

Everybody agreed, but Clare still thought it was a little odd; the cat had shown no signs whatsoever of missing Lucy while she had been in hospital, and this behaviour was very unusual. Joanna didn't usually allow Tibbles in the bedrooms but decided not to make a fuss on this occasion as it was Lucy's first night at home and the cat wasn't actually on the bed. Tibbles remained in Lucy's bedroom all evening and was still there, gazing at her intently, when the others finally went to bed, little knowing that their house would, in a few hours' time, be the scene of one of the most astonishing events in the history of the human race.

'Greetings, O Promised One.'

Lucy heard the soft, melodious voice as she struggled to wake up from her dream. It had been a curious dream in which she was sitting on a garden chair like a queen on a throne and legions of animals had paraded in front of her as though she were some kind of animal deity. There had been creatures great and small – it was what the preparations for boarding Noah's Ark must have looked like. Lions and leopards, pelicans and pangolins, rhinos and rattlesnakes, foxes and flamingos – the entire panoply of the animal kingdom had processed before her in a seemingly endless pageant. But it was not just the animals familiar to her from zoo and farm that came to pay her court. There were mammoths and other giant creatures that she could not name but looked like the pictures of creatures she had seen in books illustrating prehistoric times, and there were other, still more terrible creatures, the like of which she had never seen or imagined. But she felt no fear, for she knew that all, from the terrible to the timorous, were there to pay obeisance to her, an eleven-year-old girl. And then, towards the end of her dream, one

. . . she was sitting like a queen on a throne.

6

of the immense throng had come to her feet and spoken to her. It was a cat, looking just like her very own Tibbles. It now repeated itself.

'*Greetings, O Promised One.*'

She was just thinking how vivid her dream had been when the voice spoke yet again.

'*Welcome back. I never before realized that you were to be She Who Speaks. I am immensely honoured to be the first to speak to Her.*'

Lucy was becoming alarmed. She sat up and winced a little as she moved. She had broken several ribs in her accident and though they were healing well they still ached if she had been lying on them. The twinge convinced her that she was awake, but what on earth was this voice doing if she was awake? Then she saw that Tibbles was sitting at the end of the bed, looking at her intently, her eyes open wide, and her fur slightly raised on the neck and shoulders as it was sometimes when she saw a dog through the window. She was clearly very excited.

'Hello, Tibs . . .' Lucy started, but she suddenly knew that she didn't need to speak aloud. She knew with absolute

certainty that she could speak to Tibbles from her head just by *thinking* of what she wanted her to hear.

'What's happened, Tibs?' Somehow she knew that, if she so wished, only Tibbles could hear what she said.

'You have returned and now I can see that you are She,' said Tibbles.

'But who is She?' asked Lucy with a mixture of fear and excitement. *'And how do you know it's anything to do with me?'*

'You have the beacon which I can see and feel from afar. Even before you entered the house I could feel you. All living creatures know of the Promised One but you must speak with greater minds than mine to learn more about Her. I am just a furriclaws and know only what furriclaws know.'

'Can you speak to other animals?' Lucy asked, intrigued by the thought that other creatures already knew about her.

'Only sometimes,' the cat replied. *'If I am stalking fledgiquills*

in the garden I cannot understand their chatter among themselves, but when I get near and they fly away, I can understand when they shout "danger" to each other. Sometimes in the house I hear the scurripods in the kitchen or the understairs cupboard. If I creep down and listen or pretend to be asleep I cannot understand what they say, but if I chase one I can understand his alarm calls to the others.'

Lucy still didn't completely understand, but at that moment the cat suddenly pricked up her ears and looked to the half-open door. Her tail twitched and she jumped to the floor, sat down and started to clean herself. A few seconds later Lucy heard her mother's step on the stair.

'Hello, love,' her mother said, leaning over and kissing her. 'Here's a cup of tea and your tablets. How did you sleep back in your own bed?'

'Oh, I slept like a log – though I had a funny dream. It's great to be home, Mum.'

'Tibbles seems to have taken a special interest in you,' her mother said, looking at the cat, who gave an uninterested yawn and gazed out of the window. 'Fancy her missing you like that – and I can't ever remember her wanting to sleep in your bedroom before!' For a moment Lucy wondered whether to tell her mother what had happened, but decided that she had to think things out on her own before talking to anyone.

'I expect she thinks I'll spoil her a bit as I've been away,' she said. 'She's always looking for a bit of extra attention.'

'Come on, Tibbles,' said her mother, 'breakfast time!' But Tibbles had heard Sarah putting her bowl down on the kitchen floor and she was already on her way downstairs.

Left alone, Lucy began to wonder if she had fallen asleep again for a few moments during which she had experienced a short, vivid dream. She got up and splashed her face with cold water, brushed her teeth and put on her dressing gown. It was a sunny September morning and she went to the window and opened it for a moment to try to clear her mind with some fresh air. As she opened the window the noises hit her once again. She had noticed them when getting out of the car and coming up the path the day before, but now they were clearer and more strident than ever before.

Suddenly, she knew what the noises were. She 'heard' them in the same way as she had heard Tibbles and now she realized that she was listening to a hundred different animal voices: birds, large and small; stoats and squirrels; moles and mice; and countless other wild things. Her bedroom looked out on to their large back garden with its lawn and flower beds and shrubs. Beyond the garden was a patch of unspoilt woodland that belonged to the electricity company. Never before had Lucy been aware how many different creatures lived in this suburban garden and its adjacent copse. She felt as though she had become tuned in to the entire animal kingdom.

Bewildered by everything that had happened, Lucy shut the window and sat on the edge of her bed. What on earth had caused all this and should she tell anyone about it? She quietly sipped her tea and started to go over everything again in her mind; she clearly needed to work out a plan of action.

Downstairs Joanna brewed some coffee while her parents started packing to go home. Her thoughts turned to her husband who was still unaware of Lucy's accident. Richard had recently taken up a new post as scientific adviser to a timber company and had been posted to South America almost two months ago. He had first gone to the company's general headquarters in Rio de Janeiro, to be trained in the company systems, then to the river office at Macapá near the mouth of the Amazon. During that time he had communicated regularly – daily, in fact – by phone, fax or e-mail but three weeks ago all news from him had suddenly stopped. After a week of becoming increasingly worried Joanna had finally rung the company site manager in Macapá. He had explained that Richard had gone on a long field trip in previously unexplored jungle and was uncontactable. It was thought that his radio must have broken and there was now no way of contacting him until he returned to the base camp.

As it happened, Richard couldn't have been away at a worse time. His good luck card to Lucy – his last communication before disappearing in the jungle – had arrived on her first day at secondary school. She was leaving the primary school she went to with eight-year-old Sarah and starting at Clare's school, St Sapientia's. That morning she had been very excited as she set off for school. She had firmly refused her mother's offer to drive her, having decided that from now on she would walk with her friend Rachel. Halfway to school the girls had heard the squealing of tyres and turned to see a large, powerful car roaring up the road towards them. It was being driven by a fifteen-year-old boy who had stolen it for a joyride after an all-night party involving both alcohol and drugs. The girls did not, of course, know this – they had just thought it was yet another driver going too fast on a suburban street. Suddenly, too late, they had realized that the car was out of control as it mounted the pavement and hurtled towards them, just missing Rachel but knocking Lucy to the ground before crashing to a stop against a lamp-post. A piece of metal from the radiator grille of the car had pierced Lucy's head, causing bleeding into her brain, and in the hospital the doctors had operated on her for several hours until they were satisfied they had done all that they could. Joanna had then gone through the worst time of her life as she waited for Lucy to recover, praying that she would not have suffered any permanent damage to her brain, and unable to contact Richard to tell him what had happened. Now, with Lucy home safe and sound at last, having made a complete recovery from the accident and the operation, Joanna felt an overwhelming sense of relief. She was sure that they would soon have news from Richard and then life would, at last, get back to normal.

That afternoon Clare had a couple of free periods and she came home early.

'Good, you're back,' said Joanna when she saw her, 'perhaps you can stay with Lucy while I go out for a few things?'

When their mother had left, Lucy looked at Clare. Since the astonishing events of that morning she had thought long and hard about what to do and had decided against telling her mother who, she knew, would immediately start worrying that Lucy was suffering from some serious after-effect of her accident. On the other hand, she felt she *had* to tell someone who would really listen and understand, so she had decided to confide in her older sister. They had always been very close despite the big difference in their ages – Clare was seventeen and Lucy eleven – and Lucy was confident that Clare would know what to do.

'Clare,' she began, 'I really don't know how to tell you this but please listen, and try to let me finish before you ask any questions.' She then told Clare everything that had happened that day. Then, before Clare could speak, she said:

'I've not tried this before but I have a feeling that Tibs will do anything I say. I am going to call her now and ask her to fetch me a tissue. Don't say a word.'

Clare, who by now was seriously worried about her sister, decided to humour her a little longer and sat with a look of tolerant disbelief on her face.

Within a few seconds they heard the clunk of the cat-flap and Tibbles appeared. She went straight to Lucy and sat at her feet gazing up at her. To Clare's eyes Lucy did nothing but look at the cat. Tibbles then got up and went into the kitchen. Clare heard her jump on to the kitchen worktop – something she was forbidden to do – and then a rustling sound. A moment later Tibbles appeared with a mouthful of tissues and laid them at Lucy's feet. She sat back proudly, unaware that she had a small piece of torn tissue stuck to her chin which made her appear slightly ridiculous. Lucy glanced at Clare and said aloud:

'We can't have you looking silly when you've been such a clever pussy, Tibbles.' Then she fell silent and stared once more at the cat. The cat immediately twisted herself so as to reach her chin with her hind-paw and removed the fragment of tissue.

Clare was stupefied. It was simply not possible that what she had just seen could have happened purely by chance, and she knew it.

'I don't wish to feel I'm just using Tibbles,' said Lucy, 'but it's important that you really believe me, so I'm going to ask her to do one more thing. You know how she always sits in her favourite tree next to the Bolands' fence?' Clare nodded, speechless. Tibbles always sat in a fork of this tree so she could keep an eye on both gardens. She never went to the tree on the other side of the garden because the Browns on that side had a dog, Jumble, who always got very excited at the sight of Tibbles.

'I'm going to send her to say hello to Jumble,' she said mischievously. She then turned her attention back to Tibbles, who had curled up and was beginning to close her eyes for a nap. The cat suddenly sprang to her feet and looked up at Lucy. She then turned, a little reluctantly, Clare thought – or was it her imagination? – and disappeared. Once more the cat-flap clunked and a few seconds later the girls, now at the French windows, saw Tibbles, who was putting on weight, scrambling with some effort up the tree, placing her front paws on the Browns' fence and miaowing into their garden. Soon they heard Jumble barking frantically from next door and Tibbles withdrew from the fence into the safety of the tree. There was a long pause during which the sisters looked at each other. Clare had gone pale.

'What on earth has happened to you?' she eventually whispered, now utterly convinced of her sister's powers as a result of what she had seen.

'I dunno. It must be something to do with the accident or the operation. I feel perfectly OK.'

'Have you told Mum or Grandma?'

'No, Grandma and Grandpa left for home just after you went to school this morning and I daren't tell Mum. She'll think I've gone nuts and she's got enough to worry about just now what with not hearing from Daddy.'

'You're right,' said Clare. 'We mustn't tell her – not yet anyway. What are you going to do?'

'Well, there's nothing I can do. It's happened. You know I want to be a vet and if the power lasts it'll obviously be very useful. I would like to know more about it though, and Tibbles seems to think that some more intelligent animals – well, she didn't say it quite like that, but it's what she meant – may be able to tell me more.'

'Wow,' said Clare, 'what a thing to say to people – it would be really cool to do things in front of everyone at school.' She paused and then frowned. 'I don't know though. It might be a mistake to tell anyone else just yet. Maybe we should keep it secret for the time being.'

Lucy nodded in agreement.

'One thing I must do,' she said, 'is to find another animal to talk to. Do you think I can get to see an owl?'

'Did Tibbles suggest an owl?' said Clare, doubtfully.

'Well, no,' said Lucy, 'but they're meant to be wise, aren't they?'

Clare wasn't sure if they were or not, but agreed it might be worth a try and then went off to attempt to do her homework. She had a lot of work to do in her final year at school, but it was difficult to concentrate when such exciting things were happening to Lucy. She tried to put these out of her mind and eventually opened her chemistry books and got started.

That night Lucy woke up thirsty and decided to go down for a drink. She got out of bed and, tiptoeing past her mother's room and Clare's room, went downstairs. The kitchen door was ajar and as she got near she could hear 'voices' in the kitchen. In her mind's eye they were tiny little sounds and Lucy was in no doubt that they came from the 'scurripods' that Tibbles had mentioned. Quiet as a scurripod herself, she crept nearer to the door and listened. To her astonishment she could understand every word.

'*Old Furriclaws came back with a limp tonight,*' one little voice said.

'*I think she must have hurt her paw chasing a hedgiquill,*' said another. '*They're getting slow now it's time for their snowsleep, so they are about the only things she can chase with her weight problem. One of these days she's going to get stuck in the flap-that-cut-off-Minnie's-tail.*'

'*Yes, well, don't you get too clever,*' said one with an older voice. '*She can still move quickly when you don't expect it, as poor Babybel could tell you if she were still here.*' There was a sorrowful silence as the mice thought of their dead relative and Lucy wondered if the little tail Clare had found in Tibbles's bowl, which she had told Lucy about while she was in hospital, had been the last earthly remains of a scurripod named after its favourite food. As the conversation started again Lucy suddenly realized that there was no reason for her to hide. Tentatively, she switched on her 'beacon'. This was how she had come to think of what she did, but in reality it just meant that she opened her mind to the animal kingdom. The effect was dramatic. There was instant silence, then, after a very long pause, the eldest voice, trembling slightly in awe, began to speak.

'*Greetings, O Promised One. What dost thou desire?*'

Lucy opened the kitchen door and turned on the light. Several mice sat looking at her: three on the floor eating a fragment of boiled potato, two in a cupboard and one on the worktop in front of the breadbin near a little pile of crumbs – the remains of one of Clare's late night snacks.

'. . . and from now on there are to be no poos anywhere my mother can see them.'

Their eyes were wide with attention and their ears pricked up.

'Greetings, O scurripods, I come not to harm you. Since I learnt to speak I have spoken only to Furriclaws, and wish now to speak to some other animals.' As the mice exchanged nervous glances she added: *'Fear not, Furriclaws has gone out again despite her sore paw. She went out of my window down the sloping roof.'* The mice visibly relaxed, but Lucy noticed that the three on the floor moved further away from the cat-flap in case the cat suddenly returned. She realized that she didn't really know how to strike up a conversation with six mice so she sat down on the floor to make them feel more comfortable. Food had to be a topic that would interest them.

'What do you like best to eat?' asked Lucy.

'Crunchy peanut butter and chocolate,' said the plumpest mouse, without hesitation, and the others murmured in squeaky agreement.

'Well,' said Lucy, *'I shall put some out for you in the little hole in the floorboards in the cupboard under the stairs every night, but you mustn't go on the worktop or in the food cupboard. Oh,'* she

added, *'and from now on there are to be no poos anywhere my mother can see them.'*

'You are kind, O Promised One,' said another mouse, *'and it shall be done as you say; but,'* he hesitated, *'could . . . could you sometimes leave out some cheese as well?'* Lucy laughed and they all jumped. The one on the worktop ran behind the breadbin, those in the cupboard disappeared behind a cornflake packet and the others cowered on the floor.

'I'm sorry,' said Lucy as she realized that they didn't know what laughter was, *'we Tailless Ones sometimes make that noise with a fierce face when we are happy – I didn't mean to frighten you. Of course I will leave some cheese out if you wish.'*

Having relaxed at her reassuring words the mice suddenly became alert once more and looked in unison at the cat-flap as if they were all connected by some invisible wires. They could obviously hear something that Lucy couldn't. She got up and went to the window. Putting her head between the curtains to shut out the light behind her, she peered out into the moonlit garden just in time to see a shadowy shape flit away from the dustbins, frightened by the movement of the curtains at the window.

'It's all right,' said Lucy, rearranging the curtain and returning to the mice. *'It's just a fox at the rubbish.'*

'The henbane comes every night,' said the oldest mouse. *'Sometimes he puts his nose through the flap-that-cut-off-Minnie's-tail but he's too big to get in.'* Then he added, with quiet satisfaction, *'Furriclaws is very frightened of him.'*

Lucy decided it was time to get her water and go back to bed.

'I must leave you now and return to my place of rest,' she said, finding herself speaking in an old-fashioned way, just as they did. 'My thanks to you all for talking to me and I shall speak to you again soon. Good night.'

'Fare thee well,' they all chorused in their tiny voices.

Lucy filled her glass, put the light out and went into the hall, pulling the kitchen door almost shut behind her. She stood still for a moment, listening to the excited babble of high-pitched voices that broke out.

'Can you believe it, She lives in our house!'

'She must have been the Promised One all the time and we never knew!'

'Trust Furriclaws to get to speak to Her first.'

'Just wait till we tell next door. Having the Promised One in our house is mega-important compared with that silly secret hole into the biscuit cupboard they're always boasting about!'

'. . .and them down the road, with their nest in that posh doll's house!'

'Do you think She'll leave some cheese out every night?'

'Do you think She might shut Furriclaws out all night if we ask?'

'You know that place they take Furriclaws when they go away on holiday? Maybe they could leave her there all the time.'

'Sometimes I think they must like Furriclaws!'

'Should we have asked Her to put a bell on Furriclaws' collar?'

'Don't push your luck. Anyway, you're the one that was saying she was too fat to move a few minutes ago.'

Lucy wanted to stay and listen all night, but she felt slightly uneasy at using her power in this way and a little throb in her head and a shaky feeling in her legs reminded her that her full recovery was still a long way off. It was time to get back to bed.

In the morning she told Clare what had happened.

'Can you believe it!' she said. 'Mice in our kitchen actually joking about Tibbles getting fat. And they spoke in a funny mixture of modern and old-fashioned speech. The older ones said "thee" and the younger ones said "you".'

'What else did they say?' asked Clare.

'Well, I didn't like to listen too long,' said Lucy. 'I felt I was – what's the word? – eavesdropping.'

'No,' said Clare, 'in this case the word is mousedropping.'

'Is it really?' asked Lucy looking suspiciously at her. She was never quite sure when her big sister was making one of her silly jokes.

'Yes,' said Clare pretending to be serious, 'and I also think that you shouldn't be ratting on them like this.' With this she burst out laughing and then had to duck as the Promised One threw a pair of dirty socks at her.

The next morning, with her headmistress's permission, Clare went to the hospital. She wanted to be a doctor and when she had been visiting Lucy in hospital she had become friendly with the young doctor looking after her sister, Christine Goodward. Christine had invited her to come back and look at the pictures they had taken of Lucy's brain, as long as Lucy didn't object.

'I don't mind,' Lucy had said when Clare asked her, adding with a grin, 'It'll be good for you to know what a perfect brain looks like before you go to medical school.'

At the hospital Christine introduced Clare to Dr Pixel, the radiologist who had helped Professor Furrowhead with Lucy's operation. He told her to call him Andy and she was fascinated when he showed her a picture of the arteries in Lucy's brain.

'The arteries are tubes that carry blood to the brain just like water pipes carry water in your house. This one,' he pointed, 'feeds Lucy's pineal gland, which is a little structure the size of a pea right in the middle of her brain. The artery was damaged by the metal spike from the car but it's OK now we've fixed it. In fact it's the biggest artery I've ever seen just there so I'm quite sure she'll be all right.'

'Why is it big?' said Clare. 'And was it like that before the accident?'

'Oh yes,' said the doctor, 'but it's not important – that's just how Lucy's made. Everybody is a little bit different from everybody else on the inside, just as they are on the outside. She must have a very special pineal gland,' he said, grinning, 'just as I've got a very special nose.' Clare looked at his rather large nose and all three of them laughed.

As she returned to school Clare went over in her mind the events of the morning and her discussions with the doctors. She was particularly interested in the pineal gland, which she had never come across in her biology lessons. During lunch hour she went to the school library and got down some big books of anatomy and physiology to find out more about it. It was apparently about the size of a large pea and sat on a little stalk right in the middle of the brain. Its main function seemed to be to control the changes that occurred in the body in response to night and day, the circadian rhythm, but as she read on Clare got the feeling that it might also do things that scientists still didn't fully understand. It certainly seemed to be a very *old* part of the body in terms of the human race and evolution. Clare didn't know why but she felt curiously excited at the thought that Lucy had got an especially large artery going to her pineal gland and she wondered how certain Dr Pixel could have been when he said it wasn't important. He didn't, of course, know that Lucy could talk to animals. Was it possible that her accident had somehow changed the function of Lucy's gland in a way that had uncovered a primitive ability now lost to all other humans? She was more determined than ever to become a doctor and one day find out much more about the human brain.

While Clare was in the school library learning about the pineal gland, Lucy was having another chat with Tibbles. As she used her new faculty she was becoming more proficient in controlling it and she could talk to Tibbles even with the window open simply by shutting the other voices out. She could, she found, even pick out one of those voices to concentrate on if she wanted, and shut Tibbles out. There seemed to be a receptor or receiver that she could shut off when she wanted, and a separate 'transmitter' or outward beacon that animals could detect.

She remembered that Clare had been interested in what Tibbles thought about owls and asked the cat if she ever spoke to them, after first politely enquiring about her sore paw.

'I have seen the nightbanes during sunsleep, hunting scurripods and coneybanes,' Tibbles replied, 'but I have never dared speak to them. They do not come here very often and I think you will have to go to the great woods.' Lucy knew she couldn't go alone to any woods so she started to hatch a plan for a family outing. She resolved to get Clare's help in organizing it.

That evening Clare brought home some homework from Mrs O'Grady, Lucy's new form teacher.

'Mrs O'Grady asked me to see her,' she announced. 'She said that while you are convalescing you should try and catch up a bit on the work you've missed. It's mostly reading, apparently, but Miss Anther would like you to write up a topic for your course work.' Sheila Anther taught biology – Lucy's favourite subject. She looked through the file and found the biology page.

'I've got to write on "The woods in autumn" and "The pros and cons of zoos" – whatever that means,' said Lucy.

'Pros and cons means things for and things against,' explained Clare, 'so you have to say what's good and bad about zoos and farms and keeping pets. Sounds quite interesting but it'll be frustrating for you not to be able to say what the animals could *tell* you about being captive.'

'I've got an idea,' said Lucy suddenly. 'Why don't we ask Mum to take us to Richmond Park or Wimbledon

Common at the weekend? The doctor said I should get some gentle exercise and they say it's going to be sunny. I can pretend to make notes about the woods for my project and try to talk to an owl.'

'OK,' said Clare, 'but it'll have to be Sunday because I'm going shopping with Hannah in Kingston on Saturday.' As Clare agreed she found herself, for the umpteenth time, wondering if she was in a dream. Here she was calmly discussing a plan for her sister to go and have a chat with a wild owl. Maybe they were both on some kind of trip! But in her heart she knew that Lucy had turned into something very special and that she had to support her through this amazing experience.

'*Greetings, O Moonwraith.*'

Lucy was standing in a small clearing in the woods on Wimbledon Common. She was speaking to an owl and had decided that nightbane, the name Tibbles had used, sounded a bit rude. Clare had diverted her mother and Sarah to see some toadstools on a tree stump and though still in sight they were far enough away to leave her undisturbed. Lucy had wandered into the clearing and, while pretending to make notes in a small notepad, had 'switched on' her beacon. She had heard a bewildering array of voices – many of which were quite new to her – and then sent out a clear thought for an owl to respond. She had immediately received a new signal in reply and within a minute a tawny shape had swept effortlessly through the glade and landed in the fork of a nearby oak tree.

'Greetings, She Who Speaks. What is your desire?'

The owl replied to Lucy's salutation in a 'voice' that was surprisingly deep and masculine. Lucy wasn't quite sure how you started up a conversation with such an impressive-looking creature but she felt intuitively that it couldn't do any harm to start off with a bit of humility, even if they did all think she was the new mistress of creation, or whatever.

'Er, I am sorry if I disturbed you at rest,' she began, *'but I find I can speak to all creatures and wish to find out more about how this can be, and why you are all being so helpful to me.'* She immediately thought that she sounded stupid and should have spent more time in advance planning what she wanted to say. The owl, however, appeared not to notice her confusion and replied gravely:

'I am deeply honoured, O Promised One. If I had known you were to come I would not have slept for many suns. I will carry out anything within my power that you command, but fear I cannot give you the knowledge that you seek. Although I am large and my talons are feared by all the creatures of the field and forest, I am but a fledgiquill and have only the mind of a fledgiquill. If you seek enlightenment concerning The Promise, you must talk to others with greater minds than I. It is told that there are Hairy Tailless Ones imprisoned in the City of the Great Clock and they have much knowledge. The Little Great Ones are also said to possess much wisdom: they breathe the air but live like gillifins

in the Great Salt. Fare thee well in thy quest.'

'Lucy, Lucy, come on, we're going to the pond!' She heard Sarah calling and turned to see her mother and sisters waiting.

'Fare thee well also, Great Moonwraith!' she said, and went to join the others.

'Well, what did he say?' said Clare eagerly when she and Lucy were alone for a few moments while Joanna helped Sarah climb on a fallen tree. 'Did you ask him if he had delivered any mail to Harry Potter?'

'No, I jolly well didn't,' said Lucy. 'I actually found him a bit scary, if you must know, even though I realize that I'm the one they all hold in awe. I couldn't make some stupid joke he wouldn't understand, could I?'

'I was only teasing,' laughed Clare. 'How did it go?'

'Well, not very well actually,' said Lucy a little glumly. 'He basically said he was only a bird and didn't know much. It's funny really – we've always been told how clever owls are, but if you think about it there's no reason why he should be any wiser than a pigeon or a duck, is there? He did help a bit, though. He said I should see the Hairy Tailless Ones – whatever they are – or the Little Great Ones. They live in the sea but breathe air, so I suppose they're mammals of some sort.'

Clare replied after only the briefest pause:

'I think the Hairy Tailless Ones are apes – which would make sense as they are the closest relatives to humans, and the *Little* Great Ones must be dolphins – the Great Ones are presumably whales.'

'Cool!' said Lucy. 'You've completely cracked it. Thanks. Now I've just got to think how to get to speak to some of them.'

As they strolled back towards the car they stopped to admire a new baby in a pram. The mother was a few yards away helping a toddler to clamber on to the trunk of a fallen tree. Suddenly a horse appeared from over a slight rise ahead of them, racing along the path straight towards them. It was riderless, with its mane flying and eyes and nostrils flared. It pounded nearer and though the mother screamed and rushed towards the pram clutching her toddler, the horse was already within a few yards of the pram which lay directly in its path and there was no way in which anyone could reach the baby in time. Suddenly the horse stopped; it was as though it was running on electricity and somebody had switched the power off. It skidded to a halt and reared on its hind legs just short of the pram – the baby gurgling happily in blissful unawareness of what had happened – just as a rider ran

'Pegasus!' she cried.

into view, her riding coat torn and her hat askew.

'Pegasus!' she cried, and the horse turned to look at her. 'Thank heavens I've found you!' Then she saw the pram and the toddler and an expression of horror crossed her face. 'Is the baby all right – did he hurt anyone?' Once she had been reassured that no harm had been done, she explained that a car exhaust had backfired on the nearby main road and startled the inexperienced horse, who had thrown her and then galloped off in terror. She remounted, apologized once again and rode away.

On the way home their mother could talk of nothing else but the horse episode.

'The lucky coincidences that occur in life really are quite amazing,' she said. 'I'm sure that it was seeing that pram that stopped the horse: he obviously thought it was an immovable object. If it hadn't been there he would have stampeded right through us – poor Lucy could have been hurt again. Just think, that pram could even have saved our lives.' Lucy and Clare looked at each other in the back seat

and grinned. They both now realized that all animals did as the Promised One bid them and knew that Lucy's urgent request – inaudible to the other humans present – had brought the runaway horse to an immediate stop. One day, perhaps, they would tell their mother what had really happened that day.

Later, when they were alone, Lucy asked for Clare's advice on how she could arrange to speak to some apes or dolphins. Clare thought for a moment, then her face lit up.

'I've an idea and I think it's one you're going to like. You know you can't go back to school while you're convalescing; well, why don't you go and spend some time with Grandma and Grandpa down in Littleporkton? While you were ill Grandpa told me that they've just refurbished the dolphinarium down there, so you could spend all the time you want talking to some dolphins.'

'What a great idea,' said Lucy. 'And it fits in perfectly with my homework project. Let's go and ask Mum.'

Her mother told them that her parents had already suggested that Lucy should spend some time at the seaside and immediately rang them to fix it up. At Lucy's request she also rang the school the next day to ask if Miss Anther could write a letter to the director of the dolphinarium explaining that Lucy had been ill and asking if she could do a special biology project at the dolphinarium during her convalescence.

The following weekend Grandma and Grandpa came to stay and when they returned to the seaside they took Lucy with them. She told them about the project she wanted to do on the dolphins and Grandpa promised to go with her to the dolphinarium when it reopened the following week.

2

A Villa of Villainy

Three months to the day before Lucy's accident a meeting took place, thousands of miles away in South America, that was to have a profound effect upon her life and the lives of many others.

On that day Alf Sawyer rose as dawn was breaking and went for a dip in the private pool of his villa. As he swam, the sun rose from the sea and bathed Rio de Janeiro in a brilliant rosy glow. The 'Cidade Maravilhosa', or Marvellous City, with its stunning backdrop of mountains and miles of golden beaches, sat like a jewel on the edge of the Atlantic Ocean. But this jewel was not without its flaws. A considerable number of drug barons, thieves and assorted war criminals spent their ill-gotten gains here on villas, beautiful gardens, exotic swimming pools and servants, and made themselves feel respectable.

A self-made man, Alf – 'Chopper' to his friends and associates in the illegal logging business – had risen from humble beginnings in south-east London to sit at the head of a multi-million-pound company making a fortune from drugs and illegal gold mining. The organization operated under the cover of a legal timber company which was run by a network of Chopper's henchmen, who kept the company's activities apparently on the right side of the law while ruthlessly exterminating any person or rival company that got in Chopper's way.

Despite the origins of his wealth, Chopper had never been caught by the police or even charged with any crime. He always put on a show of outward respectability and with financial success he had indulged himself to the full. His extensive villa and grounds looked out over its own beach, and a sophisticated security system ensured that his spoils could not be shared by others, for he strongly disapproved of any criminality directed against himself.

The decorating and furnishings of the villa had all been executed in the worst possible taste and comprised a collection of the most expensive trash that money could buy. Chopper was particularly proud of his large collection of gold-plated garden gnomes, specially made to illustrate his own career and interests, and arranged in a variety of little scenes depicting criminal activities.

Chopper was the eldest of four brothers, all criminals, and he was by far the most successful of the bunch. The next in age, Sam, was his deputy in the company and had no talent other than mindless violence. The other brothers were twins and Chopper had not seen them for over five years. He knew they had gone to jail somewhere in the Far East but since then had heard nothing until they had contacted him out of the blue a week earlier and requested a family meeting to discuss 'business'. Chopper had immediately suspected that they had heard of his success and were anxious to tap into his fortune, but could hardly refuse to see them. They were due to arrive with a business colleague, Mr Song, that very morning, and Chopper had arranged a business meeting in the villa boardroom for 11 a.m. He now sat on a lounger on the patio overlooking the swimming pool, basking in the morning sunshine. It would be a long day for, following the arrival of the twins and the family meeting, he would be holding the annual board meeting for his timber company in the afternoon and there was to be a family reunion dinner in the evening. He wondered what exactly his brothers wanted and where they had been during the past five years, apart from jail.

Chopper had been six when Sid and Fred had been born. They had been criminals since early childhood. Starting with cruelty to animals at a young age, they had terrorized first their schoolmates, then their teachers and then their entire neighbourhood. After several convictions for car theft and mugging with extreme violence they had eventually ended up abroad as 'minders', protecting the boss of an organization that sold animal parts for use in Asian folk medicine. Their new career turn had happened by chance and came about because of their being arrested by customs officials in the Far East when returning from a package trip, the package in this instance being two kilograms of drugs.

The twins had been convicted and jailed for life, having only narrowly escaped death sentences. On being imprisoned they had found themselves in a small compound containing fifty or so other criminals ranging from petty thieves to murderous cut-throats. Within a few weeks these inmates were divided roughly into two groups: those who had in some way offended the twins – a group readily identified by their limps, makeshift crutches and a variety of interesting dental and facial disfigurements – and the rest, who avoided becoming members of the first group by supplying the twins with extra food, cigarettes and the best places in the shade. For a training in survival in an unfriendly world, the playgrounds of south-east London and residence in a number of Her Majesty's correctional institutions were clearly more than a match for the backstreets and crowded bazaars of the Orient. This interesting social observation did not escape the notice of a certain Mr Song, a fellow prisoner who had made certain he remained on the right side of the twins. One day, after they had left a particularly vicious and sneaky thug called Saddhu the Sadist looking even more unattractive than he had looked before stepping accidentally on Sid's toe, Song had approached them.

'I like your people skills,' he said. 'I could use you boys in my outfit if we ever get out of this place. The money, by the way, is good.' The twins were immediately interested. They had already noticed that Song's scam, whatever it was, was extremely lucrative, for he bribed the guards generously for various favours including an endless supply of cigarettes for Sid and Fred. Mr Song, they learnt, ran an organization which slaughtered tigers in the wild, selling their skins to the fur trade and their body parts for use in a wide range of Asian folk medicines. Tigers were a protected species and the trade in tiger parts was illegal in India and had been banned in China in 1993 and in Japan – an end-market for the products – in 1999. There was a thriving underground market, however, and the prices that could be obtained for such products were enormous. Song and his men paid villagers near the few remaining jungles in which tigers survived to trap or poison the animals. These poor villagers received what was only a pittance compared with the money Song would eventually receive for the animals, but for them the pay seemed handsome and well worth the risk of illegal hunting. From a single tiger Song could make hundreds of thousands of pounds. The skin alone was worth a fortune and there seemed to be no part of the animal that was not used in traditional medicine: the meat to treat nausea; the whiskers for toothache; the bones for rheumatism; the fat for leprosy; the nose for dog bites; the brain for spots; the eyeballs for epilepsy, malaria and cataracts; the teeth for asthma, rabies and fevers; the tail for skin disease; the claws for sedation; and the skin for mental illness. Song had bases in Madhya Pradesh, Bengal, Nepal, China and Bhutan, smuggling the tiger parts across the various international borders to his base in Hong Kong where, under the guise of a butcher's shop, they were sold from under the counter. In a back room the bones and teeth were ground into powder, 'diluted' with chalk to increase the volume, and then sold around the world to a variety of dealers in folk medicine. It was ironic that Song was not in jail for conducting this dreadful trade, but had been arrested for evading tax on his cover trade, the butcher's shop. While he was in jail his lucrative tiger business, long the envy of other animal dealers, was being run by his son but was under threat from a number of rival gangs eager to share in the rich pickings from the illegal trade, and Song felt that the twins were just what he needed to preserve his empire.

Shortly following this discussion the president of the small country in which they were imprisoned died suddenly from food poisoning (the twins were never quite sure if this news came as a complete surprise to Song's organization), the government was overthrown and an amnesty was declared for all prisoners.

Following their unexpected release from jail the twins took up Song's offer of employment and for two years Song's terrible trade had continued under the protection of the twins and wreaked havoc on the tiger populations of the countries in which they worked. With the supply of tigers running out, however, and the governments of those countries coming under increasing pressure from animal organizations and the media to put an end to the killing of rare and threatened species, Song had finally decided to hold a crisis meeting to discuss the future of the business. During that meeting the twins had happened to mention their brother in South America and Song's fertile brain had immediately worked out a plan to rescue his organization. He had persuaded the twins to arrange a meeting with Chopper and the three of them were even now in a taxi speeding from Rio airport towards Chopper's villa.

Chopper's thoughts as he sat by the pool were suddenly interrupted by the maid.

'Excuse me, Senhor,' she said. 'Your guests have arrived. Shall I show them to their rooms now and call you later?'

'No,' said Chopper. 'They're late and I've got a company board meeting this afternoon. Show them straight into the boardroom and give them coffee.'

'Very well, Senhor.' She turned and left to do his bidding. Chopper heaved his massive bulk out of the lounger and went in to change. A few minutes later he strode into the boardroom and greeted his brothers and Mr Song.

Mr Song bowed slightly and said:

'I am delighted to meet you and see your beautiful home – but please call me Sing – it is the nickname your brothers seem to have given me and I am very happy with it.' Despite his sinister appearance, his voice had a soft, musical quality.

'Thank you, Sing,' replied Chopper. 'Now,' he continued, 'let's sit down and get straight to business. What's all this about?'

Sing began by explaining the tiger business that he had built up and which the twins had helped him with during the last two years. Then he came to the point.

'Unfortunately all good things must come to an end, and we are going to have to stop all our operations in Asia.'

'Why?' asked Chopper.

'The supply of tigers is running out,' said Sing in a resentful tone, as though these magnificent creatures had been put on the planet solely for the benefit of his business.

'The supply of tigers is running out,' said Sing.

'But I thought there were millions of tigers in the jungle,' said Chopper.

'No, there are probably fewer than five thousand left in the world,' said Sing. 'That's enough to keep us going for a while but international opinion and, in particular, the Wildlife Protection Society of India, is making our life so difficult that we feel the business is no longer economic.'

'Where do I fit into all this?' asked Chopper.

'As the tigers are becoming extinct,' Song explained, 'the demand for their bits and pieces is higher than ever; the rarer they are the higher the price goes.' Chopper nodded; that certainly made sense. 'Jaguars, however, though they are also declining rapidly in number, still live in such remote areas that if we can get into those areas we can probably continue in business for as long as we all need to become rich, without the authorities ever noticing. We think that jaguar parts will be just as good as tiger parts and, in any case, the market we are selling into isn't exactly high-tech. They won't be doing DNA tests on the teeth and other organs we give them, as long as they look like tiger bits. So, what we are proposing is to move our supply service from Asia to South America. We'll still sell the stuff into the Asian market where we have a network of dealers who'll be delighted to find that we've got a new source of material. When your esteemed brothers' – he glanced at Sid and Fred – 'told me that their brother ran a large lumber business in the Amazon, everything fell into place. If you can give me a base in one of your remote camps we'll catch the jaguars and give you a percentage on each animal – remember, each specimen is worth a significant amount by the time I've finished with it. A well-cured skin alone can fetch up to a million dollars and a skeleton worth ten thousand dollars is worth many times that amount when ground up into powder for medicine.'

Chopper was looking more interested every minute.

'There's been a recent development which makes things even better,' continued Sing, who had originally trained as a vet. He went on to explain how he could operate on the jaguars to insert a tube through the skin into the liver from which bile – highly sought after in oriental medicine – could be collected in a plastic bag every day for several months. He showed Chopper a diagram on his laptop computer and pointed to the screen.

'You just keep emptying the bag – it's like collecting liquid gold. When the animal eventually dies you can still sell all its other bits: skin, teeth, glands and so on, but by then you've already made a small fortune out of it.'

Chopper leant forward, his piggy eyes gleaming.

'How do you catch the jaguars?' he asked. 'Aren't they very dangerous?'

'They are, but the local tribes have techniques for catching them. We'll bribe the villagers with drugs and guns and, if they don't co-operate, burn down their village. The method seemed to work quite well in India and Malaysia and I've no doubt it will here.'

Chopper looked at the vile man with growing respect. Here was someone who had got it all worked out and would be ruthless in implementing his plans.

'It so happens,' he said, 'that I'm opening a new secret camp close to Colombia. It will have an airstrip because certain ... hmmm ... trading commodities are going to be flown in there from across the border. If we're hacking a bit of jungle down I don't see why we can't hack a bit more out for your zoo.' He leant forward and shook Song's hand. His grip was like a vice.

'You've got a deal. My brother Sam will sort out the percentages with you later.'

'When can we start?' asked Song, rubbing his pale, numb hand with the other.

'The camp is already being cleared,' replied Chopper. 'We're going to call it Cayman Creek. I suggest the twins start out for there tomorrow with a list of what you need and stay there until it's ready. They can start catching jaguars as soon as the compound is secure. You can go out there to operate as soon as there are enough cats to make your trip worthwhile.' His face relaxed into a crocodilian grin. 'Well, I think that just about wraps things up for the time being. After lunch I'll tell the board why we're adding zoo-keeping to our other activities.'

At the company meeting in the afternoon Chopper positioned himself at the head of the table and surveyed the assembled board of the Ecocidal Timber Company. He was inordinately proud of the company name which he had composed himself. He had seen the word 'ecocide' in a government pamphlet circulated to the timber industry and had thought, spelling not being his best subject, that it meant being on the side of ecology.

Chopper now called the meeting to order and informed the board of three proposals. The first concerned a major drug-smuggling operation which required the setting up of a secret logging site, with an airstrip, in very remote territory. The second was that the company would employ a scientist to search for new trees that might help medical science. This would look good to the government. He said the third development was particularly exciting, and he explained about the proposed jaguar camp. At the end of his talk the board voted unanimously to approve his recommendations and Chopper closed the meeting.

The next day the twins left for the remote jungle camp to start preparations for their onslaught on the jaguar population of the Amazon, a venture that was to bring them into bitter conflict with a young girl who at that moment had no inkling of her future destiny.

An advertisement was placed for a company scientist and just one month later Chopper interviewed a certain

Richard Bonaventure and appointed him as botanical adviser to the Ecocidal Timber Company.

3

Discussions with Dolphins

On the Monday morning after Lucy had gone down to the seaside she and Grandpa went off to the new building on the seafront and reported to the director's office. After Grandpa had introduced himself and handed him Lucy's teacher's letter, the director, Mr Finnegan, said that the teacher had already spoken to him on the phone and that they would love to have Lucy there. He took her down and introduced her to Catherine, the woman who looked after the dolphins, and she said that Lucy could sit and watch them whenever she liked, and help to feed them. Lucy was thrilled and settled down beside the pool. Catherine called the dolphins over by slapping the surface of the water and introduced them to Lucy.

'There are eight altogether,' she said, pointing them out in turn. 'That's the eldest, Jonathan, and those are his brothers Tom, Alastair and Harry. Over there are Cordelia, Camilla and Imogen, and that one swimming past us now is Clara – she's just come from a badly run zoo that got closed down and as you can see she's got a skin problem. Fortunately the vet says it's not serious and she's on some medicine but she hates taking it.' Lucy could see that Clara had some dull white patches on her skin.

Grandpa said he would come back at lunchtime with Grandma and take Lucy out for a burger, thanked Catherine and left. After Grandpa had gone, Catherine and her assistant Steve showed Lucy round the dolphinarium of which they were very proud. It wasn't open to the public until late morning, so they had the place to themselves. As well as having large pools inside the building, the dolphins could now, as a result of the recent rebuilding, swim for part of the day in an area of real sea that was fenced off from the rest of the ocean and which connected at high tide with a tunnel underneath the building. As it got nearer to opening time Catherine and Steve had to go and check on things before the public were admitted, and they left Lucy sitting on a little balcony overlooking the dolphins. As soon as they had gone Lucy spoke.

'Greetings, O Master Swimmers, I have come to speak to you.' The dolphins raced towards her in excitement, left the water with effortless power, performed some impressive aerobatics and returned smoothly to the water. Lucy was enthralled.

'Greetings, O Promised One,' said Jonathan, the largest dolphin, resurfacing as he spoke. 'We knew that She Who was Expected had come at last and we are greatly honoured that you should come to this place. What is it that you desire of us?'

'Greetings, O wise one!' replied Lucy. 'I have much to ask of you for there are many things I do not understand.'

'I know not all that there is to know,' said the dolphin

gravely, 'but I will tell you what I can.'

'First I must know who the Promised One is, and why you were expecting her. And, how did you know that I had arrived – did the other animals tell you?' She had only partly understood what Tibbles had tried to explain to her about animal language, and was anxious to hear what the dolphin could tell her.

'Slowly, slowly, O Special One! My kin are among the cleverest of animals, but even our minds cannot run at the speed of yours. Your thoughts seem to me to flash like lightning in the sky. It is true that separate animal species have their own language. I can speak within this pool to my own kin in words that none other can understand. But there is also a common language among all proper creatures – I count not the crawlipods and such like – and this tongue is used when there is common cause or common danger such as a fire in the forest, or a flood of the river, or a massive tide in the Great Salt. It also means that there are links between all

animals across the world just like — like —' he paused to find a suitable description for what he wished to say, '— like the silken homes that the arachnopods weave.'

'A web!' exclaimed Lucy in excitement. 'A web of information — like the internet! I shall call your web the animanet.'

'We know not of the internet about which you speak but we know that the Tailless Ones can speak in mysterious ways over great distances and if you speak of the animanet we shall henceforth use this name for our web,' the dolphin replied. 'This animanet is used only in matters of importance to all creatures. Your long-awaited arrival is a great matter — possibly the greatest of all to us — and so we all know of your existence.'

'But why were you expecting me?' asked Lucy.

'In the Common Tongue there is a legend known to all animals which is that one day a Promised One would come. My mother's mother told me that her mother's mother knew of this and that,

'. . . O Master Swimmers, I have come to speak to you.'

47

'back into time unimaginable, the same story has been told.'

'But who made the promise, and what is the Promised One to do?' Lucy burst in.

'No one knows who made the promise. One day, with your mind of quicksilver, you may know the answer to that yourself, but the destiny of the Promised One is to restore the ancient harmony that once existed among all creatures, including the Tailless Ones.'

'But there is no harmony. How can there be when animals chase and kill and eat one another? How can that be changed?'

'All animals recognize the reality of life,' the dolphin continued. 'In the Great Salt the large gillifin eats the small gillifin, and the small gillifin eats the tiny crustakin. On land, the furripelt eats the scurripod and the scurripod eats the crawlipod. This is harmony: it is the true harmony of nature and creation. The Tailless Ones have destroyed this ancient balance, however, because they kill when they do not need to eat, and they destroy the places where animals live so that none can live there any more. It was not always thus and our legend says that one day a Promised One will come who will understand these things and speak to us. Yet she will also be powerful among her own kin, the Tailless Ones, and be held by them in high regard. She will change things to help us: to preserve our forests, to keep our rivers pure and to protect those who live in the Great Salt. She will restore the ancient order of things in nature and will be esteemed among both animals and the Tailless Ones. All creation has waited through countless ages for the day of your coming and I am privileged to be the first of all in the Great Salt to speak to you.'

'But how can I do all the things you have described while I'm just a schoolgirl?' Lucy asked in amazement.

'I admit that I am perplexed by your youth,' replied the dolphin. 'It was told that She would be a female but not that She might be a child. There have been four before you who we thought would be the Promised One and they lived long, long, ago. They were all bearded ones and one of them told our ancestors that the true Promised One would be beardless and fair to look upon, with eyes that reflected the Brilliant One. We never knew what this could mean, but now I understand.' Lucy realized that the dolphin was referring to her glasses. She took them off absentmindedly and rubbed some tiny splashes of water off them with a tissue.

'They also said that sometimes she would have eyes in her hands,' said the dolphin with some excitement, 'and now I see that you are indeed the one about whom untold generations have spoken.'

'Who were the bearded ones?' asked Lucy, fascinated.

'Alas, I know not the names by which they were addressed among their own kin,' replied the dolphin, 'but the oldest and greatest of them lived countless generations ago through a time when the waters consumed the earth and my own kin from the Middle Salt could even swim above the great mountains in the lands of sand. Then, much later, another came: he also lived in those lands of sand from which the Brilliant One rises from his sleep to warm the Middle Salt. He lived in the City of the Great River in the Sand, when it had trees and flowers such as had never before been seen in those desolate places. All these things my kin were told by the dromedkin who roam those lands. There were yet two more that we thought would be The One for whom all animals waited. They both lived in the land of olives and the great *fire mountain. The first of these lived in the City of the Seven Hills where many animals were cruelly used for untold moons. The second, the last of such kind, before you, O Promised One, loved animals of every kin and many thought he was truly the Promised One; but it was he who said that the true One would be of womankind. This bearded one had a ring of brilliant fire about his head, a ring which never faded until his days were over.'*

Lucy was puzzled by this description but pursued it no further; she could come back to it later. In the meantime she had plenty of other questions to ask. After some further discussions the dolphin asked:

'Do other Tailless Ones know you are the Promised One?'

'Only my sister,' said Lucy, *'and she will tell no one.'*

'That is good,' the dolphin went on. *'Because you are but a child there are many who will wish to use you for their own ends and this would end in evil for you and many animals. Is there one who is trustworthy and wise that can help you in your task, for it may yet be the case that The Promise will not be achieved until you reach full womanhood?'*

'The mother and father of my mother are those to whom I can speak,' Lucy said.

'Speak then to them,' said her companion, *'and return to me when you are able. Fare thee well.'*

For Lucy the morning had passed in a flash and she couldn't believe it was already lunchtime when her grandparents appeared.

'Well,' said Grandpa, smiling as he looked at the blank sheets of her notepad, 'you don't seem to have written much yet!'

Lucy grinned.

'I've been making some observations, Gramps, and I'll write it all up later.'

'You sound just like one of my old students,' said Grandpa, who was a retired medical professor, 'full of convincing-sounding excuses. Never mind, you're here to relax and get better. I don't care if you don't write a single word all week – but you may have to produce something for your teacher at some point.'

For the rest of the day Lucy was very thoughtful and after tea Grandma looked across at her.

'Are you homesick, Lucy? You've been very quiet all day. Or aren't you feeling well?'

'No, I'm not homesick or ill,' said Lucy. 'It's just that I've got something very special to tell you about, but you must promise not to tell Mummy.' Her grandparents looked at each other.

'I'm not sure we can do that before we've heard your problem,' said Grandma, 'but we'll listen to you and help you as we've always done.' She looked across at Grandpa who nodded in agreement.

Her grandparents sat and listened intently while she told them the whole story. They did not interrupt at any point but Lucy saw them glance at each other once or twice when she was describing something particularly extraordinary. She ended by describing the events of that very day, and the strange things the dolphin had told her.

When she had finished there was a long silence. It was eventually broken by Grandma.

'This is an amazing story you've told us, Lucy, and we need to think very carefully about all you've said. Let's sleep on it now and have another chat in the morning. Don't worry; we'll sort it all out one way or another.'

Lucy kissed them good night and went to bed, the conversation with the dolphin running round her head until eventually she fell asleep.

Grandma and Grandpa sat up late into the night discussing what they had heard. They were extremely worried, for there only seemed to be a few possible explanations for what Lucy had described. The first, which they couldn't bring themselves to believe, was that it was all true. The second was that she was teasing, but they knew her too well to think she would tease them over something so important. The only other possibility was that the accident had damaged Lucy's brain in such a way that she now really thought she could talk to animals. If this was the case they didn't know if there was any way she could be cured. They eventually went to bed but neither of them slept well that night.

The next morning at breakfast Lucy suggested that Grandpa came with her to see the dolphins if Catherine had no objections. As they neared the pool Lucy turned to him.

'I know,' she said, 'it must be almost impossible for you to believe that what I told you last night is really true and not something I just *think* is true, so I'm going to ask the dolphins to help convince you.' She was just about to call to the dolphin she had spoken to the day before when

Catherine and Steve came in. They were carrying a bucket of fish.

'Before you start your studies, Lucy,' said Steve, 'we wondered if you'd like to help us feed the dolphins.'

Lucy of course was delighted and started to help throw the fish to the hungry animals who snapped them up eagerly. Lucy noticed Steve poking a hole into one of the fish and slipping a tablet into it. Catherine saw her looking and explained.

'This one's for Clara,' she said. 'It's her skin medicine.' Steve threw the fish in the air to Clara who snapped it up but then spat it out immediately.

'Gosh, she's clever,' said Steve admiringly. 'Fancy being able to smell a pill in a couple of seconds when it's buried deep inside a fish.'

'It's all very well giving her a pat on the back for outsmarting us,' laughed Catherine, 'but we've still got to give her some medicine.'

Lucy saw a wonderful opportunity to help the dolphin, and Catherine and Steve, and at the same time to start to convince her grandfather that everything she had told him was true.

'Can I try?' she said to Steve. Steve looked enquiringly at Catherine and she shrugged her shoulders.

'Why not? Can't do any harm, I suppose – we're not doing too well so far ourselves.'

Steve gave Lucy a tablet and started to make a hole in another fish.

'I won't be needing that,' said Lucy. Her voice suddenly

sounded more authoritative, and they all looked at her in surprise.

'*Clara,*' Lucy said to the dolphin, '*please come to the edge.*' The animal swam obediently to the side.

'*Greetings, O Promised One,*' she said. Her voice was soft and languorous – it reminded Lucy of deep, tranquil waters, and exquisite fronds of seaweed waving over beautiful coral.

'*Do you know,*' Lucy continued, '*that your beautiful skin has been damaged?*'

'*I know all is not well with it. It feels as though tiny gillifins are nibbling at it but the others tell me that none can be seen.*'

'*Why didn't you eat the gillifin that was given to you just now?*'

'*It smells not as a gillifin should and I wait for one that does.*'

'*That smell does not mean the gillifin is bad,*' said Lucy. '*The Tailless Ones who care for you here and feed you have put a tiny pebble into the gillifin which will make your skin whole once again. It is this pebble that you can smell. If you eat the pebble on its own I will then give you a gillifin that smells pure.*'

'*It shall be as you command, O Promised One,*' said Clara. To the astonished onlookers Lucy appeared to be in a quiet trance, she and the dolphin looking at each other in complete silence.

Lucy held out her hand with the tablet in it and the dolphin leapt from the water and took it from her fingers so cleanly that Lucy just felt the slightest brush as the animal's beak closed on the pill. The others gazed in stupefaction as Lucy then took the biggest fish remaining in the bucket and threw it to Clara.

'I think she's earned a fat one for being so good, don't you?' she said, turning to them with a happy grin.

'How on earth . . .' Steve began to splutter out a question but didn't really know what to say. Catherine took over.

'Well, you've certainly got a way with dolphins, Lucy! You can give Clara her medicine every day; let's just hope she continues to co-operate.'

'She will,' said Lucy, simply. Catherine and Steve glanced at each other; they were as amazed by the girl's confidence as they were by the little drama they had just witnessed, but they had work to do so they left Lucy to finish the feed and went off about their other duties. When they had gone Grandpa looked at Lucy.

'I'm puzzled and impressed,' he said. 'Is that the dolphin you spoke to –' he stopped and corrected himself, '– you *saw* yesterday?'

'No, that was Jonathan; see, he's over there.' She pointed to him, cavorting with one of his brothers. 'This is the first time I have spoken to Clara. She has a lovely voice.' She said it so naturally that Grandpa almost found himself believing that a conversation had really taken place between his granddaughter and a dolphin – and yet, how could it possibly be true?

'As I was saying before those two arrived with breakfast,' said Lucy brightly, 'I really need you on my side, so tell me what must I do to convince you?'

Grandpa was somewhat taken aback. He thought for a few moments before speaking.

'You must do something that couldn't have been planned and practised in advance,' he said eventually, 'even though I know you haven't really had time to plan anything anyway. And they shouldn't be able to see you,' he added, 'in case they get clues from your expression or your gestures – oh, and you mustn't make any sounds or vibrations. Can you think of something along those lines?'

'Well, it's best if it involves you, Grandpa,' said Lucy, 'then it certainly couldn't have been planned.' She lay down on the cold tiled floor of the little balcony they were standing on, put her cardigan behind her head for a pillow and looked up at her grandfather. She was completely concealed from the view of the dolphins by the balcony wall. 'I'm going to tell them all to dive,' she said, 'and then you show me with your fingers how many you want to come up – and make sure you keep your hands below the wall, so only I can see.'

As she spoke the waters churned and all the animals disappeared.

'I must be completely bonkers doing this,' thought Grandpa to himself. He was glad that the members of his golf club couldn't see him now, as he showed Lucy three fingers.

Three dolphins surfaced immediately. Grandpa folded one finger down, watching the dolphins intently, and suddenly there were only two. He closed his fist and they all disappeared again. A strange and spooky sensation began to creep through him. It was a thrill of excitement mixed with a tinge of fear. He felt as if the corner of an immense and awesome mystery was being lifted so that he could peep into an unknown and unimaginable other reality. He bent down and whispered to Lucy.

'If it's the fingers on my right hand ask them to do something special; if it's those on my left hand they can just come to the surface.' Lucy nodded. He showed her one finger on his left hand and Jonathan appeared on the surface. He next showed her two fingers of his right hand; there was a short interval and then Grandpa jumped back in surprise as Tom and Harry barrelled out of the water at an amazing speed, somersaulted in the air and landed with a resounding smack, flat on their backs, sending up a splash that splattered the entire pool, and soaked Grandpa's shirt.

'Go to the edge of the pool and they'll come and say sorry for splashing you,' said Lucy, laughing. Grandpa left the little balcony and went down to the pool edge. The dolphins all swam up to him and then Tom and Harry, the splashing culprits, moved back from the others and supported themselves vertically in the water, the upper halves of their bodies sticking up in the air like mermaids. They nodded their heads mischievously at Grandpa before sinking back into the water.

Lucy came down to the edge of the pool and took Grandpa's arm as she spoke to him.

'I hate to use the animals like a circus, but Jonathan was keen that I talked to you and he said that they wouldn't mind doing something to convince you. Do you believe me now?'

It was a big question and she looked straight up into his

eyes as she asked it. He did not hesitate.

'Yes, I do, pet. It's almost impossible to believe but you've completely convinced me. I need to go home and talk to Grandma now because she's been very concerned and this will be wonderful news for her. Then, later, we need to have a long chat about what it all means for us. Now I'll leave you to talk to your new friends.' He kissed her and hugged her and left.

Lucy sat down, tears of relief streaming down her face. She had been terribly worried about telling her grandparents and when she had seen their initial reaction to her story, had begun to have second thoughts about whether she should ever have confided in them. She knew, though, that she needed the advice and support of a grown-up she trusted, and now she felt completely reassured. She looked at her watch. Grandma had given her a packed lunch and she decided that eleven o'clock was just about the right time to get started on it while she thought of what she wanted to say to Jonathan.

4
Some Mysteries Solved

That afternoon Lucy sat down with her grandparents while they had a cup of tea. She had just got back from the dolphinarium and was bursting with questions.

'There's so much I want to talk about,' she said. 'Clare's been fantastic, but there are some things she couldn't help me with and I'm sure you'll both have some useful ideas; it's so nice to be able to talk normally with you now that you really understand what's happened to me.' She was aware that her grandparents had spoken about her during the day and that they were both now completely convinced by her story. As it happened, they were both particularly interested in language. Her grandmother had been a classics teacher and her grandfather had been a doctor, specializing in speech disorders. They both now sat fascinated as Lucy described her conversations with Jonathan that day.

When she had finished Grandma got up.

'I think I'll make a start on getting dinner ready – even though it's your grandpa's turn to cook,' she said, looking at Grandpa who gave a sheepish grin. 'I can see you two are going to be at this for hours.' When she had left,

Grandpa sat deep in thought for a few moments.

'Grandma and I have some ideas about what might have happened to you,' he eventually began, 'but they are only guesswork on our part – which may be completely wrong.' Lucy nodded.

'I know,' she said, 'but I'd just like to hear what you think.'

'We know from what the doctors told Clare,' said Grandpa, 'that the pineal gland in your brain is a little bit different to everyone else's and it must have been like that when you were born. That could mean that you were *always* going to be the Promised One but you probably weren't meant to know about it until you were grown-up. I think that when you had your accident the special bit of your brain that lets you speak to animals got jogged into action and it started to work a few years earlier than it was meant to. Sometimes, if a watch has stopped, you can get it to start by shaking it and I think something similar must have happened to your brain.'

'That makes good sense,' said Lucy, 'but how can I do all the things the animals may want me to do while I'm still only eleven?'

'I think the animals are as surprised as you are that you are just a child,' replied Grandpa, 'and I don't think they are going to expect you to do much until you are grown-up. Maybe you can help them with one or two small things you feel capable of doing now and leave the bigger things until you're an adult.'

Lucy's face lit up. She was very relieved to hear this

suggestion because she had been worried about how to help the animals at the same time as trying to go to school and pass her exams.

'That's a great idea, Gramps! I can ask Jonathan tomorrow for some ideas and then pick something I feel I can cope with. After what you've said I can see that I wasn't really meant to worry about this until I was grown-up. That stupid accident has just made me know about it sooner than I should've done.' She thought for a moment, then continued:

'There are all kinds of other questions still, and one that has bothered me ever since Tibbles first spoke to me is how the animals can speak English and know so many special words.'

Grandpa chuckled. It was clearly a question he had been expecting.

'The animals aren't speaking English of course, but what *are* they speaking? Well, I think that, as a result of your accident, you can tell what animals are *thinking*. When you receive their thoughts your brain then turns them into English, using the words you already know that most closely match the ideas they are transmitting to you. Let me give you an example. Say there was a two-year-old child in this room who also had your special powers. Let's imagine a cat came in from the garden and thought about what he had just seen. The small child might "hear" the cat say: *"There's an animal with a fluffy tail in a tree."* You might hear the cat say: *"There's a squirrel in the apple tree."* Even though the cat sent the same thought to both of you, you translated it in a different way from the younger child because you know more words than she does. Does that make sense to you?'

'Perfect sense,' replied Lucy. 'So if I were a German girl I would hear what the cat said in German, and if I were Korean I'd hear it in Korean?'

'Exactly,' said Grandpa, 'and I'm sure I'm correct when I say that no animal has ever used a word you didn't know. Tell me I'm wrong, and you will completely destroy my theory.'

Lucy thought hard for a moment.

'No–oo,' she said eventually, 'they've never used a word I didn't know, but they've used words I hardly ever say and once or twice they've used funny words that I thought I'd completely forgotten. Oh! And the other thing is that *I* sometimes use words when I'm speaking to them that I never use normally.'

'Give me an example.' Grandpa was sitting forward in his seat, completely engrossed in what she had to say. Once again, Lucy had to think for a moment. She'd had so many different conversations that it was hard to remember specific examples.

'Ah yes,' she said, 'Tibbles talked about "coneybanes" – stoats. The name came straight into my mind as she spoke. I only remembered later that coney is a very old word for a rabbit. It was in a passage we did at school from some famous book – I think it was *Lord of the Rings* – and then I remembered another story in which a wicked baron was called the bane of the countryside – Mum told me it meant everyone was frightened of him because he was cruel and nasty. The animals think of stoats as animals that chase rabbits so my brain came up with the name coneybane without my even thinking about it! Another funny thing is that when I saw the owl I called it a *moonwraith*. I had no idea why – it just seemed more complimentary than nightbane and I didn't want to upset him. Later I remembered that Miss Reedwright, our English teacher, had told us that wraith was an old word for ghost and the owl swooped in such a silent and shadowy way I suppose he reminded me of a ghost.' She paused, then continued.

'Your theory also explains something else, which is that animals name other animals by describing them – so a cat is a "furriclaws" and a bird is a "fledgiquill". I must turn the animals' thoughts about each other into my own descriptive words –' she paused and thought for a moment, '– but they are usually *old-fashioned* words – and the animals say things like *"thee"* and *"thou"*. Why is that, do you think?' Grandpa pondered briefly before replying.

'I think it's because they haven't spoken to human beings for hundreds of thousands of years and they think in an old-fashioned way. Your brain tries to tell you this by using the oldest words that you have ever seen or learnt.'

'I'm so pleased you've been able to explain all this,' said Lucy; she looked relieved. 'I couldn't make head nor tail of it but now it's beginning to make some sense. I just couldn't understand how they knew all these words and spoke so perfectly, but –' she paused '– if these words come from *me*, how is it that the animals have different voices – like the lovely voice of Clara today?'

'That's even more interesting,' said Grandpa. 'I think that the thought waves from any individual animal must be distinctive in some way – just as distinctive as the normal sounds we detect with our ears. Those differences in thought waves are what distinguishes one animal from another when they can't see or smell each other or when several are "speaking" at the same time. Let me give you an example of what I mean: do you think the *volume* of thought waves sent out from a tiny mouse brain would be different from the volume sent out by a lion?'

'Of course,' said Lucy.

'That means that if you were to hear both mouse and lion "talking" using your new skill you might be able to guess which was which even if you couldn't see them. Your brain would use the experience it has gained with *sound* images to help you analyse your new *thought* images.'

'*Now* I see what you're saying –' Lucy's face lit up, '– and it's true. I knew the mice at home must be tiny creatures even before I saw them; when I was on Wimbledon Common I could hear dozens of voices and though I didn't know which animals they came from I found I could roughly guess what the owner of any particular voice must be like.'

'Now it's my turn to ask a question,' said Grandpa. 'Can you talk equally well to all animals?'

'No, they're all different. The dolphins were easily the best, then Tibbles, then the mice. Birds are much more difficult – I spoke to some little birds in the garden and an owl on the common. It was like speaking to a young child or a very stupid person. I haven't really tried with any more basic animals – though I've just remembered about a spider in the bathroom last week. It was in the middle of the floor and I don't really like them at all; I spoke to it but it didn't reply. The funny thing is though, I asked it to go away and hide and that's just what it did. I don't really know if it was just a coincidence or whether it actually did what I said, but it certainly didn't speak to me.'

'I think that the animals you can talk to best are the ones closest to us in evolutionary terms,' said Grandpa. 'I'd love to know how you'd get on with chimpanzees or gorillas. Scientists would be fascinated by all this, but whether it would be wise ever to tell them . . .'

Lucy never found out what he was going to say, because at that moment a car screeched to an emergency stop outside in the street and they both rushed to the window. A sour-faced man was standing in the road shaking his fist at a car that was just starting again, after obviously having stopped for him.

'Isn't he that horrid Mr Whitehead?' asked Lucy.

'Yes,' said Grandpa. 'I'm afraid he always just walks out into the road and expects the cars to stop for him.' Mr Whitehead was the neighbourhood nuisance. He lived opposite Grandma and Grandpa and made it his life's work to complain about everyone and everything in the road. In the previous summer he had crossed the road to shout at poor Sarah for making too much noise in the front garden on her birthday. She had been terribly upset and frightened and Lucy had never forgiven him for the incident.

'Watch this, Gramps,' she said, and he saw her looking at two seagulls sitting on the roof of the house opposite, Whitehead's own house, in fact. Suddenly one of the gulls flew low across the road, and as it passed over Whitehead a white blob descended on to his head. It was a very large blob and it splashed all over his head and shoulders.

'That's from Sarah . . .' Grandpa heard Lucy mutter under her breath. Whitehead, who was beside himself with rage, stamped his foot and looked up into the sky to give the bird a glare and a curse. This happened to be most unwise, for at that moment the second gull flew over and this time the droppings hit him full in the face.

' . . . and that's from me,' Lucy added with great satisfaction. Grandpa had never seen the man looking so angry. The sash window was open a few inches, top and bottom, and they could clearly hear him shouting and swearing. His face was covered in white goo streaked with black and grey and he looked like a circus clown. He saw Grandpa and Lucy looking at him and Grandpa started back guiltily as though he had been found out. Then he remembered that what had happened couldn't possibly be blamed on him or Lucy, and for the first time the truly awesome and anonymous nature of her power dawned on him.

Lucy laughed in glee and clapped her hands.

'Serves you right, you horrid old creep,' she said, then stopped and looked at her grandfather.

'Oh gosh,' she said, 'that was a really wicked thing to do, wasn't it?' She didn't look in the slightest bit sorry, however, and though at first Grandpa pretended to be stern, he suddenly pointed out of the window and started to giggle.

On their side of the road, to which Mr Whitehead was crossing, there was a drain with a damaged cover. The council had placed warning lanterns round it so that traffic would not drive over it until it had been repaired. Mr Whitehead had stumbled across the road, his face dripping, tripped over a lantern and got his foot stuck in the drain. He looked up again and, seeing Grandpa and Lucy still watching him, immediately stopped struggling to remove his foot and stood looking at his wrist watch, as though he regularly stood with one foot on the kerb and the other in a drain. At that moment a large grey rat appeared from the drain, jumped on to his trapped foot and started sniffing and nibbling at his shoe lace. Whitehead gave a cry of fear and disgust and tried to kick it off with his free foot, almost overbalancing as he did so. The rat then sprang on to his good foot and put its head under his trouser hem as if to run up inside his trouser leg. Whitehead shook his foot frantically to try to dislodge it. Then, just as quickly as it had arrived, the rat disappeared down the drain. Whitehead looked up to the window immediately and saw Grandpa and Lucy pretending to gaze up at the sky as though discussing the weather.

Soon an old lady crossed the street pulling a small poodle behind her on a very long lead. Mr Whitehead was

now pretending to read his newspaper, and she walked past him without taking any notice of him. When the dog came up to him, however, he sniffed eagerly at the drain and Whitehead's feet – he could smell the rat. Having decided the rat had gone he then casually cocked his leg against Mr Whitehead's trapped leg as though he routinely came across short, fat, trouser-covered lampposts on his evening walks. The old lady waited patiently for a while then tugged at the lead. Half-turning she called back over her shoulder:

'Come along, Walter, it's almost time for your tea. What a great big wee-wee for such a little doggy!'

'. . . What a great big wee-wee for such a little doggy!'

Lucy looked at Grandpa whose face was contorted with laughter.

'I didn't do that dog, Grandpa, honestly! But it was a really cool finish, wasn't it?' They were both convulsed with laughter and had to crouch down behind the windowsill so Mr Whitehead couldn't see them. He looked up to check and heard muffled hoots and shrieks floating through the window.

'What on earth are you two up to?' Grandma, hearing the commotion, came through from the kitchen and found the pair hiding like naughty children under the window. Then she looked out, and soon all three of them were giggling together on the floor.

Eventually Grandma returned to the kitchen to check on her cooking and Lucy went to the telephone. A few moments later Grandpa heard her peals of laughter as she told Clare and Sarah about Mr Whitehead. As he started to lay the table, he pondered over the extraordinary situation that had come about in which she was at one moment someone with apparently complete dominion over the animal kingdom, and the next, just a mischievous little girl.

The next day Lucy went off to the dolphinarium again. Grandma was going shopping and they set off together. As they left the house some workmen were repairing the drain in the road outside and Lucy was amused to see that Mr Whitehead's shoe was still stuck in it. While she and

Grandpa were hiding he must have hopped home with one shoe missing, a sight she would have loved to have seen. She decided to arrange some further entertainment involving animals and Mr Whitehead before she went home and to borrow Grandpa's camcorder so she could take a record of the fun back for her sisters.

Jonathan and his companions were overjoyed to see Lucy again and Catherine, still looking somewhat puzzled by the events of the previous day, reported that Clara had taken her tablet that morning without any fuss at all. Soon Lucy was able to sit down and chat in peace with Jonathan and tell him about her conversation with her grandparents.

'The Sagacious Ones have said many wise things,' said the dolphin when she had finished, 'and it is well that you have spoken to them. It was never said that the Promised One would be a child and they are right that we should wait until the proper time before you fulfil your destiny; we have waited for many aeons hitherto and in comparison with the immensity of those ages you will become a woman in the flutter of a dolphin's tail. Yet it would be good for us all if you could do something even now and it would be best if you chose to assist some animals that are close to your heart. It is said that there are two that you hold particularly dear: one is a marsupihop and the other is one of the Terrible Ones. These you keep at your side while the Brilliant One sleeps.'

Lucy gaped at him. He must be talking about her cuddly bedtime toys, Kanga Kangaroo and Jackie Jaguar.

'How can you know of these things?' she said at last.

'We spoke yesterday of what you called the animanet,' the dolphin replied. 'This is only used in very special times but the life and movements of the Promised One are special to all animals. There is nothing on earth that we value more highly than your well-being. We know about your home and your possessions and henceforth your whereabouts will always be known to us.'

'So,' thought Lucy, 'blabbermouth Tibbles has been talking about my toys over the animanet.'

The dolphin continued.

'I shall be speaking today to those who know the marsupihops to see if they need your help; I cannot, however, speak yet to the Terrible Ones for I know not what kind of Terrible One it is that you cherish. We know of the great manefang that lives south of the Great Sands on the plains where run the striped horse and the endless herds of clovenkin; the fleetfang that can outrun even the clovenkin, and the spotfang that hunts from the trees; then there is the stripedfang who lives where the Brilliant One rises, or there are the Terrible Ones over the Great Salt where the Brilliant One sleeps – the mountainfang in the north and the junglefang in the south. Which of these Terrible Ones is it your desire to assist?'

'Hmmm,' thought Lucy, 'so clever-clogs Tibbles isn't so hot on her big cats – she doesn't know exactly what Jackie is.' The dolphin obviously didn't know whether Tibbles meant a lion, a cheetah, a leopard, a tiger, a cougar or a jaguar. She spoke to the dolphin.

'I respect and admire all those Terrible Ones of which you speak, but the one that I have loved since I was very young is the junglefang.'

'I shall speak to those who know the junglefang today,' he replied. 'My own kin live in the great river of the junglefang, and I shall speak with you again after the Brilliant One has slept.'

'But how can you speak to those so far away? Is it with the fledgiquills you do this?'

'No, O Promised One, the fledgiquills can fly at great speed – faster than any other living creature – but even they cannot reach us from the lands of the marsupihop or the junglefang in but a single sunsleep. No, it is through the Great Ones that we speak. They learn of matters far away through the Great Salt and when I swim in the Great Salt today I can speak to them.'

Lucy remembered that the dolphinarium was now connected to the sea, so Jonathan would be able to speak to wild dolphins and whales, but she had no idea how that was going to help him to communicate overnight with Australia and South America.

'We will speak again when the Brilliant One rises once more,' continued the dolphin, 'but before you take your leave I have a question that has perplexed the Great Ones and all their kin since the beginning of time. Perhaps you would ask the Sagacious Ones, though I fear that even they may not know the answer to the mystery of which I speak.' Lucy was fascinated.

'What is the mystery?' she asked.

'The Great Ones that pass for league upon league through the Great Salt have discovered a secret that is known only to those that can journey for many moons across waters far from those that they know and love. It is said – and I only know what others have told me – that if a Great One follows the path of the Brilliant One, then after many, many leagues there are other lands – the lands where live the junglefang and the mountainfang.'

Lucy nodded; she had already noticed that the dolphin recognized her head movements for what they were.

'The Great Salt flows around those lands, close to the Great Ice,' the dolphin continued, 'and if, beyond them, the Brilliant One is followed once more for an immense distance there are yet other lands which the Great Salt also passes. It is said – and here is the great mystery – that, when many such lands have been passed, the Great Salt once again becomes that part from which this great journey began. I know not if this can be true for it seems as if nothing could be so – yet my father, and my father's father, told me that they had heard this from many Great Ones and I have also heard it tell that there are fledgiquills who say the same: if they fly always towards the Brilliant One and never turn back, then one day they arrive once more in the place whence they came. Do you think the Sagacious Ones will believe what I have told you?'

Lucy was in a quandary. Should she herself embark upon an explanation of the dolphin's 'mystery' or should she pretend to consult her grandparents? The latter course seemed like a bit of a cop-out and she thought that it might be easier to do things first hand – it would in any case enhance the profile of the Promised One in the eyes of the animals for her to know the answer to such mysteries even when not yet grown to full womanhood. She went to the side of the pool where there was a netted pen containing rings and other inflatable playthings that Catherine used when the public came to see the dolphins performing. There was a large ball in the pen and Lucy brought this over to Jonathan.

'The mystery of which you speak is known to us Tailless Ones,' she said, 'and in the houses we build to sail on the Great Salt and the steel thunderquills that roar in the air we have found all that you have heard to be true. I can tell you why it is so, but I know not if you will understand.' She then successfully explained the spherical nature of the earth using the ball, but Jonathan was unable to understand why the Great Salt didn't fall off the bottom, despite his effortless use of gravity in his aquabatic and aerobatic feats. Finally he spoke:

'It is said that the Tailless Ones know of many things that we can never know and I see that this is true – that, indeed, is why we need one of you to help us in our task. It is sufficient for me to know that the mysterious thing that Great Ones and their kin have told me is true, and I can now tell them that this has been said by the Promised One.'

Lucy then answered several more questions that he had obviously been saving up to ask her.

The time had passed so quickly while they were talking that Lucy was astonished when Grandma and Grandpa appeared to take her to lunch.

'I'd no idea it was lunchtime already,' she said. 'We've talked about so many things – I can't wait to tell you about them!'

They went to a pizza parlour on the seafront that Lucy had had her eye on for a couple of days and she wasn't disappointed. Between mouthfuls of her favourite pizza combination, ham and pineapple, she told her grandparents about her morning and, as they listened to their granddaughter talking earnestly about the difficulty of explaining that the world wasn't flat to a dolphin, they had to keep reminding themselves that they weren't in some bizarre dream. After lunch Grandma left to take the old lady next door to a hospital appointment, and Grandpa and Lucy went for a walk along the seafront.

5
Some Lessons in History and Geography

'I've so much to tell you about today,' started Lucy, 'but first I must ask you about something Jonathan said a couple of days ago which I forgot during our chat yesterday.'

'Go on,' said Grandpa, his interest already aroused. He was finding these discussions with his granddaughter fascinating.

'Well, when I asked him about the Promised One, he said something very strange. He said that there had been four others before me that the animals had thought to be The One. From what he said they were all men, but one of them, the most recent one, said that the real Promised One would be a woman – a *woman*, by the way, not a girl.'

'Did he give you any details?' Grandpa was beside himself with interest.

'Yes, but I didn't understand them. The first man lived what Jonathan called "long, long ago" and at a time when dolphins from the "Middle Salt" could swim across mountains rising from the sand. What on earth does that all mean?'

'The Middle Salt must be the Mediterranean Sea,' said

Grandpa excitedly. 'The dolphins would have known even before man that it is almost completely enclosed by land – in the middle of the land – and the only way in and out before the Suez Canal was built was through the straits of Gibraltar. As for swimming over mountains that Mediterranean dolphins could get to – well, you know the answer to that one, Lucy!'

She thought for a moment.

'Give me a clue.'

'When you get home look in the Old Testament of the Bible. The Book of Genesis.'

'Don't be mean, Gramps. I can't wait till we get home! Give me an easier clue.'

Grandpa grinned.

'OK, who springs to your mind when you think about somebody who could get animals – lots of different animals – to do what he wanted? And who lived during a period when the waters covered the land so deep that dolphins could swim over mountains?'

'Noah!' exclaimed Lucy. 'Of course, he must have been able to do things just the same as I can. How else could he have got the animals to go into the Ark – and not eat each other up during the voyage? No wonder the animals thought the Promised One had arrived! I should really've got that one myself, shouldn't I?'

'Never mind,' said Grandpa. 'It's very difficult to connect what you are hearing in the reality of here and now with stories relating to things that happened thousands of years ago. What I'm totally amazed by is the fact that an ancient legend that humans have passed down through the ages in the Bible has also been preserved in the animal kingdom solely by word of mouth. It's all but incredible. Who's next? This is just like a quiz show!'

'The next sounded very interesting and I'm sure you'll know the answer. He lived in the lands of sand from which the Brilliant One rises to warm the Middle Salt.'

'So,' said Grandpa. 'He lived in the desert lands to the east of the Mediterranean. That narrows it down, but it still covers an awful lot of countries. Did he give any other clues?'

'Well, he said something about a city on a great river in the sand with lots of flowers – oh yes, he said, "trees and flowers such as had never been seen before in those desolate places".'

Grandpa strolled along, deep in thought.

'"such as had never been seen",' he murmured, 'Of course!' His face lit up. 'The Hanging Gardens of Babylon – one of the Seven Wonders of the World. This was the city built in the middle of the desert on the river Euphrates by a famous king called Nebuchadrezzar. But who on earth . . .? I've got it!' he said in triumph. 'It's Daniel. Have you heard of Daniel?' He turned to Lucy.

'Do you mean the man in the story of Daniel and the Lions' Den?'

'Yes,' said Grandpa. 'Well done! Nebuchadrezzar had Daniel thrown into a den of lions expecting him to be torn to pieces, but he walked out completely unharmed. The power given to him to do that was presumably the same power that you've been given. There's no other explanation. Who's next?' he asked eagerly. They had come to a bench in a stone shelter facing the sea and they sat down as they talked.

'I can't believe how well you're solving these puzzles,' said Lucy. 'I wasn't sure if we'd get any, and now there's only two to go. They both lived in the land of olives and the great mountain of fire – or something like that – and the first lived in the City of the Seven Hills.'

'The Seven Hills is another name for Rome,' said Grandpa, 'and of course the mountain of fire must be the great volcano Vesuvius – we're talking about Italy.'

'Well, that's all I know about him,' said Lucy. 'Any ideas?'

'None at the moment; let's leave him and come back to him. Who came last?'

'Now, he's *really* mysterious. He talked to lots of animals and – wait for this – he had a ring of fire round his head that stayed there till the day he died.'

Grandpa fell deep into thought once again.

'I know who this is,' he said after a few moments, 'and so do you. But I can see why you didn't understand the ring of fire. Pictures with rings of fire in them aren't so much in fashion as they used to be and you probably haven't seen many.'

'Many? I don't think I've seen any!' said Lucy, mystified.

'I think the "ring of fire" must be a halo,' said Grandpa. 'Does that help?'

'A saint!' exclaimed Lucy. 'He was a saint. I know – it was St Francis of Assisi!'

'. . . he had a ring of fire round his head that stayed there till the day he died.'

'Well done,' said Grandpa. 'I'm sure that's who it must have been.' He paused for a moment. 'It's fascinating that the animals could actually *see* his halo — they obviously do have some kind of sixth sense that enables them to detect things that are invisible to humans.' They both fell silent for a few moments, marvelling at the thought of animals being able to perceive the halo of a saint.

'Wasn't there a story,' said Lucy, returning to their discussion, 'about someone who took a thorn out of a lion's paw? It always seemed a bit unlikely to me that the lion would have let him get anywhere near a sore paw, never mind poke around at it!'

'You've got it!' exclaimed Grandpa. 'Androcles and the lion. He was a Roman slave — so that fits perfectly with the Seven Hills story. Like you, I've always wondered about that thorn-in-the-paw story. It makes so much more sense if we assume Androcles possessed your power.'

'I'm really glad that we've solved these "mystery men",' said Lucy. 'Knowing about these famous people and thinking that they had the same power as I have makes me feel less of an oddity and more part of a plan which is somehow going to end in something good.'

Grandpa was thrilled to hear her say this. He and Grandma had been very worried by the fact that her powers seemed to make her different from all other humans

'Wasn't there a story,' said Lucy, 'about someone who took a thorn out of a lion's paw?'

— even her own family. Yet now she could relate to other people, all of them apparently good or even saintly, who had shared her gifts, and this made her part of something she clearly believed would be of benefit to all creatures.

They sat thinking for a while, looking at the sea and the waves crashing endlessly on the shore.

'Now,' Grandpa said eventually, 'what about today's developments?'

'Well, Jonathan seemed very comfortable with your idea of my only doing something I can cope with while I'm still at school. They've already asked Tibbles about my cuddly toys – can you believe it? – and he's going to find out whether the kangaroos or the jaguars have any problems for me to think about. Now that's something I need to ask you about; well, two things really. The first is that he said his own kin lived in the great river of the junglefangs – that's jaguars by the way. I thought that dolphins only lived in the sea.'

'The great river of the junglefangs has to be the Amazon and its tributaries,' said Grandpa, 'but I certainly didn't know dolphins went up it. Let's look it up after tea. What was the other thing?'

'That's even more intriguing. He says he's going to check out things with the kangaroos and the jaguars and let me know *tomorrow*. When I asked him how he could do that, he said he did it through the whales; that they spoke *through* the Great Salt. What does that mean, and how can it possibly work faster than a bird can fly?'

Once more Grandpa became excited by what she had said.

'Whale song,' he said. 'Of course! Whales can sing under water,' he explained to Lucy, 'and they use the special noises they make to communicate over thousands of miles.

Sound travels more than four times as fast under water as it does through the air, so it travels vast distances very quickly. Not only that, but there's a special "sound channel" about one kilometre below the surface that's something to do with the physics of seawater and temperature and all sorts of complicated things. Anyway this channel – I think the scientists call it the SOFAR channel – can transmit sounds for thousands and thousands of miles around the earth under the water and it's thought that whales use this channel for their songs.'

'What does SOFAR stand for?' asked Lucy, fascinated. She wasn't quite sure if she believed what Grandpa was telling her.

'I'm not sure exactly – something like "sound fixing and ranging" – we can look it up on the internet when we get home. The physicists have known about it for ages and submarines used to use it if their radios didn't work. Once, the noise of an underwater bomb set off in Australia was heard over three hours later in Bermuda; the noise had travelled round half the world under the sea. It's thought that, before ships' engines made so much noise, whales could use sound and infrasound to communicate over thousands of miles. Now it's much more difficult for them because of all the noise generated by manmade things – another example of how man, even unconsciously, can mess up things that animals have taken millions of years of evolution to attain. Apparently whales can "shout", however. A blue whale can generate more noise than a jet aeroplane, so we think they can still communicate over vast distances despite man's interference with their systems, and that, presumably, is how your Jonathan will find out overnight what's happening in Australia and South America.'

Lucy was impressed. 'That's really spooky,' she said at last, 'and I'm just thinking how useful that's going to be in the future.'

'How do you mean?' asked Grandpa.

'Well, I don't know exactly what I'm going to end up doing for the animals,' said Lucy, 'but whatever it is, it has to be a good thing for me to be able to use that kind of long-distance messaging service.'

Grandpa agreed and was struck by the fact that she was already thinking about the future possible use of her special powers. That evening he took down his big book on the River Amazon and gave it to Lucy.

'Dolphins – here we are,' said Lucy, running her finger down the index. She turned to the appropriate page and began to read. 'Gosh,' she said, 'Jonathan was right. There are special river dolphins that go deep into the jungle along the river.'

Her eye wandered down the page which was full of interesting details of the many other creatures inhabiting the river: half of all the freshwater species of fish; giant otters and electric eels that could stun or even kill a man with a shock of several hundred volts. Fascinated, Lucy decided to read the book properly and turned to the beginning where she read about the Amazon itself. The river, the largest in the world, apparently carried one-fifth of all the running fresh water on the planet and was up to sixty-five kilometres wide in places. The Amazon rainforest was by far the largest on earth and contained the greatest diversity of animal and plant species to be found anywhere. She read of the many different benefits that had come from the plants of the rainforest: rubber, which had changed the world in countless ways; hundreds of medicines including the first cure for malaria; *chicle,* the sap from which chewing gum was made; the *cacao* tree from which chocolate was made; and how there were vast numbers of unknown plants, fungi and insects that might produce new foods or medicines.

Lucy read on, utterly absorbed in the incredible world of the Amazon, but then she came to a new chapter and her enjoyment was shattered. For the chapter was about the destruction of the rainforest as it was cleared for timber, for ranching, for development, for access, for mining – much of it illegal – and many other reasons. Lucy stared at the page in disbelief; apparently an area of rainforest larger than the country of Wales was being destroyed every year. The book went on to say that, as the forest was destroyed, thousands of species, many of which were completely unknown, were being extinguished.

Scientists estimate, she read with horror, *that across the world something between 20,000 and 80,000 species are driven into extinction every year – probably about 100 a day. As well over half the species on earth exist in the tropical rainforests, that is where most of the extinction is occurring. While you have been reading this chapter a species has become extinct.*

Lucy took the book over to Grandpa.

'How can this be true, Grandpa?' she said, pointing to the terrible statistics. 'If all those species are becoming extinct how can there possibly be any left?'

Grandpa read the page in detail before answering.

'Don't forget', he said, 'that they are talking about *all* species, including thousands of plants and thousands of different tiny mites and bugs, which make the figures seem much worse than you might at first think.'

Lucy was somewhat relieved by this but was still shaken by what she had learnt.

'Can I take this book to bed, Grandpa?' she asked. 'In fact, can I take it home with me when I go?'

'As long as you don't read any more of that particular chapter tonight,' said Grandpa. 'You're tired and it's making you depressed. Read about all the wonderful animals and plants and remember that somebody, somehow, will make sure that most of them survive. Nothing really bad lasts for ever.'

Lucy went to bed and followed his advice. She read about the magnificent jaguar, lord of the jungle; the sloth, hanging upside down in the trees; the anteaters; the giant ten-metre-long anaconda, the largest snake in the world; the cayman – a type of crocodile – that grew over six metres long; the armour-plated armadillo; the amazing variety of monkeys ranging from spider monkeys using their prehensile tails as a fifth limb, down to the tiny pygmy marmoset, the size of a mouse and the smallest monkey in the world. She read about the herds of peccaries or wild pigs who could attack large snakes with their razor-sharp hooves and long, sharp tusks; the tapir, looking like a bizarre cross between a small elephant, a rhino and a hippopotamus; and the coati mundi, a playful creature related to racoons and pandas with a long bushy tail and a delightful nature that made it popular as a pet in almost every village.

Eventually she fell asleep and dreamed of the tropical paradise where her jaguars roamed and ruled.

Lucy was bleary-eyed after her late-night reading and received a gentle scolding from her grandmother when she appeared late for breakfast.

'What will your mother say to me when you go back looking worse?' she said. 'You're meant to be here to get your strength back, not to stay up half the night reading Grandpa's animal books.'

Lucy promised to have an early night that evening and then persuaded Grandpa to give her a lift to the dolphinarium so she would be in time to feed the animals.

'*Greetings, O Promised One,*' said Jonathan after she had finished helping Catherine and Steve and settled down to talk to him. '*The Great Ones have told me many things while the Brilliant One slept beneath the Great Salt. From the marsupihops in the Great Southern Land there is nothing new to report but there is news from the junglefangs, news of great concern to all that live near the mighty river of the West. Some wicked Tailless Ones have captured many of their kin and are keeping* them in one place. There are more of them there than have ever been gathered together before; they are treated very badly and they fear greatly what is to become of them.'

Lucy couldn't imagine why somebody should be collecting large numbers of jaguars, but the animals clearly believed that something sinister was going on and she trusted their instincts.

'I will make a plan to help,' she told Jonathan, 'but I need to know exactly where the junglefangs are held.'

'My kin have already told me this,' said the dolphin, 'but the way in which we understand these things is very different to your own and I know not how best to make it clear to you.' He then told her many things, to help her identify the campsite, all of which she wrote down. They included the colour of the water in the river, the islands and forks in the river, natural features in the landscape and, of major importance as it turned out, information that the birds had provided concerning the exact time the sun rose at the campsite. This was expressed in terms of other places north and south where the sun rose at the same time. One of these was a great city near the shore of the Salt of the Many Islands which Lucy was sure Grandpa would recognize from its description.

'We know not how the fledgiquills are aware of these things,' the dolphin had said, 'but just as I can feel from the water upon my body whither I go and whence I come in the Great Salt, the fledgiquills know deep in their bones about the Brilliant One and its ways.'

Soon Grandma and Grandpa came to collect her for the

last time and she thanked Catherine and Steve and all the dolphins for their help as she said goodbye.

At home, over tea, Lucy told her grandparents about her discussions with Jonathan that day and they were astonished by the apparent scale of the jaguar operation described by the dolphins. Grandpa became very interested when Lucy produced her notes relating to the location of the campsite where the animals were being kept and sat at the table and started to pore over them while Lucy went off to start packing for home.

'Got it!' Grandpa suddenly exclaimed in great excitement later that evening. He had been busy for hours with maps and reference books and had twice disappeared to his study to look things up on the internet.

'Got what?' asked Lucy.

'I think I know where the jaguar camp must be,' he explained. Lucy was delighted.

'That's brilliant! Where is it? How did you work it out?' She went round and stood behind him, looking over his shoulder at the map spread out before him*. Her notes from the dolphinarium were scattered around the map.

'It's a bit like solving a special puzzle,' said Grandpa. 'The key information was from the birds. They said that sunrise occurs at the camp at the same time as it does in a great city on the coastline of the sea of many islands. What the birds are telling us is effectively the time zone or longitude on which the camp is situated.' He pointed to the vertical lines of longitude on the map before him. 'As you can see, the lines of longitude crossing the Amazon basin also cross

* See map at front of book.

the Pacific coastlines of Peru and Chile, the Caribbean in the north, and the North Atlantic in the north-east. Now the interesting bit is the mention of islands. Out of the three oceans I've mentioned, which do you think is the "Salt of the Many Islands"?' Lucy looked at the map.

'Wow!' she exclaimed. 'I'd never really looked properly at this part of the world before. It must be the Caribbean Sea. There are dozens and dozens of islands. No wonder the pirates liked it so much for hiding treasure.'

'Exactly,' smiled Grandpa. 'And from the description the birds gave of the city, I think it must be . . .' He pointed to a city★ on the coast then picked up a ruler and laid it vertically on the map with one edge passing through the city he had mentioned. With a pencil he drew a line along the ruler down through the entire Amazon basin.

'Now,' he continued, 'the sun rises at the same time everywhere along this line and the camp we know to be situated on a river, so it has to be where one of the tributaries of the Amazon crosses this line.'

Lucy was fascinated. She leant forward to pore over the map, pushing the ruler away so she could see better. Then she frowned.

'But there are lots of places where that's true,' she said rather disappointedly.

'Ah yes, but don't forget all these wonderful notes you made,' said Grandpa looking over the sheets scattered around the table. Finding the one he wanted, he showed it

★ *Author's note: The name of the city is not given at the request of Lucy and Richard who wish the anonymity of the site of the former jaguar camp to be preserved.*

to Lucy. 'The most important clue to start with is here,' he pointed, 'where Jonathan says that, as a dolphin swims up the Amazon, it comes to a great confluence of two rivers where the river is black.' He turned to the map and pointed to a city called Manaus; Lucy saw that two rivers joined there to become one great river.

'That confluence is here,' he continued, 'and the dolphin is explicit that the camp lies up the black river. That's the one coming down from the north-west.' He traced the river with his finger.

'It's called the Rio Negro which is Spanish for "black river". The river looks black because of optical effects produced by a special pigment in it derived from decomposed plant material. As you can see from our pencil line, we've now narrowed down considerably the number of possible sites for your jaguar camp — it can only be on one of the tributaries of the Rio Negro. Using these other notes,' he picked up more sheets off the table, 'which give details of islands and vegetation and various other clues, I think the camp is here.' He planted his forefinger firmly on a spot where his pencil line crossed a tiny blue line representing a tributary of the river they had been focusing on. 'I've looked up this area in my various books and on the internet and can find nothing about it. It's incredibly remote and, as far as anyone knows, remains unexplored. Heaven only knows what anyone is doing with captive jaguars out there, but whatever it is they are obviously very keen that nobody finds out. There can be few better places on earth to hide something.' He replaced his right forefinger with his left, on the same spot, pulled a pad towards him and picked up the pencil again. 'While we've got it pinned down let's note the map reference so we won't ever have to go through all the clues again.' He wrote down the exact location of the spot in degrees of latitude and longitude and gave the pad to Lucy. 'There it is. That's your spot.' Lucy glanced from the numbers on the pad in her hand to the map on the table in wonderment.

'It's amazing, isn't it? A dolphin tells me a few details about a place in the middle of the largest jungle on earth and now we know exactly where it is.' She paused and turned and a furrow appeared in her brow.

'What do you think I should do next? Who should I tell, and what do I say?'

Grandpa thought for a moment.

'The camp is in Brazil,' he said eventually, 'so ultimately any action will be taken by the Brazilian authorities, but it might be easier for you to ring the Foreign Office in London. The one thing that will guarantee their attention is the fact that you can give them an exact map reference. They'll have to check on that site – the information is so specific – and we *know* they'll find something.'

'But they're bound to ask how I heard about this in the first place,' said Lucy. 'I obviously can't tell them I can talk to animals, and it's going to seem pretty odd that I should know about this place when I live in a London suburb.'

'That's simple,' broke in Grandma who had been following the conversation with quiet interest. Lucy and

Grandpa both turned to look at her.

'You say that you have a penfriend who lives in an Amazonian village and that she – or he – has told you about rumours they have heard about this place, far up-river in the jungle, but they are frightened and have made you promise not to reveal who they are or where they live.'

'That's brilliant, Grandma!' said Lucy, 'It's foolproof!'

'Well,' said Grandpa, 'there's your plan of action worked out; all that remains is for you to go and do it – but first –' he stopped and Lucy looked in alarm at his stern expression. Then he grinned. 'Remember your promise to Grandma this morning. It's time you were in bed, or your mum'll be after us.'

Lucy kissed them both good night and went to bed, excited at the thought that, at last, she was really going to do something to help her animals.

6

A Crash in the Jungle

Two months earlier, just before Lucy's accident, her father was starting in his new job in South America. After spending a few days at Ecocidal Timber Company's headquarters in Rio, Richard flew to the company's river office in Macapá and he was now sitting chatting to the branch manager, José Verdade, and his wife Francesca, who had invited Richard to stay at their home before he began work in the jungle. José told Richard how he had come to work for ETC.

'I was born in Brazil and even as a boy I was interested in our forests and knew how important they were for the environment. As a young man I was determined to try to prevent their destruction so I studied forestry at university then joined the company because it claimed to obtain timber in a sustainable fashion. I felt I could help preserve the forest by working with such a company.' José then asked how Richard had joined the company.

'I'm really a botanist,' Richard replied, 'and I've never worked for a commercial company before. I was a university senior lecturer until three months ago when my department closed down because of government cuts. The very next day I saw, by chance, an advertisement in the paper for a biologist to work with ETC to help discover types of tree that might produce brand-new medicines to cure cancer and other diseases. I was offered the job and here I am, ready to fly to your most remote logging site tomorrow. I have to confess I wasn't that keen on Sawyer – Chopper I think you all call him – the boss in Rio, but meeting you and Francesca has reassured me and I'm getting really excited.'

They chatted for a little longer but soon Richard began to yawn and Francesca suggested that he should have an early night. Richard needed no further prompting: he was still suffering from the effects of jet-lag and, remembering that it was now 4 a.m. in London, he collapsed gratefully into his comfortable bed.

After Richard had retired José and Francesca continued to talk, now reverting to Portuguese, their native language. They were discussing a problem that had bothered José greatly during the last few weeks. He had joined the company in the belief that he could help with forest conservation, but had soon discovered that his company was just as bad as any other in terms of its destructive behaviour towards the environment. He had also found out that ETC was using the timber business as a cover for drug smuggling and illegal gold mining. He had consulted Francesca who had cautioned him not to do anything hasty and not to allow anyone to know of his suspicions.

'Drugs mean death,' she had said, 'and not just to those who take them, but to anyone who crosses the dealers.'

José knew she was right and they had decided to wait a little and hope that in some way the wrongdoings of the company might be exposed without José putting himself or his family at risk.

The next day Richard said goodbye to Francesca and José and boarded the little company plane that would take him to the furthest company site, which was to be his base for the next few months while he searched for unknown trees and plants. As they took off from Macapá the plane turned and rose above the mouth of the mighty river. The pilot saw Richard gazing down in wonder and smiled.

'Impressive, isn't it?' he said. 'The river mouth we are flying over is just one of many mouths forming an enormous delta which is nearly three hundred kilometres wide. The river drains the Amazon basin which is an area bigger than the whole of Western Europe. It pours so much mud and silt into the sea that it changes the colour of the ocean for three hundred kilometres!' Richard could see the giant muddy stain of the river spreading in the sea out to the horizon.

The journey was one of a thousand miles across the Amazon basin and after a while the plane landed at a small airfield where they could refuel and take the opportunity to rest and have a meal. Richard had noticed several times on the journey that they had passed over areas of reduced visibility and now, as they sat outdoors in a local village restaurant, the air, at first hazy, became dark with smoke and a fine ash settled on their food and clothes.

'They're burning the forest,' said the pilot, as if in answer to Richard's unspoken query. 'It's the quickest and cheapest way of clearing the ground and it goes on all the time. Often I can't land because an airport is closed by the smoke, especially when I go further south to places like Port Velho, Imperatriz and Cuiabá. The burning is a double whammy in terms of global warming and climate change. It not only removes valuable forest but the act of burning releases millions of tonnes of carbon into the atmosphere. The scale at which this is going on is almost unimaginable – the scientists think that every minute of every hour, day and night, an area of forest equivalent to seven or eight football fields is being destroyed by burning and clearing. Just think how much has gone since we have been sitting here!'

Richard was depressed by the pilot's words and became more determined than ever to use his new job to try to correct things: little did he suspect that the company he worked for was one of the worst offenders and that it would be his daughter, not himself, who would eventually start to reverse the destructive process.

Eventually they reached the camp that would be Richard's base for the next few months. As the pilot expertly guided the plane on to the narrow airstrip that had been cleared in the forest he suddenly swore and wrenched at the controls. Richard heard a skidding noise and felt a clunk under the plane, but soon they came safely to a stop. The pilot sighed in relief, then turned to Richard with a nervous grin.

'Some fool left a log on the strip – could have finished

us, but we're OK!'

The next day Richard was very excited. He was, at last, going to start on the real scientific work he had come to do, and after spending the morning on final preparations, he set off in the plane with the company pilot. Soon they were flying over the most remote jungle on earth. The green canopy stretched, apparently endlessly, to every horizon, broken only by the glistening ribbon of an Amazon tributary whose meandering path the pilot was using to guide him ever further into the interior. After a while the pilot pointed down at the river which was now shrunk to a thread as they neared its source.

'This is the furthest I've ever been,' he shouted over the noise of the engine. 'It's unknown territory from now on, so keep your eyes strained for your fancy trees.' He handed Richard a pair of powerful binoculars and flew lower, just above the treetops, to give Richard a better view. If he could see an area with unknown and promising tree species he would note its position on his global positioning system receiver, and return later with a canoe and an overland expedition to obtain his specimens.

Suddenly the pilot tapped Richard on the knee and pointed to the fuel gauge.

'We were OK until a few minutes ago but it's suddenly gone down. A fuel line must have been damaged by that wretched log I hit on landing last night. We don't have enough juice to make it back to camp. I'm heading for those hills on the horizon; it looks as though there's a more open area just before them where I may be able to make a go at a landing.'

Without further warning, and when they were still at least a couple of miles from the hills, the engine cut out and the little plane glided swiftly into the canopy. Richard braced himself as the trunks of enormous trees loomed ahead and as the plane passed between two forest giants there was a sickening crunch and the scream of ripping metal as both the wings tore off. The remaining fuselage hurtled down towards the forest floor, miraculously avoiding any further major trees and then crashed through smaller trees and shrubs to the ground, finally skidding to a stop with a violent jolt in the dense undergrowth.

Richard was unconscious for no more than a few seconds but as he came to he felt as if he had been asleep for much longer. As he regained his faculties he realized he had a bad headache. Blood was trickling into his eye, and touching his forehead he could feel a large bump where he must have crashed into the instrument panel. Gradually the events immediately prior to the crash came flooding back into his memory. He turned to speak to the pilot but as soon as he saw the unnatural angle at which his neck was lying he knew that he was dead. He sat and thought about his situation. The radio was smashed beyond recognition and the GPS receiver had disappeared in the tangled wreck of the cockpit floor. The plane had penetrated the forest canopy and come to rest several hundred yards from its point of entry through the thick roof of leaves and branches. He knew it would be completely invisible from the air.

The more he thought about his situation the more he realized that the normal rule of survival, to stay at the crash site until help arrived, probably did not apply in this case. He decided his best chance was to try to reach the high plateau that the pilot had been aiming for, with the intention of reaching a rocky area free of trees where he might light a beacon in the hope that the smoke might attract the attention of any search plane. As he was a non-smoker he went through the pilot's pockets to see if he had any matches or a lighter. It was a horrible feeling invading the privacy of the dead man's clothing but he forced himself to do so; in the event his search was fruitless. He looked around the shattered cockpit, then cursed himself for his stupidity. The entire cockpit floor was covered in shards of glass from the broken instrument panel. Using one of these he could easily make fire by focusing the rays of the sun. He collected some suitable fragments and put them in his pocket. He thought briefly of struggling to extract the pilot and bury him but immediately realized that the task was beyond him. The pilot was a big man and he was inextricably trapped in the wreckage. He gently closed the dead man's eyes and removed a gold identity bracelet from his wrist which was inscribed with his name: 'Domingos Icares'. He also took his wedding ring with the vague thought that he ought to try to give the man's family some personal mementoes should he ever reach civilization again. He arranged two struts from the broken hatch in the shape of a cross on the man's chest, said a brief prayer of committal, and then felt he could do no more.

Turning to the matter of his own survival, he twisted round and managed to pull his rucksack out from behind his seat. He kept his compass and Swiss army knife but then emptied the bag of its remaining contents – all his scientific reference books and other items representing unnecessary weight. He replaced these with two bottles of water from a holder on the inside of the plane door, some emergency flares and as many tools as he could fit into the bag from an emergency kit bolted to the nearby bulkhead. Getting out of the plane was no problem for most of the cockpit canopy had been ripped off. As he began to clamber out, however, the thought struck him that it was already late afternoon and that soon he would be in the jungle at night. Uninviting as the prospect was of spending the night next to a corpse, he knew that it would be sensible to stay in the relative safety of the plane and then set out for the plateau at first light. His head was, in any case, already pounding from the brief physical exertion he had just undertaken and he knew that it would be wise for him to rest before embarking on what would inevitably be a gruelling expedition. He pulled back the remnants of the cockpit cover to give as much protection as possible, then leant back to sit out what he knew would be a long and scary night.

As darkness fell the sounds of creatures of the day diminished and all kinds of new noises began. On several occasions he froze in fear as he heard claws scratching at the fuselage and the paws of unknown creatures scampering across the plane. On one occasion a large animal, taken unawares by an object lying on its favourite night path, bumped into the plane and actually shifted its position slightly in the undergrowth. The night was punctuated with the growls and hisses of the hunters and the screams and squawks of the hunted. Eventually Richard fell into a fitful sleep, fearful of the challenge ahead of him and wondering if he would ever see his family again.

He woke to the sound of a repeated, melodious, bell-like chime. At first he thought it was an early caller at the front door at home, ringing the bell while the family were still asleep. As he came to he quickly remembered where he was, however, and found himself face to face with a monkey peering through one of the cracks in the perspex cockpit cover. Richard jumped in fright and the startled monkey fled into the trees.

The bell-chime started again and now Richard could see that it came not from a postman with a parcel, but from a pure white bird the size of a jay, sitting on a nearby branch. As Richard pushed the broken canopy back the bell-bird flew off, and a little later he heard the characteristic 'dong-dong' of its call from further away. Then there came a sound that chilled him to the marrow. A moaning sound came from somewhere above him; it grew louder and louder and became a howling that seemed to make the entire jungle pulsate with shattering noise. Terrified,

Richard pulled the canopy over him again and, as the noise began to diminish, he peeped up into the treetops. There was a rustling in the highest branches and then a troop of brownish-black monkeys suddenly appeared, leaping from tree to tree. They stopped, nearer to Richard, and then he saw the largest individual sit back on a branch, open his mouth wide and restart the dreadful noise. He was joined by all the others until once again the jungle was deafened by their howling and shrieking.

Relieved to find the authors of the noise were howler monkeys and nothing worse, Richard started to make preparations to leave. Amidst all the excitement since first waking Richard had gradually become aware of an

Richard set off into the jungle.

intermittent buzzing noise in the cockpit and he turned to see that large flies were already settling on the pilot's face. It was definitely time to go. He picked up his rucksack, clambered down to the ground, checked his compass and set off into the jungle.

The journey was a nightmare. The canopy above shut out most of the sun so he travelled in a kind of gloom broken here and there by dappled sunlight trying to penetrate the dense foliage. The effect was similar to the interior of a cathedral, partially lit by sunlight streaming through stained-glass windows. The ground cover in this undisturbed forest was thinner than he had imagined it would be, but his progress was obstructed by tangles of immense roots and fallen branches. As he walked and scrambled through the forest the exposed parts of his body became covered in scratches and he soon had a livid rash on one arm which stung worse than a dozen stinging nettles where he had brushed against some poisonous plant.

He was soon drenched in sweat as he thrust his way though the giant ferns that covered the forest floor. Everything was wet. Countless drops of water dripped ceaselessly from every twig and branch and an unbelievable variety of lichens and mosses adorned the boles and branches of every tree, whether alive or dead. Exotic tropical flowers were everywhere to be seen, most of which even a botanist such as Richard could not begin to identify. The air was full of noise from insects, birds and monkeys, and giant, spectacularly coloured butterflies flitted in front of his face as he stumbled across the forest floor. Although the overall impression on the senses of this jungle scene was one of awesome beauty Richard was not deceived by appearances. He had heard the forest described as an 'emerald mansion' but he knew that for a lone traveller it was really a green hell: a place where death lurked at every turn – not just from pumas or jaguars or other predators but from snakes, venomous frogs and toads, spiders and centipedes, and parasites and insects whose bites or stings could cause all kinds of loathsome diseases.

He first became aware of the jaguar by a stroke of good fortune; normally the master stalker of the jungle would have been upon him without warning. He stopped to sit on a branch to remove some leeches from his legs and arms when he suddenly saw a large porcupine break cover and, for a normally slow-moving animal, scurry remarkably quickly towards him. Its quills were stiffened in alarm and it passed within a few feet of him before disappearing into the undergrowth. At the same time there were frantic alarm calls from a flock of birds in the trees above the bushes from which the large rodent had emerged, and looking over he just caught a sight of yellow fur in the branches. Even in a brief glimpse the beautiful markings of the jaguar were unmistakable and he knew he was about to face his greatest challenge. There was nowhere he could seek refuge; his stalker was truly in its own element and had Richard completely at its mercy.

Richard knew from his reading that jaguars rarely attacked humans and that even being followed by one was not necessarily a sign of danger – they sometimes followed villagers through the forest simply out of curiosity. All that book knowledge, however, suddenly gave him no reassurance whatsoever and his worst fears were confirmed when the creature gave a long, low growl, then a series of moaning coughs. It was obviously closing in for the kill. His skin crawled at the thought of those long sharp claws suddenly sinking into his flesh and those jaws closing round his neck. He knew that his remaining life could probably be measured in minutes.

As Richard turned to try to escape he saw, for the first time that day, patchy sunlight straight ahead of him between the bushes. At the same instant he was aware of a rapid movement behind him and he ran headlong towards the light in a panic, filled with the primitive childhood terror of being chased by a deadly foe. He suddenly emerged into brilliant sunlight and plunged headlong down a precipice, to be caught in the branches of a tree growing almost horizontally from a crack in the rock face. He could see other trees jutting out from the crack further down, but the gap to the next one below was impossibly far for him to climb. Looking up he saw the jaguar peering over the edge one hundred feet above him. Its head appeared in different places along the edge as though seeking a way down but eventually it gave up and disappeared. Richard looked round. He was on the side of a cliff, which stretched down below him at a precipitous angle to the floor of a great valley a thousand feet below. The other side of the valley was so far away that it was only just visible through the tropical haze. A large, strange bird slowly flapped its way across the abyss and muttered a harsh cry, which was answered by another, far away. Turning his attention to his perilous plight he realized with horror that it was impossible even to contemplate climbing back up to the top. Quite apart from the fact that there was a large and hungry cat waiting up there, the near-vertical cliff face was unscalable. He started to disentangle himself from the branches so as to get nearer to the cliff and see if he might make his way down. As soon as he moved, however, the tree, already almost completely dislodged from its tenuous hold on the rocks by Richard's fall, finally parted from the crack and slid down the cliff at an ever-increasing pace. The last thing Richard remembered was hurtling down, down, down.

7

Kidnap!

As soon as Lucy got home from her fortnight at the seaside she talked to Clare about how she should approach the Foreign Office. The principal problem was how she could remain anonymous, for she was terrified of anybody even suspecting her of having unusual powers. As always, Clare gave her sound advice. She suggested that Lucy rang up from a public telephone, not on a mobile or domestic phone from which a call could be traced, that she gave a false name, and that she used Grandma's idea of saying that the information had come from a penfriend in a remote Amazon village.

The next day they went to a public telephone booth at Waterloo Station in London and Lucy rang the Foreign and Commonwealth Office.

'Hello,' she said, 'I'd like to inform someone about a problem related to jaguars in Brazil.' In a few moments she was transferred to someone who obviously dealt with Brazil.

'Hello, Pauline Fairfax here, how can I help you?' Lucy faltered – Miss Fairfax sounded rather fierce. Clare gave her a shove.

'Go on,' she hissed. 'Stop being such a wimp. You're the Promised One – in case you hadn't remembered?'

Lucy cleared her throat. 'Er, I'm ringing up to tell you of some serious news affecting jaguars in the Amazon.' She went on to tell the woman all she knew, but did not give her name or address. The woman sounded very uninterested in the whole thing, especially as Lucy wouldn't tell her who she was. She obviously thought it was some kind of time-wasting hoax.

'Oh dear,' said Lucy to Clare as she put the phone down, 'I don't think I did that very well; that horrid woman isn't going to do anything. She just told me to ring back tomorrow.' Clare wasn't so sure. At the woman's request Lucy had been asked to repeat the exact details of where the campsite was, and Clare thought that this was significant.

'There's nothing more to do now,' she reassured Lucy. 'Let's see what she says tomorrow.'

Back at the ministry, the Honourable Edward Tawkin-Tosh, Teddy to his friends, was just arriving in his office. He was the senior civil servant in charge of South American matters and Pauline Fairfax had been his personal assistant for several years. She liked his kindly, easygoing nature and did her best to conceal from others his lamentable ignorance about most subjects.

'Mornin', Pauline,' he said cheerily as he hung his umbrella on the stand. It was 11 a.m.

'Good morning, sir,' she replied. 'You're bright and early today.'

Her gentle sarcasm was completely wasted on him.

'Well, I'm going to lunch at the club in an hour or so, so I thought I'd pop in for a coffee first. It's good for the staff to see me pulling my weight. Anything urgent?'

'Yes – well, I'm not sure whether it's important or not. I've just had a most unusual call from someone who sounded like a young girl. She has a penfriend in Amazonia and says something terrible is going on there with jaguars.'

'Amazonia eh? Shouldn't our Africa chaps get on to that?' said Tawkin-Tosh.

'No, the Amazon is a river in Brazil – well, most of it's in Brazil anyway – and that means it's in our section.'

'Most of it?' Tawkin-Tosh didn't like anything that sounded complicated and seized upon the possibility that the problem might still not be his responsibility. 'Where's the rest of it?'

'Lots of countries,' said his PA patiently. 'Venezuela, Colombia, Ecuador, Peru, Bolivia, Guyana and one or two others.'

'Surely they're not all in our section, are they?' Tawkin-Tosh had no idea he looked after so many strange places.

'Yes sir, they're all in South America.'

'Hmm,' said Tawkin-Tosh thoughtfully. 'Trouble with jaguars in the Amazon. Well, we can't interfere in the way in which these blighters treat their own fish. You'd best send a letter to whichever embassy you think. Braziador or Venezilia sound the most promising to me. Just send something off – you know how I like to phrase these tricky memos.'

'Yes sir,' she replied.

She knew only too well how he liked to phrase a tricky memo, and would not be sending anything remotely similar to one of his childish compositions.

He consulted his gold watch.

'Good Lord,' he exclaimed, 'doesn't time fly when you're under pressure! Mustn't be late at the club. Toodle-oo, old thing,' he took his brolly off the stand and walked to the door, 'and don't forget that call to Bulimia . . .'

'No sir, goodbye sir and enjoy your lunch.' The door closed behind him.

That afternoon Pauline Fairfax rang the Brazilian embassy and asked to be put through to someone who dealt with Amazon wildlife. Eventually she spoke to a Don-Juan Enganador.

'Hello, Senhor Enganador,' she said, 'I am passing on some information given to us by a young girl. It may just be a hoax but we thought you ought to know what she says in case it fits in with anything else you know about.'

'It's kind of you to ring,' said Mr Enganador; he sounded charming. Miss Fairfax wondered how old he was and decided to look up exactly where the Brazilian embassy was. 'Please tell me all about it.'

Miss Fairfax told him everything Lucy had said and he listened with what was polite interest until she reached Lucy's description of the location of the problem; he then became extremely attentive. Miss Fairfax finished off by apologizing for taking up his time with what was probably a frivolous matter.

'Not at all,' he said gravely. 'The location that the young

lady has described to you is in an extremely remote part of the Amazon and the details are very specific. I would very much like to speak to her – is this possible?'

'She's going to ring me back tomorrow,' said Miss Fairfax. She had thought that he would have been dismissive of what she had told him but, on the contrary, he seemed extremely interested.

'When she rings,' he said, 'please give her this number – it's a private line, not the one you came in on just now – and ask her to call me at once.'

Miss Fairfax took down the number and thanked him. 'If you're ever over this way,' she added, 'we'd love to show you round our South American section – just give me a call.'

'Thank you, I will most certainly think about that,' said Don-Juan, and rang off. He then told his secretary that she could have the rest of the afternoon off and as soon as she had gone he picked up the phone and rang Chopper in Rio. Chopper maintained a network of spies in key positions in the police, the legal system and the government. His government informers included an official in each of the major embassies abroad and his man in London was Don-Juan Enganador. In return for keeping Chopper informed of developments that might affect his illegal timber, drug and mining interests, Enganador received a generous cash reward every week in addition to his regular government salary. Chopper knew that greed did not guarantee loyalty, however, and the brown envelope of cash was not delivered to Don-Juan personally in London, but was taken every Friday evening to his small home in the suburbs of Brasilia where his wife and two young children lived. It was delivered by two big men who came in a large black car with darkened windows, and Don-Juan was in no doubt whatsoever that if he crossed Chopper in any way his family would soon be receiving a visit of a very different nature from those same two men. He was now through to Chopper.

'What's up, Don-Juan? It'd better be good – I'm in the middle of a golf match with the new Chief of Police.'

'It may be nothing, boss,' said Don-Juan, 'but I think you should hear this.' He recounted Lucy's story and in particular the location she had described. He knew that Chopper had logging sites at various points along the Amazon, but he knew nothing of Cayman Creek with its captive jaguar colony and its importance to Chopper as a drug-peddling base. His instinct to ring Chopper had been perfectly correct and Chopper dropped all thoughts of golf for the moment. He gesticulated to his fellow player to take his next stroke and quickly moved out of earshot.

'Well done, Don-Juan,' he said. 'Now listen – and listen carefully. The camp the girl mentioned – that exists exactly where she said, but there's just one little problem. Nobody, *nobody* outside my organization knows about its existence! That means I've a traitor in my group. I'll see to him later . . .' Don-Juan shuddered. He wouldn't change places with that man for a million pounds. 'And that traitor,' Chopper continued, 'has obviously betrayed us to a rival organization. Now they have been clever – very clever.

Without exposing themselves in any way, they are using this girl – either by bribing, or more likely threatening, her family – to draw the attention of the authorities to the existence of our site. When they investigate, we are closed down and the rival organization takes over all our drug deals. Are you following me?'

Don-Juan was following him, and said so.

'Right, the first thing is that the Brazilian authorities must know nothing about this. That means that all embassy records of your conversation today do not exist. Am I making myself clear?' Don-Juan thought of his duty to the Ambassador, then thought of his wife and two daughters.

'Perfectly clear, boss.'

'Next, I need that girl over here. That will serve two purposes – firstly, if she's here she can't blab to anyone else and, secondly, I can . . .' there was an almost imperceptible pause, '. . . interrogate her and find out who's behind all this.' Don-Juan shuddered again, but said nothing.

'When's she due to ring again?'

'Tomorrow, boss.'

'Perfect, tell her that you must see her – you can agree that she remains anonymous – before you are able to take any action. Remember, she thinks you are part of the government and can actually do something. Tell me exactly when she is coming – but you must arrange it for Thursday afternoon or early Friday morning so I can arrange to have her snatched as she leaves the embassy. She can come back on Friday's flight.'

Don-Juan knew all about the flight he referred to. Every

Thursday a private company jet flew from Rio via Grand Canaria to a small club airport near the M25 motorway. The man it carried posed as a businessman, coming to discuss trading problems with experts in the City of London. He actually brought in drugs and returned the following day with a considerable sum in cash from the London dealers.

'But . . .' Don-Juan hesitated.

'Spit it out, man!' snarled Chopper. He had made his decision and now he wanted to get back to his golf.

'What if the girl won't agree to come and see me?'

There was a brief pause, then Chopper's voice came over slowly and deliberately.

'I was reading in the paper this morning that there has been a disturbing increase in family fatalities from suburban houses catching fire. It said that, at present, Brasilia is the least affected city of those in the survey. I do hope those statistics don't change over the weekend.'

The line went dead as Chopper switched off and returned to his game. Don-Juan looked at the phone and slowly replaced it on the receiver. He was desperately worried but could do nothing until the girl rang. But what if, having rung Miss Fairfax, she didn't even ring him? That at least he could do something about. He was fully aware of the effect of his Latin charm on Miss Fairfax. He quickly looked her up in the Foreign Office directory and then rang her straight back.

'Miss Fairfax – or Pauline, if I may,' he said, 'I am so sorry to bother you but I have had an idea about your young mystery caller.'

'Do go on, Senhor – or can I say Don-Juan?' Miss Fairfax said coyly.

'I think it might be best if I actually meet your young girl rather than just speak to her on the phone. There could be a problem though – she may be nervous about coming here alone to see me. Perhaps . . .?'

'Yes?' said Miss Fairfax, a little too eagerly.

' . . . perhaps if you were to come with her she might feel happier. You must already have won a degree of trust from her.'

'Oh, that is so clever of you, Don-Juan,' she replied in her most gushing voice. 'Of course I shall suggest that. I'll contact you after she rings tomorrow.'

After giving her details of how to get to the embassy and what time they should meet, Don-Juan felt he had done everything possible and now could only wait. He tore out the notes he had made on a pad during his conversation with Miss Fairfax and burnt them in the green metal wastepaper basket under his desk. He wondered whether to ring his wife and warn her but decided not to – all calls to his house were almost certainly monitored by Chopper.

The next day was Thursday and Lucy and Clare phoned Miss Fairfax as promised, though this time on her direct line.

The secretary was extremely kind and friendly to Lucy.

'We are making good progress, my dear,' she said warmly. 'I have spoken to a nice man in charge of these things at the Brazilian embassy. He's going to help but he needs to see you. I'll come with you if it would make you feel happier about seeing him.' Lucy put her hand over the phone and consulted Clare.

'Seems OK,' said Clare. 'They're both government officials after all and they can't force your name and address out of you if you don't want them to. It sounds as if it's the only way you can get to help your jaguars.'

Lucy nodded and resumed her phone conversation.

'OK,' she said, 'if you promise to not to ask my name, I'll come.'

'You must be here early on Friday morning though. He's squeezing you in as an emergency case and is going to see you before the proper work of the day starts.' Miss Fairfax then gave Lucy directions and said she would see her on the doorstep of the embassy the following morning.

The next morning Clare waited in a coffee bar near the Brazilian embassy and swotted for her exams while Lucy talked to Don-Juan. The meeting with Miss Fairfax had gone smoothly; she seemed a nice woman and Lucy had taken to her immediately. The sisters had arranged to meet at the coffee bar after Lucy's visit to the embassy.

After about half an hour Lucy appeared on the other side of the road. She was alone: Don-Juan had not wanted Miss Fairfax to be a witness to the kidnapping and draw any police investigation back to him and, as he had correctly anticipated, she had eagerly accepted his offer for her to stay on at the embassy for coffee after Lucy had left.

Clare waved to her sister across the busy road and as

Lucy waited at a pedestrian crossing for the traffic to stop, she was hidden from Clare's view by a double-decker bus.

The first clue that Clare had of anything going wrong was when she saw several dogs from different parts of the pavement tear themselves away from their owners and dash across the road between hooting cars with squealing brakes, leads trailing behind them. At the same time a flock of pigeons left the roofs opposite and dived towards the pavement. A cold chill struck into her heart as she suddenly realized the reason for the unusual behaviour of these animals and, as the bus moved on, Lucy was no longer to be seen. The dogs and pigeons disappeared at speed down the road, clearly in pursuit of her, but in the busy traffic they were lost to sight within a few seconds and Clare was unable to make out any details of the vehicle that had been used to kidnap her.

Clare immediately informed the police of Lucy's kidnap. There was a police station near by, and soon cars with sirens wailing and lights flashing were speeding off in the direction that Lucy had disappeared. A very kind

Kidnap!

policewoman took Clare home in a car and they broke the news to Joanna. Clare had already decided that she would have to tell Joanna about Lucy's power because it was the only way she could reassure her that Lucy was not completely without protection and support. As soon as the WPC left she turned to her mother.

'Mum, there's something you need to know and it's going to take some time. Don't ring Grandma yet; sit down while I make us a cup of tea, and then I've got a story to tell you.'

A little while later Joanna was in a state of emotional exhaustion. Her mood had swung from black despair at the news of Lucy's disappearance, to relief that she was not completely without help, and back to utter disbelief at the tale she was being told. Then, as Clare's calm and factual account of the events of the last few weeks had gradually unfolded, she could do nothing except accept the story as being true, even though she could not begin to understand how and why it had all happened.

'I think you should speak to Grandma and Grandpa

now,' said Clare. 'Like us, they didn't want you to worry that Lucy had cracked up after the operation; they didn't believe it at first, but I think they really understand the situation now and it would help if you could talk to them.'

On hearing the news Grandma and Grandpa drove up from the coast immediately, and joined them late in the afternoon. They all had a miserable night, hoping against hope that Lucy's abduction was somehow related to her animal powers and not some random crime. Then, in the morning newspaper, Clare saw what she had been looking for. An article described the mobbing of a small private plane by an enormous flock of birds of various species as it had prepared to take off from a club airfield in Buckinghamshire the previous day.

An expert on bird behaviour, the lengthy article concluded, *says that the mobbing of large birds such as buzzards by small birds is not uncommon, but she has never seen the mobbing of an aeroplane, and never seen so many birds of different species in such a co-ordinated and frenzied attack. The plane, fortunately, managed to take off without mishap, and our expert says that the birds' extraordinary behaviour was almost certainly down to the unusual weather patterns we have been experiencing in recent weeks.*

Clare showed the article to her mother and grand-parents.

'Lucy was on that plane,' she said. 'That means she is being kept alive. Whenever she gets off the plane, and wherever that is, she will have animals and birds looking after her.'

As she spoke Grandma pointed out of the window. 'Well,

look at that!' she exclaimed. The others followed her gaze. On the lawn Tibbles was crouching in front of a large pigeon. She made no move to attack the bird and soon the bird flew off. A few seconds later the cat-flap clunked and Tibbles appeared. She came straight over to Clare and dropped something on the floor at her feet. Clare picked it up.

'It's Lucy's new dolphin ring,' she said excitedly. 'The one she got on holiday. She was on that plane, I'm sure – she dropped this so we'd know she's able to communicate with us. I'm now *certain* she'll be OK. We just have to wait for news and keep our fingers crossed.'

8

An Unplanned Trip for Lucy

It was Saturday in Rio. Lucy was being tied into a chair while Chopper paced up and down the room puffing at a cigar, impatient to question her. When she had been secured and her gag removed he stopped and faced her. He thought she reminded him of someone but told himself it must be his imagination.

'You're quite a pretty little chick –' he started.

'*Quite* pretty?' thought Lucy. From that moment she hated the fat slob.

'– and it would be a shame if all that was to change,' he continued. Lucy's heart suddenly chilled. 'You see, I've got one or two mates who are a bit out of control. They get a bit careless with acid and razors and stuff – if you get my drift.' Lucy certainly did get his drift. She waited and he continued.

'– but nothing unpleasant needs to happen if you tell us who told you to ring up about our little jaguars' rest home and dental clinic.' He mentioned some names but Lucy just looked blank. Chopper was disappointed: the names he had given her belonged to the three main drug dealers working in south-west London. He fired more names at Lucy but she had no idea what he was talking about and said so.

'Well, one of those gangs is trying to put me out of business and one of them must have put you up to it. What are they doing – giving you a new bike or paying your posh school fees?' He suddenly thought of a different approach and tried to smile reassuringly. The effort made him look like a sick wolf. 'Listen, if they're threatening you or your family, that's something I can take care of. Just tell me who it is and I'll sort it.'

Lucy did not doubt for one moment that he could sort out anyone he chose to sort out but she still didn't know what he was on about and said so again.

He leant forward close to her face and she almost retched as a waft of his foul breath engulfed her.

'Look, kiddo, I haven't got time for games,' he hissed. 'There's no way on earth you could have heard about that jaguar camp except from one of my rivals. Now who was it? You'd better start talking or things are going to get extremely unpleasant very quickly.'

Lucy tried desperately to think. She couldn't tell him about the animals. Suddenly she had a brainwave. If she could reassure this dreadful man that her knowledge about the jaguars was nothing to do with these rival gangs it might be all right.

'It must have been my dad who told me,' she said. 'He works for a timber company in South America and maybe he'd heard about the camp. He . . .'

She stopped as she saw Chopper's face. He had suddenly realized who she reminded him of.

'Your dad,' he said slowly. 'Of course! He works for my company and he's betrayed me!' His voice rose to a shout as he spoke. Lucy was stunned. So *this* was the company that her father had joined. She now remembered where she had seen the logo on the villa gate before – it had been on the envelope of Dad's last letter before his field trip. Then she realized she had made a terrible mistake. In her anxiety to protect her precious secret she had now landed her father in terrible trouble – possibly even put his life in danger, judging by what she had seen of Chopper so far. What rotten luck, she thought, of all the timber companies in South America he had to work for this one! But there was no time for self-pity.

'Actually, I don't think he did mention the camp. He wouldn't if he wasn't meant to, so I think I've made a mistake.'

'You must think I'm a complete idiot,' shouted Chopper. 'Of *course* he told you.' Chopper's eyes narrowed as he thought more about what he had just learnt.

'Who else knows about this – besides your father and you?'

'Nobody,' Lucy said firmly, desperate now to protect the rest of the family. 'My mum and my sisters get very emotional about animals being mistreated and I couldn't bear to see them upset. I made the phone calls all on my own.'

The effect of the sedative she had been drugged with on the plane had now finally worn off under the pressure of Chopper's questions and the full horror of her situation had become clear to her. The dreadful interrogation and the fact that she had mentioned her father were all too much and she began to weep. She didn't want to cry in front of this beast of a man but she couldn't help it.

'I only wanted to help the poor jaguars,' she sobbed, 'and I don't know anything about your stupid company or any stupid gangs. Please don't tell my daddy off and please let me go home.'

Chopper said nothing. He was completely unmoved by the distress of the lonely and frightened girl and was thinking only of what to do next. Finally he called someone to take Lucy away.

She was locked in a small bedroom on the third floor. The wallpaper had been stripped from two of the walls and some tiles had been removed from the en suite bathroom. High up on the wall of the bedroom, immediately above a French window, was a video surveillance camera; it obviously usually pointed down at the window to detect intruders but was now turned inwards to cover the room, and what looked like a new camera had been installed in the bathroom. The room was empty apart from a bed and a jug of water. It was obviously a guest bedroom that had been emptied for redecoration and then hurriedly converted into a cell. A French window led out on to a small balcony overlooking the garden and the space between the balcony wall and the overhanging roof was enclosed by a steel mesh fence. The villa's security system had been designed to stop an intruder from getting on to the balcony but it was just as effective in preventing anyone escaping. The door out to the balcony was shut. It was locked with a simple hook and eye catch to prevent the door swinging in the breeze but it was too high for her to reach and there was nothing in the room that she could use to stand on. She tried to move the bed, but it had been screwed to the floor.

She had stopped crying and now felt angry. She had to do something to warn her father as soon as he returned from his expedition because she was sure that Chopper would seek revenge on him for telling her about the secret camp and putting his business deals at risk.

Out of the corner of her eye Lucy saw some movement. A large lizard had crept out of a broken ventilation brick near the ceiling and was eyeing an insect on the window. Lucy called him and asked if he could open the hook and eye. He obeyed her immediately, flicking up the latch with his head, and then returned to eat the insect in a movement so fast that Lucy only saw him swallow. Lucy opened the door and slipped out on to the balcony. As she breathed in the cool evening air she suddenly froze as she heard voices below. Peeping through the wire mesh she saw Chopper and Sam sitting on the patio below. They were in reclining chairs enjoying the evening sun, smoking fat cigars and drinking large exotic drinks. She shut her mind to the evening cacophony of animal voices and tried to concentrate on the conversation below. Chopper was in mid-sentence.

' . . . clearly not anything to do with our rivals. Her father must have told her about the camp and she rang up the

Foreign Office to try to save the cats. She's one of those bleeding-heart animal lovers. I just hope neither of them has told anyone else. He was told that the existence of the camp was to be kept secret for scientific reasons, but if he's been blabbing to his snotty kid he might have blabbed to others. Any news about him, by the way?' Lucy held her breath and strained to catch every word.

'No, the plane never returned from an exploratory flight over unknown territory. The camp was the only landing strip within fuelling range, so it must have crashed in the jungle.' Lucy's heart stopped.

'Please, please, God, let Daddy be all right,' she prayed. She told herself that people often survived small plane crashes – it might even have made a forced landing – and that she had to concentrate on what was else was being said, for everybody's sake.

'What have you told the family?' said Chopper.

'They think he's on an expedition into the remote interior so there'll be no questions for a while. We can keep pretending to wait for news, then just say he's tragically lost. By then the big drug delivery will be safely out of the way – it's due on New Year's Day, which is exactly two months today.'

'Well, *nothing* is to go wrong with that,' said Chopper. 'It's worth five million.' They talked for a few moments about drug trafficking and Lucy realized that the timber industry was simply a cover for their true business. Soon Chopper returned to the subject of her father. He was clearly worried that no loose ends should be left untied.

'What are Bonaventure's chances of surviving the crash?' he asked Sam.

'It's possible of course; others have survived a crash in the jungle, but he'd have to be pretty tough and resourceful ever to get back to camp.'

'Well, I don't want to take any chances of his talking to anyone else. If he reappears make sure he disappears again – permanently. What about the pilot?'

'We've already told his wife she's probably a widow. She asked us for compensation but she soon shut up when we reminded her that he was wanted for drug offences in four countries, had no legal passport and was flying without a current licence. If the drug deal goes through I suppose we could give her something.'

'We could, but we won't,' said Chopper who had no interest whatsoever in helping anyone who couldn't help him or threaten him.

'Either way she's going to end up as jaguar grub . . .'

'Bring me up to date on the cats,' said Chopper, changing the subject yet again. Lucy pricked up her ears.

'The twins have done well – better, I must admit, than I'd expected. They've collected over thirty jaguars and pumas. They ransacked a couple of villages early on and since then there's been nothing but co-operation from the locals. You remember Sing Song and his fancy operation to drain their bile?' Chopper nodded. 'He's going to do all the cats they've collected so far as a job lot. He flew in yesterday and starts operating tomorrow at Cayman Creek. He reckons on doing two or three a day so it'll take him about a fortnight. I'm flying there tomorrow to see our little animal goldmine get started.'

'How much is he costing us?' asked Chopper.

'Too much – but he's the best in the business. We'll soon get it back, though. The animals can live for months after they've been operated on, and their bile is collected every day. When they finally croak we get all their other bits and pieces, teeth and stuff, which are worth a small fortune. One cat alone will pay all this guy's costs and then we're into pure profit, which we split with him and the twins. While the bile from this batch of cats is being collected, the twins can catch some more and he can come over and do another lot when we need him.'

Lucy was sick with horror at what she had learnt. The only good thing was that it sounded as if most of the jaguars that had been captured so far were still alive and unharmed. If she could find a way to help them, most might yet escape. She forced herself to put the jaguars out of her mind for the time being and concentrate again on the continuing conversation below her.

'Well, that's the father, the pilot, the drugs and the cats sorted,' Sam was saying. 'What about the kid?'

'It's too dangerous to keep her in Rio – I doubt if her disappearance will make the news over here, but if it does we can't risk the maids or the gardeners recognizing her. On the other hand, we can't let her go. She knows too much because I had to ask her about the other drug gangs. As soon as she tells anyone we're sunk. I'd also like to know whether she's told anyone else – though she says she hasn't. The best thing to do is to get her off to the camp out of sight and sound. She can go and be locked up with her precious jaguars – I'm sure we can find a spare cage, and while she's there Sid and Fred can find out if she's blabbed to anyone else. There's nothing those two will enjoy more than extracting some information from a young girl and if she doesn't survive the experience – well, that's one less disposal problem for us. Either way she's going to end up as jaguar grub, so she'll have done her precious animals some good after all.' They both laughed and Lucy shuddered.

'When I go tomorrow to check on things,' said Sam, 'I'll take her with me and get in touch in a few days to let you know how things are going.'

With that, they went in to dinner leaving Lucy to her thoughts. She had been upset and frightened by what she had heard but at least she now had a clear idea of what was going on. There was just a chance her dad was still alive and she needed somehow to find him and warn him of the danger he was in. They were taking her to the camp – well, that was fine, it was her best chance of contacting her father. As for the plans concerning her own torture and death, she felt much less concerned about these than she did about her dad. The incident with the lizard and the balcony door-latch had reminded her that she could call on immediate assistance from the animal kingdom, and she knew that she could use her powers to protect herself when the need arose. What she particularly wanted to avoid was any further sedation so she planned to appear to co-operate as much as possible with Chopper and Sam in the hope that she wouldn't have any more injections. She slipped back into the room and called the lizard, who obligingly restored the latch to its former state.

Just then someone knocked on the door. Lucy was uncertain what to do but when the knock was repeated she told whoever it was to come in.

The person outside tried to open the door as though ignorant of the fact that it was locked, then, after some rattling of the handle, the lock was turned and a middle-aged woman stepped into the room carrying a tray.

Maria Arrumadeira had lived in Rio all her life. She had been raised in poor circumstances and, with little in the way of formal education, had worked hard in domestic service. She had been thrilled to be offered a job as housekeeper to Senhor Chopper in his large villa and, having been recently widowed, she was now dependent on the job as the only means of support for herself and her eleven-year-old daughter.

When Maria was told to prepare a room she had assumed it was for one of the many visitors and business associates that came to the villa. She was surprised, however, when she was asked to make up a bed in one of the bedrooms being redecorated and told that the guest would only be having meals in her room. She was even more surprised to find, when she took Lucy's supper up, that the door was locked and the guest was a girl, the same age as her own daughter, apparently completely on her own and looking very distressed. She spoke only a word or two of English and Lucy of course spoke no Portuguese, but after she had put the tray of supper down Maria pointed to her chest and said, 'Maria.'

Lucy told her what her name was in the same way. Maria looked at Lucy's distressed little face and red-rimmed eyes and her heart went out to her. She instinctively leant over and hugged the girl and kissed her on both cheeks.

'*Bua noite*,' she whispered, then turned and, pointing encouragingly at the food, went out, locking the door behind her.

After leaving Lucy, Maria went straight to Chopper's wife Nandita, and spoke to her in the local dialect that was, for both of them, their mother tongue.

'What's going on?' Maria demanded. 'There's a young girl locked in one of the rooms being redecorated.'

Nandita knew enough about her husband's business not to ask too many questions and she certainly wasn't going to allow a nosy maid to interrupt her life of opulence and uninterrupted luxury. On the other hand it wouldn't do to have Maria going about saying things that might attract unwelcome attention from the authorities. She thought she would start by reminding Maria just how vulnerable she was.

'I was so sorry to hear about your husband's tragic death,' she said casually. 'You must be so pleased to have a secure position now that jobs are becoming scarce in domestic service with the downturn in the economy.'

Maria said nothing. She knew that if this monstrous woman said a word to Chopper, she would be out of a job and unable to support her daughter.

'What was it you said?' Nandita continued. 'Ah, the girl. Her parents are old friends of Chopper from England. They have gone on a river trip in the Pantanal but children under fifteen are not included; only adults and older children experienced in boating are allowed. She has had some emotional troubles and run away from home on several occasions, so we've been advised to keep her under lock and key. She's very fond of wildlife so tomorrow Senhor Sam is going to take her to see some of our logging sites along the Amazon.'

'I understand, Senora Sawyer,' Maria replied. 'Please tell Senhor Sam that I will prepare a small bag for the child; it is a long journey and she will need some things. She seems to have brought very little with her.'

Nandita was happy with this. What Maria said made sense and as long as she co-operated without a fuss there was no harm done.

'Thank you. You may go. Take the evening off if you like.'

Maria went home. She lived just a few streets away in an old part of the town set behind the luxurious new villas on the seafront. As she went she wondered what she should do. She found it hard to believe that the child was not in danger and she was obviously being held against her will. There was little point in going to the authorities: she knew that Chopper's money and influence would prevail and all that would happen was that she would lose her job – or worse. She had seen Chopper in a temper once or twice and it was not a sight ever to forget. Perhaps she could get the child to give her a note with her name and address on it and she could at least somehow check out Nandita's story. She decided to take a pencil and paper to Lucy and, if her suspicions were correct and the girl was being held against her will, she would surely know that Maria was trying to help her.

Early the next morning the villa security guard reviewed, as usual, the reports from the night staff and checked the video surveillance tapes for the entire property. He saw Maria embracing Lucy and reported the finding to Chopper.

'Well, she's a soft-hearted old cow,' said Chopper, 'but she doesn't speak any English so there's probably no harm done in the way of an information leak. Get someone else to take up the kid's breakfast though, just in case she's thought up something overnight.'

When Maria came in to work she was surprised when

Nandita asked her to go straight out again to get some fish from the market.

'We've decided to entertain tonight and I want some nice fresh shrimp for a special recipe. Dolores can take the girl her breakfast.'

Maria was disappointed but there was nothing she could do. Dolores was new and she didn't dare confide in her but she told her to make Lucy a nice breakfast and to give her the bag Maria had prepared at home.

Lucy, thinking along the same lines as Maria, had planned to pass her a note to send to her family and was bitterly disappointed when a different woman appeared with her breakfast. Dolores gave her a small embroidered bag, pointed at it and said 'Maria,' and Lucy immediately understood that it was a present from the kind housekeeper. In it were some clean shorts and underclothes which Lucy guessed must be her daughter's or niece's, some spare sandals, a tube of suncream, a bottle of insect repellent, a hair brush and hair bands, a bar of soap, a toothbrush and toothpaste, some tissues, several packets of sweets, some magazines and comics – obviously chosen for their picture content because the text was in Portuguese, and a drawing puzzle book with pencil attached. Lucy was quite overcome with emotion at this thoughtful act and resolved that one day she would thank Maria and try to repay her kindness. She was particularly excited to have the pencil, for she had been hatching an alternative plan should she be unable to pass a note to Maria. She was concerned that it might be confiscated so when Dolores had left the room she bit a tiny hole in the waistband of her shorts and slid the pencil into the puckered elastic binding. It was completely invisible.

Soon Sam appeared. He and Chopper had agreed that for the time being it was best that Lucy should not be too frightened so that she would co-operate for the journey.

'Hallo,' he said, 'I'm Chopper's brother. He's not very good with kids, I'm afraid, but his bark is worse than his bite. I'm going to take you up the Amazon to the logging site where we keep the jaguars. When you've seen they're OK and your dad gets back from his trip, you'll both be off home.' Lucy couldn't help being impressed by the skill with which the man lied to her. He'd clearly had a great deal of practice.

'Can we ring up Mum and tell her I'm OK then?' she replied.

'I don't think we should do that from here,' Sam replied. 'As you probably noticed yesterday, Chopper is a bit funny about anyone knowing about his camp. Maybe we can get in touch once we get to the camp and well away from Chopper. I'm a bit wary of him myself,' he added confidentially, as if he were really on Lucy's side. He leant forward and gave her a conspiratorial leer, revealing a set of broken, yellowing teeth.

Lucy thought he was despicable. Chopper had been nasty but this guy was a complete slime ball.

'Now let's check that Maria's given you everything you might need for the journey,' he said jovially, but Lucy knew he was really checking on both of them. He fumbled through the bag and Lucy decided she'd try to wash the clothes before she wore them if she possibly could.

'What a kind lady,' he said, taking one of the packets of sweets and putting it in his pocket. 'Saved me the trouble of getting all this for you myself. Now, let's get going!'

9

An Eventful Flight to Cayman Creek

Sam drove Lucy to a nearby airfield and they got into the company's private jet to fly to the river office at Macapá. The pilot told her to call him Hermes and once they were airborne he invited her to sit next to him and see the controls. She liked him and wondered if she could slip him a note. He was employed by the company, however, and she decided not to risk confiding in him, but to wait until she got to the camp and then use her animal friends – at least she could put her absolute trust in them.

She returned to her seat eventually and ate one of the packed meals the pilot had left out for her and Sam. While looking at Maria's magazines after her lunch she suddenly noticed a fly inside the plane. Jonathan, the dolphin, had been somewhat dismissive of the crawlipods, as he described all insects, spiders and other creepy-crawlies, implying that they were so unintelligent that they would be of little interest to Lucy. She was still interested to see whether they would respond to her and she 'switched on' her mental beacon. The fly, which was resting on the back of Sam's chair – the place it decided had the most interesting smells on the plane – suddenly stiffened and raised its head. Lucy listened intently for its voice but could only hear a high-pitched crackle that sounded like radio static. She spoke to the fly.

'*Greetings, O flying one. I am the Promised One.*' The crackle increased slightly in intensity but was still meaningless to Lucy. The fly had turned towards her. It could obviously understand her at some level but could not speak back to her. She asked it to land on Sam's balding head which it immediately did. She then told it to land on his lunch which he had just opened, and it obeyed her again. She then amused herself for the next two hours by asking the fly to buzz round Sam's head, land on his food just as he was putting it into his mouth and dive bomb his eyes. He got progressively more furious.

'You've got a fly in this plane,' he eventually shouted to the pilot. The pilot turned with an amused look on his face.

'Really? Fancy that happening in tropical South America! You have my full permission to swat it – though we don't usually approve of violence in the cabin.' He laughed and turned back to the controls. He knew Sam was the vice-president of the company but couldn't help wondering what kind of an idiot felt he had to report a fly to the pilot.

Every time Lucy saw Sam making preparations to swat the fly she warned it to hide under her seat where she had left a speck of jam as a reward. For her the flight had been very useful for two reasons: she had discovered that crawlipods were able and willing to assist her – something she felt might be vitally important; and she had been able to torment Sam for two hours without lifting a finger. She felt he deserved every buzz.

As they landed, Lucy couldn't resist commenting on how much the fly seemed to have been attracted to Sam while completely ignoring the pilot and herself. Sam immediately started to curse and swear once more and demanded that the pilot ensure that in future the cabin was fly-free. The pilot said he would do his best, making sure Sam didn't see the amused wink he gave Lucy as he spoke.

'At least it was only a fly,' Sam continued. 'The things I really can't stand are spiders. Ever since I was a kid I've had a real phobia about them. It's funny how people react to different things – Chopper hates lizards and my twin brothers are terrified of snakes.'

To the pilot's surprise Sam insisted that Lucy stay in the plane overnight. He didn't want anybody in the Macapá offices to see her. He told Lucy that they would be flying in a different, smaller plane up the Amazon to the camp at Cayman Creek the next morning. Hermes unscrewed the back of Lucy's seat on the plane and rearranged it so she could lie down. He then left and returned in an hour or so with a pizza, some apple pie, a hot drink and some English newspapers.

'I don't know what all this is about,' he said. 'None of my business, you understand, but while you're in my plane I want you to be comfortable.' She thanked him sincerely, then he said good night and left for the local hotel where he usually stayed. As soon as he had gone Lucy switched on her beacon and waited. Within a few moments she heard a scrambling noise and, looking out, saw three large monkeys sitting on the wing.

'*Greetings, O Promised One,*' one of them said. '*The arborikin are here and await thy commands.*'

'*Greetings, O Agile Ones,*' Lucy replied. '*I wish you to inform the animanet of my whereabouts and that I am the prisoner of wicked ones. I also wish to send a message to my family,*' she continued. '*I could give you a tiny parcel to be taken to my home — is this possible?*'

'*It is told that thou liv'st across the Great Salt, in the City of the Great Clock, in the Isles of Albion. Thy precious burden will pass through many paws and jaws and beaks but all will be well, unless some calamity should befall one of the carriers. Where is the package?*'

'*I believe that when the Brilliant One rises I shall leave this thunderquill and get into a smaller one which will fly up the great river. When I get out of this door tomorrow I will drop the parcel on the ground — it will be very light.*'

'*One will be waiting to receive it — either a scurripod or a fledgiquill.*'

'*At the end of the mighty river I go to the place where the junglefangs are imprisoned. There I will need the help of many creatures and will fulfil my promise to release the junglefangs. Thank you for coming to speak to me and for all your help.*'

'*We hear thy precious voice and understand. Have no fear this sunsleep; the Malevolent Ones will keep thee safe. There are both stranglekin and fellfangs among them. Fare thee well.*'

'Have no fear this sunsleep; the Malevolent Ones will keep thee safe.'

Lucy craned her neck to look down at the ground. She could just make out in the moonlight a long shape on the ground, then another and another; the longer she looked the more sinuous shapes she could discern, of every shape and size. The plane was completely surrounded by snakes. Some were very large, which she guessed must be boa constrictors – the stranglekin – and the rest were various venomous species – the fellfangs. If she had worried about the plane being broken into and her being attacked by thieves or worse, she could sleep soundly. Nobody would get within yards of the machine without receiving a very nasty surprise, almost certainly their last.

Lucy retrieved her pencil and tore a blank page from the little puzzle book. She tried out the pencil with a scribble on the back of the paper then turned it over and wrote:

Dear Mummy,
  Clare and Sarah,

Am in Brazil, kidnapped by ETC
Going to Cayman Creek, a real place up the
Amazon. Will look for Daddy.
Am safe and well and expect to remain so. Clare
knows all. Don't worry
              Love Lucy xxx
  P.S. Keep a very close eye on Tibbles.

She wanted to tell her mother as much as possible, but knew that the parcel must be kept light, so she kept her message brief and when she had written it tore the paper so there was no blank space around the writing.

During her planning she had decided the message must be waterproof. She didn't know if it would go by sea or air but either way it was likely to get wet. She also remembered that some seabirds swallowed fish at sea and then regurgitated the food for their young when they reached the nest and it seemed possible that the parcel might spend some time in a bird's gullet or stomach. She folded the note up as tightly as possible, then wrapped it up in a plastic wrapper from one of the sweets. Using her teeth she loosened a thread from the piping of one of the plane's seat cushions and carefully unravelled a long length which she then bound tightly round the plastic until it looked like a small cocoon. She knotted it several times and cut the loose ends of the thread by rubbing them against the steel rim of the cockpit door.

The final package was the size of a large bean and looked very secure. It was all she could do for the moment, so she stretched out and fell into a restless sleep, tormented by worries about her father.

The next day the pilot came with a carton of juice, some fresh bread rolls and a Danish pastry.

'I took a doggy bag to breakfast in the hotel,' he explained, 'and there's a drinks machine in the lobby.' Lucy thanked him and gratefully tucked in.

When she had finished breakfast and washed in the jet's tiny toilet facility the pilot said he had to take her across to the other plane, which Sam had just boarded. He opened the door and clambered down. Before he could turn to help Lucy out she quickly dropped her parcel on to the ground behind his back. As they began to walk to the other plane the pilot pointed to a far corner of the airfield where a very large bird stood silently watching a flock of smaller birds near the plane.

'Look at that – I've never seen one on land before.'

'What is it?' asked Lucy.

'Well, it looks different on the ground but I could swear it's an albatross; what it's doing here is anyone's guess. Maybe it's injured or has been blown inland by a storm at sea. It has the largest wingspan of any flying bird – almost four metres – and can fly enormous distances over the ocean.'

'And what are those others?' said Lucy pointing to the little flock near the plane.

'They look like arctic terns,' said the pilot, who was a

keen birdwatcher, 'and those two on the edge are Manx shearwaters. I've never seen them here before either. Like the albatross, both species fly for thousands of miles over the ocean. Something very funny must be going on out at sea.'

Maybe the birds were going to decide which species was best to take the message when they saw how big it was, thought Lucy. She was impressed and comforted by the degree of organization that the animals seemed capable of on her behalf. She glanced back towards the jet. One of the birds had detached itself from the group and was pecking around under the door of the plane. As she watched, it suddenly flew over to where the albatross waited. Lucy knew that her message was about to start on its amazing journey.

She said goodbye to Hermes and climbed on board the little plane that would take her up the Amazon to Cayman Creek. She eased herself into a bucket seat and fastened her seat belt as the plane manoeuvred to one end of the field to obtain the maximum distance for take-off and turned into the wind beside the wood adjoining the airstrip. As the plane turned, Lucy heard the monkey calling to her from a nearby tree.

'Thy message has gone with the Great Saltiquill, O Promised One. Fare thee well.'

They flew all day and all night, pausing every few hours to land on even smaller landing strips to refuel, stretch their legs and eat meals at little company offices or logging huts. Sam also inspected all the company sites they visited.

They eventually reached Cayman Creek late in the afternoon of the following day. The camp consisted of a few wooden shacks with wire mesh windows instead of glass. Sam took Lucy to the largest of these, which turned out to be the site office, and locked her in a small storeroom while he spoke to the camp manager – a lumberjack called Pollard. She could clearly hear their conversation through the door. Sam asked where Sid and Fred were and was told they had gone down the river to collect a new jaguar caught the day before and that they wouldn't be back until nightfall.

'Well, they can speak to the kid tomorrow,' he said. 'They'll probably get more out of her then. Stick her in a hut and give her some grub. I'm going to get a bit of kip now so don't disturb me. Some wretched spider got into the plane and I couldn't sleep a wink the whole journey.'

Lucy toyed with the idea of further preventing him from sleeping by arranging a visitation of fleas and ticks to his bed, but reluctantly decided against it. Her escape plan would work best if he slept soundly that night. She could hardly believe her luck: Sid and Fred were away and she had the rest of the evening and all night to talk to the animals about her plans.

Without warning the storeroom door was flung open and Pollard appeared. He was a vicious-looking thug: six foot tall, unwashed, unshaven with dirty hair, and he stank of beer. He grabbed Lucy roughly by the arm and hissed in her ear:

'Come on, you little toerag – time to go to your kennel!'

He dragged her over to the nearest hut, opened the door and gave her a violent shove. She tripped over the doorstep and fell headlong into the dark, hitting her head on the far wall. It was just eight weeks since she had fractured her skull in the accident. There was a shattering surge of pain through her head and then everything went black.

Pollard looked down at her inert body.

'Come on,' he sneered, poking her with his foot. 'I haven't got time for your stupid tricks – get up!' He bent down and shook her impatiently, then he saw her deathly pallor and blood trickling through her hair from her operation scar. Suddenly he panicked. He was aware that Chopper and Sam wanted the twins to interrogate her. If she died . . . Pollard ran his tongue over his dry lips; he knew without a shadow of doubt who would be the next to go. He rushed out of the hut to fetch some water, soaked his filthy handkerchief and then knelt beside her, dabbing frantically at the blood oozing from her scalp. He slapped her cheeks.

'Come on, kid,' he said hoarsely. 'I didn't mean no harm!' It was no use; she was deeply unconscious and seemed to be barely breathing. Pollard stumbled out and locked the door behind him. He went and sat in his hut and opened another beer while he tried to think what to do. His cabin-mate Barker was over in the workshop repairing a saw, which was good; Pollard didn't want anyone to know what had happened.

A few moments after Pollard had left, Lucy gradually regained consciousness. She had a splitting headache and it took her some time to recall where she was and what had happened. Then everything came flooding back to her and she knew she must speak to the animals at once. She tried to switch on her beacon and then made a dreadful discovery. Try as she might she couldn't make her power work. Her blood ran cold as the terrible situation she was in gradually dawned on her. She realized that until now she had been apprehensive but in control, utterly confident in the protection the animals would provide for her. Now, for the first time since her capture, she was truly terrified – a lonely, helpless little girl in the hands of a ruthless gang who were going to do frightful things to her and then kill her. If her father were still alive they would kill him too, when he reappeared. She tried desperately again and again to talk to the animals but nothing happened. Then the hut seemed to start spinning round her, faster and faster, and she lapsed back into unconsciousness.

Meanwhile Pollard had finished his beer and plucked up the courage to have another look at Lucy – maybe the kid had just fainted, he tried to reassure himself. He opened her door and saw to his horror that she was lying just as he had left her. His heart sank as he decided he must have killed her. Tomorrow he would have to face Sam and he knew there was no way he was going to believe the kid had fallen over while trying to escape. He fingered his throat nervously: he knew, as did everyone in the company, Sam's favourite method of disposing of those who had outlived their usefulness. He had a bad night.

Sam, in contrast, had a very good night. He woke up at

sunrise following a long and refreshing sleep after his nerve-racking flight worrying about the spider on the plane. It had been extraordinarily active, hiding for a while and then suddenly darting out towards him when he least expected it. He'd had the feeling that the girl had been amused by the whole thing – he'd turned round once or twice and caught her trying to hide a smile. It even crossed his mind that she might have brought it on to the plane but he dismissed the thought as being too fanciful. Well, the twins would soon wipe the smile off her face and the sooner the better. He was looking forward to handing her over to them as soon as they got back.

Across in the next cabin Lucy had woken with a bad headache but she felt much better than the night before. She immediately tried again to switch on her beacon but nothing happened. She realized that the blow on her head must have somehow affected her power, and the thought that it might never return made her intensely depressed. Then she heard Pollard at the door. He had got up early and crept to her hut for a final check on her while the others were still asleep. She huddled, trembling, into a corner as he came in. He was almost sick with relief to find her still alive.

'It's all right,' he said. 'Just came to check you're OK.' His eyes narrowed for an instant, then he put on the nearest thing to a smile he could manage:

'About your little accident last night – I saw you trip. I expect you were a bit tired after your flight.' Despite her terror Lucy sensed that the man was uneasy and suddenly realized why. She looked straight at him and lifted her chin.

'I wasn't tired and it wasn't an accident,' she said as firmly as she could. 'You pushed me!'

'Well,' he replied nervously, 'I might've bumped into you in the dark but I didn't mean nothin'. No need to mention it to anyone, eh?' As soon as he spoke she knew her instincts had been right: he was terrified of Sam. She thought quickly and felt a tiny spark of hope – she could use this awful man to gain a little time.

'That depends,' she said, more boldly, deliberately fingering the dried blood and large bruise she could feel on her head. 'Maybe you should tell them I'm very ill with a temperature and it would be a waste of time trying to question me before I'm better. Oh – and I'm very thirsty and can I have some pills for my headache?'

Pollard and Lucy understood each other perfectly. In a little while he returned with several cans of Coke and some painkillers.

'I've told Sam you've got a fever – probably malaria. The others have just radioed to say they've been delayed and won't be back till tomorrow anyway.'

When he had gone Lucy heaved a sigh of relief. She had another day to try to think of something. By the afternoon her head felt a little better. Pollard brought her some food and more painkillers, and a bowl of water so she could clean the matted blood from her hair. She despised him for his apparent concern, which she knew was only to save his own neck. When he had gone she felt well enough to start looking around for a means of escape but after a while her heart sank. The hut was built of stout planks and the roof was bolted on. The window was made of sturdy wire mesh nailed to the wood and she could barely shake it, never mind think of prising it free. The door was barred on the outside and there was no way she could escape without help. She finally fell asleep, worn out by fear and physical exhaustion.

The next day Pollard continued to bring her food and drink. Sam looked in once and Lucy pretended not to recognize him, as if delirious with fever. She twisted from side to side and moaned pitifully. Sam withdrew rapidly – he didn't want to catch anything nasty. She spent the rest of the day wondering when the twins would come and towards evening she went and stood at the window mesh, dreading any signs of their return.

As she strained her eyes in the fading light, her face was pressed close to the wood next to the mesh. It had been treated with creosote – a strong preservative to protect the wood from being attacked by insects – and soon the irritant smell made her give an enormous sneeze. It shook her head violently and as it did so she felt something go click inside, and instantly she heard the myriad sounds of the forest animals. Suddenly there was complete silence and she was immediately aware of intense excitement among the animals captured in the camp and in the surrounding forest as they sensed the switching on of her power. A thrill ran through her when she heard a deep and awesome voice that could only be that of a jaguar.

'Welcome, O Promised One. You have travelled many leagues across the mighty jungle to reach us and we have been concerned about your silence. We await your instructions.'

Lucy could have wept with relief at having recovered her ability to talk to the animals but she knew that there was no time to lose. In the plane she had thought long and hard about her strategy when reaching the camp and now, at last, she was able to put her plans into action. She had been impressed by the monkeys she had spoken to in Macapá and had decided, if she could, to speak to the monkeys at Cayman Creek. She would need their help to release the captive jaguars, to escape herself and to find out what had happened to her father. If he were still alive they could then set about bringing Chopper and his gang to justice and plan to return home. She started by replying to the jaguar who had called her.

'Thank you, O Lord of the Jungle. I have been unwell and unable to speak until now. To free you I must seek help from the arborikin and others and will speak to you again soon. Are you all able to survive in the forest?' She knew that because of the terrible things Song might have done to the creatures, some might be in need of veterinary care before they could survive unaided.

'All of us can walk,' the jaguar replied, *'but some are grievously hurt and cannot hunt.'*

'When you escape, the injured must hide in the forest and, though I know the junglefang normally lives alone, the fit must bring food to those who cannot hunt. I have to go away, but when I return the evil ones will soon be gone and I will then bring help

to your injured kin.'

'It shall be done as you say, O Great One.'

Lucy then called the monkeys.

'Hallo, O Agile Ones of the trees!' Several monkey voices replied immediately and Lucy sensed the feverish desire to assist that her arrival had created.

'Who is the wisest among you?' she asked.

'I am she,' replied one of the monkeys. 'Welcome to you, O Promised One. What are your wishes?'

'I have many requests,' said Lucy. 'First I must find my father. He left here with one other Tailless One in a thunderquill two moons ago. I fear the thunderquill may have become injured and fallen into the forest. How can I find it?'

'We need the assistance of the fledgiquills in this matter. The best of their kin for your quest would be —' here Lucy detected a slight tremor in the monkey's voice '— the great hunter of the forest known as the arboribane for he flies far and wide above the trees.'

'I will speak to him,' said Lucy, immediately sensing that this was not a task the monkeys would relish. The arboribane was clearly a monkeybane; a hawk or eagle that preyed on them. ' . . . but there are other favours that I would beg of you and your kin. When the sun sleeps, and after all the evil ones have returned and are asleep, you must free the junglefangs from their enclosures and release me from this prison. First, though, you must creep into the huts of the evil ones and remove all their thunder-sticks — of these some will be long and some will be short. Each has a rod with a hole in it; if you hold it only by this rod it will remain silent and you will come to no harm.'

'Then,' she continued, 'a large arachnopod should stand inside the door of he who came with me yesterday and the Malevolent Ones should guard the doors of the others. Without their thunder-sticks the evil ones will fear to pass these creatures and will not disturb us as we leave. We will need to travel on the water in the house that floats.'

'All shall be done as you say, O She Who Speaks. Now you must rest. Have no fear from this moment; none shall harm you while we watch.'

Lucy then called the monkeybane.

'O great fledgiquill that is known as the arboribane, I seek your help.' Within seconds a new voice replied. It sounded like a rusty saw.

'Speak your will, O Promised One.'

Lucy explained about her father, the pilot and the plane.

'I shall go and seek the Paterpromise,' said the harpy eagle, 'but I may need the help of my cousins, the great soariquills from the far mountains of the south and west. For they can fly where I cannot, even unto the Brilliant One, and their eyes see that which no others can. Fare thee well.'

Lucy lay on her bed. Just two months ago in this situation she would have been absolutely terrified of lizards, spiders, ants and other creatures, and would have inspected every inch of her hut and bed. Now she felt that the entire animal kingdom was on her side and, for the first time, was aware of the enormity of the power she wielded. She had heard that all power corrupts and also sensed how her own power could be used to wicked ends if she so chose. She resolved at that moment never, ever, to use this strange and precious gift except in the service of mankind and the rest of the animal kingdom and the planet.

She thought about her safety instructions to the monkeys. She had never handled a real rifle or pistol but she was fairly certain that if the creatures touched only the barrel of any weapon they would not discharge it. As always at such moments she imagined what her sister would have to say, and she could hear in her imagination Clare pointing out that it wouldn't be too good for the image of the Promised One if, as a result of her advice, the chief monkey shot herself in the foot.

Long after nightfall she heard the twins return with their party and the roaring of the jaguar they brought with them.

'We should make a packet from the stuff off this one,' she heard one of the men say, and wondered what was special about the prize they had captured.

'Be silent, junglefang,' she called to the jaguar, *'for after this sunsleep you will be free.'*

The great cat immediately fell silent and after it had been caged the men went to eat their supper. At one point Lucy heard one of them coming to look through her window but she pretended to be asleep and after a while he went away. She heard coarse laughter from around the campfire and guessed that they were discussing her interrogation the next day. How she would have felt but for the protection of the animals she did not dare even to contemplate. Soon, thinking of her family, she fell asleep, tired out by her long journey, the relief of recovering her power and the excitement of her exchanges with the animals.

10

An Uncomfortable Day at the Creek

'*A*wake, *O Promised One!*' Lucy woke with a start. She had been in the middle of a complicated dream in which she had been flying over the jungle on the back of an eagle, looking for her father's crashed plane. She remembered instantly where she was and looked out of the mesh window. Dawn was just breaking but the moon was still clearly visible in the early morning sky. As night gave way to day the sounds of the jungle changed as the creatures of the day awoke to resume their incessant business of life and death. The voice that spoke to her was new but it sounded like a large creature.

'*The arborikin have already removed all the thunder-sticks; the evil ones remain asleep and all is well,*' said the voice. '*Now stand back, O Promised One, away from the door. Do you hear me?*'

'*Yes,*' said Lucy. '*I am ready.*'

The next moment giant claws splintered their way between two of the planks from which the door was made. The door was then wrenched off its hinges in a single movement.

Lucy gaped at the creature facing her. She had seen pictures of giant anteaters and knew that they could tear chunks out of termite mounds as hard as concrete, but to see this power in action was simply devastating.

'*Thank you, O Great Claws,*' was all she could think to say.

'*We must now make haste,*' said the anteater. '*Follow me and I will lead you to the arborikin.*' Lucy grabbed Maria's bag and an empty water bottle and followed the amazing creature. Soon they passed some empty compounds with large holes excavated under the fences.

'*The junglefangs have all escaped,*' said the anteater, by way of explanation. Lucy wondered what creature could have dug such holes so quickly but, before she could ask, they reached the edge of the river where a group of monkeys waited, a pile of guns on the ground beside them.

'*Welcome, Promised One,*' said the eldest female. '*The crawlibane has done well to free you and bring you here. He will now return to the forest.*' Lucy bade her saviour farewell and he disappeared into the trees.

'*Thank you, O Great Claws.*'

'What is your desire now?' the monkey continued, reaching for Lucy's bag and giving it to a younger monkey to carry. 'All that you previously commanded is done.'

'Thank you all for your help,' said Lucy. 'You are obedient and brave. Now we must obtain many of these from the hut where none sleep, for I fear that the water in the river may harm me.' She held up the empty water bottle and immediately a detachment of monkeys left to raid the store hut. The large female led Lucy to a boat moored at the bank.

'Here is the house that floats,' she said. 'We shall use this for the first part of our journey. It will take us quickly through the jungle along the water-that-always-flows and far from this place. I fear the harm the evil ones may do to you, even without their sticks of fire and despite the Malevolent Ones and the arachnopod who wait in guard as you instructed.'

As she spoke there was a rustling sound in the forest clearing next to the river bank and Lucy turned in alarm. She peered apprehensively, her eyes straining to see what was there against the inky blackness of the jungle background. She gradually became aware of dozens of jostling shapes, and now and then caught the dull glint of a tusk in the pale dawn light. It was a seemingly endless herd of wild pigs and Lucy remembered a final request she had made to the monkey queen.

'The snortikin are here,' said the monkey, 'and will do as you have commanded.' She looked a little mystified as she spoke and they both watched as the peccaries moved on towards the sleeping camp. Lucy couldn't suppress a grin at the thought of telling Clare and Sarah of the final farewell she had planned for the Sawyer brothers and their gang of ruffians. The monkey pulled her back to the present.

'*We must make haste, for soon the Brilliant One will awake from his slumber.*' Lucy gazed into the sky where the clouds were now glowing pink on the horizon. She climbed into the boat.

'*The Promised One should start the tail that roars.*' The monkey was sitting on the side of the boat and clearly expecting Lucy to start the outboard motor which was flipped up out of the water, its propeller reflecting the rosy light from the east. Lucy went over to it. It was locked upright in some way that she couldn't discern and looked awfully heavy – the prospects of her unlocking the motor and getting it started were definitely zero.

Just then the other monkeys returned, struggling to pull several plastic-wrapped cases of bottled water to the water's edge. These they managed to lift into the boat with Lucy's help and store alongside some cans of what she later realized was fuel for the outboard motor. She looked at the cache of water and started to calculate how long it might last. The lead monkey saw her and, as though reading her mind, said:

'*Fear not, Promised One. There will be sufficient here for our journey on the house that floats. We know of plants in the trees of the forest and special leaves that catch the water from the skies. You will never go thirsty while you are in our care.*' Lucy remembered that in Grandpa's book she had read of parasitic plants, bromeliads, that could hold up to eight litres of fresh water in their vase-like reservoirs. She also remembered that some of these ponds in the air were home to frogs and other creatures and resolved to try to supervise any water collections that might be made in this way. Her mind then turned back to the more immediate problem of getting the boat moving.

'*I have no knowledge of the tail that roars,*' she said. '*Is there another way we can move the house that floats?*' She looked about for some oars but with a sinking heart knew already that, even if she found some, she could never move the heavy boat unaided.

'*Call the Dreadful Ones,*' said the monkey.

Lucy immediately understood and called. Within seconds the surface of the water rippled and the backs of two giant black caymans broke the surface. Lucy had seen crocodiles and alligators at the zoo but nothing remotely the size of the six-metre-long reptiles now cruising slowly around the boat. She untied the mooring lines which were attached to the protruding roots of a riverside tree and cast them into the dark waters below the bow of the craft. The waters swirled and the ropes disappeared. The boat suddenly jerked forward as though pulled by giant hands and surged out into the river.

'*Which way, O Promise?*' asked the monkey. Lucy, amused and touched by the familiar abbreviation of her title, gave thought to the question. She knew her father had gone on an expedition into the remote interior, so they had to go upstream.

'*We must travel up the river in the direction from which the waters run. I'm sorry, for this means it is harder for the reptocools*' *to pull us.'* She couldn't bring herself to refer to any creatures as the 'Dreadful Ones' and instinctively knew the other name by which the great saurians were known.

'*You need have no concern for them,'* replied the monkey, *'for they are truly mighty in the water and their children's children will speak of the honour of this day.'*

The boat moved swiftly and silently up the river and soon the camp was lost to sight. Lucy had escaped!

Sam came to with a start. He thought he'd heard some snuffling and grunting but now he was fully awake he wasn't sure if it had just been a dream. He lay in his hammock for a moment thinking about the day ahead. The twins were back and he hoped the kid would be in a fit state for them to get to work on her. Chopper would by now be expecting some news and he was not a patient man. He thought he heard another grunt – it was definitely from outside – and then began to be aware of a revolting smell, which he hadn't noticed the night before. As he started to get up to investigate he saw what looked like a black mophead or brush on the floor just inside the door. He couldn't remember having stepped over it the day before and reached for his spectacles to have a better look. As he moved, the mop shifted position and he froze with absolute terror as he found himself looking at the largest spider he had ever imagined could exist, even in his worst nightmare. The creature was as large as a plate and its

. . . he saw what looked like a black mophead or brush on the floor . . .

legs were covered in stiff black bristles; it had raised itself
into a more upright position since seeing Sam move and
he was convinced that, in among a horrifying tangle of
gently waving feelers and jaws, he could just discern two
red eyes fixing him with a primitive and malignant stare.
He had never been so frightened in his entire life but, even
as a wave of nausea and revulsion swept over him, he had
the presence of mind to realize that he must not be sick –
any violent movement would surely bring this frightful
thing scurrying across the floor to pounce on him. It was
so large he was sure that its feet would make a pattering
sound as it ran. Sweating with fear he moved his hand very,
very slowly to the upturned dynamite case that served as a
bedside table. Without taking his eyes off the spider, which,
in its alert position, now looked like a small black woolly
dog, he felt about on the box for the gun which he always
kept by his side. He felt all over the top of the box and felt
nothing. Moving his head as little as possible he rolled his

eyes until he could just see the box and the floor around it, but his gun had gone. He was stuck until somebody came to help him.

Unfortunately, nobody was going to help him in the near future. The twins and the other camp staff were already sitting in their respective hammocks hypnotized by the sight of vividly coloured and venomous-looking snakes lying coiled up just inside their hut doors. They too had sought in vain for their revolvers and were now trapped and helpless.

Several hours passed. The radio had beeped several times in the office but nobody could answer it. In Rio, Chopper was becoming increasingly frustrated.

'Where the hell are they all?' he shouted at Nandita. 'They know that there should always be at least one person in the camp.'

Back at the camp Sid realized that he could no longer resist a call of nature that he had been fighting since he first woke up. The spicy food he had eaten the previous evening had been churning around in his stomach all night and a frightful smell wafting in through the wire mesh window was not helping in the battle to control his bowels. Eventually, he could wait no longer. Never taking his eyes off the snakes Sid crept along the wall to the mesh window. The snakes watched him intently in a way that made his flesh crawl, but apart from flicking their forked tongues they remained motionless as he slipped the catch and slowly opened the window. He scrambled up on to the ledge and as he now saw some serpentine movement out of the corner of his eye he threw caution to the wind and leapt out of the window. He had a soft landing. It was, in fact, a very soft landing, for the large pile of pig dung into which he jumped was only a few hours old and was still steaming gently in the late morning sun.

The smell floating in through the window had been bad, but at close quarters it was simply appalling. Sid choked and retched and gave up any pretence of retaining control of his digestive system. Eventually he stumbled to the path and made his way to the river, trying to pick a path through the peccary droppings. It was a difficult task for, though the pigs had been most generous with their donations around the huts, there was barely a square yard of the camp that was clear of any mess. He was heading for the only washing and bathing point at the camp. At the river a pool had been dug out of the bank, which was fenced off with steel mesh from the main stream so the men could bathe in safety. Sid was just about to plunge in when he noticed that the mesh fence had been torn away and he could see a shoal of piranha fish cruising nonchalantly around the pool. He knew that their razor-sharp teeth could reduce a man to a skeleton in a few moments and he was going to have to wash as best he could with bottled water from the store. Glancing along the bank he saw that one of the two company boats had gone and the other was half submerged, its stern and one side smashed to pieces. He ran back to tell Sam the bad news; if he had waited a moment longer he would have seen a giant cayman surface and thrash another large section of boat away with a swipe of its powerful tail.

Reaching Sam's hut he opened the door and stepped back hurriedly as he saw the spider. Seeing Sid, it moved away from the door and further into the room towards the bed. It moved with astonishing speed and this was the final straw for Sam, who catapulted from his hammock and hurled himself straight through the mesh window; there was a ripping sound as his shorts and part of his left buttock remained behind on the torn wire, followed by a loud slurping noise as he landed face down in a small lake of pig manure underneath the window.

Some time later the men, six in all, were gathered in the radio hut. Pollard, the site manager and Barker, the other lumberjack, had eventually managed to chase the snakes and the spider into the forest using brooms and sticks and now, having ineffectually washed with what was left of the bottled water, the unhappy band were radioing Chopper with the bad news. Sam had tentatively suggested that they drew lots to see who should have the pleasure of speaking to Chopper, but the others would have none of it. They had unanimously agreed that, as Chopper's deputy, the honour belonged to Sam. He held a moistened handkerchief to his face as he spoke – the stench of pig excrement in the midday sun was beyond description – and, stuttering with apprehension, gave Chopper a brief and semi-coherent account of recent events at the camp.

'What do you mean she's *escaped*?' said Chopper. He was pacing up and down the patio outside his villa, a portable phone clamped to his ear. 'How the hell can an eleven-year-old girl, supposedly under constant supervision, tear a door off its hinges, dig holes big enough to let out every jaguar in the camp, destroy your bathing facilities, nick most of your water supplies and escape in a boat, all in the middle of the night and without you dumb bozos hearing a thing?'

'Well . . .' began Sam. He wondered whether to mention the pigs in an attempt to win over Chopper's sympathy, but immediately decided against it.

'I'm sorry for being so dense,' Chopper interrupted in a pseudo-apologetic tone. 'I had this silly idea that she was going to be tortured for information and that six grown men would just, conceivably, be able to subdue her. Silly old over-optimistic Chopper not to know she was going to tear my camp to pieces.' His voice reverted to a vicious snarl. 'Listen, you bunch of big girls' blouses, I don't give a stuff about your stupid bloody animals, but I *do* care about the drug consignment that's due in January. The Bionic Girl can't have got far. Get after the little bitch in the other boat.'

'Actually, we can't. You see, she seems to have smashed up the spare boat and . . .' He held the phone away from his ear as Chopper went completely berserk at the other end.

'Then make a raft and get after her,' he shouted. He was purple in the face and so much saliva was spraying from his mouth that, as the phone receiver became progressively waterlogged, he was practically incomprehensible. 'She can't possibly have started the outboard motor so she *must* have gone downstream; follow her and shoot her to pieces.

But –' he paused and his voice turned heavy with sarcasm. 'Don't tell me – you can't, because Xena the Warrior Schoolgirl stole all your guns while you were asleep.'

There was a breathless moment of silence while Sam nervously rubbed his nose; it had a small lump of pig dung on it, which he smeared across his face and into one eye which started watering.

He cleared his throat apprehensively.

'It's funny you should say that, Chopper, because . . .'

The line went dead as Chopper crushed the phone in his hand and threw it across the garden. Chopper lashed out savagely with his foot at the nearest garden gnome who was engaged in mugging a smaller gnome for a tiny golden mobile phone. These particular gnomes, being nearest to the terrace, had been repeatedly knocked over and the gardener, fed up with restoring them to an upright position, had cemented them permanently in place on a little concrete platform. He was rather proud of the result and was looking forward to telling Chopper but, unfortunately, hadn't yet had the opportunity to do so.

The villa windows were all open in the morning sunshine and the sudden crack as Chopper's big toe snapped could be

. . . the gardener had cemented them permanently in place . . .

167

heard all over the house. His howls of pain and fury could be heard all over the neighbourhood. For some time Chopper remained alone; nobody in the household wanted to be the first to approach him, but eventually his secretary ventured out. He was sitting on the ground clutching his foot, his hand bleeding from where a sharp fragment of plastic from the phone was embedded in his palm. He was leaning for support against the wooden pole of a bird table which was in the process of being felled by another gnome with a miniature golden chain-saw.

'Get a bloody doctor,' he hissed through foam-filled lips, 'and get the bloody plane ready. As usual, I'm going to have to sort this out myself.' He paused and looked at his rapidly swelling foot; he was going to need help on his journey to the camp. He turned back to his secretary.

'Oh, and find that little new bloke I took on yesterday – Bert Shrunkshorts, or whatever. Tell him to get his bag packed: he's coming with me.'

His secretary helped him limp back into the house and then picked up the phone. As she dialled she looked out of the window at the haze of pollution hanging over the city. 'At least you'll get some fresh air at the camp,' she murmured comfortingly to her boss.

11

Jungle Telegraph

Joanna Bonaventure was ironing. She was frantic with worry about Lucy and she always ironed when she was worried. She said it gave her something to do but didn't require any concentration. The police searches and enquiries had so far all proved fruitless and they were now in the process of arranging a reconstruction of Lucy's last movements using a child actress in order to try to jog the memories of any possible additional witnesses to her abduction. Joanna's parents, who were staying with her, were out shopping and Sarah had gone to stay with her aunt and uncle and her cousins, Ben, Henry and Christopher. Ben was the same age as Sarah and they were very good friends.

Joanna always ironed in front of the window so she could see the garden, and her attention now focused on Tibbles who was just reappearing through her favourite gap in the fence at the end of the garden. Until a few minutes ago she had been quietly snoozing on her mat when she had suddenly woken and pricked up her ears. She had got to her feet, intensely alert, with her head cocked slightly to one side. Then she had scrambled through her cat-flap and hurried down the garden and through the fence as fast as she could waddle.

As she returned Joanna could see that she had something in her mouth. The cat-flap rattled and Tibbles disappeared upstairs. Intrigued, Joanna put down the iron and followed the cat into Lucy's bedroom to see her jump on to the bed, something that she knew she was forbidden to do, and put something on Lucy's pillow.

'What on earth do you think you're doing, Tibbles?' exclaimed Joanna, picking up the little parcel. 'Putting rubbish on Lucy's pillow indeed!' She threw the little screwed-up bit of paper into the wastepaper basket and swept Tibbles off the bed on to the floor. Tibbles, usually shamefaced if caught on the bed, immediately went to the basket, knocked it over and started pawing frantically at its contents to retrieve the parcel. Clare, intrigued by the activity and noise, came in from her own bedroom where she had been studying. She was amused at Tibbles's antics.

'She just ran down the garden to get something,' said Joanna in bewilderment, 'and now she's trying to put it on Lucy's pillow.'

'What on earth do you think you're doing, Tibbles?'

Clare suddenly stopped laughing and her eyes widened in anticipation. She knew that if Lucy was alive and well she would somehow use her special powers to get in touch with the family, but hadn't been able to think of how she would do it. Now she thought she knew.

'Stop, Mum!' she said, as Joanna started to pick Tibbles up and take her downstairs. 'Quick, let me see what she brought in.' She crouched by the contents of the basket strewn over the floor and, taking Tibbles from her mother, put her down in front of the mess.

'Good girl, Tibbles. What is it you brought?' Tibbles immediately picked up the little parcel and, jumping up on to the bed, put it once more on Lucy's pillow. Clare snatched it up, looked at it and ran to the bathroom to get some nail scissors from her make-up bag.

'Will someone please tell me what's going on?' said Joanna. 'Have you and this cat gone completely mad, or is it me?'

'Wait two ticks, Mum, and I think all will be clear,' said Clare, as with fingers trembling from excitement she snipped the tightly bound thread and opened the sweet wrapper it had surrounded. Inside was Lucy's note, which Clare opened and flattened on the dressing table top.

'I thought so,' she said triumphantly, her voice breaking with relief. 'It's from Lucy. She must be OK.'

They read the note together and Joanna was the first to speak, through tears of relief.

'Hang on a minute – ETC is the company Daddy works for. What on earth are they doing kidnapping Lucy? And what's this bit?' She pointed to the note and read out: 'Clare knows all.'

'Lucy wasn't sure if I would have told you about her secret yet,' Clare explained, 'and she's just giving me permission to do so.'

'We must tell the police about this note,' said her mother. 'They've got a massive hunt going on and this will tell them that Lucy's in Brazil. They need to get the police over there on to ETC as soon as possible.' Clare agreed that the police had to know, and her mother rang the special number that the investigation team had given her.

While they waited for the police to arrive Clare re-read the note.

'What's this about keeping an eye on Tibbles?' she said. 'It must be important or she wouldn't have wasted words on it in such a tiny note.' Her mother thought for a moment. 'I think,' she said slowly, as she looked again at the note, 'that she feels she may not always be able to send us a note, but may be able somehow to let us know something through Tibbles.'

'Of course. That's it! Good thinking, Mum! We'll watch Tibbles like hawks from now on.'

Within half an hour the door bell rang and Joanna Bonaventure opened the door. On the doorstep stood a policeman. His car was parked outside the gate. One of the back wheels was on the kerb and just behind it an old man was cursing and struggling to remount his electric wheelchair.

'Mrs Bonaventure?' said her visitor, showing her his ID

card. 'I'm Detective Constable Noholmes.' As he leant forward to take his card back Joanna was impressed to see what she took to be a small gold medal just above his tunic pocket but it proved, on closer inspection, to be a blob of breakfast marmalade.

'I hear you have a note from your missing daughter – may I see it?' He took the note and read it slowly, his brow furrowed. His finger moved slowly but steadily along each line, his lips soundlessly forming the words as he read. When he had finished he read the note once more.

'Who's this Tibbles you've got to watch?' he asked guardedly.

'That's the cat,' said Clare. 'Lucy's very fond of her and is reminding us to look after her.' The constable seemed satisfied by this explanation.

'And what's this stuff about "Clare knows Al"? Who's Clare and what's she going to say to Al?'

'I'm Clare,' said Clare. 'Lucy's sister, and it doesn't say "Al" it says "all": "Clare knows all." It means that I will explain things.'

The constable looked suspicious.

'What will you explain?' he asked. Clare thought quickly. She couldn't say anything about the animals. She glanced at the note again and then had a brainwave. The constable was holding it up as he looked at it, and on the back she could see the little scribble where Lucy had checked her pencil was working. She took the note and turned it over so the constable could see.

'You see this symbol?' She pointed to the scribble and

' . . . that's a secret sign that we've used since we were little.'

her voice dropped to a confidential whisper. 'That's a secret sign we've used since we were little. Only the two of us know about it. It proves the note comes from her. That's what only I could explain.'

The constable was impressed.

'Very good planning,' he said. 'It would make our job a lot easier if more people arranged secret symbols in case they got kidnapped.'

Then he snatched the note away from her.

'You mustn't touch this – it may have fingerprints on it. We'll send it to the lab'. Clare thought that they would be better looking for paw prints but said nothing.

'But we've already touched it,' said Joanna. 'That's how we read it.'

'Well, you'd better not touch it again,' said the constable, trying to look important. He folded the note, rubbing the crease firmly between his thumb and forefinger and then slipped it into his tunic pocket, neatly scraping off the blob of marmalade as he did so.

'Where's the envelope?' he asked.

'There wasn't an envelope – it just came like that,' said Joanna. She wondered whether to say it was just something the cat brought in but decided against it. 'I expect you'll be getting in touch with the police in Brazil through Interpol,' she continued.

'That almost certainly won't be necessary,' replied the constable. 'In fact I'm prepared to stake my professional reputation on the fact that Lucy has never left the country. This note was delivered by hand, and as you seem certain that it was written by your daughter, she must be being kept in hiding near by. I expect we'll get a ransom note in the next few days. She was forced to write that stuff about Brazil to put us off the scent. It's an open-and-shut case.'

Clare thought that the only things that had opened and shut in the case were the various beaks and jaws that had carried the note across land, air and sea but she said nothing. She knew now that Lucy would be safe and that was all that mattered. She had seen with her own eyes the immense power that her sister could wield through her control of the animal kingdom, and her quick brain was already imagining the many ways in which Lucy could use those powers to outwit her captors. In her heart she knew that all she needed to do now was to reassure her mother and await further news.

Soon the constable left. On the way out he took a photograph of the letterbox on the front door and said he would send forensics round to dust it for prints.

'The villains will have touched this flap as they posted the note,' he explained, opening the flap as he spoke and running his hand along the edge.

At the local police headquarters Chief Inspector Lestrade sat at his desk. His office was on the ground floor with a large window overlooking the staff car park so he could see at what time his staff came and went. His vantage point was particularly useful today as he was able now and then to glance lovingly at his new car – picked up from the showroom that very morning. Noholmes stood on the other side of the desk with the window behind him. The chief studied once again the crumpled, marmalade-stained note in front of him before picking it up with a pair of tweezers and carefully sliding it into a plastic bag. Heaven only knew what Noholmes had been doing to it; it looked as if it had been dragged through a tropical jungle and halfway round the world.

He went over once again in his mind the garbled story he had heard from Noholmes. The fellow had only been working under him for a fortnight and already Lestrade was wondering how on earth the man had managed to get into the force. It was a windy day and the window in front of which Noholmes was standing rattled as a particularly violent gust swept through the police compound. Glancing up from across his desk the Inspector suddenly pointed, apparently at the constable's shoulder. Noholmes looked at his shoulder. There on his epaulette was his constable's insignia. Suddenly he understood. He was about to be promoted. Admittedly the case wasn't quite wrapped up − the kid still had to be found − but he remembered that the chief had a reputation for recognizing early talent and rewarding it. He looked back to the chief, a knowing smile playing round his lips. Nothing was being said in the open at this stage; the finger said it all, he understood the code.

The chief jabbed his finger more urgently.

'Outside, you fool!'

Noholmes turned and looked through the window. His car, in which, in his excitement, he had forgotten to set the handbrake, was starting to move. The gust of wind seemed to have set his car in motion, and it was now moving slowly down the inclined yard towards the chief inspector's new car some twenty yards away.

Noholmes rushed out of the office. The inspector picked up the phone and pressed a button.

'Yes, sir?' a voice answered immediately.

'Ah, Inspector Fetterson, Lestrade here. There are several matters that require urgent attention. Can you see to them immediately, please?' The chief's tone of voice was not one that invited any reply.

'First of all, you may know of Noholmes − he's on a detective training attachment from Uniformed Branch − part of the new joined-up policing plan.'

'Ye-es', replied the voice cautiously.

'Well, I think he's got as much as he can out of us. I want him to start in your section on the first of next month.' Through the window came the sound of crumpling metal and breaking glass.

'Make that first thing tomorrow morning. We don't want to hold a good chap back and I think he's ready to move on. The other matters relate to the case of the missing schoolgirl. First, I want you to intensify searches in the local neighbourhood. She is almost certainly alive and a prisoner. Next, have you put in place the protection for the family I asked for?'

'Yes. Nothing larger than a fox has been near the place in the last forty-eight hours. The fox seemed to be after their cat – in broad daylight too, cheeky beggar! Was there anything else, sir?'

The chief sighed. There was something funny about this case and it wasn't just Noholmes. The story didn't yet add up and he could leave no stone unturned in the search for Lucy.

'Yes. Put me through to Interpol.'

12

Richard Drops in to Stay

'I think the Miracle Man is coming round, Julian.' Richard heard the woman's voice as though from a great distance. He could feel a burning sensation as she dabbed at him with something. The left side of his face felt like a football and when he tried to open his eyes he could not open the left one. With his tongue he could feel gaping holes where his upper left molar teeth used to be. He put his hand up to touch his face and experienced an excruciating jab of pain in his middle finger.

'Don't do that,' said the woman who was now coming into focus. 'I think you've broken that finger.' Richard was now fully alert and desperately trying to recall where he was. He could remember being chased by a jaguar and running towards a sunlit gap in the bushes but after that his mind was a complete blank.

'Where am I – and who's the Miracle Man?'

The woman laughed. 'Why you, of course! You just fell nearly a thousand feet down an almost sheer cliff face and are still here to tell the tale – and we're dying to hear it.'

Richard sat up and managed to prop himself against the

wall behind him. Every muscle and bone in his body seemed to ache; he felt as though he had just done three rounds with a heavyweight boxer who wasn't too fussy about the rules. He was relieved to find he could move all four limbs and if he kept still the only parts that really bothered him were his upper jaw and his finger, both throbbing with pain, and his left side and left arm and leg which were stinging and burning. Gingerly turning his head he saw that his skin was raw and bleeding down that side: the biggest graze he had ever had or was ever likely to have.

He was in a cave, which looked out over a plain stretching to a line of dark hills on the far horizon. Here and there were dense clumps of forest but there was a great deal of open savannah dotted with herds of grazing animals. He had two companions: a man, and the woman who had spoken to him, both in their early forties. She was kneeling next to Richard and dabbing at his torn skin with gauze and spirit from a first-aid box, which Richard recognized as being from a plane – there'd been an identical one in his own plane. Her companion was tall and powerfully built, and his hair and beard were unkempt. He came over, smiling, and shook Richard's uninjured hand.

'Hello. I'm Julian and this is Helen, my wife. Welcome – if that's the right word – to our crater. We never thought we'd speak to anyone else again.' Richard introduced himself and then started to ask some questions but Helen interrupted him.

'Sorry, Richard, but we can talk later. We must see if you can walk; we have to get back to the plane before nightfall.'

Julian and Helen helped Richard struggle to his feet and they moved slowly out of the cave. Helen, who was limping badly, was clutching her first-aid kit in her free hand and Julian held a formidable spear fashioned from a three-metre stake of wood. The end had been sharpened to a point and was blackened from being hardened in a fire. Looking back Richard saw that the cave was at the base of an immense escarpment. Julian pointed to a spot a little way along, where some broken trees lay on the ground at the foot of a giant vertical crack in the cliff face and a vulture-like bird walked about poking among a pile of bones.

'That's where you were lying. Those trees came down with you – they broke your fall and undoubtedly saved your life.'

'How on earth did you find me?' said Richard, looking along the immense cliff stretching into the distance.

'We've found two or three places along the cliff where animals are most likely to fall – we think the edge at the top is hidden by the undergrowth in some way at these places. The place you fell is the nearest one to our plane. We come here because occasionally a wild pig falls down and it's an easy source of fresh meat. In fact, we probably wouldn't have survived if it weren't for this spot. Hunting on my own –' he glanced at his wife's foot '– with makeshift weapons would be difficult and dangerous, and fishing is out of the question.' Richard wondered why, but

Julian continued without pausing.

'Searching for fruit and nuts sounds fine in storybooks, but actually finding enough food to live on every day is extremely difficult. Foraging is also dangerous because of the . . .' He paused almost imperceptibly and looked again at his wife, '. . . wild animals, and we daren't go too far from the plane. Fortunately there is a banana grove quite nearby, but to have an occasional gift of fresh meat land virtually on our doorstep has been a lifesaver.'

Soon they topped a small rise and the plane came into view about a hundred yards away on a flat plain. As far as Richard could see it had not crashed but seemed to have used the flat plain as a landing site. A mile beyond the plane was a strip of dense forest which wound its way into the far distance and, as Richard correctly decided, marked the course of a river. The heat haze of the day had disappeared and the evening was still and clear.

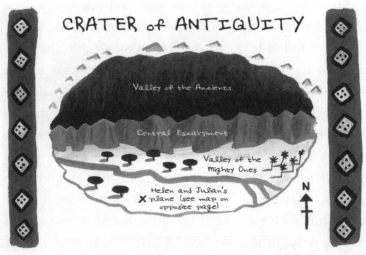

Map of the Crater of Antiquity

Richard looked across to the other side of the valley where in the distance he could see a forbidding and uninterrupted range of cliffs.

'Wow!' he said. 'It's difficult to judge distances with only one eye working but this valley must be ten miles across.'

'You're right,' said Julian. 'It is very wide – but it's not a valley. Remember we've had the advantage of seeing it from the air. It's actually a giant crater – a bit like the one near the Serengeti national park in East Africa.' Richard nodded. He'd been there as a medical student in Tanzania. The great Ngorongoro crater with its teeming herds of game was like a world within a world on the vast African plains.

'Except,' Julian continued, 'this crater is a very curious shape – that's why you think it's a valley. From the air you can see that the place where we are standing now is only one half of a super oval-shaped crater – divided down the middle by that range of cliffs you are looking at now.'

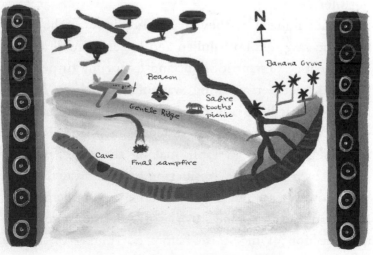

Detail from the Valley of the Mighty Ones

183

'That means . . .' said Richard, looking along the length of the 'valley' in both directions. 'Yes,' interrupted Julian, 'it means that both ends are blocked – but the crater is so large you can't see them from here. We don't know how this curious geological formation occurred, but it created twin valleys and we're trapped in one of them. It's an enclosed space that looks roughly the shape of a bath from the air – and there's no way out. The cliff is unscalable at any point so far as we can tell. That's why we're still here after three months – not that we could go anywhere even if we could get out; when Helen's foot got worse we didn't even think of trying to leave any more. She seems to have picked up some chronic tropical infection following an insect bite and her foot is gradually getting more swollen and painful. There's nothing but wild dense jungle in every direction outside the crater and we'd be lucky if we lasted a couple of days out there.'

Richard noticed as they made their way to the plane from the cave that both Julian and Helen were ill at ease. They kept a constant lookout and frequently turned as if to check whether anything was following them. At one point on their little trek there was a crashing sound in a stand of trees quite some distance away and Richard assumed it must be a tapir making the noise, pursued perhaps by a predator. Considering how far away the trees were, however, the noise was certainly very loud and both Helen and Julian stopped in alarm and gazed intently in the direction of the noise before continuing on to the plane at a faster pace than before.

Eventually they reached the plane, an unusual design that Richard hadn't seen before with large pods slung under each wing. Helen and Julian were clearly relieved to be back and they helped Richard into the cabin.

'Not much room, I'm afraid,' said Julian with a crooked smile, 'but we'll all have to cram in at night.' He made as much space for Richard as possible and offered him a drink of water, which he took gratefully. His face throbbed relentlessly and he was sure he had fractured his cheekbone.

'We've got some paracetamol too. The first-aid box was full of it – the pilot must have had a permanent headache.' He handed Richard the painkillers. 'Then, if you feel up to it,' Julian continued, 'we're dying to hear your story.'

Richard swallowed the tablets and settled himself as comfortably as possible to tell the tale of his adventures. Despite the pain in his jaw and his side, however, the exhaustion of the day was catching up with him. Helen and Julian watched him in amused silence as his head began to nod and within minutes he was fast asleep.

Richard slept for over ten hours and awoke to a gentle shake on the shoulder from Helen. Julian had already been out for water and bananas, which Richard started to eat, slowly and painfully, for his injured jaw had swelled up during his sleep.

'Where did I get up to last night?' he said eventually, as he finished his last banana. The others both smiled.

'Nowhere,' said Helen. 'You fell straight asleep which we thought was pretty rude of you considering we hadn't spoken to anyone for three months.' They all laughed and Richard felt himself warming to these nice people.

'Better late than never,' he said. 'I'll have another go, and try to stay awake this time.' He then told them about his adventures up to his arrival at the crater. Just as he finished he remembered something that might save them.

'There's something else you should know,' he said hopefully. 'I know where we are. I recorded the position of our plane almost constantly using a global positioning device. In my notes I still have the GPS fixing co-ordinates for where the plane crashed and I can't have made more than a few miles on foot through the jungle. Your plane looks OK. If it just ran out of fuel or needs a spare part we can radio my base and get whatever we need dropped to us. Which one of you's the pilot?'

'Neither of us,' Julian replied. 'That's the problem. You're quite right about the plane, it's fine – we made a deliberate landing here and we've got fuel. Those pods –' he pointed to the wings '– are extra fuel tanks for remote explorations.' He paused and Richard asked the obvious question.

'Where *is* the pilot then?'

'He was eaten –' said Julian slowly. He glanced at his wife as if seeking reassurance that he wasn't living in a fairytale and she gave him a nod of encouragement. He looked back at Richard and continued.

'– he was eaten by a sabre-toothed tiger.'

It was mid-afternoon and the three of them were sitting outside on canvas camping chairs in the shade cast by the plane. Richard was spellbound by the story that he had just heard.

'Helen and I are palaeontologists – fossil hunters,' Julian had started once they were settled outside. 'We met and married while still at college and after years of working at the university we managed to get a United Nations research scholarship to study abroad in unexplored regions of potential palaeontological interest. We'd always been interested in South America because people have thought for years that some animal species which are extinct everywhere else might still be alive in remote areas of the jungle. Sir Arthur Conan Doyle wrote his famous story *The Lost World* about a land that time forgot in the Brazilian wilderness and, though that was of course just fiction, there've been occasional reports right up to the present day of native tribes seeing unknown creatures in the Amazon basin. Helen and I didn't really believe that any weird and wonderful creatures could have survived, but we did think we might find a more complete fossil record here than has been found so far in East Africa, Mongolia and Arizona. We were delighted to learn that our application for a field study grant had been successful, the only stipulation being that we should study at four different sites in at least two continents so that any research benefits resulting from our work could be spread across several different countries. We obtained a year's sabbatical leave from our university posts and then started on our adventure, making three-month visits to West Africa, Patagonia and Colombia in turn. We saved our final three-month period for the task we thought would be the most exciting – the search for new sites in remote Amazonia. After only a week of flying over unexplored territory we found the crater in which we are now stranded. It'd been the first place we'd seen where the plane could land, and the landscape – mixed forest, savannah and rocky outcrops – was so similar in appearance to the famous Olduvai gorge in Tanzania that we both became excited at the possibility of finding some outstanding fossils.

'The pilot, David, had a problem with some tricky air currents below the rim of the crater, but we eventually landed safely and decided to set up an overnight camp to do some preliminary exploration. When David tried to radio back to base to tell them what we were up to, he found he couldn't. He thought the nearby cliff was causing radio interference so he took the radio from the plane with its back-up battery and set out alone, away from the cliff, to see if he could find a better spot for transmission and reception.

'After a couple of hours had passed Helen and I had finished putting up the tent and began to wonder where he'd got to. We were worried he might have broken an ankle or something; anyway, we set off in the direction he had gone and the first thing we noticed were some herds of completely unfamiliar animals. We also saw groups of large flightless birds that we thought must be rheas – the ostriches of the pampas – though this is further north than we ever thought they existed. After about a mile we saw the radio on the ground, its leather strap still partially slung over David's shoulder. No David – just his shoulder. It was lying there with the arm, collarbone and bits of chest still attached. His entire forequarter had just been torn out of his body.' Julian paused. Richard was listening intently to every word.

'Our first thought was to try to find his other remains but then we realized that he couldn't possibly have survived such an injury and that we ourselves were probably in grave danger. We decided a jaguar or puma must have attacked him: it was too far from the river for a cayman, which was the only other creature – as we then imagined – that could possibly have killed him. We slept in the plane that night – we didn't dare stay in the tent in case the jaguar followed our tracks or scent and attacked us as we slept. It was just as well we did because in the morning the tent was slashed to pieces and our belongings scattered.'

He paused for a drink then continued. Richard listened agog.

'The next day we felt we ought to try to get the radio back, just in case we could make it work. I took the axe that was part of our camping equipment, though quite how effectively I could defend two of us with it against a determined jaguar I wasn't sure. We had no choice, though: without the radio we were doomed to stay here for ever. As we got near to the place where he'd had been attacked we saw a gigantic bird – much larger than the rhea that I'd first thought it must be, bigger in fact than the biggest ostrich you could ever imagine – and it had a massive head and beak. It was pecking at something on the ground and as we watched it raised its head with David's entire arm in its great beak. I realized with a sensation I can't possibly describe to you that I was looking at a terror bird – phorusrhacos – supposedly extinct for thousands of years. As it lifted its head it stared straight at us – we were standing about a hundred yards away, I would guess – dropped the arm and started striding towards us. We both stood stock still, absolutely petrified with fear: I could feel the axe handle beginning to slip through my palms, which were drenched with sweat. I suppose we could've started to run

'. . . a sabre-toothed tiger hurled itself at the bird.'

but I'm sure it would have been useless – the creature was ten feet high and, with its enormous legs, would have overtaken us in a minute. Anyway, we didn't need to for at that instant there was a ferocious roar and a sabre-toothed tiger hurled himself at the bird. He'd obviously returned to see if any of his previous day's kill remained and caught the terror bird in the process of stealing it.

'I had of course seen sketches of sabre-toothed cats in museums but in real life the animal was much bigger than I'd imagined and those massive eight-inch fangs were truly amazing. They're not true tigers – their scientific name is *Smilodon* and they're supposed to have been extinct for over a hundred thousand years. While the cat and the bird were fighting we dropped to the ground behind some rocks; we then crawled away until we thought it was safe to crouch and eventually got back to the plane as best we could with Helen hobbling along on her bad foot. Once in the plane we had to think seriously about our situation. I think that at this point, at the risk of boring you, Richard, you need to know something about the pre-history of South America so that what I tell you makes more sense.'

'There isn't a chance in a million that you could bore me,' said Richard. 'Tell me everything I need to know.'

'It's best if I hand over to Helen at this point,' Julian said. 'She's the expert on this stuff.' He stopped and looked past Richard. 'Look!' he said, pointing into the distance.

Richard turned. About half a mile away was a cluster of trees that stuck out from the forest surrounding the river.

A creature the size of a small house was standing upright on its hind limbs and tearing the vegetation from one of the trees. Even at that distance they could just hear the crashing and rending sounds of its activity.

'What in heaven's name . . .' started Richard – he had leapt to his feet and knocked his chair over.

'It's OK. You can sit down, they don't come near the plane any more – not since destroying the camp the first night and finding nothing that interested them. It's a giant ground sloth, *Megatherium americanum*. It weighs almost four tons. You're looking at a creature that's supposed to have been extinct for eight thousand years. It looks remarkably like the museum models, doesn't it?' Both he and Helen seemed quite relaxed and Richard sat down again – though Julian and Helen noticed that he turned his chair so he could keep his good eye on the distant monster, and for the rest of the conversation he occasionally glanced in that direction.

Helen took a sip from her plastic camping cup and turned to Richard. 'For thirty million years South America was isolated from all other land masses and its animals and plants evolved independently into unique forms – just as they did in Australia. Then, about three million years ago, the continent of what is now North America collided with South America and the animals of the two lands intermingled. What a time that must have been.' She looked wistful and Richard realized how utterly absorbed she was in her subject.

'Just think what it would have been like. Predators and

prey meeting species they had never seen before in their entire history. Some species must have disappeared almost overnight; others would have taken longer, with the whole process eventually resulting in the present-day mix of South American animals. Except, that is, in this crater. As you can see, its walls form an impassable barrier to both animals and humans; nothing except birds can get in or out, and the funny air currents around the rim that caused trouble for our pilot seem to bother the birds as well. We haven't actually *seen* anything fly in or out since we've been here. The crater seems to be a true "lost world" as described by Conan Doyle – a miniature ecosystem in which the animals and plants have remained undisturbed by outside influences since the mid-Pliocene – about three million years ago. It continued to develop on its own, however, and the final result is a mixture of the Pliocene and Pleistocene epochs – that's up to about ten thousand years ago. It's a palaeontologist's dream come true – a zoo of living fossils which has exceeded our wildest expectations. The trouble is, we're trapped here and our situation is getting worse. Every day we risk our lives for food and water and it's only a matter of time before one of us is caught by an animal or has an accident. It's a curious twist of fate that after making the greatest biological discovery of our age – probably of all time – we can't tell anyone about it. It seems ridiculous that we actually have a means of escape right in front of us,' she nodded at the plane, 'but we can't use it. We even thought of trying to teach ourselves to fly in short hops around the crater but we realized the risk of crashing was too great. Even if we survived the crash we'd almost certainly be worse off than we are now.'

The sun had sunk over the western rim of the crater and Helen said that soon they should get back into the plane for the night.

'How safe are we in there?' Richard asked. He was thinking of the massive ground sloth he had seen; it could crush the plane with a single blow of its giant paw.

'The animals don't pay any attention to it, thank God,' said Julian. 'We noticed similar behaviour in the big game on our safaris in Africa. Even when you're in an open Land Rover the animals leave you alone as long as you don't get out. It's as though the vehicle is part of the landscape.'

They clambered into the plane on this reassuring note and talked long into the night. When they finally settled to sleep Richard's mind was buzzing with all he had seen and heard; it had, without question, been the most unusual day in his life. He eventually fell into a fitful sleep in the

cramped conditions of the plane that was at the same time their defensive fortress and their prison.

The next day Helen and Julian fetched food and water but Richard stayed behind. Because his side was painful and inflamed he had difficulty in moving and while the others were away he had the opportunity, for the first time since arriving in the crater, to assess their situation quietly and calmly. On the positive side they were all alive and relatively well, though Helen's foot was clearly going to be a serious problem if it carried on getting worse. They had the safety of the plane, which the animals genuinely appeared to ignore. Fresh water was no problem for it streamed in rivulets at hundreds of places down the cliff face from the rainforest above and the plane, mercifully, was quite close to one of these. About two hundred yards from the plane there was a grove of bananas and other trees next to a small stream which was formed from several of the rivulets coming off the cliff and ran to the main river a mile away. This grove was their main source of food. As

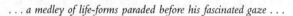

. . . a medley of life-forms paraded before his fascinated gaze . . .

well as the bananas Julian had mentioned there were avocados, some citrus fruits and some edible tubers, similar to potatoes or yams.

These few positive factors seemed to be overwhelmed by many negative ones. Nobody knew where they were and they had no means of communicating with the outside world. The crater was teeming with wild beasts, many of them fierce predators, and without any effective means of defending themselves they risked their lives every time they moved away from the plane. They were effectively confined to trips to the nearby cliff for water and to the banana grove for food. He could see now how the finding of an occasional fallen animal had been so helpful to Helen and Julian in their struggle to survive, despite the risk from competing scavengers. Julian had tried on one occasion to see if he could get fish from the main river, but he had never tried again. Richard recalled his words:

'As I got near the river I frightened a small herd of deer-like creatures. They scattered in front of me and the one nearest to the river simply disappeared. It vanished into the jaws of the largest crocodile you ever imagined in your worst nightmare. It must have been forty feet long with a body the height and width of a family car. The minute it saw me it started lumbering towards me – surprisingly fast. I turned and ran and I've never been back. The river itself was huge – as you'd expect from all the water coming off the rainforest. Where it goes to I've no idea as exploring is obviously out of the question, but I presume it must leave from the crater through some kind of underground cave. It would be a theoretical way of escape if there was air above it but it's not an expedition Helen or I would begin to consider.'

As he thought over all these things Richard realized the true horror of their predicament. As Helen had said, it was only a question of time before one or more of them fell prey to capture, accident or disease. They were literally living from day to day, and one day it had to come to an end. Richard's thoughts, inevitably, turned to his family and whether he would ever see them again – it seemed extremely unlikely. He would have been astonished if he had known that his only hope of survival was his daughter Lucy, lying at that very moment in the intensive care unit of a London hospital and as yet unaware of her awakening power.

The next day followed the same pattern. Richard stayed quietly recovering from his injuries while Helen and Julian went foraging for supplies. He sat out in the shade of the plane, gazing in awe and wonderment at the scene before him. As the sun rose in the sky a medley of life-forms paraded before his fascinated gaze as though inhabiting some immense free-range menagerie. Helen had given Richard some of the reference books they had brought with them for their palaeontological work. The most useful was one that described the creatures inhabiting South America during the Pleistocene – the epoch which Helen and Julian believed to be the principal source of the animals in the crater – and he was able to compare the pictures in this book with the real creatures going about their lives before his very eyes. Herds of long-nosed camel creatures and hippidiforms were preyed upon by sabre-toothed cats and packs of primitive wolves; terror birds stalked about fearlessly, preying upon smaller creatures and fighting with jackals and other scavengers for the remains left by the big cats. Strange birds flew through the air with plumage unlike any Richard had ever seen in modern species and the massive ground sloths lumbered about, walking on their knuckles with their giant claws curled away from the ground until they rose up on their hind legs and started stripping foliage from the trees.

Now that Helen and Julian had explained what the crater looked like from the air Richard was better able to understand the geography of his surroundings. He remembered that they were trapped in one of two valleys inside a giant crater. The valleys had for some reason become divided by a midline ridge of rock during some cataclysmic geological event. That ridge was an almost perpendicular escarpment rising hundreds of feet above the crater plain and surmounted by jagged crags, some peaking up to thousands of feet. It was impassable to any living creature that could not fly or walk up a vertical rock face. As he gazed across at the distant feature Richard became consumed with curiosity as to what lay beyond it in the other valley. If only he could somehow get there and look . . . but his train of thought was interrupted by Helen and Julian coming into view and Richard realized just how relieved he was to see them safely back. He noticed that Helen's limp seemed to be getting worse and decided to talk to her about it later.

After they had eaten and dusk was falling Richard suggested that they should build a large beacon near their plane.

'You're absolutely right, Richard,' said Julian. 'We should have thought of it before. There's only a remote chance of anyone coming but it's the only chance we have and if they do come and they miss us then we've really had it – they certainly won't search the same area twice.'

'Let's get going in the morning,' said Richard, 'but before we start tomorrow I wonder if you'd let me take a look at Helen's leg. I didn't mention it to you before but I originally qualified as a doctor before settling on botanical research as my final choice of a career. I loved the intellectual challenge of medicine but I didn't really enjoy the practical aspects of the job. Anyway, I've been watching you, Helen, and whatever is wrong with your leg it looks as if it's getting worse. I'm not sure if there's anything I can do without drugs or instruments but I think I should have a look just in case I can help.'

Helen and Julian glanced at each other in obvious relief.

'I'd be most grateful if you would', she said. 'We've been getting more and more worried about it and in the last day or two it has got really painful.' In response to Richard's questions she revealed that the trouble seemed to have started in her foot during their studies in Colombia immediately prior to this Amazon expedition, the final stage of their South American trip. There were two spots, one on the sole of her foot and the other on the top of her fourth toe. These had become infected and her entire lower leg had swelled up. Helen presumed that she had been bitten by a tick or some other jungle insect and that the bite had become infected but instead of getting better the sores had got steadily more painful.

'The really curious thing,' she added, 'was that they seemed suddenly to get worse after I had a bath. We stayed in a hotel for a couple of nights of civilization between expeditions and I luxuriated in my first bath for several weeks – it was, incidentally, to be my last until the present time, I'm afraid to say.' She grinned and pretended to sniff at herself. 'A few hours after the bath these spots became angrier and started to weep and they have oozed ever since.' Somewhat to her surprise, Richard at once became intently interested in this aspect of her story and questioned her in great detail about it. He now had his suspicions as to what she might have, but said nothing. He wanted to have a close inspection of the leg in good daylight before passing any opinion.

The next morning Richard looked at Helen's leg again. There were two angry red pustules in the sites she had indicated and he thought there might be a third spot just appearing on another toe. He thought for some time before speaking. Helen and Julian both looked at him expectantly.

'Before I go any further,' he eventually said, 'can I just check on something? Am I right in thinking that you said you'd gone to Africa before coming to South America?' Helen and Julian both looked puzzled.

'Why yes,' she replied, 'we spent three months at a site near Dinguiraye in Guinea in West Africa – but what's that got to do with it?'

Richard seemed not to hear her question but pressed on more eagerly. 'And were you near a lake or river?'

'Actually, yes. We were excavating in a river gorge, in the various beds the river had flowed in over millions of years; the course of the present river is still in the same gorge a few hundred yards away from our site.' They both looked intently at Richard who had clearly made a diagnosis.

'They may well be badly infected bites,' he said, 'but I'm suspicious that they may be something else, something I read about as a medical student but never saw a case of during my brief career of medical practice.'

'What do you think it is?' asked Helen.

'I may of course be completely wrong,' said Richard, 'but there is a worm called the Guinea worm. Its scientific name is *Dracunculus* something — yes, that's it, *Dracunculus medinensis*. It is a parasitic worm that infests humans. It lives in a minute water crustacean and when someone swallows contaminated water the larvae develop into worms that pass through the body tissues down to the legs — it may take them months to do this — and then form blisters out of which new larvae emerge, get into water, infect the crustaceans and start the whole cycle again. It only lives in the tropics, which is why I never saw a case in London. It is believed that as the worms get near the surface of the skin they can somehow sense the presence of water if the leg is immersed and become more active. That's why I was so interested in your bath story. I presume you haven't had your leg in water since then?'

'No,' said Helen. 'As you can see, it takes us all our time to carry enough to drink, never mind bathe. Can you do anything for it?' She looked terrified. 'It sounds like some horrible science fiction story about aliens.'

'Villagers in affected tribes entice the worm out with water and then start to wind it round a twig; they wind a little more each day until the whole worm is out – it's important not to hurry the process or the worm may break leaving a fragment behind that can't be removed.' He turned to Julian. 'Perhaps . . .' he started to speak, but Julian had grabbed a container and was already running to the cliff to get water. When he returned they immersed Helen's foot and within an hour they could see that Richard's diagnosis was correct: from one of the spots the end of a worm emerged and Richard gently wound it round a specimen stick from one of Helen's scientific test tubes. He then carefully wrapped a bandage around the leg to protect the twig.

'There,' he said. 'We'll get more of the little blighter tomorrow and her sisters as soon as they appear. It's a gruesome experience for you but at least we know what it is and there's a good chance we can clear it up. You may be interested to know that it's thought these worms were the 'fiery serpents' that afflicted the Children of Israel during their migration from Egypt. An ancient brass model actually exists that depicts Moses winding out such a 'serpent' on a rod.'

Helen who had turned white during the procedure had now recovered her composure.

'I think you're absolutely brilliant to have remembered that from medical school and I can't thank you enough for what you've done – even though it's just about the worst thing I could imagine having.' Julian nodded in agreement, then insisted that she sat and rested for the rest of the day while he and Richard set to work on the beacon.

By nightfall they had put together a pile of wood from fallen trees and branches that would have graced the most ambitious of Guy Fawkes parties. Julian used a climbing rope to haul the larger branches to the site and Richard, who was gradually getting more mobile, stacked the wood into a bonfire mound. Helen and Julian had fire-lighters and matches as part of their camping equipment and these items were now kept next to the beacon in a waterproof box.

They fell asleep that night weary, but encouraged by the thought that they had at least done something positive towards their possible survival.

The days passed and soon Richard felt fit enough to replace Helen on her foraging trips with Julian. This meant that she could rest her leg, and that both the food-gatherers could run back quickly to the plane should the need arise.

For the next three months life followed a similar pattern for the trio, the men collecting food and water while Helen stayed near the plane and the nearby beacon. They had agreed that one of them should always remain close to it just in case a search plane appeared in the sky one magic day. As the weeks passed, however, they all knew in their hearts that this was never going to happen and that they were doomed to spend the rest of their days in their lost world.

13

Cruising with Crocodiles

As Lucy cruised up the river, following her escape from the camp, the rising sun finally escaped from the clouds of dawn on the eastern horizon. She thought she had never seen such a beautiful sight as the morning sun shining through the canopy of the immense forest, a million dewdrops glistening like diamonds on every tree. Soon, brilliantly coloured parrots flew above searching for their breakfast fruits and Lucy was startled as a troop of howler monkeys started their deafening morning chorus. Tinkling sounds like a mandolin came from the roots of the giant trees lining the river as musical frogs greeted the day, and countless insects filled the air with humming and buzzing. At the sound of these Lucy scrabbled in her bag and took out the insect repellent that Maria had kindly provided. She didn't know whether the insect world in general was sufficiently aware of her exalted position to leave her alone, but it seemed wise to be on the safe side.

The monkey that Lucy had come to think of as the queen animal saw what she was doing and, coming to her side, sniffed in curiosity at the repellent. Lucy explained its purpose and the monkey reassured her.

'You now need have no fear, O Promise, of any creature that is not sick. Even the squitohums and the buzzithorns will not harm you. All you need fear is the Brilliant One, for your skin is fair and without fur.' Lucy was relieved to hear this and swapped her repellent for the tube of suncream. Now in full daylight she could see her rescuers properly for the first time. The black spider monkeys had long hairy limbs and faces surmounted by stiff, black, ragged caps of fur which Lucy could only think of as being 'punk' haircuts. Their most striking feature, however, was their tail. Much longer than the body, it was like a fifth limb and curled automatically round anything it touched. The monkeys sat around the sides of the boat and chattered excitedly among themselves, never taking their eyes off Lucy for very long.

After a couple of hours the queen spoke to the caymans and they pulled the boat into the bank.

'We will stop for a while,' said the queen turning to Lucy, *'for there are three that wish to join us, and we will gather some food for you to eat.'*

Lucy jumped out on to the bank and as she did so heard a deep and wonderful voice which she recognized as being that of the female jaguar that had been brought into the camp the previous evening.

'Welcome, O Precious One, I come to guard thee on thy journey,' said the jaguar and Lucy became aware of a shadow moving silently through the undergrowth. The bushes parted and she caught her breath: before her stood the most beautiful creature she had ever laid eyes on. It was a black panther with eyes as green as emeralds,

glistening fangs and muscles rippling effortlessly under its stunning fur. Lucy had read a great deal about her favourite animal and knew that occasionally both jaguars and leopards were born black, a melanistic variant. She had never seen such an animal, however, and was lost in amazement at its savage beauty.

'*Thy beauty puts all creatures to shame, O Dark One,*' said Lucy, horrified to think of the agony and degradation that had been the fate intended for this animal by Chopper's gang at the camp. '*I shall fear naught with thee by my side.*' The animal purred with pleasure at her words and when Lucy sat on the root of a giant tree she stretched herself at her feet.

Soon the monkeys brought her fruits and plants to eat. Most she did not recognize but they were all delicious and for the first time since being taken captive she felt relaxed and truly hungry. One monkey had brought some nuts and Lucy tried ineffectually to break one open with a stone. She heard the queen call into the forest and soon an agouti appeared through the undergrowth. The rabbit-sized rodent seized the nut and cracked it as though it were a peapod, then proffered the kernel to Lucy. It systematically cracked a dozen nuts, leaving them in a neat pile, and then disappeared without a word. The queen monkey noticed how impressed Lucy had been by this feat.

'*The scurridents speak but little,*' she said, '*but they can rend asunder the fruits of wood that the jaws of greater creatures cannot breach.*' Lucy was grateful for the explanation and felt she should comment on the range of animal skills being put at her disposal.

'*The different creatures of the forest have already done many things to assist me,*' she said to the queen, '*and all are masters of their skills, but why . . .*' she looked across at the panther '*. . . why do I need the protection of the ebony junglefang? No animals seem to wish to harm me once they are aware of who I am.*'

'*We cannot be sure that every creature will be aware of you in time,*' replied the queen, '*and if an animal has been bitten by one of the flitterkin it may take leave of its senses and attack you. We must take the junglefang to guard you. There is nothing in the forest that she fears.*'

Lucy did not understand the full import of this remark at the time, but years later, when in her veterinary studies she learnt that vampire bats could transmit rabies to animals, she was to remember this conversation and marvel once again at the care and concern the animals of the forest had shown her.

Later, another group of monkeys returned with some massive moriche palm leaves and attempted to arrange them in the boat as a shelter from the sun for Lucy. When Lucy saw what they were trying to do she asked them to fetch some springy saplings and some vine tendrils and showed them how to fashion an archway across the boat, covered with the large leaves to form a sun canopy. Just as they finished the monkey spoke again:

'*The others who would serve thee approach.*' At the queen's words Lucy looked up to see a cross between a panda and a raccoon bounding towards her. It was the size of a dog with a long tail marked with beautiful rings. It was restless and inquisitive, sniffing all the members of the party in turn before sitting at Lucy's feet looking up at her with bright, intelligent eyes.

'We know the Tailless Ones make special friends such as the furriclaws and the wolfkin,' the queen explained, *'and as you are alone I have asked the coatikin to serve you.'* Lucy was enchanted; she had recognized the coati mundi immediately from the pictures in Grandpa's book and she was impressed at the monkey's kindness in providing her with a substitute for a cat or dog.

'Greetings, O Promised One. I will be at your side throughout your quest.' The coati had a silvery, melodious voice that Lucy fell in love with on the spot. The animal asked permission to touch her and then came and nuzzled her, licking her hands and rubbing her legs with its soft fur.

'I shall call you Katherine,' said Lucy. *'In fact, Katy Coati.'*

'I am honoured to be so named,' replied the coati proudly, leaving Lucy's side for a moment to scamper round the group several times like a playful puppy, giving yelps of delight. Lucy had already been thinking about names – it seemed rather rude not to call her travelling companions by individual names – and she turned to the queen and her two daughters.

'And, if I may, I shall call you Queenie,' she said to the mother, *'because I think of you as a queen among monkeys. Your daughters I shall call Sophie and Clio.'*

Queenie and her daughters were just as pleased as the coati to have names of their own and Lucy felt happy that her instincts had been correct.

'And you,' she turned to the panther, *'I shall call Melanie.'*

The great cat once again purred with pleasure and, overcome with embarrassment, started grooming itself.

'*And now,*' said Queenie, '*I have something else for you.*' She stood with her forepaw behind her back and her daughters watched and fidgeted with excitement. Lucy was overcome with curiosity as the monkey brought her paw round and quickly cupped her other paw over whatever it was she was holding, so Lucy couldn't see. Then she gradually opened a gap between her fingers and a tiny face peeped out, surrounded by a little mane of golden–black hair. The pygmy marmoset was only the size of a mouse but looked exactly like a miniature lion. Lucy squealed with delight and held out her hands. The little creature sat up in the monkey's hands and said in a tiny, tinkling voice, '*Greetings, O Special One!*' Then, somewhat shyly Lucy

'I am fortunate indeed to have a lion at my side as well as a panther.'

thought, *'May I touch your exquisite locks?'* Lucy, of course, gave permission, though not without some embarrassment. She did have beautiful, dark-brown hair but after several days of kidnap and untold hours flying in prison class she couldn't help feeling that the marmoset's description was a little over the top. The tiny creature, ignoring her outstretched hands, sprang straight on to her shoulder and stroked her hair with its tiny paws. She could feel its furry mane tickling her ear and started giggling – much to the astonishment of the entire group, who had never before observed this phenomenon in any creature. Lucy, realizing the cause of their consternation, reassured them that it only meant she was happy and not to worry if she did it again. She carefully removed the diminutive monkey from her shoulder and spoke to her.

'I am fortunate indeed to have a lion at my side as well as a panther. I shall call you Michelle – Michelle Marmoset.' The tiny creature frolicked with delight on the palm of Lucy's hand and then leapt back on to her shoulder. She was so light Lucy was hardly aware of her tiny burden.

When they were ready to leave one of the caymans spoke.

'Fare thee well, O Promised One. We return now to our own waters. Our cousins will assist thee in thy further quest.' His voice was like the cold, black, forbidding depths of an ancient, hostile river. Lucy shuddered at the very thought of what it would be like to have these reptiles as foes rather than friends. With a flick of their tails they swept away down the river and as they did so two nearby shapes,

which Lucy had until then imagined to be the timber of fallen trees, revealed themselves to be caymans by suddenly moving and slithering into the river to take up the mooring ropes in their formidable jaws.

The heat of the tropical afternoon was almost unbearable. Lucy was thankful for the canopy that had been erected but the humidity of the air in the jungle was very oppressive and she was soaked in perspiration. As the boat glided along under the lazy power of the caymans the air was filled with exotic sights and sounds. Immense trees came right to the water's edge and sometimes overhung the river almost to its centre. Long creepers hung from many of the trees and Lucy could easily imagine a Tarzan-like figure swinging from rope to rope above the impenetrable undergrowth. Some creepers trailed right across the river above their heads, and monkeys and other creatures could be seen using them as bridges. Macaws, cockatoos, toucans with their giant beaks and humming birds flashed across the river with feathers of dazzling hues. Iridescent dragonflies as large as small birds darted hither and thither and butterflies, cicadas and myriad unnamed insects filled the still air with their sounds and flutterings. These ceaseless noises of nature were the only ones to be heard and for a girl who had spent her entire life in the suburbs of a great city the absence of any man-made noise from traffic, trains or aeroplanes was almost uncanny. After a while there was some discussion among the monkeys and Queenie turned tentatively towards Lucy.

'*Promised One* —' she began '— *the remainder of my kin*

would be greatly honoured to be given names by She Who Speaks.' Lucy looked around the little group of eager faces. There were three females and two males. She quickly thought of the names of some of her classmates.

'Of course,' she smiled, pointing to them in turn. *'You're Elizabeth, you're Julia, you're Eloise, you're Dominic and you're Ed.'* The monkeys fidgeted with pride and pleasure and Lucy prayed that she would be able to remember which one was which.

Lucy was entranced by the beautiful butterflies, of which there seemed to be countless different species. The morpho butterflies were particularly striking in that they were as large as birds, some blue, some white, and they fluttered incessantly across the river. After watching her with interest for a while Queenie spoke:

'You keep watching the flutterkin. Do you wish me to catch some for you?'

'Oh no,' said Lucy, *'I just like to watch them.'*

'But why should you watch them if you do not wish to eat them and they cannot hurt you?'

'Because they are beautiful,' replied Lucy.

Queenie did not reply. Lucy wondered what was going on in her mind and whether the concept of beauty for its own sake was utterly beyond her comprehension.

Lucy sat in the stern of the boat, her hand on the rudder, enjoying the power of steering the craft as she chose. She looked at her lithe protectress stretched at her feet. The cat was washing herself, licking and biting at her claws and now and then licking her paws and the inside of her forelegs and using them to wash her ears and face. She looked for all the world like Tibbles on the mat at home. Sitting near to the great cat Lucy now saw that her coat was not uniformly black but that the blotches and patches that formed the beautiful markings of a normal jaguar were just visible as slightly different shades within her fur. The effect made the coat even more attractive at close quarters. The monkeys sat at the front of the boat and Lucy noticed that they all kept a respectable distance between themselves and the cat. For an instant she was overwhelmed by the sheer wonder of her situation. Here she was in the middle of a remote jungle, a savage panther at her feet and a troop of vicious-looking monkeys for companions, being towed by caymans along a river teeming with flesh-eating piranha fish and untold weird creatures such as sea cows, sting-rays, turtles, giant otters, electric eels and water snakes. For a moment she wondered if she was still under anaesthesia after her accident and would soon wake up to real life in a London hospital. But she touched the scar on her head and felt the swellings where her fractured ribs were almost healed and knew that this was the real world – one that for her would never be the same as the one she had left for ever as she crashed to a suburban pavement. The boat thrust silently on through the interminable jungle as Lucy gradually nodded and then slept, utterly secure among the paws and claws of her devoted guardians.

14

Waiting to be Eaten

In the crater the three marooned scientists had settled into a survival routine that, apart from one or two unexpected encounters with animals during their foraging trips – fortunately none serious – had succeeded in keeping them alive and unharmed. They did their best to keep up one anothers' spirits but the near-certainty that they would never escape from their terrible situation preyed constantly on their minds.

Finally, inevitably, tragedy struck. By patient application of the stick technique Richard had finally removed the worms from the sole of Helen's foot and one of her toes, but the blister marking the site of the third worm had suddenly become very inflamed and sore and her lower leg was very swollen making it extremely painful for her to walk. One night Julian was ill, and though he felt better in the morning he didn't feel strong enough to go out on the food expedition, so Richard went by himself.

It was the first time he had walked alone in the crater, and as he got further and further from the plane he felt progressively more uneasy. He told himself that it was silly to be more frightened on his own than in company: if a pack of sabre-tooths fancied a meal it didn't really make any difference whether he was with Julian or not, but it was an eerie feeling just the same, walking alone through prehistory. On the way to the grove he passed a herd of the hose-nosed camel-like creatures he now knew to be machrauchenia and they gave him a wide berth, fearing him to be some unusual predator. He reached the grove safely and spent an hour digging up some wild yams, gathering different kinds of nuts and fruit and collecting botanical specimens for himself. He was on the point of leaving the grove when he heard a curious noise. It sounded just like a cricket ball being hit by a bat but it was repeated at regular intervals, sometimes louder, sometimes softer. It was a noise that saved his life for, instead of walking out of the grove, he peeped out between two trees at the edge to see what the source of the noise was. An amazing sight met his eyes.

Two giant armadillo-like creatures faced each other just beyond the trees concealing Richard. The creatures were massive in comparison with the modern armadillos

Richard had seen in zoos, and from Helen's books he recognized them as glyptodonts. Each was three metres long and the size of a small car. As Richard watched, the origin of the curious sound he had heard soon became apparent. The giants were hitting each other with swipes of their formidable tails, each of which ended in a knobbly horn like a mace, or a knobkerrie with spikes on it. Any one of those blows would have felled an ox but the creatures' armour was so thick that most of the blows seemed to have little effect. Clearly this would go on until one of the antagonists was hit in a vulnerable spot or became exhausted. As they swivelled and jockeyed for position clouds of dust rose from the ground and one or two jackal-like creatures began to circle the adversaries, clearly hoping that one of them might be injured enough to end up as a meal.

As he watched, fascinated by the titanic struggle, Richard became aware of something moving along the path he had just been going to take towards the plane. He turned to get a better look and then froze in his tracks. Barely a hundred

An amazing sight met his eyes.

yards away four sabre-toothed cats were tearing apart the carcass of one of the 'camels' Richard had passed on his way to the grove. They must have killed it just after he had entered the trees and he realized he was extremely fortunate that it was a camel and not him being ripped to pieces. He had also been lucky that the glyptodonts had decided to disagree about something. If he'd blundered out of the grove instead of furtively watching them he would undoubtedly have provided the big cats with their after-camel pudding. But now he was trapped. As he watched, one of the cats looked straight towards the grove and sniffed the air. Richard remained as still as a statue, his heart beating like a drum until the cat returned to its meal. He breathed a fervent prayer of thanks that he was downwind of the feeding party. But now he had the problem of getting back to the plane. The cats looked set for a long meal and lay directly in his path. Moving desperately slowly and watching the sabre-tooths all the time, Richard backed away deeper into the grove. When he was invisible to them he moved as fast as he dared and followed the line of trees back towards the cliff. Once at the cliff he knew he would be hidden from the cats by the slight rise in the ground that he had limped across on the first day with the help of Julian and Helen. Sure enough, when he reached the crater wall the cats were invisible and he then moved at a crouch along the base of the escarpment, praying that he wouldn't break a twig or kick a stone as he edged towards the part of the cliff containing the cave where Helen and Julian had first tended to him.

He knew that it was close to the plane, which was also now concealed from his view. As he drew near the cave he was astonished to see Helen and Julian standing in front of it. He waved to them and put a finger to his mouth to warn them to remain silent. When he got close he whispered to them what had happened. Then he added, 'What are you guys doing here, anyway, aren't you both supposed to be invalids?' He had been so taken up with telling them about the sabre-tooths, he hadn't really looked at them but now he realized that they were both out of breath and empty-handed – Julian went nowhere without his spear. He felt a sudden chill of fear.

'What's happened?' he whispered. Julian simply pointed in the direction of the plane, dropped to a crouch and indicated to Richard that they should move forward. As they crept nearer he could hear roaring and crashing and as he peeped cautiously over the ridge he saw three ground sloths, a female and two males, the males engaged in fierce combat. As they reared and roared and slashed at each other with their giant claws they were oblivious to their surroundings, and trees and bushes were crushed and swept aside in their struggle. Julian leant over and whispered in Richard's ear.

'They've been at this for twenty minutes. Fortunately they're making such a row that we heard them in time to make our escape, but they're getting nearer and nearer to the plane.'

Even as he spoke the men watched in horror and disbelief as the titans blundered into the plane and sent it crashing over. One of them put his gargantuan hind paw straight through a wing and the other, losing his balance, fell against the fuselage, splitting it wide open. In their pain and fury the beasts temporarily ignored each other and focused their attention on the plane, smashing it to pieces before resuming their fight. Suddenly one turned and lumbered off on his knuckles, chased by the victor. Their path took them straight to where the sabre-tooths were still at their feast and as the sloths burst through the scrub Richard saw the cats scattering away from the oncoming leviathans and disappearing into the banana grove.

Helen had by now appeared beside them and seen the plane's final moments. The three were speechless. Their one protection from the predators was irretrievably damaged and dusk would be upon them in an hour or so.

Helen was the first eventually to speak.

'We've got to make a fire. It's our only chance of surviving the night.' She saw Richard glancing at the ashes of one of their small cooking fires. 'No, something far bigger than that – a campfire, just like the old explorers used to make on the plains of Africa to keep the lions away. Thank God we built the beacon; we can use the wood from that but only as much as we need so it lasts as long as possible. We must build it near the cliff so we can sit with the crater wall behind us and the fire in front of us. The cave would be ideal but it's a bit too far – we must just go to that nearest bit of cliff.' She pointed as she spoke. 'The cats could return at any moment and we have to get as much wood as possible from the beacon before nightfall –

oh, and we mustn't forget the matches and fire-lighters.'
Nobody argued. Richard and Julian worked frantically to transfer wood from the beacon to a spot near the cliff, keeping a constant eye out for any returning sabre-tooths. Helen stacked the wood against the cliff and used some to make a fire a few yards from the rock face.

She lit the fire and they huddled close to it and ate the fruit Richard had brought. They took it in turns to remain awake and keep the fire going. They couldn't possibly risk all falling asleep together, so two kept each other awake while the third slept.

During the night they saw several pairs of eyes reflecting in the light of the fire but no animals attempted to come near. As dawn broke they all felt an intense sense of relief at having successfully survived their first night outside the security of the plane, now wrecked beyond repair.

They were shocked to see how much their supply of wood had dwindled, and during the morning the men made repeated journeys to the beacon to replenish their store of fuel. Helen remained near the fire, which they had decided to keep burning even during the day, as they no longer had the plane as a final refuge.

At about midday the last piece of the disaster jigsaw fell into place. The scattered pride of sabre-toothed cats returned to their kill, which lay downwind of the humans, and they immediately came towards the remnants of the plane to investigate. Helen fortunately spotted them and shrieked a warning to Richard and Julian, who dropped their loads of wood and ran towards the cliff and the safety of the fire. The four cats came towards the fire but were cautious of it and, instinctively separating as if working to a plan, settled themselves in a neat semicircle each about thirty yards away from the fire, completely cutting off access to the beacon and the shattered fragments of the plane. The three marooned companions looked askance at each other.

'Well, that's it,' said Julian. 'We've got plenty of water from the cliff but no food and no chance of getting any.' He turned to Richard. 'You're the doctor. How long can we survive on water without food?' Before Richard could answer Helen broke in.

'Food isn't the problem, Julian – it's wood. When the fire dies out, so do we. We can't get to the beacon because the game plan the pussycats out there have for us certainly doesn't include trips to the woodpile. We've probably got enough fuel to keep them at bay for tonight and most of tomorrow. Then – I just don't know.'

But they all did know and there was nothing, absolutely nothing, they could do to help themselves.

After the most wretched night of their lives dawn eventually arrived, only to reveal that their worst fears had been realized. The cats were still waiting, but they had been joined by two others, making a total of six, and had moved considerably closer to the fire – the nearest was now just ten yards away.

'One of the worst things about this,' said Richard as they sat looking out at the sabre-tooths, 'is that I have made a discovery in this crater that could make an enormous contribution to the world's food supply.' He drew his rucksack towards him and started to open it. Then he paused. 'But I suppose there's really no point in telling you now. We certainly aren't going to tell anyone else.'

Helen and Julian leant forward.

'No,' said Helen, 'you must tell us. What is it?'

'Yes,' said Julian, grimly, 'as it so happens, we haven't got any other plans for the day, so fire away.'

'Well, you gave me a short lecture on the Pliocene and Pleistocene epochs,' said Richard, 'so I'm going to get my own back and give a short lecture on the banana. It so happens that it's the world's favourite fruit and, quite apart from the additional eating pleasure it gives to millions who have quite enough to eat anyway, it provides almost half the daily calorie intake of countless people in Africa, Asia and Central America – for them it is an *essential* food. There's a problem, however – a big problem.' Helen and Julian looked at Richard expectantly. It was remarkable that scientific curiosity could temporarily displace from their minds the fact that this was their last day on earth, but it did.

'Most of the bananas we eat in the world today are descendants of a seedless variety dating from the Stone Age. As they are seedless they can't change to resist the pests and diseases which are devastating crops all over the world. The bananas you've been eating from the grove are delicious but they also contain seeds. I've little doubt that these plants . . .' He opened his rucksack and withdrew some specimens. '. . . could improve plantations across the globe and provide more food for hundreds of millions of people. The only problem,' he concluded with a rueful smile, 'is that between the grove and here they have probably already completed the longest journey they are ever likely to make.'

They all sat silently for a while. It was a bizarre scene: three scientists who had made world-shattering discoveries sitting next to a dwindling fuel pile waiting to be eaten by creatures thought to have been extinct for one hundred thousand years.

The sun rose higher in the sky. There was no shade, for the long axis of the crater valley ran from east to west and a sabre-tooth now sat at the entrance to the cave a little way along the cliff. Their final day would be a hot one: Richard couldn't help wondering if the cats preferred their food medium or well done.

15
Jungle Quest

Lucy was asleep on the boat, dreaming of her home and family. She dreamt that she was sitting at her mother's dressing table trying on her mother's make-up and had spilt powder on to her shoulder. For some reason Tibbles was sitting on her knee during this activity. She heard her mother coming up the stairs and Clare, who now magically materialized in her dream, started to brush off the powder.

'Promised One!' she heard her mother call out. 'That's funny,' she thought. 'Mum's never called me that before.'

'*Wake up, O Promised One!*' Suddenly she awoke. The queen monkey, not Clare, was pawing at her shoulder and speaking to her. Katy, her coati, was snuggled up to her in her lap. For an instant Lucy felt a pang of intense homesickness – how nice it would be if she *were* at home and it *had* been Clare brushing her down, with Mum about to appear at the door.

The monkeys were very excited. Sitting on the other end of the boat was the harpy eagle and Lucy noticed that all the monkeys were now clustered in her part of the boat, even though that meant they were nearer to the panther.

There was no doubt which of the predators they feared most. The eagle was a magnificent bird. It stood over a metre high, dark grey and black with a white breast and a vivid black ruff on its throat. On its head was a double crest of feathers that looked like the headdress of a native American chieftain on the warpath.

'. . . I bring good tidings . . .'

'*Greetings, Promised One!*' grated the eagle. Lucy found his voice really scary. '*I bring good tidings.*' Lucy's heart leapt for joy – her daddy must be alive. The harpy glanced up to the sky and Lucy instinctively followed his gaze. At first she could see nothing, but shielding her eyes against the glare, she could just make out a tiny black dot, unbelievably high, slowly gliding in a great circle. '*I sought the aid of the soariquills,*' the harpy continued. '*When they heard the Promised One needed their assistance they flew from the great mountains of the west where they soar and glide. Their sight is matchless in a quest such as ours. They can see a thunderquill resting in the Crater of Antiquity and there are three Tailless Ones, one of whom is beardless.*'

'*Three* people, and one of them a woman,' Lucy thought in astonishment. Chopper and Sam had only mentioned her father and the pilot during their conversation in Rio. But the coincidence was too great. One of them had to be her father. Maybe the pilot had taken his daughter for a day out or maybe she was a relief pilot. The harpy continued:

'*The soariquills will guide us to that place before they return to their mountain crags. I will stay with you now for I can fly where the forest is dense and yet still see where the soariquills wish to lead us.*' Lucy was sure she detected a flutter of dismay among the monkeys at this news. '*And now,*' the eagle continued, '*the river becomes very narrow and turns away from the path you need to tread. You must leave the house that floats and the arborikin will help you through the jungle.*' The animals leapt out of the boat and two monkeys assisted Lucy to the shore. She turned to the caymans; she still couldn't bring herself to call them Dreadful Ones even though she knew it was their name in the animal kingdom.

'*Thank you for your strength and patience, O ye with the*

mighty tails. I will return one day when I reach full womanhood and assist your kin in their struggle against the evil that men do for your beautiful skins.'

The great reptiles flicked their tails in pleasure.

'It has been the greatest honour of our lives to serve She Who Speaks. Fare thee well in thy quest for the Paterpromise.' And with a swirl of the dark waters they were gone.

After they had gone Lucy asked Queenie about the Crater of Antiquity.

'The soarquills and the arboribane call this place a crater because they can see things from on high which others cannot,' said the monkey. *'My own kin know only that there are two valleys in this place: the Valley of the Mighty Ones and the Valley of the Ancients; the thunderquill must lie in one of these. They are many, many sunsleeps from here but the arboribane will guide our path.'*

As soon as the boat was moored on the bank, the monkeys took off into the trees to find food, and to jump and climb after their long hours sitting restlessly in the boat. They looked just like a class of children rushing from their classroom to spend playtime on a climbing frame. Lucy had read how their prehensile tails acted like a fifth limb but now, seeing them swinging and scampering through the trees, she fully appreciated for the first time what this meant in practice. The tail was used in effortless combination with the arms and legs as they swung and climbed and jumped, and Lucy was spellbound by their agility and acrobatic feats.

Lucy looked in wonder at the forest through which they must pass and wondered how on earth she would manage.

Immensely tall trees such as fig, teak, kapok and mahogany towered into the sky through the canopy. Other trees making up the canopy itself formed a second layer, and beneath them an incalculable number of vines and lianas, some thicker than her leg, hung down like a green curtain. Among the shrubs and bushes on the forest floor grew ferns and lichens interspersed with lilies and orchids, and mushrooms and mosses growing on fallen and decaying branches. The ground was teeming with life. Beetles of every description, termites and millipedes feasted on the organic litter of dead and decaying wood and leaves and were feasted on in turn by centipedes, spiders and scorpions. As she watched, the coati sniffed and suddenly unearthed a two-metre-long earthworm from beneath the carpet of leaves. Lucy glanced away – she didn't think she wanted to watch what would happen next. She looked at the wall of green before her and wondered about the journey they had to make. At the edge of the river, where light could penetrate right down to the forest floor, the dense tangle of jungle growth formed a forbidding and apparently impenetrable barrier. As if reading her thoughts the queen monkey spoke:

'*This is not a land that is suitable for the dainty steps of the Promised One. We have arranged some help for you. The hippophant draws nigh.*'

Just as Lucy made a mental note to tell her sisters and Paula, her ballet teacher, of her 'dainty steps', the bushes parted and the strangest creature Lucy had ever seen appeared. It looked like a very large pig or a very small hippopotamus. Mainly black in colour but with a white back, it had an elongated snout that looked like the beginnings of an elephant's trunk. It stood almost as high as Lucy and was very, very solid in shape. It stepped back and trembled a little as it saw the panther, but Lucy spoke immediately.

'The junglefang will not harm you while I am here. Thank you for coming to help me.'

The tapir knelt on its forelegs and said: *'I am told that I am the first creature in all of countless aeons to bear the Promised One on my back. It is something that shall be wondered at for all generations yet to come amongst my kin.'*

The queen monkey then told Lucy to sit astride the shoulders of the tapir and the entire incongruous party set off through the jungle: the Promised One on the tapir with her loyal coati scampering alongside, her marmoset on her shoulder, the black panther stalking majestically behind, the chattering monkeys swinging through the trees, the fearsome harpy eagle flying above the canopy, occasionally swooping down through the trees to check on the progress of the strange caravan, and the condors, unchallenged masters of flight and sight, directing the expedition from on high. The tapir moved effortlessly through the undergrowth. For such a large and apparently lumbering creature it was remarkably agile and seemed by instinct to know where the green curtain would part to admit it with its precious burden. The journey for Lucy was quite enchanting, particularly as she now knew her father was alive and she was able to enjoy the experience.

'. . . I am the first creature in all of countless aeons to bear
the Promised One on my back.'

She felt as though she were being transported through a series of green mansions, each with a new sight to thrill the senses. As they moved further into the forest the animals and birds that would normally have fled from humans and the predators in their party could sense the mystical presence of the Promised One and, as they gathered for a glimpse of Lucy, she passed through what must surely have been one of the most spectacular wildlife gatherings of all time. She was reminded vividly of her dream in bed back at home when all the creatures of the earth had come to pay her homage.

A multitude of monkeys scampered and swung through the branches and vines above them, and slow-moving, upside-down sloths struggled to get into a suitable vantage point. On the jungle floor an astonishing variety of birds seemed suddenly to find they were going the same way as the party: jungle turkeys, scarlet ibises, white herons and ducks. An ear-shattering blast of noise came from a group of trumpeter birds, standing in a row as if on parade and delivering a trumpet fanfare for a visiting empress, and, with every new spectacle of the pageant that unfolded, Lucy felt a pang of regret that Clare and Sarah were not there to share this amazing experience.

Towards evening the ground began to get marshy and the tapir had to pick her way carefully to remain on solid ground. Soon, however, the ground became completely waterlogged and eventually opened into a lake.

'There is always water here; it wells up from the ground in this place,' said the tapir. 'Hold tight for I must swim. You need have *no fear, the Dreadful Ones will not harm me while I bear Thee. Hold on to my ears, O Radiant One.'*

Lucy held on as requested and was astonished to see what a powerful and expert swimmer the ungainly-looking beast proved to be. Several caymans slid silently into the water from the surrounding marshy edges but none came near. Eventually they reached dry land again and resumed their passage through the dense jungle. Soon they reached a ravine where the ground fell away steeply but the tall forest trees rooted in the sides of the steep valley still grew to a dizzy height across the chasm with long ropes of lianas falling down out of sight. The tapir knelt and asked Lucy to dismount.

'I cannot cross this place,' she said, *'but the arborikin will take you.'*

Lucy wasn't quite sure what this meant but she was soon to find out as she embarked upon the most exciting experience in her life – an adventure far more exciting than the rollercoaster she had been on at Alton Towers theme park, or the skiing holiday she had gone on with the school last year. After courteously asking her permission, Queenie removed Lucy's glasses and then a troop of monkeys took hold of Lucy. Clutched by a dozen hands and tails she was swept off into a breathtaking flight across the ravine, the band swinging from liana to liana and branch to branch, and sometimes flying through the air unsupported until agile limbs made contact with another green curtain of vines and branches. The speed with which they moved, the death-defying distances they jumped and the narrowness of the gaps through which they continued to pass, despite their unusual burden, left Lucy breathless with a mixture of fear and exhilaration and when, eventually, the tree-high traverse of the immense gulf was accomplished, Lucy knew that she would give anything to repeat the experience.

Soon a new tapir appeared, another female, and after respectfully greeting Lucy she knelt to receive her burden for the next stage of this amazing journey. Lucy noticed that her coati was still with them — she must somehow have crossed the ravine on her lightning feet — and was sitting behind her on the tapir, and her little marmoset who had clung to her like a limpet during the arboreal flight across the ravine was now sitting contentedly on her shoulder.

Every now and then they stopped and the monkeys brought Lucy fruit and nuts to eat. The nuts were always cracked for her by a scurrident; the rodents seemed able to open the hardest of nuts with a single bite. The monkeys also showed Lucy how to find fresh water trapped in the bromeliad plants which grew as parasites in the forks of the forest trees and which looked just like one of her mother's house plants. Remembering Grandpa's book she was careful to check their contents before drinking. As night fell the monkeys gathered soft ferns and leaves and made a bed upon which Lucy could lie. She lay between the forelegs of the panther and felt utterly secure in the embrace of the unchallenged queen of the Amazonian jungle.

The next day they climbed higher and higher and soon came to a plateau where the trees were fewer in number and where the soft, moist forest floor gave way to volcanic rock. Far above the great condors floated effortlessly on their immense wings, after the bustards the heaviest flying birds in the world. Throughout their journey the harpy eagle had passed tirelessly up and down through the forest canopy to guide Lucy and her companions in the direction indicated by the all-seeing eyes of the condors in the sky, and now, as the forest thinned, Lucy could see them again, tiny black dots circling endlessly in the blue sky.

Soon there was agitated chattering among the monkeys and the reason was soon apparent. The rocks upon which they stood were rent by a giant crevice which ran as far as the eye could see in both directions, a geological fault that completely barred their progress. The fissure was about two metres wide and creeping to the edge on her hands and knees Lucy shuddered as she peered down into inky blackness. She threw a stone into its seemingly unfathomable depths and though she strained her ears she was unable to detect any sound of its landing. The panther coiled itself like a spring and leapt over that ghastly crack as if it were a join between paving slabs on a suburban pavement. She turned and looked at Lucy and the animals as if expecting them all to follow. Lucy's heart started pounding. She was good at long jump and thought that on the school playing field, with a sandpit to land in, she would comfortably jump the distance. But this was very different.

She looked back to the forest. The nearest trees were

too far away to use to bridge the gap – even if the animals could gnaw one to the ground. She felt her mouth beginning to dry with fear but then, to her immense relief, Queenie spoke.

'*Nothing, O Promised One, shall put your life at risk while you are in my care. Rest here awhile and all shall be well.*' And with that she disappeared with some of her troop back into the forest while the remainder foraged for a while and brought her food. The panther sprang gracefully back and looked back into the jungle as if uncertain as to what the monkeys were up to.

Within an hour the troop reappeared and sat looking expectantly towards the undergrowth. Lucy noticed that they all stayed close to her, even though she was alongside the panther, and wondered what on earth was about to appear from the forest. Soon a large, black, diamond-shaped head appeared through the ferns to be followed by a seemingly endless body that eventually slid clear of the bushes and moved effortlessly towards Lucy, its greenish-brown skin shining with large black spots in the brilliant sunshine. Lucy knew that the great stranglekin must be an anaconda, for she had read about these creatures in her book about jaguars and other denizens of the Amazon. The

giant water boa grew to a greater size than any other snake on earth and the creature now gliding towards her must have been one of the largest of its kind. It was over ten metres long and its girth at its maximum thickness was almost a metre – the size of a good-sized barrel. This was an animal that could swallow whole a calf or a cayman. As Lucy gazed in awe at the monster, a second, almost as large, emerged from the bushes and slid alongside its companion. The larger of the two spoke to Lucy. The anaconda's voice was not quite like any animal voice that Lucy had heard before. It was clearly reptilian and in that respect reminded her of the alligators, but it was in some subtle way more refined and its long, drawling delivery somehow reflected the immense, sinuous length of the creature itself.

'Welcome, O Promised One. We are honoured to help you bridge a gap.' The snake glided effortlessly over the chasm to the other side, then turned and came back until the thickest part of its body lay across the gap. The second snake moved in beside the first, head to tail, so that their bodies lay together like two giant cables; it would have been impossible to slide a piece of paper between them, so snugly did they fit together. The queen monkey leapt on to one of the snakes and a second monkey on to the other.

'Walk behind us and hold our tails, Promised One . . .'

The queen turned to Lucy:

'*Walk behind us and hold our tails, Promised One. All will be well.*' Lucy climbed on to the living bridge. The skin of the snakes was smoother than she had expected, and dry; not in the slightest bit slippery. She could feel the immense muscular power holding the two bodies together and knew that there was no chance whatsoever that she could fall between them into that dreadful abyss. She was over the bridge in a few seconds, the marmoset as always on her shoulder, followed shortly by the coati who scampered across in an instant. One or two of the bolder monkeys also used the snake bridge but most simply leapt over the gap, preferring to stay as far as possible from the great serpents which could swallow them whole for breakfast. Soon the party was back in thick forest once again with Lucy on the back of yet another tapir. She was growing to love these gentle animals and their hoofed feet seemed magically to find the easiest and safest way through the tangled undergrowth.

In the late afternoon there was great excitement as the vanguard of monkeys who had been constantly scouting ahead under the guidance of the harpy eagle returned to report that they had reached the Valley of the Mighty Ones. Lucy was agog to know what the Mighty Ones could be. She knew that the great mammals of Africa were not to be found in the Amazon, and what on earth could be mightier than the tapirs, jaguars, caymans and anacondas she had already seen?

After dismounting she followed the queen monkey who

suddenly stopped and prevented Lucy moving forward. Peeping over the animal's shoulder she realized the reason why. They were standing on the edge of an immense cliff and she could see across a vast valley to a sharp, high ridge on the other side. The monkey prevented her from looking at what lay below as the edge was crumbly and Lucy saw that some loose stones dislodged by the queen's paws disappeared soundlessly over the edge. The monkey turned and spoke.

'There is a great precipice, O Promised One. My kin have gone in both directions to find a path down. The Brilliant One now sinks below the earth so we should stay here for the sunsleep and enter the valley tomorrow.'

Lucy lay in the nest of leaves the monkeys prepared for her as usual, and fell asleep almost immediately, worn out by the long and eventful journey.

16

Into the Valley of the Mighty Ones

In the morning Lucy woke in her nest, high above the valley, to find that both the scouting parties of monkeys had returned. They chattered to the queen who turned to Lucy.

'There is no passage down, O Promised One, but there is a place where the precipice is not so high. That is where we shall go.'

Lucy remounted her trusty tapir and they trekked westwards with the morning sun behind them for twenty minutes. Then they went downhill a little way and came to a rocky outcrop clear of trees. The monkey led Lucy near to the rim of the crater and she gazed in wonder at the spectacle before her.

'The arboribane says the thunderquill is here in the Valley of the Mighty Ones,' she told Lucy. 'It is as well, for the Valley of the Ancients lies far yonder, beyond those hills —' she pointed to the horizon, '— and it would have taken us many more sunsleeps to reach it.' She stopped and suddenly pointed down into the valley. 'Here are the Mighty Ones below us.' She pointed to the crater valley and Lucy gasped. In the distance on the plain below she could see the black shape of a creature as big as the tree it was stripping. It was so far away that it was difficult to estimate its true size, but from where Lucy stood she guessed it must be as big as an elephant.

'What is it?' she said, realising the instant she had asked the question that there was no logical answer, for it was a creature she did not know and the monkey would only have her own name for it.

'It is one of the Mighty Ones,' said the queen simply. 'Its kin are to be found nowhere except in this place and none of my kin nor any of the forest creatures knows of a time when they did not exist here.' She paused and turned to Lucy. 'But now we need your help, O Promised One. Nothing except a crawlipod or a fledgiquill can descend to the valley floor and that is where the three Tailless Ones are living. Even the mighty wings of the soariquills have not the strength to bear you down. We know that the Tailless Ones can think of things that we cannot and we hope you can find a way down.' Lucy peeped down from the rocks. The place the monkeys had found was indeed the lowest point on the rim of the visible crater, but it was still a sheer drop of thirty metres – about a hundred feet – to the plain below.

Lucy sat down and thought hard. What they needed was rope and the nearest rope was hundreds of miles away – but was it? In a flash she thought of the thousands of lianas they had pushed their way through and swung on during their journey. They hung like cables from the tallest trees and looked immensely strong.

'I have an idea,' she said to the queen, 'but it will take much work by your kin and others.'

'Your wish is our command!' was the immediate reply.

Soon sharp teeth were gnawing through six of the longest and strongest lianas that Lucy could find in the adjacent forest. A party of monkeys was gathering straight sticks and saplings and another group was finding supple reeds, strong grasses and the petioles of palms to act as ties.

Lucy tied a harness around the tapir so it could drag the severed lianas from the forest to the rocky plateau above the crater rim. Under Lucy's instruction the first two lianas were laid side by side like a miniature railway line separated by the width of a ladder rung. Another two were laid at the ends of the first with sufficient overlap to be tied securely, and the final two were added in the same way, bringing the total length to almost three liana lengths. The sticks and saplings were broken or bitten into ladder rungs and Lucy then showed the monkeys how to tie them to the lianas. She checked every knot herself and by mid-afternoon they had constructed an immense flexible rope ladder. Two more lianas were obtained and the ends of these were tied securely with loops around the base of the nearest trees. The other ends were tied to the top of the rope ladder which the tapir then pulled to the edge of the cliff as Lucy and the monkeys fed the bottom end steadily over. When the entire ladder had been lowered the monkeys surged forward and swarmed down – they reached the crater floor in less than a minute – the first of their kind to have entered the crater alive since time immemorial.

Just as Lucy was plucking up the courage to start her own descent a dark shape appeared from above the trees and swooped down to the rocks. It was the harpy eagle. Lucy saw a little piece of bloodstained monkey fur stuck to one of his talons and felt slightly sick. She knew that life in the jungle consisted of a constant cycle of 'eat and be eaten', but it was upsetting to think that this beautiful eagle had just devoured a cousin of one of her new friends.

'*The great soariquills have just departed,*' said the harpy in his fearful grating voice. '*They said that the Mighty Ones have destroyed the thunderquill in the crater, but that the Tailless Ones are safe; they sit near a fire which the arborikin will find. The air moves in curious ways near this crater, not as it does in the forest. It is best if I remain up here lest I injure my wing against the rocks.*'

'*I understand,*' said Lucy; she could feel the unusual turbulence tugging at her clothes and hair. '*You have brought us safely to this place and I would not have you hurt. I have, however, one more favour to ask of you before we depart.*'

'*Ask, O Promised One!*'

'*Can I speak to the great soariquills?*' asked Lucy.

'*I fear not,*' replied the eagle, '*for they now already fly high, near the Brilliant One where I cannot reach them.*'

Lucy looked up, her hand above her eyes: there were the tiny circling dots. She had never tried to project her voice thoughts such a distance but there was no physical obstruction and she thought it worth a try. She watched the condors and concentrated intensely on projecting her thought beam directly at them.

'*Can you hear me, O masters of the sky? Please come to me if you can.*' She listened intently but there was no reply.

Disappointed, she tried once more and then turned her attention to the task of her descent into the valley. Suddenly the queen monkey tugged at her shorts.

'Look. They come!' she said. Lucy looked and sure enough the birds seemed nearer. As she watched they grew larger and within a few minutes two of the great condors were gliding on to her rock. Their wingspan was almost three metres — exceeding that of any bird but the albatross — and looking at their great bodies Lucy wondered how anything of such bulk could fly with such consummate grace high above the earth. Their plumage was black with a ruff of white at the base of their long naked necks. Their heads and necks were blood red.

'You called us, O Promised One, and we are here,' said the larger of the two. Lucy glanced at its great hooked beak and gave a mental shudder; but she pulled herself together — without the help of these creatures and their incredible eyesight she would never have found the people below, one of whom she was certain was her father.

'I am deeply in your debt,' said Lucy. 'I know you flew many leagues from the mountains in the west to assist me and I wanted to thank you. You must now return to your kin.'

'We have found rising air here such as we feel in our own mountains,' said the condor, 'but we knew not of the existence of the place until we came to you. Our kin may return, for we see food below such as we have never seen before. Fare thee well.' The birds then ran towards the cliff, their wings making a swishing noise like satin curtains, and launched themselves into space. Once in the air they became transformed from clumsy land creatures into masters of flight, and as they picked up a rising thermal from the valley they began to rise in ever-widening circles. Lucy watched, fascinated, until once again they were but specks in the sky and then she lost them as they flew west into the rays of the afternoon sun.

The panther spoke. She had been lying quietly in the shade at the edge of the forest, unable to help in the construction of the rope ladder.

'It is time for you to go, O Promised One, for the Brilliant One already begins to fall to his sleep; the raspihops are falling silent and the croakihops begin their songs of the night. I cannot come, but I will be here with Katy Coati to protect you and greet you once again when you return with the Paterpromise.' Lucy thanked her for all she had done and then turned her attention to the challenge that now awaited her.

She was not particularly afraid of heights but the prospect of descending that terrible precipice on the makeshift ladder was a daunting one. She had constructed a strong reed harness to go round her chest, like a baby's seat harness but with a loop sticking up above each of her shoulders. She indicated to the queen that two monkeys might follow her down, holding on to these loops in case she lost her foothold.

Lucy then stepped to the edge. The monkeys had been playing incessantly on the ladder while she had been speaking to the condors, running up and down, sometimes running down headfirst, even jumping over one another and catching the ladder further down. Lucy

*She climbed steadily
down the ladder.*

envied their fearless agility. She turned so that she faced the ladder and the cliff to go down and as she moved down she felt a soft scratching as the tails of the spider monkeys above her came down past her ears and wound around her shoulder loops. Greatly reassured by this additional support she climbed steadily down the ladder, the monkeys babbling excitedly above and below.

About halfway down her arms and shoulder began to ache and she realized she was gripping too fiercely with her hands instead of letting her feet take all her weight. She gradually relaxed and moved more easily and efficiently, and only once did she partly lose her footing. As she did so she felt the tail of the spider monkey on that side instantly tense and steady her and she soon resumed her steady progress.

When she had started her descent Michelle, her little marmoset, had jumped off her shoulder and scampered down the ladder ahead of her; now, the instant she set foot on solid ground, she leapt back up on to her shoulder again.

The queen monkey was sniffing the air for smoke.

'The fire is back along the cliff,' she said, and set off towards it. After a while the monkeys started the excited chattering that Lucy had now come to recognize as an indication that something of interest was afoot, and soon the queen came to her.

'The Tailless Ones are ahead,' she said, 'but they are surrounded by the greatfangs. Look! One approaches us.' Lucy looked ahead and at first could see nothing among the scrub and bushes but soon she made out the shape of an enormous feline sauntering majestically towards them.

The monkeys grouped closely around Lucy and the marmoset disappeared into the pocket of her shorts. One or two monkeys scampered back to the ladder and waited cautiously to see what would happen.

The enormous, sabre-like yellow fangs of the smilodon glistened in the evening sunlight and Lucy gulped in apprehension and wondered what kind of big cat this was. She had seen

The queen monkey was sniffing the air for smoke.

pictures of sabre-tooths but didn't realise that any still existed. She then remembered the Mighty Ones she had seen and the thought struck her for the first time that this crater must be an area of specialized ecology with unusual animals in it. Close on that idea came the horrifying thought that these creatures in their isolated world might never have heard of the Promised One. If that was the case they all had a serious problem and one that would be apparent in the next few seconds. Gathering her nerve she stopped and looked straight at the approaching beast.

'Greetings, O magnificent cat with fangs of ivory. I come in peace with my companions.' The great cat paused for what seemed like an age to Lucy and her trembling companions, but was in reality just a few seconds. Then, to Lucy's indescribable relief he replied, in a majestic and sonorous voice:

'So there is indeed a Promised One. We have heard tell of such a one through many ages but we knew not that She would ever grace this place with Her presence. What is your desire, O Great One?'

'I seek my father and his companions,' replied Lucy, *'for I believe that they are here in this place. I hope that I, my kin and all these animal companions can pass freely through your domain without danger or hindrance.'*

'It shall be as thou command,' replied the cat. Lucy felt she detected a distinct note of disappointment in his voice.

'Thy kin sit yonder by the tongues that burn.'

He turned his head and Lucy then saw, through a gap in the bushes, the smouldering fire and beyond it her father, bearded and tanned almost beyond recognition.

'Daddy!' she shouted, and rushed through the bushes, ran round the fire and flung her arms around him. Then she burst into tears and he held her tight, saying nothing as all the accumulated stress of their months of separation poured out of her. When, eventually, she calmed down, the questions poured out of him in a torrent.

'What on earth are you doing here? How did you find me? How did you get into the crater? And how, in heaven's name, did you get past the sabre-tooths?'

Lucy laughed through her tears of joy and said:

'There's a lot to tell you, Dad, but first you need to see something!' She turned to look out from the fire then, suddenly remembering her manners, looked at Helen and Julian. 'I'm sorry,' she said. 'I'm Lucy and this is my dad.' She clung to her father. Helen smiled.

'We'd just about worked that one out,' she said, 'and like your dad we can't understand how you possibly got here.' Lucy left her father and started to walk out beyond the fire. 'Watch!' she said.

'Stop!' said Helen, moving forward and grabbing Lucy's arm. 'I know that somehow you came here safely but you were unbelievably lucky. There are dangerous animals out there.'

Lucy laughed and was about to call the sabre-tooth when she suddenly remembered that she should guard her secret from these strangers. She paused, uncertain as to what to do next. Her father looked at her and, even though he did not understand what had happened, his father's instinct told him why Lucy was hesitating.

'It's all right,' he said to Lucy. 'Helen and Julian are scientists who saved my life and I trust them absolutely. There's nothing you can't tell them.'

Lucy turned back to the bush. 'Come, O mighty fang and pay homage to the Promised One.' It was a dramatic gesture but Lucy knew that her story would be literally incredible unless those about to hear it had seen irrefutable evidence of its truth. She had spoken the words out loud for the benefit of the onlookers but now she called silently to the cats.

The nearest sabre-tooth, a female, walked towards Lucy. Julian started forward to pull her back but Richard put a restraining hand on his shoulder. He had complete confidence in his wonderful daughter.

'Just watch!' he said quietly.

The great cat came to Lucy then lay at her feet, its head resting on its forepaws, looking up at her. At her command it rolled on its back and she leant forward and stroked its belly.

'Thank you, O mighty fang. Now return to your kin and protect us from all that might come to harm us this night.'

'As thou command,' the cat replied. *'I shall be honoured among all my tribe for having felt the hand of the Promised One upon my flank.'* She then rose and stalked back to the waiting circle of her kind. She moved from one to another and as she did so each cat turned to face outwards from the fire, now keeping guard over those within their fearful circle.

Lucy returned to the speechless adults and sat down. Before speaking to them she called Queenie.

*'I shall be honoured among all my tribe for having felt
the hand of the Promised One upon my flank.'*

'This is my father,' she said. The queen regarded Richard
with grave respect. *'And these are his companions.'* The
monkey looked in turn at Helen and Julian.

*'Thank you for all you did this day. Go now and rest with your
kin. The greatfangs will not harm you. Please bring us food when
the Brilliant One rises from his place of rest.'*

The monkey scampered away. After she had gone Lucy
turned back to the others. As she did so Helen suddenly
shouted in alarm.

'What's that?' She pointed at Lucy's shorts where the tiny
marmoset was peeping out. She soon came out completely
and darted up to her usual vantage point on Lucy's left
shoulder.

'That's Michelle, my little cuddly pet,' said Lucy. 'She
wants to come back to England with me – if it's allowed,'

she added hurriedly, glancing at her father, suddenly an eleven-year-old once again in his presence. 'And just so you can all relax before we tell our stories, those funny lions or whatever they are won't hurt you and the monkeys will bring our breakfast in the morning.'

'Those funny lions are sabre-tooths,' said Richard, 'and though I'm sure you know you've saved all our lives you probably don't know that you arrived just in the nick of time. We don't have enough wood to last the night and if you hadn't turned up when you did we would have ended up as cat food some time in the next few hours.' Lucy laughed spontaneously for the first time since she had been kidnapped a month earlier.

'Just imagine the giant tins in the pet food section of the Crater Superstore with a special offer notice above them. "*Buy Sabretibbles a nice toothy snack! When we say our new fang-smacking formula is scientifically balanced we mean just that. Every tin contains no fewer than three real scientists!*" '

They all laughed – in a slightly hysterical way as months of relentless trauma evaporated.

'That's definitely one to tell your big sister,' said Richard, wiping tears of laughter and relief from his face.

Lucy sat down next to him and cuddled up to him. 'Now, Dad,' she said, 'tell me how you got here and how Mr and . . .'

Julian interrupted, 'Julian and Helen to you, Lucy.'

' . . . how Julian and Helen saved your life.'

The four sat round the dying embers of the fire until late

into the night as they told their amazing tales.

In the morning the monkeys appeared with all kinds of food, including fruits that even those who had lived for some time in the crater had not seen before.

'Some of these are unknown to us,' said the queen, 'but we have tried all that you see here and they are good to eat.'

After breakfast they had a long discussion. Lucy had told them that they could all return to the camp with the help of the animals, but Julian was concerned about Helen's leg.

'Helen can't climb a cliff and trek through the jungle, even with the help you describe. If you're sure that the animals here won't attack us any more, then I think I'll stay here with Helen until you and Lucy get back to civilization and send help. While you are gone we can clear the wreckage of the plane enough to make a landing strip.'

'That last job won't be necessary,' said Lucy firmly. The others looked at her. She spoke with an authority beyond her years.

'What d'you mean?' asked Julian.

'I shall ask the Mighty Ones to clear the landing strip. They certainly look big enough.'

'The Mighty Ones?' said Helen.

'Those things like large brown bears that go round ripping trees down. I saw one yesterday from the cliff.'

'The giant ground sloths!' exclaimed Richard.

'Is that what they are?' said Lucy. 'The ones who bust up your plane. Well, I'll talk to one before we leave and ask him to clear up the mess.' She misinterpreted the glances of sheer astonishment that the grown-ups exchanged, for looks of disapproval.

'Well,' she added, as if to give moral justification for the use of animal labour, 'it won't hurt them and they caused the mess in the first place, didn't they?'

Everyone laughed and Richard felt proud of his daughter and the way she was coping with her extraordinary powers. Lucy then enquired about Helen's leg and was very interested to hear what Richard described to her.

'I think I can help, Dad. Insects and worms and things don't talk to me but they do seem to obey me.' She turned to Helen.

'Can I see your leg?' Helen was only too happy for Lucy to look at her leg and having heard Richard's description of the condition Lucy asked him to bring a container of water. Then Lucy addressed the leg.

'Come forth from your hiding place, O long and slender one, and there will be water for your sons and daughters.' Helen stifled a grunt of pain as she felt movement in her leg. The final worm in her affected foot emerged, bursting through the inflamed boil under which it had lain. As promised, Lucy held the water for it to enter. Helen then cried out in pain. 'My other foot, my other foot!' And from a tiny inconspicuous spot that Helen had previously thought to be a bite or sting yet another worm emerged and Lucy held the container so that it too could enter the water.

'We shall return these to the river,' Lucy said, 'and then they can fend for themselves once again.'

Helen, Julian and Richard were astonished at what they

had witnessed and Helen was grateful beyond words.

'The legs still need to heal,' said Richard, 'so I think we should stick to plan A, but at least we know that you are now on the road to recovery.' The men and Lucy then spent the rest of the day moving whatever was salvageable from the wreck of the plane into the cave, which would be Helen and Julian's new shelter until help arrived. Much to everybody's amusement the monkeys carried everything to the cave that they thought would be useful such as pieces of broken glass, nuts and bolts and pieces of torn canvas. Nobody had the heart to stop them and Helen arranged them carefully along one side of the cave floor.

Towards evening a crashing noise could be heard in the distance as a giant sloth hove into view stripping foliage off the surrounding trees. Lucy called to it and it lumbered over on its great knuckles. One of the enduring memories of Richard's life was to be the sight of his small daughter

It was like a scene from King Kong *or* Godzilla.

standing in front of a monster wagging her finger and giving it instructions. It was like a scene from *King Kong* or *Godzilla*, except that the heroine was in complete charge of the situation.

When Lucy returned she and Richard had a chat. Helen and Julian were at the cave preparing a special farewell evening meal and it was their first opportunity to talk alone.

'Mummy and the girls must be frantic with worry about us,' Richard said. 'If only we could let them know we are safe.'

'They already know I'm safe,' replied Lucy with a grin, "cos I sent them a letter.'

Richard's jaw dropped. 'You what?'

'I sent them a letter. Are you deaf or something?' She grinned again, then relented and explained how she had contrived to get a message back to the family.

'It's funny you should mention it,' she continued, 'because I was just thinking we should send them another saying we've met up. Let's go and do it. It should be easier to prepare this time. I had to do it in secret before – but it will still need to be short so it's not too heavy. It should arrive in time for Clare's birthday. I've no idea of today's date but it must be getting close.'

Richard was thrilled beyond words to hear that they could communicate with home, and arm-in-arm they hurried back to the cave to write a note.

Ten minutes later Clio was scaling the liana ladder, clutching a tiny parcel in her mouth.

Now that Richard and Helen and Julian had grasped the

reality of their new situation they could all relax for the first time for many months, and during their meal that evening the conversation turned eventually to home, a place they could all believe – at last – that they might see again. Helen and Julian explained how they had not seen their two sons for almost a year. The elder was at university studying medicine and the younger was still at school. By one of those extraordinary coincidences in life they lived in London, not far from the Bonaventures, and they agreed that when they all got home the two families should meet up. Richard took down the necessary details and promised to contact Helen and Julian's family to say they were safe as soon as they were able to.

The next day they awoke to the sound of four giant sloths clearing plane fragments and rocks from the areas Lucy had pointed out, and once again the monkeys were waiting with fresh food for breakfast. Helen and Julian were looking forward to resuming their scientific explorations now that they had the protection of the sabre-tooths and Lucy explained to Helen that if she wanted to move far while her legs were healing, the sabre-tooths would allow her to ride on them. Helen seemed extremely doubtful about this but said she would think about it.

Then it was time to go. The three adults had grown very close during their period of enforced companionship and Helen wept a little as she bade goodbye to Richard. Then she took Lucy on one side and talked quietly to her for a few minutes. Her expression was serious and Richard saw

Lucy nodding in agreement. As the two came back to join the group Lucy spoke to Queenie who scampered off into the bush.

'What was all that about?' said Richard when Lucy returned, instantly regretting this question as it was perfectly obvious that it was something that Helen wished to be discreet about.

'Oh, just girls' talk,' said Lucy lightly, and Richard dropped the matter.

Helen and Julian came with Lucy and Richard to the foot of the rope ladder and watched nervously as they climbed to the top, two monkeys going in front of Lucy and steadying her with their tails as before. Just as they reached the top Queenie reappeared at the foot of the ladder and clambered up after them in a few seconds. As Lucy reached the top Katy Coati scampered over to her yelping with delight, chasing her own tail and then running round and round Lucy's feet. Lucy had some difficulty in reassuring Richard that the black panther sitting at the top waiting for them was not the mate of the jaguar who had chased him over the cliff, but as Melanie came over purring and rubbing herself against Lucy, he had no choice but to be convinced.

There had been some considerable discussion concerning the fate of the rope ladder so laboriously constructed by Lucy and her animal assistants. Should some disaster befall Richard and Lucy, then help would never come for Helen and Julian and the ladder would be a potential route of escape for them from the crater, assuming Helen's legs were by then fully healed. Having seen the ease with which the monkeys swarmed up and down the ladder, however, Helen was adamant that Richard and Lucy should cut it free once they had climbed out, so as to avoid contamination of the crater's ecology by the normal forest fauna and vice versa.

'These habitats have been isolated from each other for over three million years,' she said. 'We can't possibly allow them to mix just for our convenience – if they do the crater creatures will inevitably be wiped out just as they did in the rest of the continent, and if some crater animals get out they may unbalance the outside environment in ways we don't know; they may even have diseases to which ordinary animals have no resistance. No, Julian and I will just have to hope that you make it safely back and arrange help for us. Anyway, even if we did climb up the ladder our chances of safely reaching civilization on our own would be negligible.'

Julian looked somewhat doubtful at losing this slender link with the outside world but in the end agreed with Helen's unselfish and unarguable scientific logic, so it was decided that the steps would be removed. When Richard and Lucy reached the top they pulled the ladder up rather than cutting it and letting it fall, just in case something happened that meant they wanted to return to the crater instead of continuing their journey.

As they laid the ladder on the plateau Lucy saw Queenie looking at it pensively and stroking the rungs with her paw.

Just think,' the monkey said wistfully, catching Lucy's

glance, '*it was within our capacity to build such a tree-that-bends before you came and for generations we could have entered the Valley of the Mighty Ones and eaten the strange and delicious fruits therein. Yet we did not, because we knew not how. Truly, the Tailless Ones are the masters of all creation.*'

Lucy was a little saddened by the monkey's remarks but the conversation suddenly made her think of one more precaution she had to take. After she and Richard had waved a final goodbye to Helen and Julian far below on the crater floor she asked Queenie to muster all the monkeys and other animals that had helped to build the ladder. They assembled in front of her and she addressed them all.

'*This special tree that you made has saved the lives of the Paterpromise and his companions. No such tree must ever again be made in this place, for if animals of the forest mingle with those in the crater, many creatures will be doomed. Do you all follow my words?*'

'*Your command shall always be obeyed by all that stand here,*' replied Queenie, '*for we know that there are matters within your ken that we shall never comprehend.*'

Richard stood mystified by this exchange which, for him had consisted of Lucy and a band of monkeys and assorted other animals standing looking at each other in complete silence. When it was over she explained to her father what had been said. Richard said nothing but realized that when it came to organizing and planning for the future his daughter was wise beyond her years. In the event, Richard's fears that they might need to return to the crater proved unfounded – as Lucy had always known they would – and within a few weeks the ladder, like all other fallen branches in the jungle, had disappeared under the never-ending onslaught of the myriad insects and moulds of the forest floor.

17

Christmas in the Jungle

Lucy and Richard retraced the journey she had taken previously under the guidance of the condors. The monkeys seemed to have an infallible memory for the route and the return journey was undertaken in much the same way as the outward one a few days earlier. There was now a very large tapir for Richard, and the only serious problem they faced was in crossing the jungle-clad ravine over which the monkeys had carried Lucy. It was impossible for them to assist Richard in the same way as he was a large man, and it took almost a week of additional journey time to circumvent this natural obstacle that the monkeys had traversed with Lucy in less than an hour.

One night, after journeying for two weeks, they sat after supper in the rapidly fading light when Lucy remembered something she had forgotten to tell her father.

'Dad, I know this sounds stupid, but I don't suppose you've any idea what the exact date is? I heard Chopper say that they were expecting the biggest drugs delivery they've ever had on New Year's Day – they thought it was the ideal day not to get noticed doing something criminal.'

Richard took his diary out of his rucksack.

'I must say, it's becoming a novel experience to be one up on you, but as it so happens I do have a diary and I know exactly what day it is. I nearly told you in the crater when you mentioned Clare's birthday, but I got distracted by the thought of writing a letter home.' He handed the diary over and pointed to where he had been conscientiously marking off the days since his crash in the jungle.

'I wasn't going to tell you until tomorrow as a surprise,' he continued with a smile, 'but, now you've asked, tomorrow is Christmas Eve. Happy pre-Christmas!' And he leant over and gave her a kiss and a hug.

'Christmas! – I can't believe that I'd forgotten all about it. Normally I think of nothing else for weeks beforehand.' Then she smiled. 'Do you think Santa Claws will visit us in the jungle?' Richard looked slightly mystified. 'Oh, come on, Dad. Santa *Claws!*' They both laughed as he eventually twigged and their thoughts turned at once to Clare, the chief punster in the family. Richard saw Lucy's eyes beginning to glisten with tears.

'It'll be my first Christmas away from Clare, Sarah and Mummy. I wonder what they'll all be doing.'

At that moment Queenie stiffened and looked up into the treetops. It was now almost dark. As Richard and Lucy watched, a shape detached itself from the canopy and glided silently down to them. The screech owl perched on a nearby shrub and spoke.

'*I bring sad tidings to thee, O Promised One.*' The voice reminded Lucy instantly of this bird's distant cousin on Wimbledon Common. '*The henbane that was the last to bear a message to thy kin did not return to his den for many sunsleeps. Now he has been found by the side of the great path that carries the moving houses with paws of rubber that roar. He may have been distracted by a coneyhop, for the remains of one lay near by. His own kin know not whether he perished before his duty to thee was fulfilled. They greatly fear thy wrath.'*

Lucy turned to Richard tearfully.

'They may not have got our message from the crater. The fox carrying it on its last leg got run over.' Richard was trying to console her when suddenly she sat up straight and wiped her eyes with a leaf.

'Of course!' she exclaimed. 'How could I forget! We must use the animanet.' She ignored Richard's mystified expression and turned quickly back to the owl who was waiting patiently to be dismissed.

'Thanks to thee who rend the night with thy great cry. I have a further errand. First my kin must know that the Paterpromise is with me and that we are safe from all evil. Then the kin of the henbane who sacrificed himself in my cause must be thanked. I feel only gratitude, not wrath. They shall come and speak to me when I return to Albion. Now go in haste: tell the swiftest of the fledgiquills in the forest to fly to the Great Salt and give these messages to the Great Ones. Thank thee and fare thee well!'

'I fly even now to do thy will.' The owl rose with a clatter of wings and sped off into the black night.

When he had gone Richard turned to Lucy:

'I want to know all about this animanet, or whatever it is you said – it sounds fascinating – but first let's go back to our discussion about Chopper and the drugs delivery on New Year's Day. We've got to try to get to the camp in time to warn the cops so they can stop the drug switch and catch both sets of villains. Do you think we can make the camp within a week?'

Lucy consulted Queenie, then turned back to Richard.

'She says we'll be there just after the new moon. I remember it was a full moon about a week ago – so we should be OK.' They both peered into the night sky for confirmation, and could just see a half-crescent through a gap in the canopy.

'You're right,' said her father. 'Clever girl! But it's going to be close: we can't afford to lose any time in the next few days.'

Christmas morning started off as a sad affair in the Bonaventure household. The family were all together at Joanna's house and the absence of Richard and Lucy seemed even more poignant on a day that, over the years, had been filled with such happiness in the family. Joanna had decided that, for the sake of Sarah, Ben, Henry and Christopher, they should try to celebrate as best they could in the circumstances with a traditional Christmas meal. Just before lunch, as she was taking the turkey out of the oven, Tibbles came up to her and started purring and rubbing her head against her leg in a most insistent fashion.

'Out of the way, Tibs,' she said. 'I'm really busy just now, we'll talk to you later.' But the cat grew even more

Clare . . . suddenly . . . turned to watch the cat.

insistent, mewing incessantly and deliberately moving in front of Joanna's feet, so that she practically tripped over her.

'What on earth's the matter?' said Joanna. 'You've already had your breakfast. You don't have lunch as well just because it's Christmas.'

Clare, who had been making some cranberry sauce and only half paying attention to this little interchange, suddenly stopped and turned to watch the cat. The cat, seeing Clare's movement, immediately came over to her and started to do the same as she had to Joanna, then went to and fro between the two of them.

'It's Lucy!' exclaimed Clare, practically in a shout. 'It's a message from Lucy!'

The cat, seeing it had at last got their attention, turned and raced upstairs, followed by Clare and Joanna. The other members of the family, putting the finishing touches to the table in the dining room, were puzzled to see, through the serving hatch, their sudden disappearance, but presumed it was some kind of surprise they had forgotten to get for the younger children.

Tibbles first went to Lucy's bedroom and found Jackie, the favourite soft toy from which Lucy was normally inseparable. She then led the curious pair to Joanna and Richard's room and, jumping up on their bed, laid the toy on Richard's pillow. Next she went to the wardrobe where Richard kept his clothes and shoes and mewed and pawed at the door. Clare opened it and the cat immediately rummaged inside and emerged with one of Richard's slippers in her mouth. She then deliberately placed it next to the soft toy on Richard's pillow, sat by the pillow and started purring as loudly as the astonished mother and daughter had ever heard her purr before.

'Lucy and Daddy are together in a safe place!' Clare said, her voice now almost a whisper and trembling with emotion.

Joanna looked at her and nodded, an ecstatic smile crossing her face. 'You're right,' she said. 'It just can't mean anything else.'

They hugged each other and wept for joy, with Tibbles purring and rubbing herself against their legs. Then they went downstairs and Joanna told her parents the news.

'What a wonderful Christmas present – the best any of us could have hoped for,' said Grandma, crying happily into a tissue.

Clare took Sarah, Ben, Henry and Christopher aside and told them simply that they had heard that Lucy and Richard were safe. The family had decided that none of them should know Lucy's secret until they were much older.

18

An Even More Uncomfortable
Day at the Creek

When at last they reached the river, Lucy and Richard found the boat guarded by the caymans. Following Lucy's instructions the monkeys had covered it in large fronds to protect it from the rain and hide it from any observer plane that might be sent out from the camp. After several minutes of backbreaking tugging at the starter cord Richard was eventually able to start the outboard motor. They chugged off down the river, accompanied by all the animals.

During their long journey Lucy had recounted in full detail her experiences in Rio and the camp, and Richard had gone cold with anger at the thought of the fate that Chopper and his associates had planned for his daughter. He was also appalled to learn the truth about the company, though he was convinced that José Verdade was not involved in any of the shady side of the business, and decided he would contact him as soon as he could.

When they got to within a couple of miles of the camp Richard shut off the engine so that its throbbing would not be heard and they floated silently down towards the jetty and the wreck of the spare boat. When they eventually moored the boat it was almost evening on New Year's Eve and they held a council of war. The first thing they decided they must do was to find out how many men were in the camp and where they were. Lucy was particularly interested to know whether Chopper had come from Rio and whether he was armed.

'None of the animals must get hurt,' she said. 'They have done everything they can to help us and it wouldn't be fair to send them into danger. I'm going to talk to Queenie about the safest plan of action.' Richard agreed and watched, fascinated, as his daughter sat down and discussed tactics with a monkey — neither of them apparently speaking; they just looked intently at each other with Lucy nodding now and then. She had started the conversation by taking off her glasses and giving them to the monkey who had immediately put them on and worn them throughout the interchange, adding a final, surreal touch to the scene. Richard wished he had a camcorder to record everything. Soon the monkey got up, gently replaced Lucy's spectacles, being careful not to knock Michelle off her shoulder, and disappeared towards the camp.

'What was going on with your specs?' asked Richard.

'Oh, she loves them,' said Lucy. 'At first she made me take them off when I was about to get into a situation where they might get broken, then I noticed she started to ask me to remove them for more and more trivial reasons just as an excuse to try them on. Now I just give them to her whenever we have a chat.'

As Richard laughed a gentle breeze drifted towards them from the camp. He wrinkled up his nose.

'Phew! What's that pong?'

Lucy gave a wicked grin.

'Oh, that's a little present I left behind.' She told her father about the pigs and he burst out laughing. 'It's amazing it's still so strong after all this time,' Lucy said, laughing. 'I didn't specifically ask them to, but it looks as though they went a bit dung-ho and have been back now and then to keep things topped up.' For a few minutes neither could speak for laughing.

'But now to business,' Richard said wiping tears from his eyes. 'What have you been hatching up with your monkey friends?'

'It's all arranged,' said Lucy. 'The scurripods are going to suss the place out tonight . . .'

'Scurripods?' interrupted Richard.

'Sorry, rats and mice – I'm beginning to talk like an animal myself. Anyway, they can tell us who's where and then Queenie is going to get Chopper's revolver if he has one. She did it before with the others and isn't worried about it. We'll then immobilize them all in the morning and put part of the airstrip out of action after the drugs plane has landed so the police can catch them.'

Richard was looking at her open-mouthed.

'Hang on a minute. How will you immobilize heaven knows how many villains, put an airfield out of action and call the police?'

'Well, the first two problems are a secret between

Queenie and me,' grinned Lucy. 'All you have to do is to get on the radio as soon as we have the men trapped in their cabins and call the cops.'

They slept that night in the boat, protected by the panther stalking the river bank and the caymans cruising in the river. Just after dawn Queenie appeared, carrying some fruit and a revolver.

'*The evil ones sleep in three huts. All except one of those who were here before remain.*' She put down the fruit and held up one paw with the fingers outstretched.

'Five,' said Lucy. '*What happened to the other?*'

'*He who inflicted pain on the junglefangs disappeared from his cabin one moon ago while the Brilliant One slept. I know not what happened to him for this was not done at your command.*' Lucy thought it best not to enquire further about Sing Song, but suspected that the uninjured jaguars she had instructed to feed their disabled companions had not gone far for their first supply of rations. The thought that Song had probably already been converted into, among other things, several pints of jaguar bile struck her as something approaching the ultimate in poetic justice.

Queenie continued: ' . . . *and two more have come since we were last in this place.*'

'Seven altogether, then,' Lucy added.

'*The new ones sleep in the biggest hut – the others had to move. One is small, like a child; the other looks like the hippophant who bore you through the jungle. I have his thunder-stick, it was easy to remove as it was hanging in its skin on the chair beside where he slept. The door opened easily and he heard nothing for he was making a sound like a great snortikin. I have left him a surprise in the skin as you suggested.'*

As the sun rose the men stirred. Fred rose and went to the door to cross over to the mess tent to make coffee. He opened the door and was about to step out when he cursed and slammed the door shut.

'Can't you make less noise!' shouted Sid. 'Some of us are still trying to kip – what's up?' he suddenly added, seeing Fred's face.

'Ants,' said Fred. 'Millions and millions of the little bleeders. Not a square inch of ground without ants – and big ones too.' He suddenly swore and slapped at his foot. 'And their bites are like red-hot needles!' His brother jumped up and rushed to the window.

'My God!' breathed Sid. 'I've never seen anything like it!'

The entire camp except the radio shack was carpeted with ants. They covered every surface like a seething black coat of treacle and extended along the path leading to the dynamite store and the airstrip.

'I've heard about these ant armies,' said Fred. 'When they go on the move they destroy everything in their path, large and small. Nothing that can't escape survives.'

His brother didn't seem to find this observation particularly comforting. 'Well, *we* can't escape,' said Sid. 'They're all around us for as far as I can see, in every direction. The only weird thing is, they're not coming in the doors and windows, even though they'd easily fit through the cracks.'

'Well, just be grateful they're not,' said Fred, 'and don't go attracting their attention. I expect they'll move on when they've cleared out all our grub and then we'll be OK. We'd better just sit tight.'

A similar scene was taking place in the second hut, occupied by Pollard, Barker and Sam. Barker rushed out with a shovel and started beating the ground outside the door. Within seconds he was covered in ants from head to toe and was carried screaming back into the cabin by Sam, who himself got bitten as he attempted to brush the insects off his companion.

'Where's Pollard?' Sam asked when they had finally removed the insects.

'He got up before dawn and went to the gelly shack. He's probably got trapped there by the ants. Chopper told him to have a gelignite pack ready from first thing, in case the drugs plane came early. His instructions were to hide near the airstrip all day. He's to blow their plane up if they try to double-cross us.'

'Phew! Chopper certainly thinks of everything,' said Sam.

'Well – almost everything,' replied Barker bitterly, rubbing the angry red bites already swelling on his legs. 'It's just a pity he didn't remember to bring a zillion tons of ant powder with him.'

'We'd better tell Chopper about the ants,' said Sam. 'We've got to get this lot clear before the plane arrives.'

'Well, I don't know what Chopper can do,' said Barker. 'He's not a bleedin' anteater, even though his nose is the right shape. Still, I suppose you're right, he needs to know.' They started shouting through the window across to Chopper's cabin, a larger hut behind the two smaller ones.

Chopper had gone to bed exhausted as usual. He found the humidity and heat of the camp intensely uncomfortable and since his arrival almost two months earlier had been permanently nauseated by the lingering and all-pervasive stench of peccary ordure. He had been desperately keen, however, that the drugs delivery planned for the next day should go smoothly and had realized that the only way to ensure this was to remain at the camp and supervise things himself. Before getting into his hammock he had finally removed the strapping from the foot he had injured on his garden gnome. His foot had felt much easier once he had taken the strapping off, and he was now in a deep sleep lying flat on his back in the hammock, after having had his first really comfortable night since his injury.

The large black lizard left by Queenie had also spent a very comfortable night in the gun holster slung over the chair next to Chopper's hammock and, with his head cocked slightly to one side, looked for all the world like a gun. The holster was a perfect spot for, without moving, he had passed the early morning picking off the flies buzzing around Chopper, many of which unwisely stopped for a brief and final rest on the holster or the chair.

'Chopper . . . Chopper . . . Chopper!' Chopper awoke to the sound of distant shouting. His first thought was that there was a raid by the police or a rival gang, and he attempted to snatch his revolver from its holster, knocking a plastic bottle of water to the floor as he did so. The lizard was more than a little affronted by this interruption to his breakfast, and not only scrabbled violently with front and back legs in Chopper's hand but bit him hard on the ear for good measure. Chopper gave a howl of fright and disgust and, dropping the reptile, ran straight for the door in his bare feet. In his panic he didn't notice the large rat standing guard near the door and stampeded past it on the way out, his foot missing its tail by millimetres. The rat did notice Chopper, however, and when, a few seconds later, he came back inside cursing and rubbing at his ant-covered feet, it bit deep into his healing toe, guided by some unerring primitive instinct to his victim's most vulnerable spot and instantly refracturing the bone. Chopper screamed and, clutching his bleeding toe, hopped around the cabin floor. He hopped into the pool of spilt water and skidded across the cabin towards his cabin mate, the lizard and the rat jumping for their lives as his enormous bulk hurtled towards them.

Chopper was a large man − very large, in fact 'obscenely fat-arsed git' was the phrase that crossed most people's lips once they were safely out of earshot. His momentum when he had been precipitated into motion, usually inadvertently, was prodigious. He now hurtled through the air towards the hammock in which his small hut-mate, Bert Shortshanks, was sleeping soundly.

Bert had been working hard the previous day trying to clear the remains of the most recent delivery of pig dung from the camp. It was hard and disgusting work and, as the washing facilities had still not been restored in the camp since Lucy's last visit, he had retired to his hammock smelly and exhausted. He was so deeply asleep that Chopper's snoring had not disturbed him, and even while Chopper was confronting the lizard, the ants and the rat, he remained engrossed in an absorbing dream. Whatever dream he was dreaming it seems unlikely that, under normal circumstances, it would have ended with his being hit by a human bulldozer, but when Chopper's massive bulk came hurtling across the room and collided with Bert's diminutive form, there was only one possible outcome. Bert left his hammock as though someone had pressed the ejector seat button in a fighter aircraft, and sailed through the air to land headfirst in the corner. The hut was very sparsely furnished: apart from the two hammocks and Chopper's bedside chair there was only a bucket and a small cupboard. The bucket was used by the men as a chamberpot during the night to avoid them having to go out across the unlit compound with the risk of attack by snakes, poisonous insects or larger animals. It stood in the far corner of the room and was ideally positioned to break Bert's fall as he landed headfirst in its welcoming depths.

Meanwhile Chopper had made a perfect two-point landing. His bottom hit the floor of the hut, making a noise that sounded like the end of the world. The impact shook the entire hut and the surrounding ground for several yards and the floorboards splintered as if made of matchwood, a very large fragment disappearing into the

. . . when Chopper's massive bulk came hurtling across the room . . .
there was only one possible outcome.

blubbery depths of Chopper's buttock; two days later it would take a prison doctor, two nurses and a hospital porter to remove it. While his buttocks were demolishing the floor Chopper's right foot, hitherto his good foot, smashed through the door of the little cupboard, breaking two of his toes. The screams of rage and pain emitted by Chopper and Bert carried to the jetty, where Richard looked in concern at Lucy.

'You're not having them killed, are you?' he said as Chopper's howls floated across the clearing. 'I mean, I know they're a crowd of so-and-sos, but we should try to bring them to justice.'

'Chill out, Dad!' said Lucy laughing. 'Queenie and I have just arranged a little early morning entertainment, but nothing that's against the Geneva Convention.'

Richard smiled nervously in relief and instantly

regretted having let such a terrible thought even cross his mind. The fact that it had, however, did bring home to him the true power and responsibility that his daughter now exercised. She was the first person in history who could commit the perfect unsolved murder – or a thousand – without being at any risk of discovery or even suspicion. She could, for instance, easily arrange for every man in the camp to be exterminated by snakes, scorpions, caymans, jaguars or any other lethal creatures. Far from being under any suspicion she would, in all probability, even end up being seen as an innocent and fortunate survivor. In his mind's eye he saw a headline from one of the tabloid newspapers:

PLUCKY KIDNAP GIRL AND FATHER
SOLE SURVIVORS OF AMAZON TOOTH
AND CLAW CARNAGE

Our South American correspondent flew into what is now being referred to as the 'Camp of Terror' to establish why up to thirty jaguars ate seven men yesterday in an inexplicable display of ferocious savagery. Here is his exclusive account of his conversation at the blood-drenched scene with one of the only two survivors, Lucy Bonaventure, who emerged as the heroine of the incident. She told him of her kidnap ordeal and the horror of the massacre.

'I found Lucy sitting on a log cuddling a small marmoset for comfort and obviously too numbed by the horrific experience to show any real grief. "Daddy

tried to rescue me from the camp but when the villains caught him too I almost gave up hope of ever escaping alive," she told me, her amazing blue eyes misting over at the memory. "Then, one day, the jaguars appeared from nowhere. I was a *bit* scared," she admitted modestly with true British pluck, "but the animals just seemed to ignore me and Daddy. It was almost as if somebody had *told* them who the bad guys were. While I was a prisoner I had thought of lots of ways I might get free, but the way it finally happened . . ." Her voice trembled with emotion and a grimace of anguish crossed her face which, if I hadn't known better from my long years in trauma journalism, I could easily have mistaken for a ghastly smile.'

'Dad . . . Dad!' Richard was jerked out of his reverie by Lucy. 'What on earth are you daydreaming about? We've things to do!' With a guilty start Richard was relieved to remember that his daughter could only read animal thoughts and not his own.

'I think you'll find it's all clear in the radio shack now,' she continued briskly. 'I'll come with you in case we need to call up more reinforcements but somehow I don't think it'll be necessary.' Lucy threw Chopper's gun into the river and they strolled across to the radio hut. Richard gaped in astonishment when he saw the seething carpet of ants and the enraged faces of the men at the cabin windows. The panther strolled nonchalantly up and down outside the radio shack just in case anyone felt like making a dash across the sea of ants. She had been joined in her patrols by the jaguars operated on by Sing Song, which had been recalled from the jungle by Lucy in preparation for their veterinary treatment.

'Don't tread on any ants, Dad,' said Lucy. 'They think we're the good guys and we don't want to confuse them.'

They went into the shack and Richard called José Verdade back in Macapá.

'José? It's Richard. Thank heavens you're there, even on New Year's Day! I was worried about what Chopper might have done. Are you OK?'

'I'm fine,' José replied against a background of noisy static. 'I've been coming in every day in case you called. It's great to hear you again – thank God you're safe. Where are you?'

'I'm at Cayman Creek,' said Richard. 'Listen, I need to fire a lot of information at you so get a pen and paper ready.'

'OK, but first I must tell you that there've been a lot of developments here. I'll give you a quick summary. Apparently the police in London got a garbled story about the kidnapping of a girl in which the Ecocidal Timber Company was involved.'

Richard turned to Lucy. 'Looks as if at least one of your messages got through – well done!'

'Anyway,' continued José, 'it turns out that the Brazilian authorities have had their eye on Chopper and his crew for some time – something to do with drugs – and this kidnapping was the final straw. They've got warrants to arrest Chopper, his brothers and some associates. I'm the most senior innocent manager in the company, so it looks as if I'm now in charge. Someone flew over from Scotland Yard a couple of days ago – nice chap – and he's been through all the company records with me. He flew to Manaus yesterday to join the local police and drug enforcement people. The company pilot, I'm pleased to say, is also innocent and he'll guide the police and customs officers to Cayman Creek, so they should all be with you later today. There'll probably be three planes in all.'

'That's great news,' said Richard, 'and the kidnapped girl, by the way, is my daughter Lucy who is standing here right next to me. Her adventures are a story on their own, which I'll tell you when we meet. There are urgent matters to deal with first, though. Are you ready?'

'Fire away!'

Richard then asked José to warn the police about the drug consignment due that day, to arrange a rescue plane for Helen and Julian, to fly a vet out to treat the jaguars, to obtain an emergency passport for Lucy and, of course, to contact the two sets of families at home.

'Phew!' said Richard as they left the shack, 'I feel as if life is at last beginning to sort itself out. Now, what about this plane?'

'All you have to do just now, Dad, is relax and enjoy the show. I'll tell you when you need to do your bit. Let's go and sit by the airstrip, eat our bananas and wait for the fun to start.'

Richard stumbled after his daughter in disbelief. He couldn't begin to understand how his little girl had been transformed into this decisive, resourceful young woman but he was intensely proud of her. He hugged her.

'I feel so confident with you around,' he said. 'I'm quite enjoying a bit of role reversal after looking after you for nearly twelve years.'

'It makes a change for me too,' said Lucy. 'You don't think I enjoyed being a child slave for all that time, do you?' She ducked to dodge a banana skin. 'And my animals don't want to see your rubbish around thank you very much, even if it is biodegradable!'

They sat in the shade by the little airstrip, Michelle, as ever, on Lucy's shoulder, Katy curled up on her knees and Melanie now sprawled languidly alongside Richard. The monkeys chattered in the branches, taking it in turns to go and check on the prisoners. It was an unnecessary precaution, however, since the men had all seen the jaguars prowling around through their windows and none of them fancied a bare-handed grapple with the big cats.

Richard suddenly made an exclamation and slapped his forehead.

'What is it, Dad?' Lucy looked concerned and Richard quickly reassured her.

'Oh, nothing too serious; it's just something else I meant to say to José – boys' talk!' He grinned at Lucy as if to remind her of her own private chat with Helen at the crater. 'I'll nip back and call him again – back soon!' Richard returned to the radio shack and made his call, then set off towards the airstrip.

As he hurried back along the path leading to the airstrip

he passed the dynamite store, which was situated some distance from the main camp for obvious reasons. The men all called it the 'gelly' shack as it was packed with cases of gelignite – the explosive that was used for ground clearance and illegal mining. As Richard passed the hut he suddenly felt his neck completely encircled by sharp, cold steel. He stopped instantly as the grip of the instrument tightened and bit into his flesh.

'What's the big hurry, mate?' A coarse cockney voice came from somewhere to the side. Turning his head as best he could to the direction of the sound he saw Pollard standing in the doorway of the store. A rucksack was slung over his shoulder and he was holding a four-metre polling hook, on the end of which Richard was trapped by its encircling blades as securely as a gaffed fish. Richard had a similar tool at home for pruning high branches but this was something different: it was a heavy-duty power tool capable of slicing through very large branches – branches as large as Richard's neck in fact, and at the moment it sat snugly around it. Richard's mouth ran dry as he felt the serrated edge of the massive blade millimetres from his windpipe. It was so sharp that he could feel the teeth tearing the surface of his skin just from the slight movement he had made to bring Pollard into view. The length of the pole meant it was of the question for him to try to grapple with the man.

'Well, if I'm not mistaken, you seem to have a way with ants. This is the second time I've seen you strolling past as if they didn't exist. What is it? Don't they like the smell of your feet or something?' His face cracked into a toothless grin at his own wit. Richard's first thought was one of relief that the fellow obviously hadn't seen him with Lucy on their first trip along the path together.

'Well, whatever it is,' Pollard continued, his face reverting to its natural scowl, 'you've come at just the right time to see me over to the radio shack. I need to call up a spray plane to clobber this lot.' He took his hand off the pruning hook to gesture at the sea of ants. He paused and looked at the unwieldy tool; it was going to be impossible for him to use it to control Richard while he went into the radio shack and operated the equipment. His face lit up as he thought of a hands-free solution to the problem.

'I can't hold on to this thing all the time so I think I'll just take one little precaution to make sure you stay on your best behaviour. Oh, and I advise you to keep very still while I get things ready – you don't want to go losing your head over this, do you?' Once again he laughed at his own joke as he lowered the handle of the pruning tool to the floor. Richard winced as the blade bit deeper into his flesh with the change of angle. Pollard slid the rucksack off his shoulder to the ground and opened it.

'Enough gelly in here to take out a plane, but this stick looks just your size.' He took a stick of gelignite from the bag and grinned at Richard's horrified expression.

'I must say,' he continued with obvious sadistic pleasure, 'this could all be a bit of a blow for you.'

He fumbled in the bag again and withdrew a tiny electronic detonating device which he attached to the stick of explosive. He then moved behind Richard who felt him tie the little package to his belt. Pollard once again took hold of the hook, but this time it was to remove it from Richard's neck. He laid it on the ground and, before Richard could move, he took a remote control from his bush-shirt pocket and waved it threateningly in the air.

'Now,' he said grimly, 'we're going for a little walk. Any attempt at heroics and I press this little button. And make sure you stay a polite distance away from me, I've got this thing about getting blood and guts on my clothes. Get moving!' He picked up the rucksack and slung it over his shoulder.

Richard started back to the radio shack. The ants parted for him and immediately began to surge behind him to close the gap. Pollard stayed as far behind Richard as this gap would allow – about five paces – and behind him there was once again an uninterrupted sea of black. He was intent upon watching Richard and avoiding the ants, so was unaware of the jaguars silently patrolling the camp. They, of course, saw him, but assumed that he was accompanying Richard and left the pair unmolested.

As they neared the shack Lucy reappeared. Fearless of any animals, she had taken a short cut through the forest rather than the winding path past the dynamite hut. She had returned to see where Richard had got to, concerned that the drugs plane could arrive at any moment, and stopped in surprise and horror when she saw the two men. Pollard recognized her instantly: as site manager he had taken all the blame for Lucy's escape and he felt he had a large score to settle with her. It was a task he was going to relish.

'You!' he exclaimed. 'Couldn't manage out there on your own any longer and came back to throw yourself on our mercy, eh?' He glanced at the patch of ground on which she stood, seeing that it was completely clear of ants. 'And I see you've got the magic bug repellent too. Well, I'll see to you later. In the meantime, no funny business or this bloke gets it – in the back.' He gestured with the remote control to the charge on Richard's back.

They continued to the shack and, seeing it was free from ants, Pollard told Richard to stand to one side as he passed him and went in the door.

'Come and stand where I can see you!' he called, as he slipped the half-open rucksack off his shoulder, put it down near the doorway and went over to pick up the radio transmitter. Richard stood several paces from the open door facing Pollard. He glanced at Lucy who gave a nod and, pointing to her legs, stood with them close together so there was no gap between them. Richard immediately understood and did the same thing. Anything approaching him from behind was now concealed from Pollard. A few seconds later he felt a scrabbling behind his legs and then sharp teeth tugging at the ties fastening the gelignite to his belt. Pollard, glancing at him now and then, could not see the squirrel at work. Soon he was cursing as he realized that nobody was going to answer at the other end – he'd forgotten it was New Year's Day – and, as he turned to slam the transmitter down in disgust, he didn't see the squirrel replacing the primed gelignite stick in his rucksack.

Pollard came out of the hut, blinking as he emerged into the bright sunlight. He surveyed the impassable sea of ants once again, desperately trying to think of an alternative plan of action. As he went over the various possibilities in his mind he fiddled idly with the remote control device in his hands and, as he watched, Richard broke out in a cold sweat. There was enough gelignite in the rucksack to comfortably see them both off, and probably Lucy and half the camp as well. Suddenly a crafty look crossed Pollard's face and he turned to Richard.

'How did you get here?'

Richard saw no point in telling anything but the truth. 'By boat,' he replied.

'Where is it?'

Richard pointed to the path leading through the forest to the little jetty. It was about a hundred and fifty yards to the river, which was completely invisible from the camp. 'Down there,' he said simply.

Pollard picked up the rucksack and disappeared along the path to the creek.

'I'll be back !' he shouted through the trees. As soon as he was out of sight Lucy ran to Richard and hugged him.

'What a ghastly man!' she said, her voice trembling with relief. 'I really do believe he would have killed you if necessary – he's a complete psycho.'

'He may yet try,' said Richard, who had formed the same opinion of his erstwhile captor. 'In fact . . .' His face suddenly froze in alarm. '. . . quick, run! And tell the animals to run!' He grabbed her arm and they ran across the camp and hid behind the storehouse on the far side. Animals and birds fled away from the jetty path and their alarm cries resounded through the surrounding forest.

Pollard stopped about fifty yards down the path. The remote control had a long range but he wasn't taking any chances. He grinned to himself.

'Bye bye folks!' he murmured as he pressed the button.

Even though Richard and Lucy were half expecting it, the explosion when it came was absolutely shattering. The entire camp trembled at the force of the blast and after a moment of eerie silence the forest creatures broke into a chorus of terrified noises. Lucy and Richard hugged each other tightly once again. Eventually she spoke:

'Wow! Well done, Dad – just in time! What made you suddenly realize what he was going to do?'

Richard's face was still deathly white but he pulled himself together.

'He's more cunning than he looks – though that's not saying much!' He managed a weak smile. 'I always suspected that he might kill me, but that would have left you free as a witness. He knew he couldn't catch you because of the ants and he didn't have a gun. He guessed that as soon as you judged the remote control unit was out of range you would disconnect the gelignite from me, and he thought he'd blow us both up as you were doing it. He had to pretend to get out of range, which is why he didn't set it off as soon as he was hidden by the trees. If he'd done it too soon he couldn't have been sure of getting you as well. Those vital moments gave us and the animals the opportunity to get out of range. I must say,' he added, 'life is certainly never dull with you around!'

'We should be getting back to the airstrip,' said Lucy, 'but before we go I need to give you a big kiss!' She stretched up and planted a kiss on his cheek.

'My,' said Richard, laughing, 'a kiss as well as a hug! What's that for?'

'It's for thinking about the animals as well as us. Your quick thinking must have saved hundreds and hundreds of little lives. You're a really cool dad and I love you!'

Lucy suddenly stiffened and cocked her head.

'Listen!'

Richard listened but could hear nothing but the gradually fading cries of the animals disturbed by the blast. He shrugged his shoulders. Lucy laughed. 'We are getting old, aren't we? Never mind, you'll eventually hear it; it's a plane and we'd better move. Come on!'

They ran to the airstrip and soon even Richard could hear the distant drone of a light aircraft. They knew that the police were coming in three planes, so if it was a single plane it would be the drug carriers. Shading their eyes they peered into the brilliant sky until they spotted the incoming plane. Once they were certain it was on its own, Lucy sprang into action.

'Now, Dad,' she said, 'I know you've had a boring few weeks and I know you feel a bit left out when I'm talking to Michelle and Katy and Queenie, so now's your big moment.' She turned, and taking two palm fronds off Queenie gave them to him. 'You've got to go out and wave them into their parking spot.' She pointed to a space near the trees where Richard now saw two tapirs waiting quietly in the bushes.

'Quick, off you go. Don't be a wimp, Dad,' she said, giving him a little push in the back. Richard went out into the field feeling as if he were back at school, but what Lucy had said made perfect sense. It was the most natural thing in the world for one of the men at the camp to guide the plane in.

As the plane approached for landing Richard waved the fronds with arms outstretched, just like a member of the ground staff at a large airport, and the pilot obediently taxied to the spot to which Richard guided him and the aircraft came to a stop. As it did so the tapirs came out and sat, one just in front of the wheels and one just behind.

'Run, Dad!' Lucy shouted.

Richard needed no second bidding. He ran into the adjacent bushes and then circled back under cover to where Lucy sat. When he got back Lucy was staring into the jungle with an expression he was now very familiar with: the faraway look she adopted when she was communing with animals. At that moment there was another droning sound and Richard glanced up, concerned that more planes were coming in and that he had just misdirected the first police plane. He heaved a sign of relief as the noise grew louder and its source became clear. A massive swarm of hornets swept out of the jungle and zoomed like a squadron of fighter planes towards the trapped aircraft. The cockpit door was just opening and as the cloud of hornets reached the plane it was hurriedly shut again. The swarm filled the air around the plane, so dense that it looked as though the plane was sitting in a bank of dark-brown fog.

They heard the engine start up again and saw the plane trying unsuccessfully to move against the dead weight of the tapirs obstructing the wheels. The animals were invisible to the occupants of the plane and through occasional gaps in the hornet cloud Lucy and Richard got fleeting glimpses of the anger and bewilderment on their faces as the plane refused to budge. Once again the door started to open and then it shut even more quickly than before. No human being on earth could have survived for more than a few seconds in that living, buzzing maelstrom and it was clear that those inside the aircraft were not

. . .before their very eyes, the plane started sinking into the ground . . .

about to put their survival chances to the test.

Now an anaconda's tail appeared from the bushes and coiled itself neatly around the tail fin of the little plane. It took over the job of immobilizing it from the tapirs, who moved away from the wheels, making way for four giant armadillos who emerged from the bushes and started to dig at breathtaking speed at the ground around the wheels.

'The anaconda can't stay there long,' explained Lucy gleefully, 'in case the villains dare to open the door and start shooting at it, but they don't even know it's there yet and by the time they do the flexishields – sorry, armadillos – will have finished; Queenie tells me they're the world's champion diggers.' Lucy now thought she knew what had created the massive trenches through which the jaguars had escaped on her previous visit to the camp.

Sure enough, before their very eyes, the plane started sinking into the ground as its wheels disappeared into a trench. Earth and dust flew for yards as the armadillos worked and within a few minutes the bottom of the plane was sitting flat on the ground. The anaconda unwound its tail and disappeared.

'We had to do this at the side of the strip,' explained Lucy, 'so the animals could hide, and the strip was left clear for the police planes to land safely. That's why we had to get you to trick them into parking over there.'

Richard looked once more at his daughter in speechless amazement. There seemed to be no detail that she had left unattended.

19

Operation Jungle Sting

Later in the day, they once again heard the drone of aero-engines and three planes approached and landed. Richard and Lucy were standing at the side of the airstrip and waved to the planes as they taxied towards the camp. As the planes came to a stop armed police jumped out and, seeing Lucy pointing to the drugs plane, ran towards it to surround it. As they drew near, the hornets, still clustered in an angry crowd around the cockpit, disappeared as if by magic into the adjacent jungle. Soon the men in the plane clambered out and the police made them turn and lean with their hands on the plane fuselage while they frisked and disarmed them. It looked just like a scene from an American police movie. The men from the other planes, including the liaison officer from Scotland Yard, then went over and talked briefly to the villains before the Yard man detached himself from the group and came over to Richard and Lucy.

'Hello, I'm Inspector Cockayne,' he said as they shook hands. 'Dr Bonaventure, I presume!' He smiled as he turned to Lucy, 'And you must be the intrepid Lucy. Thank heavens you're safe, my dear. Everybody has been very worried about you.' He turned and pointed to the drugs plane.

'It looks as if we've got three of the most notorious drug dealers in the region and the biggest haul of cocaine I've seen in twenty years on the force. Their plane seems to have got stuck in some kind of a hole – I don't know what the pilot was thinking of going anywhere near it. The extraordinary thing is that the wheels seem to have disturbed a massive hornets' nest – maybe it was in the hole – and the villains say it was impossible for them to get out. Funny thing is, when our men surrounded the plane the hornets flew off. Maybe they're frightened of humans in this remote spot – it's a good job the crooks didn't realize they were so harmless. Another odd thing is that our code name for this operation is "Jungle Sting". It turned out to be more appropriate than anyone could have guessed.' They all laughed and the inspector continued. 'You've been incredibly lucky. If it hadn't been for the hole and the hornets I daren't think what that lot would have done to you. They're a bunch of really nasty characters.'

'Well, we had a problem,' said Richard. 'We weren't sure who was going to get here first, you or them, so we had to stay near the airstrip to check. When we saw it was them we were terrified,' he glanced at Lucy who put on a suitably worried expression and nodded in agreement, 'so we hid in the bushes until you came. We couldn't understand why they didn't get out but now you've solved the mystery for us.' He felt the fib was justified in the circumstances. 'Tell your men to be careful when they go into the camp,' he continued. 'It seems to have been invaded by an army of ants overnight and the men have all been trapped in their huts.'

'Thanks for the warning,' said the Inspector. 'I'll let them know immediately – they look as if they're just on their way into the camp.' He took Richard and Lucy over to the Brazilian officer in charge to introduce them. 'This is Captain Colarinho. He's in overall command of the operation.' The captain was a charming man who greeted Lucy and Richard in flawless English and congratulated them on their resourcefulness in contacting José and in staying out of the clutches of the villains. Then he called two of his men over and talked to them in Portuguese, explaining about the ants. One of them crossed to the cabins and soon returned to give a brief report to the captain. He turned and courteously translated this for the benefit of his British colleague, Lucy and Richard.

'He says the ants are clearing off even now. If the villains had got out sooner they might have discovered you two and who knows what they might have done. We obviously arrived in the nick of time.' The captain shook his head in disbelief. 'I just can't get over this. What kind of coincidence gets half the insects in the Amazon trapping two bunches of thugs at the same time?'

'We do seem to have been extraordinarily lucky,' murmured Richard, and Lucy nodded in agreement, looking straight at the police officers, blue eyes wide with innocence. Then she slipped away to lock up the jaguars before the police came across them.

Richard and Inspector Cockayne watched as the police surrounded Chopper's hut. One of the police force was extremely large and tough-looking, with muscles bulging under his bullet-proof vest. Captain Colarinho explained that he was an ex-commando. Richard thought that the man looked distinctly disappointed at the somewhat uneventful nature of the arrests so far. The ex-commando eagerly kicked in the door of Chopper's hut as if anticipating a bit of rough stuff. They all gaped at the sight that greeted them.

The captain inspected the scene, then turned to the inspector and Richard.

'They've obviously been fighting,' he said, '– probably on drugs. That little guy must be tougher than he looks and he's obviously a martial arts expert – fancy being able to chuck that fat one through a cupboard! And look at that nasty wound on the big fellow's ear lobe,' he added authoritatively. 'You can always tell a knife fighter when you see one.'

Chopper's injured leg was by now so swollen that it proved impossible even for the commando to extract it from the door. The captain vetoed any further attempts despite assurances from the commando that he could definitely remove it with one final vigorous tug, so the cupboard door was unscrewed and the prisoners 'helped' out of the hut by the commando.

As the police started to break into the next hut Sam, seeing that the ants had gone, prised the window open and escaped. There was no time for the others to follow and they pushed the wire back to conceal his absence. Crouching below the window Sam glanced hurriedly round and, seeing no big cats, dashed to the nearby edge of the forest and then ran towards the jetty. Halfway to the river he was astonished to see the devastation caused by the dynamite. He had, of course, heard the massive blast while trapped in his hut and had assumed that Pollard must have had an accident with his gelignite pack. In a way he was right, but he couldn't understand what Pollard had been doing on the path to the creek. Over a wide area the trees had been completely flattened and those around the perimeter of the blast area were broken and splintered. As Sam crossed the new clearing he tripped over a boot and to his horror saw that it was still occupied by a foot. No leg – just a foot ending in a bloody mangled stump where the ankle should have been. Sam was looking at the largest remaining fragment of Pollard. Fighting back waves of nausea he stumbled on to the jetty.

The giant cayman opened one eye at the sound of approaching footsteps. She watched as Sam crept up to the boat recently vacated by Lucy and Richard and started to fumble with the moorings. She slowly raised her snout a fraction and sniffed appreciatively. Most lumberjacks and camp workers seemed to use soap, shampoo and even deodorants nowadays. She had not smelt a human being so thoroughly organic as Sam for a very long time. She slid into the black waters of the river with barely a ripple as the boat pushed off from the makeshift jetty. It was beginning to look, even to her simplistic reptilian mind, as though the destruction of the previous boat would prove to have been an invaluable educational experience.

The inspector in charge had decided that all the captured men should be evacuated by boat, and a police craft was already coming up the river to join them. Because of the remoteness of the area the nearest town with a police launch was . . . *

This launch would not reach them for at least twenty-four hours so in the meantime the men were herded into the mess hut, the largest building in the camp, so they could be kept under armed guard. The drug peddlers from the plane had been disarmed and taken to join the others. After they left the plane the pilot kept looking back at the trench into which the wheels had disappeared; he passed his hand across his eyes and shook his head repeatedly in bewilderment, muttering incoherently to himself as he was marched to the mess hut.

As the villains all stood in a group waiting to be shepherded into the hut the police were helpless with laughter, for the prisoners looked like a troupe of clowns in a travelling circus rehearsing for their next village show. Barker was standing with both feet in a bucket of water to relieve the pain of the ant stings; the pilot of the plane had been stung by hornets on his nose and both ears, which had swollen to the size of ripe tomatoes; Bert still had the bucket stuck firmly on his head, the captain having, with some difficulty, prevented the commando from trying to

* Author's note: This name has been deleted in order to respect the wishes expressed by Richard and Lucy who want to protect the site of the camp (now dismantled) from future commercial or tourist exploitation.

. . . the prisoners looked like a troupe of clowns . . .

prise it off with his combat knife. He had already made
several failed attempts to remove it with his bare hands by
gripping Bert's neck between his knees and twisting the
bucket vigorously in both directions. The handle of the
bucket had now fallen neatly over so as to form a chin
strap, making Bert look like the tin man in *The Wizard of
Oz*. Chopper stood speechless with rage, a towel wrapped
like a giant nappy around his injured bottom, a
handkerchief pressed to his bleeding ear and the cupboard
door still around his leg. Looking at him Inspector
Cockayne turned to Richard and said drily:

'Well, he's not in prison yet, but he's certainly got one
foot in the door.'

Lucy, who had by now returned from the jaguar
compound, made a mental note to pass this gem on to Clare.
She knew that the villains deserved everything that had

happened to them, but she was a kind-hearted girl and couldn't help feeling a twinge of sympathy for the dejected group. Then she thought of the miserable state of the three jaguars she had just left, tortured for greed; the months of pain ending inevitably in death that they and all those she had released would have faced; the destruction of the precious rainforest with its irreplaceable animals and plants; the destruction of thousands of species by the contamination of the rivers with mercury and other poisons from illegal mining; and the destruction of countless lives and societies by the filthy drugs these men were distributing throughout the world, and any vestiges of sympathy that she felt for them evaporated. She only hoped that it wasn't too late for them to mend their ways and start again with more useful lives.

With the villains all now grouped together, Lucy noticed immediately that Sam was missing and told the inspector. The police ran down to the jetty to find that both he and the boat were gone.

'He wouldn't have dared start the engine because of the noise, so he'll be floating downstream until he's out of earshot,' said the astute captain. 'That means the police launch will meet him on its way up. I'll call them to warn them.' When he emerged from the radio shack he beckoned to Richard.

'There's a call for you on the radio,' he said. Richard and Lucy went to the radio shack and Richard switched the receiver to 'open' so that Lucy could also hear. It was José.

'Richard? I've managed to set up a radio link with the UK. I've got some folk here who would very much like to have a word with you.' Lucy's heart leapt and a few seconds later she heard her mother's voice. Richard and Lucy spoke excitedly to her and Clare and Sarah, then to Grandma and Grandpa, Lucy's aunt and uncle, and Ben, Henry and Christopher. Lucy had never felt so happy in her life, re-united physically with her father and now with the rest of her family by radio.

Soon they said goodbye, looking forward to a grand reunion when Lucy and Richard returned, as they hoped, within the next few days.

Lucy then went to the jaguar compound to take water to the animals she had locked up when the police arrived. There were three jaguars awaiting treatment from the vets. They had lain low in the nearby forest and had been fed by their fit companions as Lucy had requested.

'*All the evil ones will soon be gone,*' she told them, '*and in one sunsleep some Tailless Ones will come to make you well. They may put a sharp straw in your leg and this will make you sleep. I will be with them and speak to you, so have no fear.*' She then returned to the main camp and rejoined her father.

'Well, young lady, it's time we started off home to see Mummy and the girls . . .' Richard stopped as he saw Lucy's face.

'We can't go today, Dad. I have to stay and comfort the sick jaguars when the vets are here – please, *please*, it's only one more day and the animals helped us so much I *have* to stay.'

'Well, we do owe our lives to all these creatures,' he said, 'and I suppose after all this time one more day or two is neither here nor there. I've a lot of business to discuss with José and I can start writing my botanical notes up. The main thing is that everybody at home now knows we are safe.'

'Thank you, Daddy, thank you!' She flung her arms round him and hugged him.

' . . . and, while we're on such matters,' he continued, 'I really don't think you can take Michelle with you.' He looked at the cute little creature. 'She would have to spend a long time in quarantine – it could be most of her remaining life span – and it would be cruel to take her away from her natural environment.'

'I know you're right,' said Lucy. 'I wouldn't really have taken her but I will miss her terribly.' She scratched the marmoset under the chin and Michelle held her finger between her paws and licked it with her tiny pink tongue.

That night Richard and Lucy were able to sleep in a hut – their first night under proper cover for weeks. The captain had allocated them Chopper's old hut but Lucy took one sniff at the hammocks and declared that she wasn't going anywhere near them.

'They're disgusting, Dad; heaven knows what you'll catch if you go in one of them.' And so saying she took them out and burned them. She washed her hands afterwards, much to the amusement of her father.

'You must have come across every known bug and parasite in the last few weeks – and even more unknown ones,' he said. 'Why the sudden fuss about hygiene?'

'Jungle dirt is clean dirt,' she replied, 'and this is *Chopper* dirt. And as far as I'm concerned there's all the difference in the world.'

They slept on the floor on sweet-smelling leaves and branches just as they had in the jungle, Michelle and Katy snuggled up close to Lucy. She slept in complete contentment for the first time since she had been kidnapped and dreamt of seeing her home and family again.

The next day a plane arrived with two vets, James and Jane Stockwell, a man and wife team. They had radioed Lucy the previous day to find out exactly what was wrong with the jaguars and they brought with them the equipment they would need. Lucy explained that the jaguars had become half-tamed – a white lie, but one she felt was justified as being the only explanation the vets would understand for the cats' docile behaviour. With Lucy's help they anaesthetized and treated the animals, then told her that the drainage tubes they had put in would probably come out on their own, but if not they should be taken out in about ten days' time.

'Unfortunately we can't come back then because we will be away on a field trip immunizing a wild herd,' Jane told Lucy, 'but anyone who feels comfortable being near the jaguars can do it.'

'What exactly needs to be done?' said Lucy.

'Well, you see this little plastic tube,' Jane said, pointing to the side of the third jaguar, which was just beginning to regain consciousness. 'If it's still there in about ten days' time it just needs a tug to remove it. It won't hurt the animal, just a twinge, and the little hole left behind will heal on its own. It doesn't need a vet, it just needs someone who can get near to the jaguar without losing an arm.'

'I think I can organize that,' said Lucy.

James and Jane assumed she meant she would help one of the company staff at the camp to do it and they had no doubt she could, having seen her amazing ability to relate to the animals.

'I don't think I've ever seen anyone as good with animals as you are,' said James. 'The way you can handle these big cats is almost unbelievable. What are you hoping to do eventually? Something working with animals, I hope.'

'Yes, I'd like to be a vet,' said Lucy, 'and I'd love to do the sort of work you do. Thank you so much for letting me help and watch today.'

'It's we who should be thanking you,' laughed Jane. 'Our job would have been twice as difficult without your help. I'm sure we'll meet again one day; maybe you'll come and help us when you are a vet – or during your studies.' She kissed Lucy goodbye and James gave her an affectionate hug; then they climbed into their aircraft, giving the half-buried drugs plane a puzzled glance as they did so.

Lucy waved until the little plane was out of sight and then returned to the camp where the police captain was supervising the removal of the fashion accessories acquired by the villains. The plastic bucket was eventually cut off Bert's head by means of a large, high-powered tree saw, wielded enthusiastically by the commando. The cupboard door was removed from around Chopper's ankle using the same tool. During these procedures the commando kept turning his head and chatting to his colleagues as he worked. The conversation clearly involved some amusing stories for it involved a great deal of raucous laughter and at one point the commando laughed so heartily that he had to remove one hand from the juddering high-speed saw to wipe the tears from his eyes. Judging by their expressions, neither Bert nor Chopper seemed to find the removal operation to be a particularly relaxing experience.

Later that day the police launch arrived and the prisoners limped down to the jetty under an armed escort. As the prisoners boarded the launch the river officer in charge stood on the deck by the rail and talked to Captain Colarinho about Sam's disappearance.

'I just don't see how we could have missed him,' said the boat officer. 'We didn't even see an empty boat so he can't have escaped on foot – though if he had we'd never find him in this lot.' He gestured to the luxuriant jungle surrounding them. He gazed into the dark waters below him and as he looked, there was a slow swirl on the surface as though something large was moving in the depths. He looked up again at the forest.

'A fellow could be neatly tucked away in some dark hidey-hole just a few feet away from you in this place,' he mused, 'and you'd never know it.'

20

Sad Farewells

That night Richard and Lucy and the company pilot were the only ones remaining in the camp. In the evening, while the pilot and Richard prepared supper, Lucy walked out to talk to the jaguars who had now fully recovered from their anaesthesia. She called Queenie, who appeared within a few minutes with Sophie and Clio, and explained about the extraction of the drainage tubes to the monkeys and the convalescent cats. She then pointed to the moon.

'See how the Great Silver One that lights the night now grows larger once again. When she is restored to her full size you must all return to this place. If the grey straws have fallen from the sides of the junglefangs there is nothing more to be done; if they remain –' She turned to Queenie. *'– you must pull them out. They will come easily.'* She then turned to the cats.

'When the arborikin removes these straws from your side you may feel a little pain but it will soon pass. It will be less than the sting of a buzzithorn. You must not hurt the arborikin, for she performs a great service for us all.'

She then explained that she would be leaving in the morning but would see them once more before she left.

She returned to the main camp and sat down to a supper of baked beans and sausages – the latter a rare treat, brought by the pilot in his cool box. Over the meal Richard told her that José had decided to close down the camp at Cayman Creek as part of the company's new policy of developing only renewable timber resources. As soon as possible all traces of the development would be removed and the jungle allowed to reclaim the site.

José had also asked Richard to become chief scientific adviser to the company, which would not only mean an increase in salary but would allow him to develop his research into bananas and other trees producing food and new medicines. The company initials would still be ETC – it would be expensive and confusing to change them – but they would now stand for the Ecofriendly Trading Company instead of the Ecocidal Timber Company.

Lucy was excited by this news and they talked about the various developments long into the night. Just as they eventually crossed towards their hut, where Lucy, with the help of Sophie and Clio, had earlier arranged beds of new fragrant leaves and fronds, there was a deafening clap of thunder that silenced even the night noises of the jungle. Michelle clung to Lucy's shoulder with all her tiny might. They dashed into the hut just as the rain started and stood at the mesh window watching the breathtaking phenomenon of a tropical thunderstorm. They had both experienced a great deal of rain of course: in the rainforest it usually rained every day, and there had been thunderstorms once or twice a week, but neither of them, even Richard in all his travels, had witnessed anything remotely as spectacular as the storm that now raged around them. Vivid flashes of sheet lightning lit up the whole sky, silhouetting the vast canopy of the jungle, alternating with jagged bolts of forked lightning, some so near that Lucy hugged closer to her father and Michelle's paws felt like a miniature vice clamped on to her shoulder. Then rain such as she had never seen before came down in what looked like continuous silver rods as thick as her fingers, pounding on the roof of the hut with such a drumming noise as to make speech impossible. Lucy hoped all the animals would be all right, then remembered that they had spent their entire lives experiencing such storms at regular intervals; storms that were an integral feature of the world they had evolved in. Eventually the storm passed and Lucy and Richard returned from the window to their nests of leaves, grateful that they had been under cover and not out in the open during the downpour.

In the morning the sun rose into a brilliantly clear sky and the camp looked clean and fresh as Richard and Lucy walked to the mess tent to meet the pilot for breakfast. The stranded drugs plane had been struck by lightning and was a smouldering wreck.

'It's as if nature has called an end to this wicked place,' said Lucy, 'and knows that today marks the start of a new era for the precious plants and creatures who live here.'

After breakfast the pilot went to the plane to prepare for their flight and Lucy excused herself for a few moments. There were tears in her eyes and Richard guessed she was going to say farewell to the animals that had become so much more to her than just willing and loyal servants.

'Just a minute, Lucy, I've something for you.' He put his hand in his pocket and pulled out a little case. Lucy opened it and inside were a pair of spectacles with bright green frames. She put them on.

'Well, Dad,' she said in a slightly embarrassed tone, 'they're an . . .' she paused imperceptibly '. . . unusual colour, but to be quite honest they're a bit small for me and they're a bit blurred.'

Richard grinned: 'Of course they're small because they're not for you, and they look blurred because those aren't lenses – they're clear plastic.'

Light dawned on Lucy.

'You must have asked José!' she exclaimed. 'Your "boys' talk". And I suppose the vets brought them yesterday!' Richard nodded, as she rushed over and hugged him. 'You're really cool,' she said happily, 'and the greatest dad anyone ever had.'

She hurried off to the edge of the forest with Katy and Michelle. All the animals congregated around her and, looking across at the gathering, Richard prayed that Tom, the pilot, would remain engrossed in his plane for the next few moments; he wasn't sure how he would begin to explain away the extraordinary scene should the pilot ask him. As he watched, his daughter hugged all the animals in turn and then, though he heard nothing, he knew she was speaking to them:

'Thank you for all you have done. I can now tell you that this

evil place will be destroyed and once again belong to you and all your kin. I also promise that one day, when I am a woman, I will return here and tell you of the changes I will then be making to benefit all animals in the world. Most of you who stand here today will not see me then, for the Great Silver One must wax and wane countless times before I return, but you can assure your young and their young that I will come.'

She beckoned to Queenie. *'You, O Queen, have been particularly helpful to me and I will always cherish the memories of our times together. Here is something that will remind you of our adventures and our quest.'* She handed the spectacle case to Queenie, who opened it and took out the glasses with an expression of delight and surprise on her face. She put them on and gave the case to Sophie who started opening and shutting it repeatedly. Clio tried to help but got her fingers trapped – not seriously – and she contented herself with removing the little yellow cleaning cloth from the

'. . . through these eyes it looks as it does on the clearest day.'

case and putting it on top of her head, making Lucy laugh through her tears.

'When I looked through the second eyes of the Promised One,' said Queenie, 'the world looked as though it were covered by the gossamer the arachnopods weave, but through these eyes it looks as it does on the clearest day. It cannot be right that I should have better second eyes than She Who Speaks.' She tried to hand the glasses back to Lucy who stopped her and smiled kindly at her.

'There are many second eyes made by the Tailless Ones and through them the world appears in many different ways. These eyes are specially for you and I hope they will give you pleasure and even greater status among your kin.'

She then turned to the assembled group and gave Michelle, Katy and Melanie final cuddles.

'And now I must bid thee farewell, for I return to my own kin in Albion, far across the Great Salt. I will never forget you all and what you have done for me.' Tears streaming down her face, she turned and went to join Richard. He put his arm round her and hugged her but said nothing. They gathered their few things and walked to the plane where Tom was starting up the engine.

Soon they were in the air and Lucy got butterflies in her stomach as the little plane lurched from side to side, buffeted by the tropical air currents as it climbed. She watched the campsite shrink to a tiny spot as they ascended higher and higher. Once again she was confronted with the breathtaking enormity of the rainforest stretching unbroken to the horizon on every side. This time, however, she was able to share her sense of wonder with her father and together they watched the unfolding panorama as the plane banked to pick up the Amazon tributary winding like a silver ribbon through the trees, the marker that they would follow as it joined successive tributaries on its way to the great river itself.

'You really did form a very special relationship with those animals, didn't you?' said Richard.

'Much closer than I ever thought possible,' she replied. 'They're so refreshingly *uncomplicated*. They know that life is hard and unfair and dangerous; they know that medium animals eat little animals, and big animals eat medium animals. They accept the reality of life as it is and I suppose that's why they're so relaxing to be with. You know that they say what they mean, and mean what they say, and that they'll never betray you. They're *so* much nicer than most people.'

Richard felt as though he were listening to an adult, so fluent and accurate was her language; then he remembered that she had always been good at language. She had learnt to speak fluently at a very early age and her vocabulary at three had already been that of a school-aged child. Perhaps . . . Richard started to explore in his mind the same ideas that Lucy's grandpa had been through a few weeks earlier. For the very first time he began to realize that Lucy must *always* have been destined for this role and that her language skills must always have been related to some special pathways in her brain that were one day going to enable her to communicate with animals. She was, in effect, a super-communicator.

It now dawned on him that the Promised One was always much more likely to have been a female than a male. He remembered a scientific article he had read just before leaving London for Rio. It had described the different types of human brain: type E for empathizing, type S for systematizing and type B for balanced. Most men were type S, leading them to understand systems and try to build them. Most women were type E which enabled them to perceive what another person was thinking and react to it appropriately. Lucy was an outstanding example of a type E brain. Richard thought that there should now be a new category, UE, or ultra-E, for those who could relate to animals as well as humans. At the moment Lucy was the only UE in the world.

Richard pulled himself back from his daydream to their conversation.

'I was amused by the vets,' he said. 'They just couldn't believe how good you were with the animals. They said that with you just standing there the jaguars seemed to know in advance what they wanted them to do and one of them even held out his foreleg to receive the anaesthetic injection. All I could do was to say, rather lamely, that you had always liked animals. Anyway, they said that their operations had gone very well and that you knew what to do about their aftercare. Something about some tubes being removed.' He suddenly stopped and frowned. 'Hang on a minute – you didn't know before they left that the camp was going to be closed down and that nobody would be there after today? I only found that out from José the same afternoon. What's going to happen to the animals?'

'Relax, Dad,' said Lucy smiling. 'You don't think I'd leave them stranded, do you? It's all arranged. Queenie's going to pull their tubes out at the end of next week. She knows to do it when the moon is full, which conveniently happens to be in nine days' time.'

Richard gaped at her.

'You what!' he exclaimed, 'I mean – you've left some monkeys to perform a veterinary operation?'

'Don't make it into a big drama, Dad. The tubes may fall out on their own and they only need a little tug if they don't. Monkeys are just as dextrous as human beings and, as there aren't going to be any people there next week, they're the obvious ones to do it. Anyway, I think it's good that animals learn to look after each other in some situations. Close your mouth, Dad, you look as if you're going to dribble in a minute.' Richard realized he was staring at her open-mouthed in amazement. He wondered if he was ever going to get used to his daughter in her new decisive and authoritarian role. She really was something special.

Later in the day they began to fly over areas of forest that were already being developed, mainly near the rivers which were the only 'roads' in this part of the jungle. Soon they saw a haze covering the forest which, as they flew on, became so dense that it completely blotted out their view of the canopy.

'What on earth is going on?' said Lucy, peering down at the swirling fog of smoke.

'They're burning the forest to clear it,' said Richard. He then told her all the depressing statistics he had learnt about the destruction of the jungle and the damage that was being done to the earth's atmosphere and climate by uncontrolled deforestation. Lucy's face grew pale with anger as she listened and looked down. She already knew some of the facts from Grandpa's books about the Amazon but seeing the destruction in real life was much worse. They had emerged from one immense bank of smoke but now she could see another coming into view ahead of them.

'One day, I'm going to stop all this,' she said simply. There was a look of frightening determination in her eyes and Richard knew that this was no schoolgirl's idle boast; no pre-teenage fantasy. This was something that she could, and probably would, actually bring about.

'My animals can achieve almost anything,' she continued. 'All they lack is someone to co-ordinate and direct them. They just need — what's that person called who bosses armies about?'

'A general?' said Richard.

'Yes, that's it! A general. And that's what I'm going to be. I'll command the largest army that anyone ever conceived of in their wildest dreams. I can't help it because it's been plonked on me, and I'm going to have to talk to you and the family about what I actually do. And I know I'll have to finish school before I do anything – anything really big, that is.'

Richard suddenly realized that he had been so busy that, until this moment, he had not really had time to think through all the implications of what he now knew about his daughter's power and, in particular, the threat it posed to her safety. He knew that there was nothing that some people would stop at to control Lucy's power by the use of money, promises or threats to herself or her loved ones. Those people included individuals from every walk of life: the greedy, the criminal and the insane; politicians; secret service agents; generals; bankers and captains of industry. And the threat was not confined to individuals: governments; tyrannical regimes; industrial concerns; traders – ranging from the corner shop to great international corporations; in fact any institution which could use Lucy's power to better itself or diminish its opponents would not hesitate to do so once her secret was out.

He turned to Lucy and tried to sound casual.

'How many people have you actually told about your secret, Lucy?'

She looked straight at him.

'Don't worry, Dad, I can guess what you're thinking about. I've told very few. There's you, Clare, Mum, Grandma and Grandpa, and Helen and Julian. That's all and that's how it must stay.'

'It's Helen and Julian I'm worried about,' said Richard. 'They seem nice enough but they're not family and when we talked to them I didn't appreciate what I realize now that I've had chance to think about things.'

'Well, I thought about it at the time, Dad, and it was a difficult decision which I had to make quickly on the spot. I don't think there was any way we could have saved ourselves and them, without their knowing my secret. I had a long talk with Helen about it and I'm sure they'll never do anything that would endanger us. We did what was right at the time and all we can do now is to trust them.'

Richard was relieved by what she said, and then remembered something else that had occurred to him when Lucy took over the camp and the airstrip:

'Lucy, those ants and hornets – can you talk to *any* animals or insects?'

Lucy started to answer but stopped abruptly and looked at the pilot. Richard followed her gaze. The pilot had taken his headphones off and was no longer speaking on the radio. Richard, who could see him better than Lucy, saw that he was writing some data in a log book and was not listening to them. As Richard watched he finished what he was doing and replaced his headphones. Lucy relaxed and started talking again. The incident brought home to Richard just how aware Lucy was of the need for secrecy and how alert she was to dangerous or unguarded situations. Richard himself hadn't even noticed the pilot taking his headphones off and realized that he was going to have to be much more careful.

'Anyway, as I was saying,' Lucy continued, 'I'm most comfortable with mammals – much more so than with reptiles or birds, but even with them I can easily hold a two-way conversation. Insects, spiders and worms are different. I get nothing back from them at all and they are very unpredictable: sometimes they respond and sometimes they don't even seem to notice me. I've noticed, though, that insects that live in colonies like bees and ants – I think they're called social insects, aren't they?' Richard nodded. 'Well, they respond to my commands much better than individual insects. Grandpa thinks that it's something to do with their brains being geared up to responding to group orders.'

'What about even tinier creatures?' asked Richard. He couldn't bring himself to say straight out what he was thinking; the implications were too great.

'I know what you're getting round to Dad, don't be shy! What you really want to know is whether I can control bacteria and viruses, isn't it?'

'Well – yes,' said Richard, smiling.

'The short answer is no. They seem to be just too primitive and Grandpa says bacteria are more like plants than animals. In a way I'm relieved, because otherwise I couldn't justify not spending the rest of my entire life in hospitals, curing people of their infections.'

Richard was relieved at what he had learnt. The thought of her being able to cure infections and yet being unable to help more than a fraction of the millions of patients who could benefit from her powers, even if she worked twenty-four hours a day, was too frightening to contemplate.

21

A Flutter on the Stock Exchange

Richard was exhausted by the emotional and physical stress of the past weeks and the past few days in particular. At last he felt able to relax, and against the background of the soothing drone of the plane's engine he quickly fell asleep. As he drifted off, his mind was full of his discussions with Lucy and soon he was lost in one of the most vivid dreams he had ever experienced.

Five years had elapsed and he was sitting in the lounge of their home in London. The room looked somehow different and it took him no longer than the average man – several minutes – to realize that it was because there was new wallpaper, a new carpet and new chair covers. It was late in the evening and he was waiting for Lucy. Clare was away on a gap-year trip after finishing at university and, as it was the school holidays, Joanna had taken Sarah and cousins Ben, Henry and Christopher to stay with her parents down at the coast.

He heard the front door slam and Lucy came in. She was now tall and her beautiful hair had been cropped very short. She came into the lounge and flopped down on to the sofa. She had been getting increasingly angry and frustrated over the failure of the government to honour the commitments it had made at successive international conferences, starting with the Kyoto Conference, to reduce national emissions of carbon dioxide and a variety of toxic pollutants.

'Are you going up to London tomorrow, Dad?' said Lucy.

'No, I'm staying at home to finish a scientific paper I'm writing,' said Richard.

'Good,' she said, 'because there's going to be chaos.'

'What do you mean?' asked Richard.

'Well, you know that one of the things I've been doing to help the animals is to minimize climatic change?'

'Of course,' said Richard.

'I issued an anonymous ultimatum to the government a month ago. If they didn't take some definite action by today I was going to show them the kind of things that might happen. They haven't done anything, so tomorrow I'm going to use the animals to close down the Stock Exchange.' She briefly explained what she was going to do and how easy it would be.

'But —' Richard didn't know where to begin '— how could any government respond to an anonymous threat? It could be just anyone trying to stir them up.'

'I gave them a code,' said Lucy, 'so though they don't know who I am they'll know when I give them the identical code tomorrow that it's the same person who spoke to them a month ago.' Richard thought for a moment. The Stock Exchange was one of the world's leading financial centres. To close it unexpectedly would cause unthinkable confusion and financial instability.

'You just can't do this!' said Richard. 'It will cause financial ruin for millions and damage the City's reputation, the government and the country.'

'Just watch me!' said Lucy. She seemed colder and harder than the sweet girl he used to know.

'But you'd be breaking all the rules of civilized behaviour,' protested Richard. 'It's a kind of anarchy and many innocent people will suffer from your actions.'

'Sometimes breaking the rules is the only way to achieve anything,' said Lucy. 'Do you call it civilized behaviour to destroy the atmosphere? If there's to be any planet left for our children and grandchildren and all the animals, then somebody has *got* to do something drastic. As for suffering – a few people always have to suffer for the benefit of the majority.'

'But it's *you* who is deciding what is best for everyone, without anyone else having had the chance to discuss it with you. That's what all the world's most ruthless dictators did – think of Hitler, Stalin, Chairman Mao, Pol Pot and all the rest.'

'Ah, but what they wanted was wrong and what I want is right,' said Lucy.

'But that's what they all thought,' said Richard, 'and they all thought that the end justified the means – that what they wanted was so important it didn't matter how they achieved it.'

'Dad, you're just a boring old git. This talk about

discussion makes me see red. People have been *discussing* global warming, ocean pollution, destruction of the rainforest and species extinction for years and years and look what's happened – just about nothing. Talking never achieved anything. The world is in a desperate situation and desperate remedies are required. Your stupid, selfish, greedy generation got us all into this mess and I'm going to get us out of it!'

'But . . .' Richard felt desperately worried and sad. 'You'll bring the City of London to its knees,' he said, 'which won't benefit anyone. Commerce will grind to a halt throughout the country.'

'Not just this country,' said Lucy grimly as she went to the door. 'The world! Through the animanet I'm going to do the same to the Stock Exchange in New York later today and Tokyo tomorrow. Good night.'

She shut the door behind her, leaving Richard struggling to cope with what he had just heard and wondering what he should do. Should he warn the authorities? He couldn't do it effectively without saying who he was, which was unthinkable – Lucy's secret power must remain secret. An anonymous call would probably have no effect whatsoever – they probably got dozens of crank calls every week. He comforted himself with the thought that Lucy was just winding him up, as did all teenagers with their parents, and that he was playing into her hands by over-reacting.

When Richard woke the next morning he was surprised to see how late it was. Joanna usually got up first, and with her being away he had overslept. He got up and went downstairs, made some coffee and sat down to read the paper. Lucy's bedroom door was shut and he presumed she was still in bed – so much for changing the world, he thought.

The scene changed and he found himself in the City of London as the invisible observer of an unfolding drama. He could see Lucy standing on the pavement of a busy street. Across the road was the entrance to the London Stock Exchange. She had dark sunglasses on and was carrying a map of London. She looked just like a tourist gazing at one of the world centres of finance. She was very attractive and received more than a few second glances from the throng of men hurrying to their city offices.

Suddenly a group of large dogs appeared – rottweilers, alsatians and bull-mastiffs. They went to a nearby pedestrian crossing and each sat on the pavement behind an unsuspecting pedestrian waiting to cross, as though accompanying a master or mistress. The traffic stopped and the dogs trotted on to the crossing with their temporary owners. The pedestrians continued on their way to the opposite pavement but the dogs remained on the crossing. Traffic started to build up in both directions and cars started hooting. A policeman moved towards the crossing but hastily retreated from the row of snarling jaws that confronted him. Most of the dogs now lay down on the crossing, those at each end of the pavement facing outwards towards the pavement to attack any pedestrians bold enough to confront them. A few dogs left the main group and began to patrol between the stationary cars in

both directions. One or two drivers who had begun to open their car doors hurriedly thought better of it after seeing one man lose an entire trouser leg and just manage to get back into his car before losing his actual leg. More dogs appeared from side streets and joined the patrols. They did not attack those who remained on the pavement or in their cars, but were aggressive if anyone came towards them or tried to leave their vehicle. Within ten minutes the whole area was paralysed. No vehicle could move on any street. A helicopter was spotted in the distance, but as immense flocks of pigeons had appeared from nowhere to wheel in great circles above the City, the pilot could not approach any nearer for fear of the birds damaging the rotor blades.

Two of the largest rottweilers now detached themselves

from the group and sauntered to the Stock Exchange. The large crowd that had by now gathered on the pavement to watch the curious spectacle melted away from the dogs like the Red Sea parting for Moses. The animals went to the sliding doors and as they opened, the dogs sat one against each door to keep them open, snarling savagely at the commissionaire who hurriedly retreated into his office. Soon, in the distance, it appeared as though a swirl of black fog was unseasonally enveloping the City on a summer morning, but as the dark cloud drew nearer a humming noise filled the air and countless swarms of bees and wasps came into view, flying just above the queues of stationary vehicles. Nearer to the Stock Exchange their buzzing sounded like a hundred electric motors run wild and the crowds fell to the ground, covering their heads and faces with jackets and cardigans. They needn't have worried, for the insects had not the slightest interest in curious crowds and casual passers-by. They zoomed like a black funnel into the open doors of the Stock Exchange and entered the old trading floor and every other open room in the building. A moment later they were followed by large flocks of jackdaws and magpies.

At the same time another flight of very large birds appeared in the sky from the north-west. It looked as though they had come from the aviary at London Zoo as well as the surrounding countryside, for there were not only buzzards but numerous large vultures and even two golden eagles, each carrying a small monkey.

The flying party swooped low in the street, passing close to the attractive young tourist who was still standing on the pavement, apparently fascinated by what was going on. Then, as if controlled by a radio signal, the strange flock abruptly changed direction and flew to the roof of the Exchange which was covered in communication aerials, transmitting rods and satellite dishes. There they settled and immediately started wreaking havoc on the complex assortment of communication devices. Savage beaks, curved talons, teeth and eager paws ripped and tore at cables and connections, twisted and dislodged satellite dishes and uprooted aerials.

The scene changed again, so that Richard now found himself in the corridors and offices of the Exchange, where there was complete chaos. Nobody could escape from the multitude of insects that had now formed into hundreds of smaller groups that buzzed around the heads of all that could not find immediate refuge in the offices, lifts or toilets. Those who had already managed to reach their offices slammed doors behind them in relief but then gazed in dismay at the scenes before them. Rats and mice had been hard at work during the hours of darkness and all computer, fax and phone cables had been bitten through, their severed ends hanging limply from every desk and terminal. Every key left in a door, cupboard door or filing cabinet had been removed during the night by squirrels, led into the building by rats who had guided them through their regular runs from the sewers into the catering section and from there throughout the Exchange.

Even as the bewildered office workers watched, hosts of jackdaws and magpies swept through every room collecting any loose keys, keyrings and security devices that had been inaccessible to the squirrels, pecking savagely at anyone foolhardy enough to try to stop them. Many people ran to the windows to see the reason for the loud and incessant hooting from the street and were astonished by the sight below. Even while they watched, a party of police dog-handlers with rifles – presumably for firing tranquillizing darts – pushed their way through the crowds in Old Broad Street towards the pack guarding the crossing.

As they did so a flock of falcons stooped down from the sky like divebombers, and descended on the handlers, landing on their heads and shoulders and starting to attack their faces with hooked beaks and sharp talons. The onslaught was so sudden and furious that the police split up and fled for cover, dropping their rifles to leave their hands free to protect their faces and to try to beat off the attacking hawks.

Waitresses from a local pub were now passing among the crowds with large trays selling hot steak and kidney pies, sushi, pork scratchings and coffee. To the astonishment and amusement of those watching from the pavement they were allowed by the dogs to approach the cars to sell food and drink to the stranded drivers, but no one else could step on to the road without being attacked.

The scene changed back to the inside of the exchange, where the experience of Ronald Stiltskin, the security officer on the third floor, was typical of many throughout the building.

Since the tragic terrorist events of recent years an order had been issued to the effect that an Incident Cupboard was to be installed on every floor. As the wasps zoomed up the corridor, Stiltskin dashed to the cupboard in his section with his jacket over his head. He knew that the equipment in there included protective clothing for use in case of accidents or incidents involving radiation, toxic chemicals and biological hazards. If this wasn't a biological hazard he couldn't imagine what was and wrenched the door open just in time to see a long grey tail disappear into a large hole gnawed through the back of the chipboard cupboard.

In the cupboard were three face masks, three protective suits, three emergency axes, three plastic bottles of water and a wind-up portable radio. Two of the face masks were full to the brim with fresh rat droppings, while in the third a mouse was putting the finishing touches to a nest; she fled as Ronald peered in. The nest was made from shreds of the *Financial Times* and *Investment Weekly*, their edges neatly serrated by little teeth, and Ronald could just make out a fragment of an advertisement box saying: 'Cut this out and start your own little nest egg.'

He seized one of the protective suits but dropped it when he saw that the arms and legs had been chewed off; the others were similarly damaged, though curiously there were no fragments from the suits anywhere to be seen. The axeheads had been gnawed off their shafts, and the entire cupboard floor and its contents were soaked from the water that had seeped from the holes chewed in the plastic bottles.

Stiltskin grabbed the wind-up radio and ran for safety to the nearest lift. As the door opened he flung off his wasp-covered jacket and got in, clawing off the wasps that had got in through the gap in his jacket and were starting to sting his nose and lips. He breathed a sigh of relief as the doors closed but his deliverance was short-lived. Suddenly all the lights went out, plunging the inside of the lifts into inky blackness, and any moving lifts stopped, most of them between floors. It was as though a switch had been thrown – which was, as it happens, just what had occurred: one of the monkeys, having devastated the communications on the roof, was now in the fuse room shutting off the row of heavy-duty switches that covered an entire wall. The bewildered officer wound up the radio in the dark and switched it on.

' . . . .*and if you have just joined us,*' the commentator was saying, '*we are still reporting on one of the most bizarre events ever to have taken place in the long history of the City. Traffic is at a standstill and unconfirmed reports say that this is due to a pack of dogs blocking Old Broad Street; a pack fiercely resisting all attempts to interfere with them. It is impossible to reach the scene by road and our roving helicopter cannot approach because, by an extraordinary coincidence, large flocks of pigeons are wheeling over the area in behaviour patterns that our ornithological experts are at a loss to explain. It is, in fact, only by the greatest good fortune that we are able to bring you this report at all – one of our reporters just happened to be researching new material in the Insider Dealers' Arms, a public house not far from the scene. As I speak we are receiving even more serious and perplexing news. Reports are coming in that the Stock Exchange is in chaos. Garbled messages from mobile phones are the only source of our information so far, as we are currently unable to contact any Stock Exchange officials using our regular channels of communication. Whatever turns out to be the true explanation of what is happening, one thing is certain: the pound is plunging on world markets and millions of pounds are being wiped off shares as I speak. This is nothing short of a disaster and, when the truth comes out, I'm afraid some very senior heads are going to roll.'*

Meanwhile, in offices throughout the building, there were gurgling noises from the washbasins and sinks at coffee points as dirty waste water welled back up through plugholes, filled basins to the brim and began to spill over on to the floor. Those who had taken refuge in the toilets found themselves having to cope with problems that were similar in nature but considerably more unsavoury in detail. The instructions to the rats and squirrels had been very specific and they had carried them out painstakingly during their busy night. The hundreds of fragments of material they had chewed off the protective suits throughout the Exchange had been taken to the sewers and stuffed back into every waste outlet leading from the building.

Outside, the traffic remained solid and stagnant. In quintessential British fashion somebody had now brought a bowl of water to the dogs on the crossing and they were taking it in turns to lap it up gratefully, never leaving the crossing unattended. Incredibly, someone was already selling T-shirts saying:

They went to see Paws in the Traffic and all I got was this lousy T-shirt.

And now, once again, Richard saw Lucy in the vast throng. She finished eating a packed lunch, put the wrappings in her rucksack, replaced her sunglasses with a pair of ordinary spectacles and began to make her way through the crowd. As she did so the dogs on the crossing and among the cars melted away into the crowd and the skies cleared as the pigeons circling above disappeared into the west. The traffic slowly began to move again just as, in the distance, a detachment of troops could be seen clearing the crowd from one side of the street and making their way with an armoured troop carrier along the pavement. What they would have done – or, more probably, failed to do – was never put to the test for at that moment the bees, wasps and birds began to stream out of the building. Their numbers were so great that it took several minutes for them to leave but eventually the last intruder left and it was clear that the crisis was over.

It was the afternoon of the same day and the director of the Exchange, Graeme Midasman, had been invited by the manager of the bank nearest to the Stock Exchange to use a suite of his offices as a temporary headquarters while the Exchange was restored to some semblance of normality. He sat at his desk in front of a half-open window through which he could hear the noise of the dispersing crowds. He was a ruthless and ambitious man who was universally unpopular with his staff, and he was now reading the reports on what had taken place to see if he could plant the entire blame for what had happened on one of his section chiefs.

The phone rang on his desk: it was his secretary in the adjoining office:

'A call from Whitehall, sir. Shall I put it through?'

'It's not the Chancellor yet again, is it?' The Chancellor of the Exchequer had rung three times in the past hour.

'No sir, it's the Prime Minister.'

'For heaven's sake – put him through straight away!'

'Graeme?' It was the unmistakable voice of the PM and he did not sound like a happy bunny. 'What the hell's going on? Every time there's a financial crisis I get some cock-and-bull story from the Chancellor but this one is really way out – he's blaming it on an invasion of your place by a bunch of animals.'

'For once he's telling you the truth, sir,' said the director. 'You've heard of bear markets and bull markets? Well, today has been an entire zoo market. We've had wasps, bees, dogs, birds, monkeys – I've never seen anything like it.'

'The pound's dropping like a stone,' said the PM tersely, 'and my five-year plan is disintegrating by the minute. When are you going to be back in action?'

'Well, every computer and phone in the building has got to be reconnected and the IT people can't give me a firm prediction as to how long that's going to take. The entire place needs cleaning up, of course, and recarpeting – you've never seen so many bird droppings in your life. Then there's the plumbing. Our maintenance engineers say that every waste pipe is blocked right down to the sewers – we've ordered in some portable loos but the plumbers say it could be several days before it's fixed.'

'Plumbers!' exclaimed the PM. He sighed in resignation. He was a practical man and a householder; he now knew for certain they were dealing in weeks. 'What about the staff?' he asked. 'I understand none of the dealers was seriously hurt.' There was an unmistakable note of disappointment in his voice.

'That's right, sir,' said Midasman. 'Lots of stings of course, a couple of rat bites and three jackdaw pecks. One person is in hospital with a broken jaw. He swiped at a wasp and hit Big Bert the odd-job man on the nose by mistake. What I can't understand is what drove all these animals to do it. It's as though they were working to a plan.'

'Do you think it was terrorists?' said the PM.

'What, dressed up as animals? No, the dogs looked real and the birds and wasps and bees were so tiny that nobody would have . . .'

'No, you fool!' the PM interrupted. His voice had taken on a distinctly truculent tone. 'I don't mean dressed up as animals. I mean were terrorists behind it? Did they mastermind it? Have they been training animals in special camps?'

'Well – I've no idea. How would we know?' The director was not particularly bright but he had a distinct feeling that the conversation was not going particularly well.

'What have you done with the animals you captured?' asked the PM testily.

'Captured . . . er, I'm not sure we captured any. In fact, I know we didn't. They all just suddenly disappeared as if on a pre-arranged signal.' He felt that it was time to restore his credibility with a shrewd comment and, clearing his throat, continued: 'Er . . . with respect, sir, what difference would it have made if we had captured some animals? It's not as if we could interrogate them, is it?'

By a superhuman effort the PM just managed to control himself; he spoke through gritted teeth. 'No,' he said very slowly, as if talking to a young child. 'Curiously enough I didn't actually have interrogation in mind. In my simple way I was thinking more about looking for possible identification marks, implanting electronic chips in the dogs and then releasing them so they could be tailed back to their source, and various other methods that didn't involve engaging the animals in actual conversation.'

'Oh, that's really clever. I'd never have thought of that myself,' said the director.

'Really?' said the PM. 'Perhaps that's why I'm a Prime Minister and you're just somebody looking for a new job.'

'But I'm not looking for . . .'

There was a click and the line went dead.

The scene faded and Richard found himself back at home. He sat watching the television as shaky shots of the day's scenes outside the Stock Exchange telexed by tourists on their camcorders were displayed. He was just going to get up and make a cup of tea when a newsflash came up.

'*And now we interrupt our programme on London to go over to New York where the Stock Exchange is experiencing scenes astonishingly similar to those we have just been reporting in London. A large number of skunks have entered the building which was occupied by a swarm of killer bees a few minutes earlier. We are now going over to our New York correspondent, Magnus Appleton, to hear more details. After his report we shall be interviewing Professor Wildersage, an expert on abnormal animal behaviour, to see if there is any possible explanation for this bizarre animal behaviour across two continents . . .'*

Richard stared in stupefaction as the scenes from New York, uncannily reminiscent of those he had just witnessed in London, flashed across the scene. The only difference he could see was that many of the New Yorkers crowding the Wall Street pavements had face masks on, presumably in case the animals were infected.

Just then Lucy walked in.

'Hi, Dad!' she said, looking at the television. 'Oh great! I was never sure about whether they'd understand my animanet instructions but they certainly seem to be doing the business in New York – in fact it's going so well I think I'll do the Ministry of Defence and the Pentagon later in the week. Then I'll pick off all the Ministries one by one and see if they learn from each other how to cope. They won't, of course, 'cos I'll do something different each time. Then, the big one!'

'The big one?' said Richard. His throat was so dry that his voice came out in a croak.

'Parliament of course,' said Lucy. 'Can't you just imagine it – live on TV? I'll get some of those boring old farts moving quicker than they've done for years. It'll be the circus to end all circuses. They'll be the laughing stock of the world. And think of the headlines the next day: "THE NOAHS HAVE IT AS WHIPS FAIL TO CONTROL PARTY ANIMALS." I can't wait. And then, of course, they'll do anything I say, *anything*!'

'Lucy, we need to talk,' Richard said. He stood up to face her, his knees trembling.

'Just a minute, Dad. I must have a drink.' She disappeared into the kitchen.

Richard sat down again. His skin was cold and his heart was pounding. The situation was nothing short of catastrophic.

'Dad! Dad!' Lucy was calling him from the kitchen. 'Dad! Dad!' Her voice sounded nearer. 'Dad, wake up! The pilot says we're flying into a storm and it's best if you're awake.'

Richard suddenly realized where he was and was overcome with a feeling of intense relief. It had all been an awful dream!

'Dad, you're as white as a sheet. Are you OK?'

Lucy sounded very concerned. She was the same as ever. Her old sweet expression was back and her hair hadn't been cut off. Everything was all right.

'Yes, I'm fine, love,' said Richard. 'I've just had an incredibly long and realistic dream – a terrible nightmare in fact. It was about you.'

'Well, go on! What did I do? Tell me quickly before you forget.'

Richard felt slightly embarrassed but he recounted the whole story. Lucy listened in silence, grinning once or twice at some of the more outrageous incidents. When he had finished, he apologized for the role he had cast her in.

'Don't worry, Dad. I've had some similar dreams myself. I think that the possibilities created by my power are so mind-blowing that our subconsciousness works on them and they come out as dreams. You can be quite sure I'll never misuse my power and behave like a terrorist or an anarchist. I've thought about this a lot and there are loads of perfectly legal and moral ways of exerting influence. In fact I'd like to discuss them with you when we have a chance and see what you think.'

The little plane was bucking and jolting in the storm but Richard hardly noticed, so relieved was he to hear Lucy's reassuring words.

'By the way,' she continued, 'I like the way you used the animals. You obviously learnt a lot in a couple of days at Cayman Creek. I couldn't have done better myself.' They both laughed and Richard put his arm round her and gave her as good a hug as their seat belts would allow.

The pilot removed his headphones and turned towards them.

'Landing in five minutes,' he said. The little plane was stopping the night in Manaus and they would go on to Macapá the following day. They would spend the following night there with José and his family, and then go on to Rio for a direct flight to London.

22

Home – to More Revelations

British Airways Flight 246 touched down at Heathrow exactly on time at 8.50 a.m and there had never been such a reunion. Lucy and Richard came through customs to find the entire family waiting. Sarah had pushed her way under the barrier and rushed up to fling herself into Richard's arms, and soon everybody was hugging and kissing. Joanna was crying too much to speak at first but eventually managed to say that she had been convinced she was never going to see either of them again. Clare couldn't get over how long Lucy's hair was and how tanned she was, and told her father that his very first job was to cut off his beard. Richard had by now got used to it and was secretly rather proud of its luxuriant growth, but it seemed that Clare's views were shared unanimously by the rest of the family and it was decided that, after a final photograph, it would be ceremoniously removed the next day. Grandma and Grandpa were both in tears and Grandpa hugged Lucy so tight that he knocked her glasses off. They fell to the ground and the lenses fell out. Lucy burst out laughing.

'I just don't believe you, Gramps. In the last ten weeks

those glasses have survived kidnapping, imprisonment, jungles, rivers, swamps, storms, cliffs and a monkey, and you've bust them in ten seconds!'

'What did the monkey do to them?' asked Ben, his interest immediately aroused.

'There was a tame monkey called Queenie at the jungle camp where I was staying and she loved to play with my glasses. Daddy actually bought her a blank pair when we left so she's now the only monkey with glasses in South America!' They all laughed and Joanna then reminded Lucy that she had some spare glasses at home in her bedside cupboard.

'It's a funny feeling,' said Lucy. 'I've been so used to only having what I stand up in that the idea of having anything spare or new seems like an incredible luxury. They gave me a little bag of toiletries on the plane and it seemed like a treasure trove.'

Soon they arrived home and Lucy was overjoyed to be back in her own bedroom with her own things. Tibbles

Grandpa hugged Lucy so tight that he knocked her glasses off.

was incredibly excited to see her and told her that she had received occasional reports to say that she was well and being cared for by the animals. Tibbles seemed uncertain as to what kind of animals had been looking after Lucy, she described them as giant dreykin – squirrels. Lucy was puzzled until she remembered that Tibbles had never seen a monkey and this was how she must have imagined what they looked like from what she had been told. She had also obviously had trouble imagining the armadillos, which she sometimes referred to as giant velvetkin and sometimes as giant shieldkin.

Richard and Lucy were both weary and they went to bed for the rest of the day. In the evening Joanna prepared a special dinner to celebrate the long-awaited family reunion.

After dinner the family listened enthralled as Lucy and Richard told their incredible stories. They talked into the early hours and it was only as they recounted their stories that Lucy and Richard realized just how much there was to tell. Sarah's eyes were as wide as saucers as Lucy described her expedition to look for Richard and she insisted on Lucy describing everything in the utmost detail. She was especially interested in how Lucy had coped with everyday matters.

'What did you drink? How did you brush your teeth? Did you ever comb your hair? How did you cut your nails? Did you cry every day?' – and dozens more questions until Lucy laughed and pleaded for mercy. When Sarah kissed Lucy good night she said:

'It's lovely to have you home again but I really, really wish you could have brought Michelle and Katy with you.'

'Never mind,' Lucy said. 'Maybe one day we can go there together and find a new Michelle and Katy just for you.'

The next day Joanna spoke to Lucy:

'I know that you and Dad have had lots to tell us but you're not the only ones with some interesting news. Guess who came to see us while you were away?' She glanced at Clare as she spoke and Lucy thought she saw a faint blush on Clare's cheeks.

'I've absolutely no idea,' she said, and she hadn't.

'Tell her, Clare,' said her mother.

Clare reddened even more. 'Well, you know that boy who caused your accident? He's called Mark Fossfinder and he lives with his aunt because his parents went missing abroad last year. Anyway, his older brother Clive was away at university when the accident happened, but he was so upset when he heard the details, he got permission to come and see you to apologize on behalf of his brother and to see how you were. He rang up to find out if it was OK to come and was horrified to hear that you'd gone missing. He came anyway to see me and Mum and Sarah, and, guess what? He's doing medicine and I've just got accepted for a place in the same medical school. I'll be in the year below him. He seemed quite nice . . .'

'Correct me if I'm wrong,' her mother interrupted, 'but didn't I hear the words "gorgeous" and "fit" the last time we talked about him?'

' . . . he seemed quite nice,' continued Clare hurriedly, completely ignoring her mother's interjection. 'He said that he felt responsible for his younger brother. They had been very close and Mark had always relied on him. He seemed to go completely off the rails when Clive went off to college – apparently it was the final straw after losing his parents. He got in with a bad crowd and started on drugs and drink. He was actually high on drugs when he ran Lucy down. Clive said his aunt has now given up her flat in the city centre and moved into their parents' house, so his brother has got back to his old friends and his old school. Because of his circumstances the magistrate said he didn't have to be locked up but could do community service instead. Now he's with his old friends he's back to his old self and has made a fresh start. He's very clever, apparently, and is doing really well at school.'

'How exciting,' said Lucy, 'and well done for getting into medical school – fancy not telling me before!'

'Well, we had to hear all your news first; mine could wait – and anyway I've got to get the right grades in my exams or I won't be going at all.'

'I wish I'd been here – I'd love to have met him,' said Lucy, thinking back to what Clare had told her.

'You will. He said he'd like to come again and, if we didn't mind, his brother would like to come too. Of course he doesn't know the good news about your return yet, so I think I ought to call him and let him know.' She blushed again and Lucy had the distinct feeling that the need to call him was not an altogether unwelcome prospect for her sister. She said nothing, but planned to have an interesting conversation later with her mother.

To say that Grandpa was fascinated by Richard's account of the lost crater was something of an understatement. The men talked about little else for several days and as they talked Richard grew more and more uneasy about the thought of telling anyone else about the discovery. They agreed not to say anything until they had seen Helen and Julian.

A week after Richard and Lucy had returned there was a call from Helen and Julian to say they were safely back in England and would love to meet up again.

'Come over to our place at the weekend,' said Richard, 'and bring your kids as well if they're free – it would be nice for the families to get together.'

Saturday was a day of great excitement and preparation for the Bonaventures. Helen and Julian and their family were arriving in the afternoon and staying for dinner in the evening. Grandma and Grandpa were coming back up from the coast for the weekend and everybody was looking forward to meeting the couple who had saved Richard's life and who in turn had themselves been saved by Lucy and Richard.

From lunchtime onwards Sarah waited at the window and at three o'clock she called out. 'They're here, they're here!' Clare and Lucy were upstairs getting ready and Lucy ran into Clare's room which was at the front of the house.

Clare was already at the window. As she looked out she stopped short and put her hand up to her mouth. 'It's not them,' she said with mounting excitement in her voice as two boys got out of the back of the car. 'It's Clive and his brother – they've come without ringing us first.' Lucy joined her sister at the window just as the front-seat occupants got out of the car.

'It *is* them,' she said 'That's Helen and Julian.'

The girls looked at each other completely puzzled; then, as the light suddenly dawned, they raced downstairs, Clare narrowly beating Lucy to the front hall. By the time they got there Sarah had already opened the front door and there stood the Fossfinder family. Helen and Julian smiling at Lucy as she appeared, Clive grinning at Clare, and Mark standing a little behind the others, looking slightly embarrassed.

'We didn't twig until we were almost here,' Clive said to Clare. 'I suddenly realized that we were near to your house and then asked Dad the exact address we were going to. I simply couldn't believe my ears when he told me.'

They had all expected that there would be a lot to talk about that evening but in the light of the revelation that

Helen and Julian were the boys' missing parents they had even more to chew over. Mark had felt a little awkward at first, confronting the girl he had so nearly killed, but Joanna kindly put him at his ease and soon he was chatting away happily with the other youngsters.

After a celebration dinner to remember, the young people disappeared to play the latest games and listen to some new tracks on Clare's computer. The grown-ups sat in the lounge over coffee chatting about the extraordinary events that had changed all their lives and what they might mean for the future.

'Talking about the future,' said Helen, 'there are two things that Julian and I want to say. The first is that we haven't told the boys about Lucy and we won't tell them, or anyone, without your permission – and Lucy's of course.' Richard felt an intense feeling of relief flood over him. His conversations with Lucy had made him even more acutely aware of the dangers Lucy and the family would be in if her secret ever fell into the wrong hands.

'The second,' she continued, 'concerns the crater.'

Richard felt he must interrupt at this point, otherwise he might never have the courage to express his point of view. 'Sorry to break in, Helen,' he said, 'but before you say what I think you are going to say, I want to say something about the crater that I've gradually come to feel more strongly about ever since I left you.'

'Go ahead,' Helen said, with an understanding smile.

'For all three of us, publishing our discovery of what is arguably the greatest find in scientific history would mean instant fame and fortune. Professorships, awards, books, lectures, films and no money worries for the rest of our lives. We have stumbled across every scientist's greatest dream.' He paused.

'Go on,' said Helen.

'Well,' Richard went on, 'this may sound very selfish but it's what I believe and I must tell you even if you disagree.' He stopped and sipped his coffee. 'When I think about how mankind is devastating virtually every part of the natural environment we know about and then think of the crater, existing as it has done for millions of years, I don't think I want to be responsible for its destruction – which is almost certainly what will happen if we tell people about it. I've discovered a new species of banana that, as far as anyone knows, I could have found in any remote spot in the Amazon and I think that will be enough to secure my academic future without my ever needing to mention the crater.' He paused and picked up his coffee cup. 'Well, I've had my say. That's what I think, but I can't speak for you two and, when all's said and done, you discovered the crater before I did.'

'We did,' said Helen, 'and if it weren't for you and Lucy we'd still be there – probably in the shape of sabre-tooth droppings. Julian and I have been thinking about this, just as you have, Richard, and we've come to the same conclusion. Like you, we are certain that if people get to know about the crater, all those special creatures that live in it will be destroyed by disease, poaching, commercial interests, "Pliocene safaris," or simply insatiable scientific curiosity. We've spent all our professional lives examining the fossils of creatures that became extinct because of changes they couldn't cope with and we can't possibly put all the crater animals at risk just so that we can become famous. The place will obviously be discovered by someone else one day, but by then the world may be behaving more sensibly – especially if Lucy is able to carry out her Promise – and at least we won't have been the ones responsible for its destruction.'

For a few moments Richard was speechless. Eventually he broke his silence. 'I've been worrying so much about what to say to you and now I find you've been thinking along exactly the same lines. It's wonderful. But there's one thing that's been bothering me ever since I started thinking this way; that is the fact that, even if you two should feel the same as I do, there is someone else involved – the pilot who came to rescue you. There is so much game in the crater he must have seen it and unless he were incredibly stupid he would have noticed that the animals were special.'

'You're right, of course,' said Helen with a little smile, 'and that's why I made sure he didn't see any animals.'

'How on earth did you do that?' said Richard. 'You can't exactly blindfold a pilot, and he would see things from the air before he even landed.'

'Simple,' she replied. 'I didn't try to stop him seeing anything, I just made sure that there was nothing for him to see.' They all looked mystified.

'You, Richard, will remember being a little impatient

when you were climbing the rope ladder to leave the crater and I called Lucy back for a chat. I told her not to tell you what it was about, because I wasn't certain of your own views at that time.'

Richard nodded. 'I remember, Lucy said it was "girls' talk" – I presumed it was just that.'

'I asked her to tell all the animals to disappear completely into hiding if they ever heard the sound of an aeroplane again and, if one landed, to remain hidden until it had gone away. She immediately understood what I was up to and did just as I asked. The effect in practice was incredible: long before Julian and I had the slightest inkling that a plane was drawing near, the game disappeared as if by magic. The ground sloths had always been my biggest worry because of their enormous size but they moved more quickly than you'd ever believe and hid among the trees. By the time our pathetic human ears heard the plane the crater was already apparently deserted. When the pilot landed and we were chatting he actually expressed surprise at the paucity of animal life. I told him the plane had frightened everything away – which, in a way, was true.'

Richard shook his head slowly from side to side in admiration and whistled softly.

'What a woman! When it comes to forward planning you run rings round us feeble males.' He looked at Julian who chuckled and said:

'Yes, by the time we were rescued she had already convinced me that it would be disastrous for the flora and fauna of that special place if we ever revealed our finds to other scientists and the public. And just as you can still publish about your bananas I think we can still benefit from our stay in the crater even if we keep it a secret. Having been there has given us a new insight into prehistory and we've already started on a major review article – it's called "The Pliocene revisited: fresh thoughts on old bones." Nobody who reads it will ever guess that we've *actually* revisited the Pliocene but they certainly won't be able to prove that anything we say is incorrect!'

The three sisters came downstairs to collect stocks of snacks and drink to take back upstairs. The lounge door was open and the adults saw them go past, chattering and giggling. When the girls had gone Helen looked across at Julian. 'And now,' she said, 'I think it's time to tell them the really big news, don't you, darling?'

'OK,' replied Julian. 'I'm glad you're all sitting down, because you're not going to believe this.'

'After what we've heard in the last few weeks we'd believe anything,' said Grandma. 'Just try us!'

'Well,' said Julian, 'as you all now know, our lives in the valley were transformed after Lucy left because we had the sabre-tooths and the ground sloths to protect us. Three days after you left we made an expedition right across the valley to the precipice separating us from the other valley in the crater. Even though we started to set off on foot, a sabre-tooth came and lay in front of Helen. Its intention to give her a ride was unmistakable and it would have seemed unkind to refuse, so she got her prehistoric cat ride after all. In the event it was just as well because the journey was difficult in several places and I think we'd have had to turn back much earlier than we did if she'd been on foot.' He broke off his story for a few moments and drew a map on

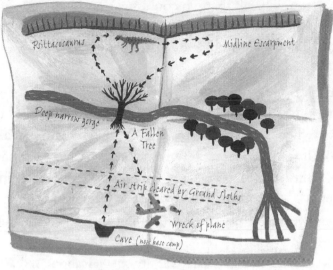

He drew a map on a paper napkin.

a paper napkin so that Joanna and her parents would understand what he was describing.

'We found that the sabre-tooths could cross the main river here,' he pointed to the map, 'where it runs through a deep narrow gully and where a massive tree has fallen across the gap – it must have fallen years ago, because the trunk is now worn bare by the feet of all the animals that have crossed it. It's too high above the river for the caymans to pose any threat.' He paused to take a long draught of the beer Richard had set in front of him, then continued. 'We had started very early and reached the cliff about midday. It was even more impressive close to than we could possibly imagine, having only once briefly seen it from the air. The wall was a sheer rock face and it ran the entire length of the crater, as we had always suspected, and without any break that we could see.'

'So the two valleys really are completely separate!' interrupted Richard. He was sitting forward on his chair listening intently.

'Exactly,' Julian nodded. 'Anyway, we started to walk along the foot of the escarpment and we'd gone only a few yards when we came across a lizard-like creature with a beak. It was lying on the ground – a perfect specimen. We'd only seen reconstructed fragments before but neither of us was in any doubt as to what it was, even though, so far as we knew, no traces of it had ever been found in South America.'

'What was it and what was so special about it?' asked

'It was lying on the ground – a perfect specimen . . .'

Joanna. 'I mean, apart from being in such good condition.'

'It was a dinosaur,' said Julian, 'a psittacosaurus or its South American equivalent, a species that dates from the Cretaceous period.'

'Phew!' said Richard, 'and to find a perfect specimen just lying on the surface! Presumably it had been exposed by a recent rock fall or something. That find alone is enough for your academic credentials – and you could have found it anywhere. You don't need to say anything about the crater.'

Julian looked at Helen and they both smiled.

'You don't quite understand what I'm saying, Richard,' he said. 'This wasn't a fossil. It was *alive* – just. It was bleeding from its beak and it died a few minutes after we found it. We think it had fallen from the top of the cliff. It had presumably clambered up the other side which, for all we know, is less steep than our side.'

'But that means . . .' Richard began; he looked very excited.

'Yes,' said Julian, 'the other valley was isolated even earlier than the one we now think of as "ours". This tiny dinosaur may just be a one-off survival freak but it probably indicates . . .' His voice trailed off. He didn't need to elaborate. His audience were all ahead of him. There was a stunned silence, broken eventually by Grandpa.

'Did you find anything else?'

'No, we spent the next couple of hours searching unsuccessfully for other finds along the base of the cliff and collecting rock fragments. As we returned to pick up our precious specimen we were just in time to see a large, vulture-like bird flying off with it. That, of course, is why

353

we didn't find anything else; it was obviously a favourite spot for scavengers and we were fortunate to have arrived just after the psittacosaurus had fallen. We couldn't stay any longer because we were keen to get back before nightfall and it was a very long way – even with the help of the big cats. We were only a short distance from the cave on our side of the valley when the sabre-tooths suddenly left us and we saw the ground sloths heading for the forest. At first we wondered what on earth was happening, then we heard the drone of the rescue plane and got back to the cleared strip just as it was landing. We never had another opportunity to go back, so it remains a tantalizing mystery.'

'We've got to go back!' said Richard, glancing apologetically at his wife.

'Tell me something I wasn't expecting,' she said with a resigned smile.

'But we need Lucy . . .' Helen started, then looked at Joanna and Richard. 'Sorry, what I mean is, it would be great if Lucy could come.'

Richard looked at Joanna. 'I've got to spend some time in Brazil every year with the new job, as you know. Why don't we arrange a family holiday during the summer holidays so Lucy doesn't miss any school? We can all visit the Pantanal – a fantastic nature reserve – and then anyone who wants can come with me and Lucy and Helen and Julian to the new valley for a short expedition – say, a week. Anyone who doesn't can stay with José and his family, who I'm sure won't mind, and see all the sights around the mouth of the Amazon.'

'Well, I know this is going to happen whatever I say,' said Joanna, 'and as long as Lucy wants to go and doesn't miss any school I don't have a problem with it. I've always wanted to visit South America and I'm quite sure Clare and Sarah will jump at it.'

'Do you think . . .' Julian began '. . . I'm jumping ahead now, but just say there *is* a valley containing dinosaurs, will Lucy be able to talk to them?' Richard looked at Grandpa, who thought for a moment before replying.

'It seems almost incredible when we're talking about periods involving tens of millions of years, but I've seen her talking to birds and I know from Richard that she can speak to alligators and lizards. It's very likely that she *could* talk to dinosaurs. Having said that, there's obviously only one way we're ever going to find out. By the way, if there's room for wrinklies on this trip I'd love to come with you – and I can help out with some of the expenses.'

Just then Lucy came down again. 'Where's the album with our holiday photos, Mum? I want to show Mark where we stay in Cornwall.'

Joanna went to a cupboard for the album and gave it to her.

'Stay just a moment, Lucy, I've something to tell you,' said Richard. He told her what Helen and Julian had discovered.

'Oh, that other valley,' said Lucy, flicking through the pages of the album. 'Queenie called it the Valley of the Ancients. I thought it must be something a bit older than the one *you* landed in. Bye now!' She rushed back upstairs clutching the album.

355

The others looked at each other in amazement; then they all laughed.

'What a kid!' said Helen.

'What a kid!' they all chorused in reply.

Richard got up and disappeared for a moment. He returned with a bottle of champagne and six glasses.

'I've been saving this for something really special,' he said, 'and if this reunion isn't it, then I don't know what is.'

As he opened the bottle hoots of laughter floated down from above and the house started vibrating to the beat of music.

Joanna gazed up at the ceiling. 'Something tells me,' she said, 'that those kids are going to have some amazing adventures together.'

'I think we all are,' said Richard, pouring out the champagne and handing the glasses round. He lifted his glass and proposed a toast:

'Here's to the Future!' he said.

'The Future,' they all echoed.

Ateles paniscus   *Homo sapiens*

Lucy's Lexicon

(The suffix -kin is both singular and plural)

Albion	England
animanet	animal communication network
arachnopod	spider
arboribane	harpy eagle
arborikin	monkey
Brilliant One	the sun
buzzithorn	bee, wasp, hornet, etc.
City of the Great Clock	London
City of the Great River in the Sand	Ancient Babylon

Cebuella pygmaea

clovenkin	antelope, gazelle, etc.
coatikin	coati mundi
coneybane	stoat, weasel, etc.
coneyhop	rabbit
crawlibane	giant anteater

Myrmecophaga tridactyla

crawlipod	crawling insect, spider, etc.
croakihop	frog, toad
crustakin	crustacean: prawn, shrimp, etc.
Dreadful One	cayman, crocodile, alligator
dreykin	squirrel
dromedkin	dromedary, camel
fellfang	any species of venomous snake
fledgiquill	bird
fleetfang	cheetah
flexishield	armadillo
flitterkin	bat
flutterkin	butterfly, moth
furriclaws	cat
furripelt	furry mammal
gillifin	fish
greatfang	sabre-tooth
Great Ice	polar region
Great One	whale
Great Salt	the sea
Great Saltiquill	albatross
Great Silver One	the moon
Great Southern Land	Australia
Hairy Tailless One	great ape
hedgiquill	hedgehog
henbane	fox
hippophant	tapir
Isles of Albion	Britain

Desmodus rotundus

Megaptera novaeangliae

Felis catus

junglefang	jaguar
Little Great One	dolphin
Malevolent One	snake
manefang	lion

Panthera onca

marsupihop	kangaroo, wallaby
Middle Salt	the Mediterranean
Mighty One	giant ground sloth
monkeybane	harpy eagle
moonwraith	owl
mountainfang	cougar
nightbane	owl

Vultus gryphus

paterpromise	Lucy's father
raspihop	cricket, grasshopper, cicada, etc.
reptocool	cayman, crocodile, alligator
Sagacious Ones	Lucy's grandparents
Salt of the Many Islands	the Caribbean Sea
scurrident	agouti
scurripod	rat, mouse, vole, shrew, etc.
shieldkin	tortoise
snortikin	peccary, pig
snowsleep	hibernation
soariquill	condor

Testudo graeca

spotfang	leopard
squitohum	mosquito, gnat, etc.
stranglekin	boa constrictor

Eunectes murinus

stripedfang	tiger
sunsleep	night
Tailless One	human being
Terrible One	any species of great cat
thunderquill	aeroplane
thunder-stick	firearm
velvetkin	mole
wolfkin	dog

Morpho menelaus

Notes on the names in the book

Many of the names that appear in the book tell you something about the character they belong to. Some are very obvious, others much less so, and some are in Portuguese, the language of Brazil. Here is a list describing them. See how many hidden meanings or associations you spotted as you read the story.

Anther *Chapter 1* Miss Anther is Lucy's biology teacher. An *anther* is part of the stamen of a flower.

Appleton *Chapter 21* Magnus Appleton is a reporter in New York – a city known as 'the big apple.' *Magnus* is the Latin word for big and *Appleton* means appletown.

Arrumadeira *Chapter 8.* This is the Portuguese word for maid. Maria *Arrumadeira* is one of Chopper's maids.

Babybel *Chapter 1* This is the name of a mouse who likes cheese!

Barker *Chapter 9* Barker is a lumberjack and cuts *bark* every day.

Bonaventure *Chapter 1* Bonaventure is Lucy's surname. Saint Bonaventure (1221–74) was a mystic and philosopher who was the author of *The Life of St. Francis*.

Brown *Chapter 1* The Browns live next door to Lucy and have a dog called Jumble. William Brown, in the famous stories by Richmal Crompton, has a dog called Jumble.

Chopper *Chapter 2* Chopper runs a logging company which *chops* down trees.

Cockayne *Chapter 19* Inspector Cockayne is from the drug squad at Scotland Yard to help catch people smuggling *cocaine*.

Colarinho *Chapter 19* Captain Colarinho is one of the Brazilian policemen. *Colarinho* is a Portuguese word for a person who catches someone.

Don-Juan *Chapter 7* Don-Juan Enganador is very friendly and charming to Miss Fairfax. The original *Don Juan* was a legendary Spanish nobleman who was a famous flirt and philanderer.

Ecocidal *Chapter 2* The Ecocidal Timber Company is owned by Chopper who thought up the name. The suffix *–cide* means killing or death (eg homi*cide* , sui*cide*), so ecocidal means causing death or destruction of the environment. This is, of course, the exact opposite of the meaning the ignorant Chopper intended for the name, but happens to be a very accurate description of the activities of the company.

Enganador *Chapter 7* Don-Juan Enganador is Chopper's 'inside man' who tricked Lucy into a trip to the Brazilian embassy and arranged her kidnap. *Enganador* is a Portuguese word for deceiver.

Fairfax *Chapter 7* Miss Fairfax works in an office and undoubtedly sends extremely good *faxes*.

Fetterson *Chapter 11* Inspector Fetterson is a policeman who might have to restrain criminals. *Fetters* are chains or ankle shackles similar to handcuffs.

Finnegan *Chapter 3* Mr. *Fin*negan is the director of the dolphinarium.

Fossfinder *Chapter 22* Helen and Julian Fossfinder are palaeontologists who look for *fossils*.

Furrowhead *Chapter 1* Professor Furrowhead is a brain surgeon who makes *furrows* in *heads*.

Goodward *Chapter 1* Dr. Christine Goodward works in the hospital and presumably runs a very *good ward*.

Hermes *Chapter 9* This was the name of Lucy's pilot on her trip from Rio to Macapá. *Hermes* was the flying messenger of the gods in ancient Greece. He wore winged sandals and was the divinity who protected travellers.

Icares *Chapter 6* Domingos Icares was the pilot who crashed to his death while flying Richard across the jungle. *Icarus* was someone in Greek mythology who had wings made of wax. He flew too near to the sun, the wax melted, and he fell to his death.

Insider *Chapter 21* The Insider Dealers' Arms is a pub

near the stock exchange. An *insider dealer* is someone who cheats on the stock market.

Jumble *Chapter 1 Jumble* is the name of William Brown's dog in the famous stories by Richmal Crompton.

Lestrade *Chapter 11* Inspector *Lestrade* is the name of the Scotland Yard detective who appears in the Sherlock Holmes stories by Sir Arthur Conan Doyle.

Littleporkton *Chapter 1* A seaside town which must be somewhere similar to Little*ham*ton.

Melanie *Chapter 13* This is the name of Lucy's panther. It comes from *melas* – the Greek word for dark or black.

Midasman *Chapter 21* Graeme Midasman is the director of the stock exchange, a place where everyone is trying to make more money. The Greek god Dionysius gave *Midas*, a legendary king of Phrygia, the power to turn anything he touched into gold.

Minnie *Chapter 1* The mouse whose tail was cut off by the cat-flap. In Walt Disney's cartoons *Minnie* mouse was Mickey Mouse's companion.

Nebuchadrezzar *Chapter 5* The correct spelling of a name usually referred to as Nebuchad*n*ezzar.

Noholmes *Chapter 11* Detective Constable No*holmes* is not a very good policeman. Certainly not as good as Sherlock (see under Lestrade).

O'Grady *Chapter 1* Mrs. O'Grady is Lucy's new form teacher and should give her a good *grade*.

Paterpromise *Chapter 9* The Paterpromise is Richard,

the Promised One's father. *Pater* is the latin word for father.

Pegasus *Chapter 1* In Greek mythology *Pegasus* is an immortal winged horse.

Pixel *Chapter 1* Dr. Andy Pixel is the radiologist who looks at Lucy's X-ray images on a display screen. A *pixel* is one of the tiny dots that make up the picture on a visual display unit or TV monitor.

Pollard *Chapter 9* The name of the lumberjack who hurts Lucy. A lumberjack cuts down trees and to *pollard* a tree means to cut its branches in such a way as to stimulate bushy growth.

Reedwright *Chapter 4* Miss Reedwright is, of course, Lucy's English teacher.

Sapienta *Chapter 1* St. Sapientia's is Lucy's new school. *Sapientia* is the Latin word for wisdom.

Sawyer *Chapter 2* Alf Sawyer is Chopper's real name. Chopper runs a timber company and *sawyer* means one who saws timber for a living.

Shortshanks *Chapter 18* Bert Shortshanks is Chopper's diminutive cabinmate. The shank is another word for the shin, so *shortshanks* means short legs.

Song *Chapter 2* Mr. Song has a musical voice, which is why the twins call him *Sing* Song.

Stiltskin *Chapter 21* Ronald Stiltskin works at the stock exchange where everyone is trying to make a fortune. *Rumpelstiltskin* was a fairytale dwarf who could spin straw into gold.

Stockwell *Chapter 19* Jane and James Stockwell are vets. *Stock* is the name given to animals on a farm and vets keep them *well*.

Tawkin-Tosh *Chapter 7* Teddy Tawkin-Tosh is a fool who seems to be *talking tosh* most of the time.

Verdade Chapter 6 José Verdade is one of the few honest men in Chopper's company. *Verdade* is the Portuguese word for truth.

Whitehead *Chapter 4* Mr Whitehead is Grandpa's unpleasant neighbour. Lucy makes sure he lives up to his name!

Wildersage *Chapter 21* Professor Wildersage is an expert on abnormal animal behaviour. Abnormal animals may exhibit *wilder* behaviour than usual and a *sage* is a wise person

Glossary

The explanations in this glossary give only the meanings of words as they are used in the book. Many of the words have other meanings as well and if a full description of a word is required the interested reader should consult a dictionary.

(n. – noun, pl. n. – plural noun, v. – verb, adj. – adjective, adv. – adverb, conj. –conjunction)

abbreviation *n.* a shortened word or phrase

abduction *n.* the removal of someone by force; kidnap

abruptly *adv.* suddenly; unexpectedly

abyss *n.* a very deep cleft in the ground; a gorge; a chasm

adamant *adj.* determined; having an unshakeable opinion about something; impervious to pleas

adjacent *adj.* next to; near; adjoining

adversary *n.* an opponent or enemy

aeon *n.* an unimaginably long period of time

affront *v.* to insult; to offend; to upset the dignity of

afoot *adj.* in operation; happening at that time

aggressive *adj.* hostile; quarrelsome; belligerent

agility *n.* speed and skill in movement; nimbleness

agitated *adj.* excited; disturbed

agog *adj.* very curious; intensely attentive

allocate *v.* to give to; to assign; to allot

all-pervasive *adj.* spreading everywhere

ambitious *adj.* Chapter 12: requiring extraordinary effort. Chapter 21: having a strong desire for success or power

ambush *n.* a trap, usually involving people waiting in hiding to catch or attack others

amnesty *n.* general pardon

anaesthesia *n.* the state of unconsciousness produced by medical drugs during a surgical operation

anarchy *n.* a state of lawlessness; disorder; chaos

anguish *n.* severe pain; misery; intense grief

anonymous *adj.* from or by an unknown person

anticipate *v.* to expect or foresee

apprehensive *adj.* anxious; fearful

arboreal *adj.* to do with trees

archaic *adj.* out of date; old-fashioned; ancient; antiquated

askance *adv.* (to look) with disapproval, doubt or mistrust

askew *adj.* tilted to one side; awry

assemble *v.* to gather together

astute *adj.* clever; shrewd; perceptive

asunder *adv.* apart; in pieces. In Chapter 13 *rend asunder* means tear apart

attain *v.* to achieve; to reach; to accomplish

automatically *adv.* without conscious effort

awesome *adj.* very impressive; amazing; outstanding

axis *n.* a reference line used to describe the location of a point or object

babble *n.* chatter; incoherent or meaningless speech

backfire *v.* to emit a loud noise from the exhaust system (usually of a car) as a result of the sudden explosion of unburnt gases from the engine

bank *v.* (of an aircraft) to tilt to one side while making a turn in the air

barrel *n.* the metal tube in a firearm from which the bullet or projectile emerges

beacon *n.* Chapters 1, 9: a signal; a shining light. Chapters 6, 12, 14: a large fire built to act as a signal or attract attention

bear market *n.* a stock exchange term for a financial market in which prices are falling (see *bull* market)

berserk *adj.* in a violent rage or frenzy

bewildered *adj.* confused; puzzled

bid *v.* to order; to decree; to command

bile *n.* a bitter, yellow-green digestive juice produced by the liver

bitch *n.* a female dog or other canine animal. The word is also used (as in Chapter 10) as a slang term of abuse for a female person meaning she is spiteful or malicious

bizarre *adj.* very unusual; odd; extraordinary

blab *v.* to give away a secret (in speech)

blabbermouth *n.* one who talks too much, especially indiscreetly

bleary *adj.* blurred; dim; unclear

bleeding–heart *adj. or n.* (slang) an excessively sentimental or soft–hearted person

blighter *n.* an old-fashioned slang word meaning an annoying or irritating person or thing

bloody *adj.* (slang; swearword) a strong imprecation used to lend particular emphasis to a phrase or statement

blubber *n.* a thick layer of insulating fat under the skin of whales and similar aquatic creatures

blunder *v.* to stumble in a clumsy fashion

BMW *n. Bayerische Motoren Werke.* Bavarian Motor Works – a famous German car company

bole *n.* the trunk of a tree

boss *n.* (informal) the person in charge; the employer; the manager or the supervisor

bozo *n.* a stupid man

brainwave *n.* a sudden good idea; an inspiration

breach *v.* to make an opening in; to break through

brolly *n.* an umbrella

Bua noite *Portuguese* Good night

buck *v.* to move with jerks and jolts

budge *v.* to move; to shift

buffet *v.* to knock about; to batter

bulk *n.* size or volume (especially when large or massive)

bull market *n.* a stock exchange term for a financial market in which prices are rising (see *bear* market)

buttock *n.* one of the two fleshy masses that form the rump or bottom

cache *n.* a hidden store

cacophony *n.* an unpleasant mixture of different sounds or notes

calamitous *adj.* disastrous

canopy *n.* Chapters 6, 15, 17, 19: the highest general level of foliage in a forest, formed by the crowns of trees and penetrated by only the tallest trees

Chapters 6, 13: an awning or roof-like covering

capacity *n.* ability; power

captor *n.* one who captures and holds another captive

caravan *n.* a group travelling together

carcass *n.* a dead body

carnage *n.* slaughter; massacre

cataclysm *n.* a violent geological upheaval

catapult *v.* to shoot out of something

catastrophic *adj.* disastrous; calamitous

cautiously *adv.* with great care; warily

cavort *v.* to jump around; to caper; to prance

chamberpot *n.* a pot used as a toilet, usually in a bedroom

chasm *n.* a very deep split or cleft in the ground

cherish *v.* to love tenderly; to hold dear

cicada *n.* an insect famous in hot countries for its 'song' which is really a loud, continuous clicking noise produced by a pair of drum-like organs in the abdomen

circumvent *v.* to go around; to bypass

civil servant *n.* one who works in a government office; a state administrator

clever-clogs *n.* a know-all; someone who thinks they are very clever and knowing

clobber *v.* (slang) to beat; to batter; to destroy or eradicate

cluster *v.* to gather round in a close group

coarse *adj.* Chapter 9: vulgar; indelicate; ribald; Chapter 18: rough; unrefined

cock-and-bull story *n.* a made-up story; an untrue tale

cockpit *n.* the pilot's compartment in an aircraft

coincidence *n.* the simultaneous chance occurrence of events that are apparently connected

combination *n.* a grouping or alliance. In Chapter 15 it means the union or integration of different bodily movements

commissionaire *n.* a uniformed doorman

committal *n.* usually, the act of burying or cremating a body. In Chapter 6, Richard can only leave the body in the plane

commune *v.* to communicate closely

composure *n.* a calm state; tranquillity; serenity

comprehension *n.* understanding

confide *v.* to share a secret with

confidential *adj.* secret; private

confirmation *n.* proof; verification

confluence *n.* a point where rivers meet and merge

congregate *v.* to come together as a crowd or group; to assemble

conscientious *adj.* taking great care; painstaking; diligent

consignment *n.* a package of goods

console *v.* to comfort

conspirator *n.* one who plots in secret with another or others

consternation *n.* worry; concern; anxiety

consummate *adj.* supremely skilled; outstandingly accomplished

contemplate *v.* to think about intently; to consider

contribution *n.* something given to a cause

convalescence *n.* a period of recovery from illness

convert *v.* to change the appearance or function of something; to transform

co-ordinate *n.* Chapter 12: one of a set of numbers or values that define an exact location

v. Chapters 7, 20: to organize; to integrate different elements; to harmonize

copse *n.* a small wood or thicket

coral *n.* a rocklike substance formed from the skeletons of certain sea animals, often beautifully shaped

corrupt *v.* to have a bad influence on; to make rotten; to deprave

courteously *adv.* politely

cower *v.* to crouch in fear; to shrink away from

cram in *v.* to squash in

crank *n.* an odd person; one with eccentric or idiosyncratic views

credential *n.* something giving a person status or authority; an entitlement

Cretaceous period *n.* the last period of the Mesozoic era, between the Jurassic and Tertiary periods, 144–65 million years ago

crevice *n.* a crack; a fissure; a cleft

croak *v.* (slang) to die

crustacean *n.* one of a class of animals having a carapace or shell

culprit *n.* one who is guilty; the perpetrator of a (specific) crime

cumulate *v.* to heap up; to add together

cumulated *adj.* built up over time; added up

dappled *adj.* marked with spots or patches

daunting *adj.* frightening; disheartening; intimidating

declining *adj.* getting smaller; reducing; diminishing

degradation *n.* being reduced to a bad state

deity *n.* a god or goddess; a god-like being

delirious *adj.* in a state of mental confusion, which can be caused by a high fever

demolish *v.* to destroy completely

denizen *n.* a person or animal living in a place; an inhabitant; a resident

desolate *adj.* deserted; uninhabited

destiny *n.* the fate determined for a person or thing; their future or fortune

detachment *n.* a separate party; a group or unit

detonator *n.* a device for setting off an explosive charge

devastate *v.* to destroy utterly; to lay waste

dextrous *adj.* physically skilful, especially with the hands

dialect *n.* a form of speech used in a particular geographical area, or by a particular group or social class

diminutive *adj.* small; tiny

discern *v.* to see; to perceive

discreet *adj.* tactful; behaving so as to avoid embarrassment

disfigurement *n.* something that spoils or defaces

disillusion *v.* to change someone's falsely hopeful ideas; to reveal the truth to someone

disintegrate *v.* to fall apart; to break up; to shatter

dismantle *v.* to take apart

dismissive *adj.* uninterested; not bothered with

displace *v.* to move out of position; to replace; to supplant

disrupt *v.* to break apart; to split; to shatter

distracted *adj.* confused; attention taken away by something

diversity *n.* the quality or state of being varied or different

divert *v.* to change the direction of someone or something; to turn aside. In Chapter 1 Clare *diverts* her mother so as to distract her attention from Lucy

DNA *n.* deoxyribonucleic acid. The substance in cells of

which genes are made and which can be used to identify species and individuals

docile *adj.* tame; easy to manage; submissive

doggy bag *n.* a bag containing leftovers from a meal – supposedly for the diner's dog

domain *n.* land or area owned or dominated by a person, family or group

dominion *n.* rule; control; authority

doomed *adj.* destined to die or suffer a terrible fate

double whammy *n.* something that has two bad effects; a double misfortune

double-cross *v.* to betray or cheat

downturn *n.* an undesirable change; a turn for the worse

drastic *adj.* severe; extreme; forceful

drift *n.* meaning

drone *n.* a continuous low sound

droppings *n.* animal dung; excrement; faeces

drug trafficking *n.* the illegal trading of drugs

dwindle *v.* to grow smaller, or fewer in number; to diminish

eavesdropping *v.* listening secretly to the conversations of others

ebony *adj.* black. A certain type of black wood is called ebony

ecosystem *n.* a system comprising various living and non-living elements; the interactions between the organic and non-organic elements of a given environment

ecstatic *adj.* in a state of rapturous delight or joy

edible *adj.* eatable

eerie *adj.* mysteriously frightening; spooky

elaborate *v.* to give more detail in a story or account; to expand upon

elongate *v.* to stretch; to make longer

embark *v.* to start out; to begin or commence

embarrassment *n.* a feeling of self-consciousness or confusion; a state of being disconcerted

embed *v.* to fix in firmly; to stick into

ember *n.* glowing fragment of wood (etc.) in a dying fire

embrace *v.* to hug

embroidered *adj.* decorated with artistic needlework

cmission *n.* a substance that is given out or emitted. In Chapter 21 the word *emissions* refers to polluting substances, particularly gases, produced by industrial processes

emit *v.* to send out; to utter

empathy *n.* the understanding of another's feelings; the ability to relate to others emotionally

en suite French phrase meaning part of a set or unit. The *en suite* bathroom in Chapter 8 is joined directly on to Lucy's bedroom

encounter *n.* a meeting, especially one that is unexpected

enduring *adj.* lasting; permanent

engrossed *adj.* completely absorbed in; occupied; taken up with

engulf *v.* to completely surround; overwhelm

enlightenment *n.* sudden understanding; knowledge

ensure *v.* to make sure; guarantee

enthral *v.* to enchant; to spellbind

entice *v.* to attract with a reward; to allure

epaulette *n.* a strip of material on the shoulder of a uniform

epilepsy *n.* a disorder in which there is loss of consciousness, sometimes accompanied by jerking movements (convulsions)

epoch *n.* a particular period of time in history

era *n.* a particular period of time in history

erstwhile *adj.* former. In Chapter 18 *his erstwhile captor* means the person who used to be his captor

escarpment *n.* a long, very steep slope

esteemed *adj.* held in high regard; respected

estimate *v.* to make a rough calculation (e.g. as to size or distance)

evade *v.* to get around; to dodge; to avoid

evaporate *v.* to fade away; to disappear

exalted *adj.* high in rank or position; noble; dignified

excavate *v.* to dig out; to remove (earth, etc.); to make a hole or cavity

exclusive *adj.* belonging to a particular individual or organization. In Chapter 18 the story about Lucy belongs to the tabloid newspaper and nobody else

excrement *n.* poo (slang); faeces; dung; droppings

excruciating *adj.* intensely painful; agonizing

exhilaration *n.* pleasurable excitement; elation

exotic *adj.* strange beauty or quality; having unusual allure

exquisite *adj.* particularly beautiful; attractive with delicate, refined qualities

exterminate *v.* to destroy completely; to wipe out; to annihilate

extraction *n.* taking out; removal; withdrawal

faculty *n.* an ability or power

fading *adj.* slowly disappearing; diminishing

fauna *n.* all the animals living at a particular time, or in a particular place

feline *n.* (or felid) any member of the cat family, Felidae

fend *v.* to look after; to support; to defend. In Chapter 16 *fend for themselves* means look after themselves; manage on their own

fervent *adj.* intense; heartfelt; ardent

fib *n.* a harmless lie

fitful *adj.* occurring in irregular spells. A *fitful* sleep (Chapter 6) is broken and restless

flank *n.* the lower part of the side of an animal or person

flaw *n.* a defect or imperfection

flexible *adj.* bendy; pliable

flit *v.* to move quickly and lightly; to dart about

flora *n.* all the plant life living in a particular place or at a particular time

focus *v.* to fix one's gaze or attention on something; to concentrate

foliage *n.* the leaves of plants

forage *v.* to search for food

forensics *pl. n.* in Chapter 11 this is short for the forensic technicians or scientists who gather clues (often microscopic) from a crime scene

forequarter *n.* part of the front portion of a carcass including an arm (or foreleg) with its attached shoulder and adjacent parts

formidable *adj.* awesome; impressive; threatening; something inspiring fear or dread because of its size, strength or ability

forth *adv.* out. In Chapter 16 *come forth* means come out of hiding

forthright *adj.* direct; frank; outspoken

fracture *n.* a break or crack, often, as in Chapter 13, of a bone

fragment *n.* a portion of something larger; a broken-off piece

fragrant *adj.* sweet-smelling

frantic *adj.* very excited; distraught with emotion; displaying frenzied behaviour

French window *n.* a long window, reaching to the floor, that opens like a door

frenzied *adj.* wild; frantically excited

frisk *v.* to feel or pat to check for concealed weapons

frivolous *adj.* not serious; silly; unimportant

frond *n.* the leaf of a palm or fern

fulfil *v.* to achieve; to complete a task; to attain an ambition; to carry out a promise

fumble *v.* to feel or grope, especially clumsily or blindly

furrow *n.* a groove; a wrinkle; a trench. In Chapter 11 *his brow furrowed* means his forehead wrinkled

furtive *adj.* sly; secretive

fuselage *n.* the main body of an aircraft

gaff *v.* to land a fish using a hooked pole

garbled *adj.* mixed up; jumbled; distorted so as to render unintelligible

gargantuan *adj.* giant; enormous

gelignite *n.* (gelly) an explosive – a type of dynamite

Geneva Convention *n.* an international agreement to do with the treatment of prisoners of war

gesticulate *v.* to send a message or signal by using body movements (usually of the hands or head)

gesture *n.* something done or said to make a point or emphasize something

ghastly *adj.* horrifying; terrifying; hideous

gingerly *adv.* gently; cautiously; timidly

git *n.* (slang) an unpleasant or contemptible person, often rather foolish

glisten *v.* to shine or gleam in the light

glumly *adv.* sadly; gloomily; dispiritedly

gnaw *v.* to chew or bite persistently, so as to wear away

gossamer *n.* a cobweb or any material having a very fine, filmy texture

GPS *n.* global positioning system. A worldwide location and navigation system based upon satellite signals

grapple *v.* to struggle in close combat; to come to grips with someone or something

grievous *adj.* serious; severe

grille *n.* In Chapter 1 it is the grating of metal bars on the front of a car that lets in air to cool the engine

grimace *n.* a twisted or contorted facial expression

gritted *adj.* in Chapter 21 the expression *gritted teeth* means the Prime Minister had his teeth clenched in anger

ground cover *n.* low level plants and shrubs that cover the surface of the ground

gruelling *adj.* extremely tiring; punishing; exhausting

gruesome *adj.* horrible; ghastly; repugnant

gullet *n.* the oesophagus or food pipe, leading from the throat to the stomach

gushing *adj.* over-effusive. In Chapter 7 *her most gushing voice* means she spoke in an affected, over-sentimental way

halo *n.* a circle or disc of bright light around the head of a saint

hammock *n.* a bed of canvas or netting, slung between ropes

harness *n.* an arrangement of straps that fits around the body and to which things can be attached

henceforth *adv.* from now on

henchman *n.* a supporter; an attendant or servant

hindrance *n.* an obstruction; an impediment

hippidiform *n.* a horse-like creature

hither and thither *adv.* here and there; this way and that

hitherto *adv.* until now; up to this point

hobble *v.* to walk in a lame, awkward way; to limp

homage *n.* an act or display of respect or allegiance to one of superior status

hostile *adj.* very unfriendly; antagonistic; inimical

hove *v.* the past tense of the verb 'to heave'. *Hove into view* (Chapter 16) is a nautical (sailing) expression meaning 'came into sight'

huddle *v.* to gather or nestle closely to one another

hue *n.* a colour or a shade of colour

humidity *n.* the amount of moisture in the air

humility *n.* humbleness; the quality of not being proud or arrogant

hysterical *adj.* in a highly emotional or excited state

ill-gotten *adj.* obtained illegally or dishonestly

immemorial *adj.* very ancient; from a time too long ago to be remembered

immobilize *v.* to make it impossible for someone or something to move, or be moved

impassable *adj.* not possible to cross or traverse

impenetrable *adj.* not possible to get through

imperceptible *adj.* too slight or subtle to be noticed

implement *v.* to carry out a task or job; to make something happen

implications *pl. n.* effects or results that might not at first be obvious

import *n.* meaning; significance

inadvertent *adj.* unintentional; not deliberate

incalculable *adj.* incapable of being determined; beyond calculation

incessant *adj.* never stopping; continual

incessantly *adv.* without stopping; unceasingly; continually

incoherent *adj.* not making sense; unclear; distorted

incomprehensible *adj.* unintelligible; incapable of being understood

incongruous *adj.* an unexpected or inappropriate mixture; unusual; bizarre; ill-matched; having disparate elements

inconspicuous *adj.* not easy to see; unlikely to be noticed

indescribable *adj.* too extreme for words; beyond description

ineffectually *adv.* without success or effect

inert *adj.* not moving; still

inevitable *adj.* certain to happen; unavoidable

inexplicable *adj.* not possible to explain

inextricable *adj.* not able to be disentangled

infallible *adj.* never wrong; incapable of making an error

inflammation *n.* redness, heat and swelling, usually painful, in an injured or infected part of the body. In Chapter 14 Helen's foot is *inflamed*

inkling *n.* a suspicion; a suggestion; a hint

inmate *n.* a person in an institution such as a home, hospital or prison

inordinately *adv.* more than usual; excessively

insatiable *adj.* incapable of being satisfied; continually hungry

insect repellent *n.* a substance that drives insects away

insignia *n.* an emblem or badge indicating rank, status or membership of a group

insistent *adj.* determined; persistent in a demand

integral *adj.* being an essential part of something

interchange *n.* an exchange of information

interjection *n.* a word or phrase used to interrupt or interpose

interminable *adj.* unending

intermingle *v.* to mix

Interpol *n.* abbreviation for *International Criminal Police Organization*

interrogation *n.* asking somebody questions

intersperse *v.* to scatter between

intrepid *adj.* fearless; bold; daring

intriguing *adj.* interesting; arousing curiosity

intuitively *adv.* instinctively

invalid *n.* one who is ill

invaluable *adj.* priceless; having a value that is too great to calculate

iridescent *adj.* having colours that shine and flash and change with movement

ironic *adj.* in Chapter 2 this word means surprising in a slightly amusing way; unexpected

irrefutable *adj.* undeniable; impossible to prove wrong

irretrievable *adj.* incapable of being recovered or repaired

isolated *adj.* cut off; set apart

IT *n.* abbreviation for *information technology*

jockey *v.* to try to gain an advantage in a struggle by changing position or manoeuvring

jolt *n.* a sudden bump; a jarring blow

jostle *v.* to push or bump into

jovial *adj.* jolly; good-humoured

juddering *adj.* shuddering; vibrating; shaking

justification *n.* a reason for doing something; a proof; a vindication

ken *n.* range of knowledge

kip *n.* (slang) sleep

knobkerrie *n.* a South African weapon consisting of a stick with a large knob on the end

laboriously *adv.* with great effort

lamentable *adj.* very bad; deplorable; pitiable

languid *adj.* inactive; lacking energy

languorous *adj.* inducing a state of dreamy relaxation

league *n.* an old unit of distance equal to 3 miles (4.8 kilometres)

leer *n.* an unpleasant, suggestive look or smile

legion *n.* a very large number or group

leprosy *n.* a chronic (long-lasting) skin disease; Hansen's disease

lest *conj.* in case; for fear that

lethal *adj.* deadly

leviathan *n.* a huge, powerful monster

liaison officer *n.* one who communicates between groups or units

liana *n.* a tropical climbing plant; a woody vine

limpet *n.* a shellfish renowned for its ability to cling to rocks

linger *v.* to persist; to continue; to remain longer than expected or desired

link *n.* a connection

lithe *adj.* flexible; supple

livid *adj.* intensely discoloured

loathsome *adj.* disgusting; abhorrent

locks *pl. n.* (poetic) hair

logical *adj.* based upon clear or valid reasoning

logo *n.* a company emblem or trademark

lucrative *adj.* profitable; financially rewarding

lumber *n.* Chapter 2: sawn timber; wood for construction and carpentry

v. Chapters 12, 15: to move in an awkward or ungainly fashion

lumbering *adj.* moving in an awkward or ungainly fashion

lumberjack *n.* one who cuts down trees

lurk *v.* to move or lie in wait in a concealed way, usually for an evil purpose

luxuriant *adj.* fertile; lush; abundant

luxuriate (in) *v.* to take intense pleasure in; to revel in

luxury *n.* in Chapter 8 *a life of luxury* means that Nandita enjoyed an extravagant and sumptuous life full of costly possessions and expensive clothes, in beautiful surroundings

mace *n.* a medieval weapon consisting of a spiked club

maelstrom *n.* an area of whirling confusion and turbulence

magistrate *n.* a public official who administers the law

makeshift *adj.* something found or put together to use when a proper tool is unavailable

malevolent *adj.* wishing evil on others, or appearing to do so

malignant *adj.* causing harm or evil

mandolin *n.* a stringed instrument similar to a lute

manoeuvre *v.* to move into a suitable position

maroon *v.* to abandon; to leave isolated

massacre *n.* the indiscriminate killing of a large number of people

matchless *adj.* incomparable; without equal; peerless

materialize *v.* to take shape; to appear; to happen

meander *v.* to wander; to follow a winding course

medley *n.* an assortment; a mixture

melanistic *adj.* black

melodious *adj.* pleasant to hear; tuneful; sweet-sounding

memento *n.* a souvenir; an object that brings back memories

memo *n.* short for *memorandum* meaning a written note or communication

menagerie *n.* a zoo

mess hut *n.* a dining hut (usually for soldiers etc.)

minder *n.* (slang) bodyguard or protector, especially of a criminal

minimize *v.* to make as small as possible

mishap *n.* an unfortunate accident

misinterpret *v.* to misread; to misunderstand

mob *v.* to surround or attack as a group

momentum *n.* the force of a moving body (in physics: the product of a body's mass and its velocity)

monitor *v.* to check on; to observe; to record

morale *n.* the level of confidence or optimism in an individual or group

multitude *n.* a very large number

muse *v.* to think; to ponder

muster *v.* to call together into a group; to assemble a party

myriad *adj.* very many; innumerable

mystified *adj.* puzzled; bewildered; confused

naught *n.* (archaic or poetic) nothing

nausea *n.* a sick feeling; the sensation preceding vomiting

nautical *adj.* relating to ships and sailors

neologism *n.* a new word

nerve-racking *adj.* intensely worrying; distressing; harrowing

nick *v.* Chapter 10: (slang) to steal

n. Chapter 16: *in the nick of time* means just in time; at the last possible moment

nonchalant *adj.* casual; unconcerned

obeisance *n.* homage; deference. In Chapter 1 the animals paid obeisance to Lucy which means that they treated her as their queen

oblivious *adj.* unaware; taking no notice

observation *n.* Chapters 2, 3: a fact learnt as a result of watching or observing

Chapter 18: a remark or comment

obstacle *n.* something in the way; a blockage

oddity *n.* someone or something unusual

onslaught *n.* a fierce attack

open-and-shut *adj.* easily solved; obvious

opulence *n.* riches; wealth; luxury; affluence

ordeal *n.* a stressful experience

ordure *n.* dung; droppings; excrement; poo (slang)

organic litter *n.* the scattered remnants of vegetable and animal matter covering the ground

ornithological *adj.* to do with the study of birds

outrageous *adj.* shocking; grossly offensive

outsmart *v.* to outwit; to get the better of

PA *n.* abbreviation for *personal assistant*

packet *n.* in Chapter 9 *make a packet* (slang) means make a lot of money

pageant *n.* a parade; an elaborate procession

painstakingly *adv.* paying great attention to fine detail

pallor *n.* a very pale colour; whiteness of the skin

pampas *n.* the grassy plains of South America

pang *n.* a sudden, sharp, brief sensation, usually unpleasant (such as of pain or hunger)

panoply *n.* a complete display or array; a collection of different items or elements

Pantanal *n.* a vast area of wetlands in South America, famous for its flora and wildlife

paucity *n.* smallness in number; dearth; fewness; scarcity

peddler *n.* one who deals in illegal drugs

penetrate *v.* to enter; to pierce; to find a way into or through something

pensive *adj.* deeply thoughtful, with an element of sadness

perilous *adj.* very dangerous; extremely hazardous

perpendicular *adj.* upright; vertical

perplex *v.* to puzzle; to confuse; to bewilder

perspex *n.* transparent, tough plastic made from acrylic resin

pervade *v.* to spread throughout; to permeate.

petiole *n.* a leaf stalk

petrify *v.* to terrify into immobility; to stun with fear

phenomenon *n.* an unusual or remarkable occurrence

philanderer *n.* one who flirts with women

phobia *n.* an intense and irrational fear

piping *n.* a thin strip of covered cord, used to edge cushions, seats, etc.

plateau *n.* a flat area on raised land

Pleistocene epoch *n.* the first epoch of the Quaternary period. It lasted from 1.8 million years ago to 10,000 years ago

Pliocene epoch *n.* the last epoch of the Tertiary period. It lasted from 5 to 1.8 million years ago, the start of the Pleistocene epoch

plonk *v.* to drop on; to place upon; to burden with

pluck *n.* courage; bravery

plumage *n.* the feathers of a bird

poetic justice *n.* an appropriate outcome in which someone gets what they deserve; fitting retribution; just deserts

poignant *adj.* emotionally distressing or painful

polling hook *n.* a long-handled tool for cutting high branches on trees

ponder *v.* to think thoroughly and deeply about something; to give careful consideration to something

pong *n.* (slang) a strong, offensive smell; a stink or stench

pore over *v.* to study something intently; to read or examine something very carefully

potential *adj.* possible

precipice *n.* a sheer, steep cliff face

precipitous *adj.* very steep

predator *n.* a carnivorous (meat-eating) animal; a hunter-killer

predicament *n.* a difficult situation

prehensile *adj.* adapted for grasping

presentiment *n.* a premonition; a sense about something that is going to happen

prevail *v.* to win; to prove superior; to overcome

prick up *v.* to start to listen with great interest. In Chapter 8 Lucy *pricked up her ears* which means she listened very intently

prime *v.* to prepare an explosive charge for detonation

primitive *adj.* early; crude; undeveloped

prise *v.* to lever or force open

prodigious *adj.* very great; vast

proffer *v.* to offer; to present

proficient *adj.* skilled; able; having great facility in doing something

project *n.* Chapter 1: a task; a plan; a job

v. Chapter 16: to throw one's voice (or, in Lucy's case, a thought) so that it can be heard at a distance

prologue *n.* an introductory section to a story, play, speech, etc.

protrude *v.* to stick out; to project beyond a surface

pseudo *adj.* pretended; fake; put on

psittacosaurus *n.* a small (2-metre) dinosaur with a parrot-like beak. It lived in what is now Asia approximately 100 million years ago

psycho *n.* (slang) a psychopath – one who commits antisocial and violent acts

pulsate *v.* to throb; to vibrate; to quiver

punctuate *v.* to occur or to insert at frequent intervals; to interrupt

punk *n.* a youth cult of the 1970s, featuring unusual clothes and hairstyles

punster *n.* one who makes puns – jokes that play on words

pustule *n.* a small spot containing pus

quandary *n.* a puzzling situation; a predicament

quarantine *n.* a period of isolated detention to prevent the spread of disease

quest *n.* a search; a mission to find something or someone

quicksilver *n.* an old name for the bright liquid metal mercury, which moves rapidly when touched. In Chapter 3 *your mind of quicksilver* means that Lucy's mind can move rapidly from thought to thought

quintessential *adj.* having the very essence of; possessing the most representative features or elements of something

rabies *n.* a viral infection of animals and man. Also known as hydrophobia, it can cause affected animals to behave abnormally and unpredictably

radiologist *n.* a doctor who specializes in images such as X-rays and body scans

random *adj.* unplanned; haphazard; occurring by chance

ransack *v.* to plunder and pillage; to take apart

rat (on) *v.* slang term meaning to betray or reveal secret information

raucous *adj.* hoarse; loud; harsh

recipe *n.* the ingredients and directions for making something, usually a meal

recognize *v.* to know someone or something as being familiar from a previous meeting

reconstructed *adj.* put back together; rebuilt; restored to a former state

recount *v.* to tell; to describe; to narrate

refined *adj.* elegant; polite; not vulgar or coarse

reflect *v.* to bounce something back (usually light). In Chapter 14 the eyes of the animals were acting like mirrors by *reflecting* the light of the fire

refracture *v.* to break again

refuge *n.* a place of safety; somewhere providing shelter or protection

refurbish *v.* to restore; to renovate and repair; to redecorate

regurgitate *v.* to bring food back from the stomach to the mouth

relentless *adj.* without stopping; sustained; unremitting

relish *v.* to enjoy; to savour

reminiscent *adj.* reviving memories of something

remnants *n.* remaining pieces or parts

remote *adj.* far away; distant; out-of-the-way

rend *v.* to tear forcefully; to rip

rent *v.* the past tense and past participle of the verb 'to rend.'

replenish *v.* to put back what has been used up; to replace; to restore to completion

resentful *adj.* feeling aggrieved or bitter about something; indignant

reservoir *n.* a store

resound *v.* to echo; to reverberate; to ring with sound

resourceful *adj.* capable; ingenious; having the ability to deal with difficult situations

restrain *v.* to hold back

resume *v.* to start again

retch *v.* to heave as if to vomit; to vomit ineffectually

retrieve *v.* to recover something; to get something back

reunion *n.* a gathering together again of people after a period of separation

revelation *n.* something revealed or disclosed, usually in a surprising way

reverie *n.* a daydream; a state of absent-mindedness

revert *v.* to go back to a previous state, practice or topic

revulsion *n.* drawing back in disgust; loathing

rheumatism *n.* pains in the joints or muscles

rival *n.* a competitor

role reversal *n.* the exchange of normal behaviour patterns between individuals. In Chapter 18, Lucy is looking after and instructing her father instead of the other way round

rueful *adj.* sorrowful; repentant

ruffian *n.* a rowdy or violent person; a villain

rummage *v.* to search carelessly or untidily

sabbatical leave *n.* a special period of leave granted to university staff to do extra research, etc.

sadist *n.* one who enjoys inflicting physical or mental pain on others

sagacious *adj.* wise

salvageable *adj.* saveable; capable of being retrieved

sarcasm *n.* a contemptuous or mocking remark, often ironically worded; a taunt

saunter *v.* to stroll at a leisurely pace

saurian *n.* a lizard-like reptile

savannah *n.* open grassland, studded with trees and bushes

scale *v.* to climb to the top of a height

scam *n.* (slang) a swindle; a method of cheating

Scotland Yard *n.* the world-famous police headquarters in London

sedation *n.* a state of drowsiness or calm induced by a hypnotic or sleep-inducing drug

see red *v.* to get very angry about something

seething *adj.* moving in an agitated state, as though boiling or foaming

self-made *adj.* to have achieved success through one's own efforts

semi-coherent *adj.* not making complete sense; illogical; inconsistent

serpentine *adj.* snake-like

serrated *adj.* having sharp teeth like a saw

shackles *pl. n.* fastenings, usually metal, used to secure the ankles or wrists

shamefaced *adj.* looking ashamed

shard *n.* a broken piece or fragment of pottery, glass or similar substance

shrewd *adj.* clever; astute; perceptive; penetrating

silhouette *n.* the outline of a solid object

sinister *adj.* threatening; suggestive of evil; ominous

sinuous *adj.* winding; twisting

slang *n.* a word or phrase that is not standard language but is used informally; jargon

smoulder *v.* to burn slowly and smokily without a flame

so–and–so *n.* an unpleasant person. The term is often used to avoid using a swearword to describe someone

sonorous *adj.* deep and resonant (sound)

sophisticated *adj.* refined; complex; classy; state-of-the-art

sparse *adj.* scanty; scattered; small in number

specimen *n.* an object of interest, collected and kept for future study or display

spectacular *adj.* dramatically impressive

spontaneous *adj.* occurring naturally, without prompting or preparation; unpremeditated

spooky *adj.* eerie; ghostly; supernaturally frightening

static *n.* unwanted hissing and crackling sounds on a radio

statistics *n.* facts and figures; quantitative data on a subject

status *n.* position or rank in a group or hierarchy; relative importance or standing

stifle *v.* to cover up or suppress a sound

stipulation *n.* a condition

stock exchange *n.* a financial market in which stocks, shares and securities are bought and sold in a regulated manner

stoop *v.* to swoop down

strewn *adj.* spread or scattered

strident *adj.* loud; harsh; insistent; clamorous

stupefaction *n.* bewildered amazement; astonishment

stupefy *v.* to astound; to astonish

subconsciousness *n.* part of the mind that operates below the level of awareness

subtle *adj.* not very obvious; difficult to detect

suburb *n.* a district on the outskirts of a town or city, usually residential (where people live)

suffix *n.* something added to the end of a word

summary *n.* a short account giving the main points of something; a precis

supervise *v.* to oversee; to watch over

supple *adj.* bendy; flexible

suppress *v.* to hold back; to keep in check; to restrain

surmount *v.* to rise above

surreal *adj.* having an unreal or dreamlike quality

surveillance *n.* watching; observation; scrutiny

suss (out) *v.* (slang) to assess a situation

sustainable *adj.* capable of being maintained at a steady level

swarm *n.* Chapters 18, 21: a large group of small animals, especially bees and other insects

v. Chapter 16: to move about in large numbers; to climb

swat *v.* to strike or hit something, especially an insect

swivel *v.* to turn or twist

symbol *n.* a sign, logo or character

sympathy *n.* emotional feelings for others (compassion, anguish, etc.)

systematically *adv.* in a methodical fashion

tabloid *n.* a newspaper written in a sensational style designed to appeal to a mass readership

taken aback *adj.* surprised; disconcerted; startled

tantalizing *adj.* frustrating; teasing; offering the hope of something desirable

tawny *adj.* having a browny-orange colour

taxi *v.* (of an aircraft) to move along the ground

teeming *adj.* full of; abounding with

tend *v.* to look after; to care for; to treat, as in *tend a wound*

tentative *adj.* hesitant; cautious; uncertain

tentatively *adv.* uncertainly; cautiously; hesitantly

tenuous *adj.* insecure; flimsy; insignificant; of little substance

termite *n.* an ant-like tropical insect. Colonies can build large strong hills which may be attacked by anteaters

terse *adj.* short; curt; abrupt

testy *adj.* touchy; irritable

theoretical *adj.* not actually tried in practice; possible in theory or thought

thermal *n.* a column of rising air produced by uneven heating of the ground and local area. May be used by birds or gliders to gain height with minimum effort

thrash *v.* to beat hard

throng *n.* a large crowd gathered closely together

tidings *n.* news; information

timorous *adj.* timid; fearful

titanic *adj.* possessing or involving colossal strength

toerag *n.* (slang) an unpleasant, despicable or contemptible person

tolerant *adj.* able to accept the behaviour of another; uncritical; indulgent; forbearing; easygoing

toodle-oo *interjection* (old-fashioned slang) goodbye

torrent *n.* a large and rapid flow of water, words, etc.

trance *n.* a dreamlike or hypnotic state

tranquil *adj.* peaceful; calm

tranquillizer *n.* a calming drug

transmit *v.* to pass on; to transfer; to impart

trauma *n.* physical or emotional injury

traverse *v.* to cross; go over

treasure trove *n.* a hidden store of valuables

trek *v.* to make a journey, often a long and difficult one

tributary *n.* a river or stream that joins a larger one

trip *n.* (slang) an abnormal state of mind caused by an hallucinogenic drug

trivial *adj.* unimportant; petty

troupe *n.* a company of travelling players or actors

truculent *adj.* aggressive

tuber *n.* a fleshy underground stem or root

turbulence *n.* gusty air currents

twig *v.* (slang) to understand suddenly; to work out what is going on; to catch on

twinge *n.* Chapter 1: a sudden, brief stab of pain
Chapter 19: a sudden pang of emotion

ultimatum *n.* a final demand

umpteenth *adj.* (slang) one of very many

unanimous *adj.* in complete agreement (of a group of people)

uncanny *adj.* having a supernatural quality; eerie

understatement *n.* a description of something that represents it as being less than it really is

unerring *adj.* consistently accurate; without any mistakes

unfathomable *adj.* immeasurably deep

ungainly *adj.* awkward; ungraceful

unison *n.* complete harmony; complete co-ordination

unkempt *adj.* untidy; ungroomed; dishevelled

unmolested *adj.* left alone; not attacked; not interfered with

unravel *v.* to untangle or undo

unsavoury *adj.* unpleasant; distasteful; disagreeable

unscalable *adj.* not possible to climb; insurmountable

unwieldy *adj.* too awkwardly shaped to be handled easily

vanguard *n.* the leading group in a party; those at the front

vantage point *n.* a position giving a favourable view of a scene or situation

vegetate *v.* to pass time monotonously and inactively

venomous *adj.* poisonous

venture *v.* to set out on a possibly hazardous undertaking; to set forth with caution or trepidation

vestige *n.* a very small amount; a trace of something larger that was there before; a remnant

veterinary *adj.* to do with the health of animals

veto *v.* to forbid; to refuse to give consent to

vile *adj.* particularly unpleasant; abominable; wicked; hateful

villa *n.* a large and often luxurious residence

villain *n.* a wicked person

vivid *adj.* bright; brilliant

vulnerable *adj.* capable of being hurt or wounded; weak

waft *n.* something carried on the air, especially a smell

warrant *n.* an official document that authorizes a course of action such as an arrest

wax and wane *both verbs* to get bigger and smaller

well *v.* to flow upwards or outwards. In Chapter 15 it means that the water comes up out of the ground like a spring

whence *adv.* (poetic) from; 'from what place'

white lie *n.* a fib; a minor untruth

whither *adv.* (poetic) 'to what place'

wide berth *n.* in Chapter 14 the machrauchenia give Richard a *wide berth* (originally a nautical expression) meaning they avoided him by staying well clear of him

wimp *n.* (slang) a feeble, ineffectual individual

wince *v.* to move or grimace suddenly because of a pain or injury; to flinch

wistful *adj.* sad; pensive

WPC *n.* abbreviation for *woman police constable*

wrath *n.* extreme anger; rage leading to retribution or vengeance

wreak *v.* to cause; to inflict (havoc, chaos, etc.)

wrinklies *pl. n.* (slang) old people

yonder *adv.* (poetic) 'over there' – often far away

zillion *n.* (slang) an unimaginably large number (based upon a million, billion, trillion . . . etc.)

zoom *v.* to move rapidly with a buzzing sound

Unit conversion table

1 inch = 2.54 centimetres
1 foot = 12 inches = 0.3 metres
1 yard = 3 feet = 0.91 metres
1 mile = 1760 yards = 1.61 kilometres
1 league = 3 miles (archaic)
1 ton = 2240 pounds (1016 kilograms)

1 centimetre = 0.39 inches
1 metre = 3.28 feet = 1.09 yards
1 kilometre = 0.62 miles